WHERE IN HELL AM I?

Mondragon could not remember what had happened to him, how long he had been here.

"Come on, come on," voices said, as they gathered him up off the bottom of a boat and a vision out of hell swung about him, oil-light and black-cloaked figures. They stumbled over a body in the bottom of the boat, someone who wasn't moving—they said, handing him on to someone else, "He killed Depagian."

He thought he was going to fall as they passed him ashore and a gap of water opened under his feet—he could not have saved himself; but they hauled him up the steps and into a great open doorway, more oil-light, blond stone, a desk, a cleric sitting there with a book open in front of him.

The priest said, "Canon court," while they held him on his feet. The priest said, in the disinterested voice of record-keepers everywhere, "Thomas Mondragon, a Falkenaer, resident of the city, charged with conspiracy, with espionage, with sedition, with theft, with murder of one Everett Depagian, with resisting arrest, with—"

The voice came and went in his hearing. He watched the pen move on the paper. The priest said, "Put him in number three," and made another note in his book—after which the cardinal's men dragged him off to a place with barred cells at one end, a place of echoes and strange noises. Mondragon felt cold of a sudden, not sure what sounds he was hearing and what he was remembering; one thing blurred with the other, one prison was very like the other, and all that kept it focused was the surety that he had no great deal of time left. . . .

C.J. CHERRYH
THE ALLIANCE-UNION UNIVERSE

The Company Wars
  DOWNBELOW STATION

The Era of Rapprochement
  SERPENT'S REACH
  FORTY THOUSAND IN GEHENNA
  MERCHANTER'S LUCK

The Chanur Novels
  THE PRIDE OF CHANUR
  CHANUR'S VENTURE
  THE KIF STRIKE BACK
  CHANUR'S HOMECOMING

The Mri Wars
  THE FADED SUN: KESRITH
  THE FADED SUN: SHON'JIR
  THE FADED SUN: KUTATH

Merovingen Nights (Mri Wars period)
  ANGEL WITH THE SWORD

Merovingen Nights—Anthologies
  FESTIVAL MOON (#1)
  FEVER SEASON (#2)
  TROUBLED WATERS (#3)
  SMUGGLER'S GOLD (#4)
  DIVINE RIGHT (#5)
  FLOOD TIDE (#6)

The Age of Exploration
  CUCKOO'S EGG
  VOYAGER IN NIGHT
  PORT ETERNITY

The Hanan Rebellion
  BROTHERS OF EARTH
  HUNTER OF WORLDS

MEROVINGEN NIGHTS

FLOOD TIDE

C.J. CHERRYH

DAW BOOKS, INC.
DONALD A. WOLLHEIM, PUBLISHER

375 Hudson Street, New York, NY 10014

First Printing, November 1990

1 2 3 4 5 6 7 8 9

DAW TRADEMARK REGISTERED
U.S. PAT. OFF. AND FOREIGN COUNTRIES
—MARCA REGISTRADA,
HECHO EN U.S.A.

Printed in the U.S.A.

CONTENTS

Because the stories in this volume overlap in time they are, by the authors' consent, printed here in a "braided" format—so that they read much more like a novel than an anthology. The reader may equally well read the short stories as originally written by reading all of a given title in order of appearance.

For those who wonder how this number of writers coincide so closely—say that certain pairs of writers involved do a lot of consultation in a few frenzied weeks of phone calls as deadline approaches, then the editor, presented with the result, has to figure out what the logical order is.

MEROVINGEN

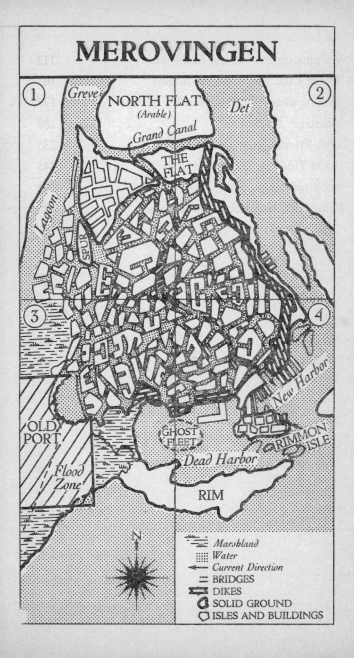

FLOOD TIDE

by C. J. Cherryh

Nights were getting cold again, stiff wind skirling down the black waters of the Grand, nights that in better times would have seen Moghi's porch crowded with skips and poleboats and even the odd fancyboat, while the noise of folk at serious drinking made a cheerful sound over the water.

The lanterns were still lit, but there was no fancyboat in sight, for damn sure, as Jones poled her skip softly up against the siding. She hopped down to the well and racked the pole with time enough, even counting the Grand's harborward current, to make a leisurely grab after the bow-rope and the ring by Moghi's steps—simple tie-up, no plans to linger. It was trade she was after. She kept at work despite the fact she went in warm clothes and often (at least in the hours before dawn) slept under a roof in a real brass bed, nor ever wanted for food these days. She still kept old customers. Mind where you can tie up to, Mama would say. Time comes, storm or flood or fever, ye got to know the spots you can get to—

Meaning there was places you could tie up without being swept to harbor and places you could sleep without your throat cut, and Moghi's was a place if you ever had a way into the back rooms, you didn't ever give it up, no, not for yourself and not for the damn fool man you took up with, even if he had gotten hisself tied-up at Kamat and all—and even if ever'body in the Trade was whisperin' about Jones' man and what in hell was he up to?

Old Mintaka Fahd outright asked, being Min, and being fond of gossip, You an' that pretty feller not havin' any trouble, are ye?

Jones had said, calm as could be, She's business, Min, pure business.

And Min: What kind o' business?

After which, Min, denied the gossip, went on to ask didn't she worry about them Kamat women and all them hightown folk and then to say, dreamily, how she had had her a hightowner once, when she was young—

Damn right, Jones worried. She carried worry up and down the canals these days, these terrible days when people disappeared right off the walkways or knocks came on doors at night. You could see, sometimes, that black poleboat going out and coming back to the College or the Signeury, at which if you got caught facing it in some dark canal you just poled past minding your business like she was any boat; and sweated a little, because you maybe got a look at a dead man's face—such as folk wasn't supposed to see, or know about, and him staring at you so scared he gave you nightmares—

She clambered barefoot up the ladder to Moghi's porch like the Dead Harbor ghosts was after her, and into the safe light that showed through the windows, a little warmer just by that.

Warmer still when she walked in the door. The

dusty-silky boards were better than fancy carpet under her feet, and the smell of Moghi's beer and whiskey was sweeter than the polishing-oil and perfume smell of Kamat House.

It was all the Trade here. In nervous times, folk tended to stick to their own kind, and the pole-boatmen that ferried hightowners here and there about town didn't bring hightowners here nowadays, didn't bring strangers here at all, or they got cold stares with their beer and they got bumped on the canals or their poles fouled, which was the Trade's way of saying a hook was next. There wasn't a face in here she didn't know, and her walking in only got a passing look, a quiet sociable nod from Willy Kandar and his brothers, which was like being told ever'thing was safe, nothing out of the ordinary.

A body came in out of the dark these days and never knew what she was going to hear or the looks she was going to get, the kind that told you right off they knew you didn't know some bit of bad news yet.

But she went to the bar and handed Jep the tally from Hafiz, and Jep slid her back a paper, crisp, first-time-used paper, the kind that all but stopped her heart.

It wasn't any more than folded. She opened it and it was writ in that fine writing she never could do, but she had learned to read. It said,

I paid for your room. I'll be there. Wait, however long. M.

She thought, Damn him. She was suddenly fluttery in the stomach. She thought, Thank the Lord—

said, "Jep, gimme a whiskey on my tab." She thought, He don't want me comin' to Kamat tonight; and then: Lord, is he comin' from there or is he out in the town t'night?

She thought about Mondragon on some kind of Kalugin business, Anastasi *damn-'im* Kalugin, who had this nasty way of calling Mondragon in and wanting to know things that could get you killed in this town. So Mondragon might not be sitting safe in Kamat tonight. That *Wait* could mean there was a real solid reason Mondragon wanted her in Moghi's safe room that had nothing whatsoever to do with the fact there was a crazy Kamat m'sera carrying a baby to her wedding and getting harder and harder to deal with—

(Hell, his door had a lock and all. And they used it, when they were in that brass bed, which had stopped one night-time visit.)

But if things in Kamat had gotten past sensible, and he was just walking over from Kamat with a notion of a little lovemaking in Moghi's upstairs Room, that was a quick walk down and over Fishmarket Bridge. He knew what time she usually got back from Satterday runs to Hafiz, he might just walk in the door. —But what did anybody do in Kamat at this hour, that he wasn't here waiting for her, instead of her sitting in that upstairs Room till he just happened to drop by?

Damn, it did sound like he was out in the town, where Tom Mondragon had no business being these days—with folk too scared even to open their mouths in their neighborhood taverns for fear of who might be listening. They'd hanged this poor crazy fool last week for no more than saying things the whole town knew anyhow, and Jamie White, a hightowner lad, no more than twenty-six, had himself a heart seizure (they said) in the Justiciary offices, but whispers said it was down in the basement of the Justiciary, where a room was that, thank the Lord, no canalsider ever saw.

She had not recognized that pale scared face in the boat tonight. It might well be some hightown man. A body wanted to forget things like that, that a body couldn't help nor do nothing about—

But she had looked at a dead man, she knew; and she had this note of Mondragon's in her fingers, and she drank her whiskey standing at the bar, because chance was Mondragon was just coming over the walk any minute now, and he was only intending a nice, quiet night where they could talk private-like and not worry about Kamat business— but damn him, he didn't put a time: Mondragon never liked to write things like that, in the case of that note getting misplaced.

So she had her whiskey—and a second, at which Jep gave her this questioning look, as if to ask was there some worrisome thing in that note. "Ney," she said, and stared at the glasses behind the bar while she sipped the second glass, trying not even to look at the door, not to have the whole damn room knowing she was waiting, and guessing it was for a damnfool man who (the Trade knew) was on the shady side of hightown and had dealings in places canalers didn't even think about—like Kalugins, like Anastasi Kalugin, in particular, who was not in a good mood since Cardinal Borey had gotten murdered; and the new head of the college, Exeter, backing Mischa Kalugin to succeed the governor, who at seventy and more gave everybody the shivers when he sneezed—

Orthodoxy, hell, Mondragon had said about the hangings, with Exeter and her sneaks being so concerned about Janes and Sharrists and other such outlaw cults getting so aboveboard in Merovingen. It's fear she's using, it's putting the fear in the canalers and the fear in the Houses, it's removing Mischa's enemies and having her people ready to make arrests and cut throats the minute the governor dies—

Hush, she'd said to him, the two of them lying abed in Kamat, where he had had to move because the Petrescu apartment was not safe anymore. And he talked like that where Kamats might hear.

It's no secret in this house, Mondragon had said.

But people died lately for things that were not secret. Mondragon worked for Anastasi Kalugin, who wanted to be governor, and Mondragon was supposedly a bastard Boregy on the one hand (but Boregy House was siding with Mischa and Exeter these days, turned against Anastasi) but Mondragon was Nev Hetteker, Sword of God like Karl Fon the governor up there, and knowing too much of Fon's business the way he knew too much of Anastasi Kalugin's here. Fon had been his best friend once, had kept him five years in prison, about which Mondragon did not talk much, but he waked with nightmares still—Mondragon had gotten away and tried to get to help from friends in Boregy, except the Sword had got there first and he had had nowhere to go and no hope at all till Anastasi took him up—

And her. She had looked that cold bastard in the

eyes and known this was a killer worse than any she had ever met on the canals, and worse than any crazy down in Dead Harbor. This was a man who smiled while he killed your friends and offered you fancy wine before he said he was going to hang you or worse; and Anastasi Kalugin was worried sick about Exeter. *That* was what she was worried for, the chance that Kalugin was likely to say to Mondragon, Go get me something on Exeter. . . .

Wait for me, he wrote, not where he was or why or why he wanted her in the safest place in Merovingen's underside, in a place even blacklegs didn't come and where the cardinal's slinks hadn't yet shown their faces.

Wait for me. Which meant stay off the water and out of sight and out of reach of certain kinds of trouble.

But he wasn't out of it, damn sure.

Mondragon had a great deal rather have been in Kamat, Marina's importunities notwithstanding, or most places in Merovingen, as happened, rather than where he was—sitting in the carpeted cabin of Anastasi's black yacht, facing Anastasi's desk, sipping a very expensive brandy.

"They arrested Delaree," Anastasi said.

Bad news.

Very bad news. Mondragon said, "He knows Ketch."

"Does he know you?"

"He doesn't," Mondragon said. "Ketch does."

"Ketch is dead, then," Anastasi said, like that. Mondragon felt both relief and revulsion, watching Anastasi tick off a name. "Who else?"

Ketch had a woman. Mondragon remembered. Frightened kid, who had no idea what her man was up to, or how life had gotten better or where the money came from. He said, "Nobody," and thought of how Rani could say her man had a blond-haired, hightown friend. One damned, *damned* encounter, the woman walking into the foundry, overhearing too much. . . .

"You're sure," Anastasi said.

"I'm sure."

"I don't pay you to have scruples, Mondragon." Anastasi looked at him a long, thoughtful moment, with that half-lidded stare behind which there was no shred of a soul. Then: "He has a girlfriend."

"So I hear. She doesn't know me. He's kept her out of it."

"We don't know what she knows." A note, a checkmark. "No chances. We've ways to get to Delaree in his cell. Ketch and the woman—no problem. —I won't put that detail up to you. You've other things to do."

"What?" His hand was shaking. He rested the glass firmly against the chair arm to conceal that fact. He thought, for one wild, Jones-inspired moment of charity, of warning Rani Spence; then broke out in sweat, wondering whether, if the tremor in his voice had just put Anastasi in doubt of his loyalties, the killers might not be on his trail tonight too—and Jones'. No doubt—Jones'. Anastasi had made him sure of that: only so long as Anastasi got whatever he wanted, Jones stayed alive.

But Anastasi occupied himself with a drawer, seeming not to notice his distress—took out a vellum envelope, held it out to him. Mondragon tossed off the brandy, stood up, thinking, Thank God. He was free, he could go, he could deliver some small piece of business to one of Anastasi's agents. . . .

"This goes to my dear sister," Anastasi said, releasing the envelope into Mondragon's hand. "Tomorrow. I'm sure there'll be an answer."

THE TESTING

by Nancy Asire

Autumn in Merovingen meant uncertain days: rain one morning, sun in the afternoon; chill temperatures one day, followed by warm winds the next. The uncertainty Justice Lee felt, however, had little to do with the weather. Something ominous had bloomed in the city during summer and now was coming to fruition.

First he had noticed little things, simple things . . . the increasingly brusque manner of the priests at the College; the way people spoke quietly now on the bridges and walkways, some going so far as to look over the shoulder before engaging in conversation. Add to this the mix of new faces among the old; the way certain folk seemed to have nothing better to do than eavesdrop.

And now the not unexpected summons had come from Father Rhajmurti, directing Justice to see him at once.

Shivering slightly in a sudden brisk wind, Justice stepped inside the College and hurried across the entryway and up the stairs that led to the priests' offices. He surreptitiously glanced at the students he passed and felt slightly better when he saw they looked as uncertain as he felt.

He paused briefly before Rhajmurti's door, straightened his shirt, and ran a hand through his windblown hair.

"Come."

Rhajmurti's calm response to the soft knock somehow reassured Justice. He stepped inside and stood facing his patron.

"Ah, Justice," Rhajmurti said, looking up from a pile of papers spread out on his desk. He gestured to a chair close by. "I'll only be a moment longer."

Justice sat down and studied his mentor as Rhajmurti flipped through one sheaf of papers, then started on the next. Though Rhajmurti's voice had sounded calm enough, Justice saw telltale marks of anxiety on the priest's face, the small lines of worry around eyes and mouth.

"So," Rhajmurti said, shoving the papers to one side and looking up, his eyes catching the sunlight falling through the window. "Thank you for being prompt." He glanced toward the door.

"It's shut tightly," Justice said, reading that look with a skill only years of association could grant.

"Good." Rhajmurti leaned back in his chair, his posture giving the outward impression of relaxed attention. The fingers of one hand drummed a moment on the armrest, shattering the pose. "I don't usually ask you to come see me between classes, but today is an exception."

Justice squirmed a bit at the seriousness in Rhajmurti's voice. Lord! What was going on now? More drugs? More—

"I'm going to ask you to hold what I say in strict confidence," the priest said. "*Strict* confidence. Events have occurred recently that I'm sure you're aware of. There's a new wind blowing through Merovingen, and not a few will be swept away by it. I want to make certain you're not among those who don't weather the storm."

"Do you mean—" Justice glanced at the door he had securely shut. "—Cardinal Exeter?"

Rhajmurti's face went very still and he nodded briefly. "Adherence to strict Revenantist credos is being tested, Justice. Merovingen has never been a city that takes kindly to those of other—religions. Oh, yes . . . Adventists here aren't bothered if they keep their heads down and don't stir up trouble. But now trouble may be hunting them and others of their ilk. Do you understand what I'm saying?"

Ancestors! Does he know that I'm not really a Revenantist? That I go through all the motions while my heart isn't really in what I'm doing?

"I think so," Justice said slowly. "A purge."

"Of sorts," Rhajmurti agreed. "I want you to be very, very careful. While it's on record that you converted to Revenantism years ago, you come from an Adventist background. This has not, of course, escaped notice by some in the College."

Justice's shoulders tensed. *Raj. Oh, Lord. What about Raj? He's only newly converted.*

"I want you to remember the recent hanging," Rhajmurti said. "I want you to remember it at all times."

"I don't think I'll forget. It was enough of a show."

Rhajmurti sat up straight. "Listen to me, Justice! I'm deadly serious. What you just said could be held against you if heard by the right ears."

"It's not that I don't believe you. It's stupid,

that's all. Some poor drunken fool stands up in some seedy tavern, curses the cardinals, and is executed for blasphemy. How civilized are we to hang him for being drunk?''

"It wasn't his being drunk that got him hanged," the priest said, "it was what he *said* while being drunk that did it. I'm telling you, in utter, complete sincerity; don't speak until you've thought everything through, and I mean *thoroughly* thought about what you're going to say. And don't think yourself safe in your usual haunts. There are eyes and ears watching and listening in the strangest places.''

Justice leaned forward in his chair. "What's caused all this turmoil, Father?"

"I couldn't tell you if I wanted to. I'm sorry. There are certain things you'll have to take on faith. This is one of them. Suffice it to say that for those citizens of Merovingen who are not born Revenantists, things could get very dangerous in the future.''

"What about Raj?" Justice asked, thinking of his roommate, the mysterious heir to House Takahashi whom he had met canalside. "He's from Nev Hettek . . . an *Adventist* city . . . and newly converted himself.''

"I'm including Raj in this warning. Especially Raj. I want you to tell him everything I've told you. Raj isn't stupid. Tell him to keep his mouth shut and to watch what he says. House Kamat has not escaped notice in the past few weeks.''

No, it had not. Rumor had it that Richard Kamat himself had been "invited" to a talk at the College, with the indomitable Willa Exeter herself. Raj, being sponsored to the College by House Kamat, would be under certain scrutiny.

"There is to be a testing," Rhajmurti said, folding his hands on his desk. "An inquiry, if you will, into the beliefs of all the students in the College. I don't know that exact date, but it's soon. Questions will be asked and individual responses recorded. If you've forgotten the teaching I gave you before you converted, I want you to study again."

A shiver snaked down Justice's spine. "I haven't forgotten," he said.

Rhajmurti smiled slightly. "I didn't think you had, but this is no time to let the slightest bit of hesitation cloud your mind. I'm going to be giving several catechism classes, and I want you and Raj to be present at all of them."

"When?"

"Starting tonight."

"Father?"

"Here, at the College. Most likely in one of the quieter classrooms."

That probably meant a room far from the major activities. Justice nodded.

"I'll be there. I'll talk to Raj—Father, if you can't tell me what's caused all the upheaval—can you at least tell me why?"

Rhajmurti smiled, but the smile did not touch his eyes. "Change, Justice. A gathering of strength into new hands. When a hurricane comes, those who ride it had best be prepared."

Rhajmurti sat staring at the wall, his mind a total blank. He sighed, stood and glanced down at his desk. There was nothing else he could do. He had said all he could say without jeopardizing his own position as a priest, and Justice's position as a student.

Justice would watch what he said, Rhajmurti was certain of that. But how much of a Revenantist *was* he? Rhajmurti prided himself on his pragmatic outlook on life, despite his priestly calling. He had never choked at gnats. But now . . . now the smallest unorthodoxy could spell death.

He had never been quite sure that Justice believed everything he had learned before converting from Adventism. Justice was a model Revenantist . . . he knew the terminology, the feast days, the—

Dammit! With things going the way they were, that was not enough. The questions asked in the testing given to the College students would be tricky, formulated to trip up all but the most fervent of believers. And he could not let his protégé—his unacknowledged son—fall victim to a well-turned phrase.

He left his room, unsure where he was going, letting his feet carry him where they would. Classes were over for him this morning; he would not be missed if no one found him in his office. He walked the halls, climbed the stairs to the residences.

It was not until he stood in front of Father Trevor Bordinov's room that he knew why he had come this way.

"Alfonso!"

Trevor stood back from the opened door and gestured into the room.

"What brings you here?" Trevor asked, closing the door.

"Events. Moodiness. Apprehension. Maybe all three."

"This is a change." Bordinov's thin face split into

a grin. "*You're* usually the one to pull me off the walls. What's happened?"

Rhajmurti glanced around the room. "Are we alone?" he asked in a low voice.

"Of course. Now, what's bothering you?"

"The same thing that's bothering you—that's bothering everyone."

Bordinov's smile disappeared. "There's little we can do about it."

"Ha! And you're the one I had to restrain from tearing the College down stone by stone not long ago."

"And I thank all the gods you did. Vishnu protect, Alfonso. If it hadn't been for your voice of reason, I could have been caught up in all this mess."

"I'm worried about my students," Rhajmurti said, rubbing the bridge of his nose. He was fighting off a growing headache.

"I don't think there's a one of us who isn't."

"I have several who used to be Adventist."

Bordinov's eyebrows rose. "Justus?" he asked.

"Yes. And then there's Raj, the medical student."

"Oh, *that* one. The Takahashi heir. That was a coup for you, Alfonso, when *he* converted, him a Nev Hetteker and all."

"It's the test, Trevor. I know how damned sticky some of those questions can be. I've decided to hold catechism classes."

Bordinov gestured Rhajmurti to a chair and took another one facing him. "Fine idea. But you won't be able to anticipate a truly malicious tester."

"*That's* what I'm worried about."

"Politics."

"What isn't any more?" Rhajmurti leaned his head back. "But I've got an idea."

"Oh?"

There might be something I can do. Like arrange to test my own students."

"How? We don't even know *who* the testers are to be, or *when* the testing's to take place."

"As for when . . . I want to get those students tested at the head of the list. The sooner, the better. I've got a feeling the worst of this is yet to come."

For a long moment, Bordinov sat silent. "How far have we fallen, Alfonso? I remember I asked you that once before. What's become of us when we value power more than spiritual learning?" He threw up his hands in resignation. "I know . . . I know. You gave me all the answers the last time we talked, but I find them damned hard to swallow."

Rhajmurti smiled. "Listen to us old ones, Trevor. We've seen a thing or two."

"You're not much older than I."

"True. But I've listened to my elders with a far more forgiving ear than you, you rebel."

Bordinov grinned sheepishly. "I know what you're going to say. Stay alive long enough to come to power yourself. *Then* you can change things."

"You learn well."

"No one's accused me of being stupid. Now what about this scheme for getting yourself set up as a tester?"

"I don't see why I can't. Any priest can ask the questions. I've taught enough catechism classes to qualify."

"That's true." The ghost of a smile touched

Trevor's face. "Who are you going after, Alfonso? Who are you going to manipulate?"

"I'm not sure yet." Rhajmurti blinked against the rising pain of his headache. Tension. He knew tension had brought it on. "But I know where I'm going to start."

Justice sat on the large, though somewhat threadbare couch that dominated the small sitting room, Sunny curled up enjoying feline dreams at his side, and watched without comment as Raj slumped down into one of the two chairs that faced the couch.

"Bad morning?" Justice asked.

"Hoo!" Raj leaned back in the chair and closed his eyes. "I thought studying to be a doctor would be difficult, but I didn't realize *how* difficult."

Justice leaned forward, balancing his arms on his knees. "You know. . . ." Justice grimaced. "Strange. Odd. Out of the ordinary."

"I saw Krishna this morning," Raj said, "acting like a normal human being, and *that's* strange. I heard his father nearly killed him when he found out his dearly beloved youngest son was involved with drugs. It's a wonder he still has his room here at Hilda's. I expected m'ser Malenkov to order his son home and never let him out of sight again."

Justice shrugged. "I guess Krishna squirmed his way out of yet another mess. He's been damned quiet lately. Maybe he got some good sense scared into him."

Raj contemplated the ceiling. "You asked about strange. The priests *are* in a rare mood, that's for sure. I haven't seen them so terse and uncommunicative since I started my studies."

"Then are you ready for some interesting news?" Justice slid forward so he sat on the edge of the couch. "And can you keep your mouth shut?"

Raj looked down from the ceiling. "What now?"

"Father Rhajmurti asked me to come to his office this morning. There's a purge of sorts starting, Raj, and I don't think I need to say anything more about it than that."

"No, you don't." Raj's eyes darkened in the dim lamp light. "House Kamat has seen a portion of it."

Justice waited, but Raj did not elaborate, which was probably for the best. "Well, it's not over and I think it's going to get worse. Especially for people like you and me."

That got Raj's attention. The heir to House Takahashi sat up straight in his chair, his expression gone deadly serious.

"How so?"

"We're former Adventists. Converted, you know." Justice ran a hand down Sunny's side and was rewarded with a deep purr. "The cardinals are going to test us, Raj, all of us at the College; Revenantist testing. We're going to be asked questions by some priest and we're going to have to answer them correctly. And I mean *correctly*."

"Is *that* all?"

"Listen to me. These questions aren't going to be the kind that you can use your damned perfect memory on, Raj. They're going to be tricky, with hidden pitfalls. We're all going to have to reason our way through them."

"Shit."

"That's what I said. Rhajmurti is having catechism classes, starting tonight and he expects us to be there. He's going to try to help us through this."

Raj rubbed his hands together. "Do you think he suspects that we're. . . ." His voice trailed off.

"Really Adventists? I don't know. Probably. But I've known him since I was a child, and he's never been anything but kind to me. If my being an Adventist mattered to him, he wouldn't have paid such close attention to me when I was growing up."

"When's this testing to take place?"

"I don't know, and I don't think Rhajmurti does, either."

Raj glanced behind at the closed door. "Is it Exeter?" he asked in a hushed whisper, as if the walls had ears.

Justice nodded. "And Rhajmurti warned me—and you, indirectly—to watch every word we say. He told us to remember the recent hanging. There are spies out there, watching and listening. Anyone who says anything slightly out of line could get hauled in by College Security."

"Lord and Ancestors!" Raj bit his lip. "I mean, gods!"

"That's what I'm afraid of, Raj. An innocent slip of the tongue. You and I aren't afraid to think or talk that way when we're alone, but we could end up at the end of a rope if some College spy heard us."

"But, House Kamat's Revenantist, and—"

"Where are you from, Raj?"

Rigel Takahaski cursed softly. "Nev Hettek. I'm damned from the start."

"And newly converted, too. You're in it deeper than *I* am. I've lived as a Revenantist long enough for people to have forgotten I was born Adventist. And I'm scared, Raj. This isn't something that's going to blow over quickly."

"Then I suggest we start studying," Raj said. "Rama bless, what's going to happen to Denny?"

"Tell him to keep out of sight and be the best damned Revenantist he can be."

Raj sighed softly. "There's always a dark lining to every silver cloud," he said, turning an old saying inside out. "Just when things have started looking up for me, *this* happens."

Justice scratched Sunny between the ears. "We'll make it. We've shared some tough times."

"I know. But we've never faced *religious* tough times before." He smiled slightly. "I hope we're both up to it."

"So do I," Justice said. "So do I."

FLOOD TIDE
(REPRISED)

by C. J. Cherryh

Mondragon left Kamat by the middle tier door, took the bridge that led toward uptown and tried not to think what Jones might be thinking by now. He had had no sleep. He reckoned that Jones had had none last night, either, waiting for him, but he had met with Anastasi in the last watches, and by then, when a cloudy, soggy dawn was threatening, he had taken a detour past Ventani on his way to Kamat and left a sealed note and a sol in Moghi's night-drop, that said only, *Sorry, Jones. Hang on. Stay where you are. I'll explain later.*

Jones might well ask Moghi's lads to find him, but he trusted Jones herself would stay put for now, no matter what she might have to say to him later—you bought a night in Moghi's upstairs Room, and with it came a boy to run your boat into someplace inconspicuous and sit watch on it; food arrived outside the door; anything you wanted did—besides which you had Moghi's connections, which were extensive in Merovingen's dingy underside. Moghi fixed things, never got his own hands dirty, and God knew, he had bought priests as well as blacklegs. Which was why Mondragon wanted Jones there, off the water, so long as the Ketch affair was running—

God only knew, too, where it would run before it was finished. Delaree was doomed. Ketch and Rani were. He sensed Anastasi's increasingly dark and worried mood, and feared . . . he had no idea what, but Anastasi's own survival was increasingly uncertain. Anastasi had made mistakes, minor ones, singly taken—but at least one or two of his enemies had consistently done the right things, chiefly encouraging Vega Boregy to slip Anastasi's ties and edge closer to Mischa Kalugin's hitherto laughable partisans—laughable no longer, now that Willa Exeter, *Cardinal* Willa Exeter, succeeded to absolute control in the College, purged her enemies under charges of heresy, and aimed at putting a malleable fool in Iosef Kalugin's office.

All of which Mondragon was sure had Iosef Kalugin's full backing. The aging governor wanted to die of natural causes—and that meant making it unprofitable for his two stronger offspring to assassinate him, by the simple expedient of nominating his feckless eldest son as vice-governor and signaling the old moneyed Families, like Boregy, of course, that he planned to pass power not to a strong successor, but to a cabal of the same moneyed interests that had kept *him* in power lifelong. If Tatiana or Anastasi got to power, Iosef would tell them, the world would shake. Tatiana favored trade with Nev Hettek; Anastasi promoted war. Not so with Mischa. Mischa would be no more than a puppet, the Families in question knew that: Mikhail the clockmaker, they called him—brilliant in his own crazed way, at

inventing gadgetry of wheels and valves and such
that (irony among others) his chief partisan the
cardinal would have called anathema and unapproved
tech had any of her enemies proposed it. Mischa
was also involved to the ears in the Cassie Boregy
lunacy, which Exeter would otherwise have denounced as heresy—nothing powerful was useful to
Exeter unless Exeter controlled it, and it was certain Exeter was watching Boregy closely on that
account and figuring what to do about it. One needed
no theology to explain Exeter's moves. Fanaticism
and religious zeal was not her motive for the purge.
Power was.

An ex-Sword understood that game very well.
And he had an idea at least why Anastasi was
sending him to deliver a personal message to Tatiana
Kalugin: approaching Tatiana was absolutely rea-
sonable at this point. It was the timing that made
Mondragon anxious—that it coincided with Delaree's
arrest by Exeter's agents—which meant threads that
led back to Anastasi's own organization.

So Delaree died; and Mondragon, who had moved,
until lately, mostly in the middle and nether tiers of
Merovingen, had a cover that involved Boregy, a
situation that Boregy might find . . . embarrassing.
Ordinary Merovingians had no connections upriver
to tell them that Mondragon was no Falkenaer name,
and that he was no bastard Boregy—but rich Families with upriver connections and extensive intelligence in the government surely knew the whole
story, how he had fled Nev Hettek, how Karl Fon
wanted him back—

Iosef Kalugin himself knew those facts. Tatiana
did. One or the other of them (Mondragon's own

suspicions leaned to Iosef lately) had had him beaten and thrown into the Grand, when he had first come to Merovingen looking for Boregy help—a quiet little signal that whoever had done it wanted no quarrel with Fon, and no dealing with possible factional feuds inside the Sword of God hierarchy— Thomas Mondragon could vanish without a trace, and Fon could simply wonder whether he was still alive somewhere.

But he had frustrated their hopes by surviving and falling into the hands of Anastasi, the Advocate Militiar, head of the army, who wanted no negotiations with Karl Fon. So he had skipped, using Anastasi's money, from Boregy House to the Petrescu apartment, and mingled in hightown society at least by day—always a jump ahead of disaster.

He did not understand, for instance, specifically *why* Richard Kamat had taken him in, though Richard had offered him plausible reasons. He had his own guess—that it was his relationship with Anastasi rather than that with Marina Kamat, who had paid his rent and taken it out in trade. Kamat, Nev Hettek ties and all, could very easily have exposed him: pregnant Marina's tantrums reminded him that she still had the means for blackmail or, failing that, revenge on him, if not for Richard Kamat's protecting him. And Richard, head of Kamat, head of the mercantile association, head of the second tier of Families in Merovingen, and ally of the Takahashis in Nev Hettek, had a great deal to lose if weak-handed Mischa and a cabal of Old Money came to power.

So Richard preserved a fugitive's life, forgave him Marina's pregnancy, and thereby signaled

Anastasi that he might deal—which put Anastasi, who took a hard line with the Fon government in Nev Hettek, in unlikely alliance with a Family whose Nev Hettek connections were ungodly public—

All of which was an exposure that put Mondragon at a giddy, dangerous height in this city. Mondragon went to the meetings, attended the soirées and the dinners, wore velvet and Chattalen silk, unarmed. He did his fencing with words, these days, while he imagined behind every pair of eyes a sure knowledge who he was and a cynical calculation of his value to Anastasi and to Richard Kamat.

Ye're crazed, Jones had cried on a certain night— he could remember the look on her sensible, sun-browned face, the plain reckoning of another survivor in rough waters, who knew the law of her Trade and the waterways, and who, as she would say— knew a fool when she saw one.

They're goin' t' kill ye, Mondragon! Ye go in an' out o' them fancy Houses an' ye smile at them sherks, and someday somebody's goin' t' lock a door an' ye ain't got no help! Ye got friends on the water, Mondragon, ye ain't got none in them places— Kamat'll sell ye as fast as Anastasi will, don't matter if he's your heart's own friend. Hightown folk just got different laws, Mondragon, friend don't mean nothin' to him, not if you ain't profitable. . . .

And Jones professed to know nothing at all about politics.

But she knew her city and she knew Kalugins and Kamats, and how once upon a not so long ago time, when someone fell afoul of the Families, most particularly the Kalugins, a body turned up floating in the Harbor—very discreet and quiet. Nowadays

Exeter disposed of her enemies on Hanging Bridge, sometimes two and three at a time this summer past, and the governor, who had the power to assume jurisdiction in capital cases, declined to do a damned thing about it.

Kalugin's executioner was the tag the canals hung on Exeter—only in whispers, God knew. Bloody Exeter. The lower tiers understood Exeter's religion better than the upper tiers gave them credit for.

Three men hanged for "heretical thinking" and "forbidden technology" because of a warehouse alarm common as doorbells in Nev Hettek.

A doctor driven out of practice for "unorthodoxy."

A teenaged girl beaten and left on the canalside walkway over on Foundry, for asking why another was being arrested . . .

That was the climate in Merovingen nowadays. Fear was working its way so deep into Merovingian thinking that very few were willing to object to arrests or question charges, or to speak of the disappeared.

So Anastasi sent to his sister, who had attempted Anastasi's life by knife and poison and subversion, a sealed envelope, in Mondragon's pocket.

And Mondragon presented himself to the grim and lately anxious blackleg guards at the Signeury's mid-level doors, with the more than slight idea he might be a deliberate sacrifice, in one sense or another. He had had that damned letter in his rooms at Kamat for hours, thought of ways to break the seal and read it—but he much doubted what he could gain that way was worth the risk of detection. He had two good and not mutually exclusive ideas what it held, and knowing it exactly made no particular difference.

So it was up to the offices where Tatiana held sway—chief of city and police operations as Anastasi was of the military arm of the blacklegs. He got as far as the front desk in that office where a blackleg officer looked him over and asked his business.

"Courier," he said, "from the Advocate Militiar."

The man got up, called aides from the office inside, and insisted on a body search. That was the level of trust between the two staffs. He said, "I don't object. But in advance of that, give m'sera the choice."

"Of what?" the blackleg asked.

One took a chance sometimes. Mondragon said, folding his arms and assuming a cold confidence he did not feel: "M'sera may say. Or not. Ask her."

The man went. Mondragon stood still, relaxed only to change his stance and the blacklegs followed every move. Footsteps sounded, returning, the door opened, the man came back and Tatiana Kalugin came with him, red-haired, elegant, and armed, a blackleg military issue.

"M'sera." Mondragon pulled his coat back delicately with two fingers, extracted the envelope, and offered it to the blackleg at his left.

"McHugh," Tatiana said. The man brought her the envelope and the attention of the other two never left its proper target. Mondragon watched her break the seal with a paper knife, not touching the seal itself, watched as, with a crisp unfolding of vellum, she read whatever was written there.

Her face did not change expression. She looked directly at Mondragon then and said, "Come into my office."

Mondragon walked past the desk. The blacklegs made to follow, but Tatiana said, "Wait outside."

Inside, she went to her desk, sat down and wrote an answer in her own hand, folded an envelope and sealed it.

She said, offering it to him, "How *is* Anastasi, by the way?"

"Healthy," Mondragon said, and took the envelope.

Tatiana laughed, quite pleasantly. "I trust," she said, and looked him over with a cold, critical stare, from the desk up. "Give him my love."

He said, refusing any interpretation, "I will, m'sera."

He wanted out of this room. He wanted to be back on the canals, far from the Signeury and its plots and its trading in human lives. He stood there while Tatiana Kalugin looked at him with God only knew what estimation of old scores, murders, attempted murders, and present opportunities.

Finally she folded her hands in front of her on the desk and said, "Do you *like* my brother?"

"I'm indebted to him."

"Of course," she said, with a slow deliberation that made him think—God, she'll wonder, she'll ask, she'll look for leverage. . . .

Jones—

She said, quietly, "All his best people are. Indebted to him, that is. Good day, ser. Do be careful."

THE TESTING (REPRISED)

by Nancy Asire

Rhajmurti sat on the end of one of the benches by the stairs, watching the flow of students and priests pass by him. The halls were growing emptier as the last classes of the day wound down. The change in the atmosphere of the College struck him stronger than before he had talked with Trevor Bordinov. A feeling of repression permeated the hall: students talked quietly to each other and left immediately after their classes, while the priests went about their business all but ignoring the non-ordained.

When Willa Exeter had come to power after Cardinal Ito Boregy passed on to a new rebirth, Rhajmurti had grown concerned, not only for himself and other priests he considered moderates, but for priests like Bordinov who were reformers at heart. He should not have worried; Trevor might be called a hothead, but he was too smart to make an example of himself.

Rhajmurti straightened, smoothed his saffron shirt, and stood. His quarry was in sight.

"Alexiev," he said, stepping out into the hall.

The heavyset priest changed course and joined Rhajmurti by the bench.

"Rama's blessing," he said. "How are you, Alfonso?"

"Outside of a headache, not bad. Do you have plans for supper?"

"No. But why don't you join me for something to drink first?"

Rhajmurti smiled and followed Alexiev up the stairs. He disliked what he was doing, but sometimes one had to undertake unpleasant duties for a worthy end.

"Hard day?" Alexiev asked, opening the door to his room and ushering Rhajmurti in.

"Actually, no. But you look like you've been through the mill."

Alexiev snorted as he poured himself and Rhajmurti each a glass of wine. "It will take more than this to get me down. Sit, Alfonso."

"How's Krishna doing?" Rhajmurti asked. "He's still in your literature class, isn't he?"

"Better. I think you scared him out of ten years' growth when you dragged him home that night. His father's *still* upset, but Krishna seems to have settled down a bit."

"I think the College getting involved in punishing drug dealers and drug takers is helping calm things."

Alexiev lifted a heavy eyebrow. "What do you want, Alfonso?"

"What do you mean, what do I want?"

"I've known you too many years not to recognize that expression in your eyes. Don't try to hide things from me."

Rhajmurti gestured briefly. "I'm worried, Pytor. About some students I know."

"Ah-h-h. The testing. Well, I can tell you right now, I don't know how soon it's going to be."

"Or *who* will be administering it?"

Alexiev took a long sip of his wine and met Rhajmurti's eyes. "Why?"

"I'd like to be one of the testers."

"You're qualified. I'm sure you've already been selected."

"But you don't know for sure?"

"Alfonso—"

"I don't want you to name names, but if you know, tell me. It's important."

"And why do you think *I'd* know anything about it?"

"Don't try to hide things from me, to quote a wise man I know. You've always been close to the circles of power, and I haven't noticed you backing off lately."

Alexiev wiped his forehead and frowned. "Gods, Alfonso. No one's sure which direction to jump now. So I've kept myself in good graces with the powerful. What of it? I might be able to do some good."

"I'm not criticizing you. I need your help, that's all. I'm trying to do some good myself."

"You're being considered as a tester," Alexiev admitted, "and that's straight from Cardinal Tremaine himself. But you never heard it from me. Swear it, Alfonso."

"I swear." Rhajmurti sipped at his wine. Tremaine. Head of the intellectual wing of the College; brilliant, cold, immersed in theory and theology.

Rhajmurti had studied with him and managed to come away with some of the highest grades Tremaine had ever given out. "You're working with him on this, aren't you, Pytor?"

Alexiev squirmed in his chair, quite a sight for someone of his build. "Do you have to ask all these questions? Especially when you've figured out the answers?"

"If events weren't on such a breakneck pace, I wouldn't be so pushy. You know I've got several students who could be singled out by the testers for no other reason than they're brilliant and full of the fire of youth. I don't want to see that happen, and I'm willing to take a risk to see that it doesn't."

Alexiev paled. "What kind of risk?"

"It's nothing that could come back on you. And I don't think it's really a risk now, after what you told me. What I'd like you to do is—"

"Now wait a minute, Alfonso. I don't want to get involved in something that could—disadvantage me."

"I'm not asking you to endanger yourself." Rhajmurti leaned forward, keeping his eyes locked with Alexiev's. "Convince Cardinal Tremaine that I should be a tester, which shouldn't be hard since you say he's already considering me. Once that's done, set me up with certain students early on in the testing."

"I don't know if I can do that. I honestly don't. Cardinal Tremaine hasn't compiled the list yet—of testers *or* students."

"Even better," Rhajmurti inserted smoothly before Alexiev could go on. "This is exactly where you can help me . . . and help yourself. Offer Tremaine your services for setting up both lists. I'm sure he'd be more than pleased to have that mundane task off his back."

Alexiev's eyes narrowed in thought. "That's all? Nothing more?"

"Nothing more. I want to make sure I'm able to test certain students early on. It's a little thing, Pytor, but it will elevate your importance in Cardinal Tremaine's eyes."

"Are you *sure* that's all?" Alexiev asked. "You're damned tricky, Alfonso."

Rhajmurti placed one hand over his heart. "I swear, by Rama, Shiva, Vishnu and all the gods above and below that I'm not doing anything nefarious or injurious to the College or Revenantism. Is that good enough for you?"

"Well, you didn't have to go *that* far." Alexiev finished off his glass of wine and stared out his window. "It's Justus you're worried about, isn't it?"

"Yes, but he isn't the only one. I don't think one should be assumed a threat because one was born an Adventist. Converts are equally precious in the sight of the gods, perhaps more so. Converts make a choice."

"All right . . . I'll try. I don't see how it could hurt me. But I can't guarantee anything. And if I *do* succeed, I think it would be best if I scattered these students out, don't you? Having too many of your proteges in one session might seem suspicious."

"I don't care how you do it, as long as it's early in the testing and *I'm* the one who questions them." Rhajmurti emptied his glass. "And for godssakes, let me know as soon as you can if I'm chosen—and when the testing begins."

Alexiev stood and looked down at Rhajmurti. "You drive a hard bargain, Father."

"And you, Father, are a pompous ass!" Rhajmurti shot his compatriot his most disarming smile. "Let's go to dinner."

Justice looked around the large classroom at the students who had gathered for the first of Father Rhajmurti's emergency evening catechism classes. Raj sat to his left at the long table, and to his right sat Sonja Keisel, though he could not for the life of him figure out why a good Revenantist like her would be included in this crash program. But then the same could be said for the other students present, good Revenantists all: Kalivera Chavez, Thomas Cromwell, Ramadanje North, and Ivan Dorjan. The only thing he could come up with that linked them was the fact their teachers considered them above-average in intelligence, and more than above-average in diverse intellectual pursuits.

Ivan was the College radical; there were times Justice swore Ivan was atheistic, at best agnostic. He very quietly made a point of questioning everything taught concerning religion. Of all the students present, Justice feared the most for Ivan. His brilliant musical career might be brought to an abrupt end if he continued in his past patterns of behavior.

"All right," Rhajmurti said, leaning back in his chair and surveying the room. "Now that we've established *why* we're here this morning, let's consider the questions you might be asked."

"Do any of the cardinals know you're giving these classes, Father?" Cromwell asked.

"I haven't made it a secret, and I'm not the only priest who's doing so."

Ivan leaned forward in his chair and propped his chin on his hand. "Why us, Father? I know why *I'm* here, but I don't understand the reason for teaching these other birds to fly."

"Everyone in this room is a Revenantist, that's true, but some are newly converted. The rest of your families have been of the faith for so long now you probably take its tenets for granted."

Justice briefly shut his eyes. The "newly converted." Lord! And let's all guess who *that* is.

"Here's a question likely to be asked by the testers. Listen to it carefully, and don't give me a quick, ready-made answer. *Think* before you speak. Will a good person who is *not* Revenantist, but who lives an exemplary life, advance through the Karmic wheel at the same rate as a Revenantist?"

The room fell silent. Justice sneaked a glance at his fellow students and saw by their expressions how truly difficult the question was.

"Yes, Kalivera?" Rhajmurti prompted.

"If this person acts according to his conscience, and he has never done anything evil, how could the gods *not* reward him after death?"

"But what if this person is Adventist? What if he doesn't believe in the gods?"

"Why are you posing a question that can't be answered?" asked Ivan. "Who really knows what happens after death? Has anyone come back to tell us?"

Rhajmurti fixed Ivan with a level stare. "If you give an answer like that, m'ser Dorjan, you won't live to see another semester! Now listen to me, all of you. Right now the only thing I'm interested in is teaching you how to *think* your way through the pitfalls of Revenantist theology. What you believe in your hearts is between you and the gods, though I could wish each of you lived your lives by their laws."

"Why should the cardinals care how we respond to trick questions if we obey those laws and give the Church due honor?" asked Ramadanje North.

Sonja stirred in her chair. "Something's going on, isn't it, Father? Something that we don't know about?"

Rhajmurti looked at Sonja, then let his eyes travel up and down the table. Justice sank a bit lower in his chair, wondering if they would all survive these classes.

"That isn't for me to say. I *can* say: if you let me help you, I'll teach you how to succeed in the testing. If you fight me. . . ." The priest shrugged. "Remember, not all your families' wealth, power, or influence can alter what is written down after the testing is complete."

"I agree with Ramadanje," Kalivera Chavez said. "Why should anyone care *what* we believe if we're decent people and obey the laws?"

Rhajmurti sighed softly. "Let me tell you something," he said, making a steeple of his hands and resting his chin on their tips. "You have grown up in a time of greater freedom of thought than has been seen for years. You've been allowed to think things that would have doomed your grandparents. The circle's come 'round, children. Times have changed. And if you value your careers, to say nothing of your lives, you'll listen to the questions I ask, and learn how to answer them."

"That's being dishonest," Ivan protested, lifting his head. "How can the gods love us if we lie just to save our skins?"

Justice caught Ivan's attention. "Remember the hanging? *That* poor man was drunk when he cursed the cardinals."

"All right. I'll grant you that, but where do we draw the line? If we acquiesce on this, if we allow someone to dictate what we think and say, the next time we'll give way on something else until all our freedom to think what we want is gone."

"Besides, the hanged man was a nobody," Thomas Cromwell said. "He had no position, no—"

"What did I just say about that?" Rhajmurti demanded. "None of you is safe by merit of *position*. And if you don't believe me, may the gods have mercy on your souls."

Silence fell heavily on the room. Justice glanced at Sonja, saw her face had gone white, then looked at Raj. Raj lifted one eyebrow in eloquent agreement to what Justice was thinking. Learn now, and learn well. Like the moment of one's death, no one knew when the testing would be.

"It's not working, Trevor," Rhajmurti said not two hours later. He sat slumped back in a chair in Trevor's room. "I got through to most of them, but I can't seem to penetrate Ivan's rebellious attitude."

Father Bordinov shrugged and turned away from the window. A morning storm had swept into Merovingen: the windowpane rattled in a gust of wind that sent raindrops running across its glass.

"He *can* be obstinate," Bordinov said, "but he's one of our smartest students."

"Smart could be dead. He looks up to you as a role model of sorts, you know."

"Oh?"

Rhajmurti smiled. "You're young—one of the youngest of the teaching priests—and everything you do has a certain flair to it. Of course he looks up to you. What student wouldn't?"

"Flatterer. I assume you want *me* to talk to him."

"Clever man. *I* don't seem to be making any headway."

Bordinov took the chair facing Rhajmurti. "What of your converts . . . Justus and Raj?"

"Everyone did quite well, once we settled down to business. Ivan's the problem." Rhajmurti spread his hands. "Look what's facing us, Trevor. The governor is aging; the government is in a flux. Iosef sees the Church as a staunch ally and possibly his eldest son's supporter. The way I see it, he'll let the Church—" He lowered his voice. "—meaning Cardinal Exeter, go on about its business without interfering. We've already seen canon law taking precedence over the secular, or at least working hand in glove with it."

"And what's the life of one student who gets caught up in the whirlwind? Is that what you're saying?"

"Yes. Exactly."

Bordinov sighed. "I never thought I'd see the day . . . me, who believes the Church should be cleansed down to its foundations, telling a student to toe the line and give answers he doesn't believe to questions he deems pointless. I know, I know. Survive.

The key word here is survive. I'll talk to him, Alfonso. Maybe he'll listen to me."

The window rattled suddenly in another gust of wind. Rhajmurti jumped at the noise, saw Bordinov react similarly. *What's happened to us that we take fright at the slightest noise?* He drew a deep breath. *Not even priests are immune to the power of reactionism.*

"What of your plan to get yourself set up as a tester?" Bordinov asked.

"I found out I'm already being considered. If things go right, I don't have to worry."

Bordinov smiled slightly. "I congratulate you on your source. It couldn't be Alexiev, could it?"

"You're too clever for your own good," Rhajmurti said. "If I don't tell you, you can never say you heard it from me."

FLOOD TIDE
(REPRISED)

by C. J. Cherryh

Day went to dusk and to night again, and Jones paced and fretted and slept in catnaps, thinking, variously: He's in trouble, or: It's that damn Marina Kamat, *she's* the trouble—

At which times she thought—What if that damn Richard puts it to 'im with bribes an' all?

Man needs money, her Mama said, sitting cross-legged at the foot of the bed. Mama's ghost hadn't bothered her for months and months, but let her be alone and worried like this and Mama got more and more forward, she did—Mama herself, Retribution Jones, sat there with that old river-rat's cap they shared (in Mama's day it had more shape) tilted back on her head and with a kind of worried I-told-you-so in her eye.

Hard on a hightown man like that, Mama said, —livin' on charity. Altair, daughter, I told ye, I did tell ye, di'n't I?

She thought at her, Mind your own business, Mama.

But Mama got nervier, and got into the matter of the engine (Ye damn fool, Altair! Ye traded 'er?

Off *my* boat?) and the tangle lilies (Lord, Altair, you been drinking Det water?) till she said, out loud, "Shut *up,* Mama, ye ain't no damn help . . ." and went downstairs to whisper at Jep through the curtain, "Gimme a bottle, Jep. Whiskey."

Jep came back with the whiskey and a glass.

"Ye ain't heard nothin'?"

"Not since mornin'. Ye want we should ask?"

"Ney. Not yet." Mondragon went places best not looked into. Lord, she wanted to know; but the chance of disturbing something and getting Mondragon hurt was too much risk.

Be downstairs next dawn, she would, catch him when he came slipping by.

Damn 'im.

She took the bottle and the glass upstairs, she poured herself half a glass and drank it, she poured herself another and she and Mama had themselves a long, long talk.

Problem with being dead, Mama said, you missed things like good whiskey.

So she drank another one, by which time she was feeling no acute pain, just a lot of heartache.

See? Mama said. Told you so. See what men's good for?

A little more went into the glass. Mama went away, disgusted, maybe, and Jones sat there and stared at the wall and drank, thinking down her list of enemies and Mondragon's. That was the kind of mood she was in.

Supper came. She picked at it and had some more whiskey, because otherwise she was going to go crazy. She hated roofs over her head, damn! she hated it, she was boxed in this damn little room and

outside there was a storm going on, with the Det
running high and the thunder and the lightning skip-
ping around the wooden towers and bridges and
dancing on the water—that was where she wanted
to be, out finding out where a certain damnfool
man was, which she could do on a night like this.

Another whiskey, the supper mostly untouched
on the table. She rolled herself into the rumpled
bedclothes, felt after her knife that was on the
bedside table, along with her belt and the barrel-
hook—never forgot where those were, no, Mama,
never forgot that. . . .

But sleep escaped her, and she had a bit more,
till she was hard put to hold the glass.

Then came this tiptoeing up the steps, not the
way a body walked who was supposed to be in
Moghi's back hallway, and her heart pounded. She
thought she might be dreaming, she was so tired
and had so much whiskey in her, but she heard the
steps reach the door and stop. Just stop—like a
fool.

She got her breath and her balance, put her feet
off the bed and reached after her knife. "Mondragon?" she asked in a voice none so steady, and
then thought that was stupid: speaking out let someone with a gun figure where she was, so she got up
fast and lurched for the wall, where there was a
bureau between her and gunshots.

The latch moved and this fuzzy door opened and
this fuzzy drowned shape stood there looking at
her.

"Sorry," Mondragon said.

"You sherk!" she cried, as her heart started this

slide from her throat to her stomach. "Wha's matter, ye can't speak up?"

Mondragon slung off a wet cloak and hung it on the chair, looking so tired she was sorry she'd yelled. He came and put his arms around her, and she had this stupid knife in her hand, so she could only use one arm.

"Ye all right?" she asked him, when he just stood there holding her. He said nothing at all, and that scared her. "Mondragon?"

"Ketch is dead," he said. "Rani Spence, too."

They were all right folk. Mondragon dealt with Ketch, something to do with business. It made no sense, or it made a bad kind of sense, that he walked in like this and said something like that in that shaky kind of voice. "You all right?" she asked him again, and held onto him very gentle, the way he seemed to want just now. "Mondragon?"

"They were good people," Mondragon said. It was as broken up as she'd ever seen him.

She said, "Ye're cold. I got a bottle, got a warm bed. I'll pour ye one, here."

He sat down on the bed, she got him the drink. He took a good mouthful of it and swallowed it down with a grimace. *That* wasn't like him. She sat down sideways on the bed, watched him while he took another swallow, while the whole room was turning around, and wondered what Ketch dying meant, or why Mondragon was so shaken up.

"Ye want t' say?" she asked. "I'll listen."

He gave no answer, only took a third big drink, set the glass down, put his arm around her and kissed her, which with the whiskey made things turn around and around, she had no idea how long.

After that they fell back on the bed. He ran his hands through her hair—it was clean, she had washed—and whispered, "Jones, I've left some money on account with Moghi. He'll do you fair—"

"What's fair?" Her heart was beating hard of a sudden. Her mind made instant, elaborate constructions, Mondragon with some damn notion of going somewhere safe, somewhere only rich folk could go, folk with polished manners and connections that could help him. "What's this 'fair,' I don't need any damn *money*—"

His hand went over her mouth. He looked down into her eyes and said, "Jones. Listen to me. If anything happens to me—"

She wanted to say that was nonsense, that he was flat broke, moving into Kamat meant a whole lot of fancy expenses, she knew that. She shoved him.

He said, "—I want you to go straight to Moghi, tell him get word to Kamat, and just figure things will happen, hear me? Kamat's got a place—"

He moved his hand. She got a whole breath.

"Hell with Kamat! Nothing's going to happen to you!"

He leaned over her, so that all she could see was his eyes and all she could feel was his weight. He said, "Jones, if it does. If it does. That's all I want to know."

"Can't promise that. Somethin' happens to you—I told you long time back what I'd do—"

"My enemies are out of your reach, Jones."

"Anastasi ain't out of my reach. I'll get 'im. So you can quit makin' your fancy plans, Mondragon, I ain't goin' anywhere on Kamat charity—"

She hurt him somehow. She had no idea how. She just stared and he looked like hell.

Eventually he wound a piece of her hair around his finger and pulled, enough to sting. "Just do what I tell you. All right?"

"I ain't. Anything happens to you, I got an account with Anastasi, is what I got, Mondragon. And I'll pay 'er. I ain't lyin'."

"Jones. . . ."

"You want t' go out t' Harbor a while, just drop out o' sight? Ain't no damn Kalugin comin' out t' the rim. Do a little fishing . . ."

"Jones—"

"Well?"

"It's a dream, Jones."

"Ain't no sayin' ye can't have one work."

"Not for me." He kissed her on the mouth, but it did nothing for the lump in her throat. He made love to her, gentle and slow, said, the bastard, when he had her all out of breath, "Promise me. Promise me you'll do what I say."

She said, "The *hell*!"

And passed out.

THE TESTING
(REPRISED)

by Nancy Asire

A member of College Security had posted the Notice of Public Execution on the entry hall bulletin board of the College. As such, it was impossible to ignore, and Justice was able to read between the lines enough to realize this meant students would be expected to attend.

He and Sonja had posted themselves close enough to the Hanging Bridge to see, but far enough away so as to avoid the crush of the crowd. Justice remembered the first hanging: the man had been a ruffian with little public sympathy. The crowd that had gathered then took some delight in seeing a no-good bastard meet his end.

Today was different. Lord, how different.

The people who stood around Justice and Sonja were silent for the most part. A cold wind blew down the canals now that the storm was gone, making the noonday sunlight glitter on the choppy water. Sonja drew her cloak closer, glanced up at Justice, and grimaced. He read the look: I don't want to be here any more than you do.

A ruffle of drums. Justice turned, his greater

height allowing him to easily see over the heads of the people around him. A slow procession wound its way through the crowd; banners snapped in the brisk wind, and sunlight glittered off bared swords carried by the College Guard. Justice could not see who was being led to his death on the windy bridge, and the Notice of Execution had not given the condemned's name.

"Justus."

He looked down at Sonja who had spoken and followed the line of her stare.

Krishna! Lord and Ancestors! He had not seen Krishna in days, and here he was at the hanging, come like all the other students to fulfill his civic duty. Some of the swagger had gone from Krishna, some of his old haughtiness. In fact, in the noonday light, Krishna's face might best be described as pale.

The drums ceased. The crowd grew silent and soon there was only the sound of the wind, the snap of the saffron banners, and the slapping of water against the pilings.

"For crimes against Church and State," boomed out a voice that carried well in the wind, "for dealing in forbidden drugs and endangering the lives of others by their sale, here today will end this incarnation of Stefan Dunham."

Justice's knees began shaking; he heard Sonja gasp softly. Ancestors! One of the College's own . . . a student he had seen not more than three days ago in the halls. *And*, one of Krishna's partying friends.

"Gods, Justus," Sonja said, gripping his arm. "Do you—"

He nodded and stared at Krishna who stood as if

turned to stone, then glanced quickly away, as if in some strange fashion he could not continue watching Krishna's personal agony. He looked back toward the bridge.

The chief of College Security gestured and two of the Guard dragged a young man toward the gibbet. The executioner, clad in traditional black, with ribbons in the colors of both the governor's family and the College tied to each arm, stepped forward and fit the noose over Dunham's head.

"May your next life be wiser than this one, young Dunham," the Security chief intoned loudly, "and may some of your karma be lessened."

Sonja turned her head, unable to watch. Justice put an arm around her shoulder, bent his head and offered up a prayer in Stefan's behalf. He heard the sudden thump, the ghastly sound of snapping bones, and the soft moan that ran through the crowd. When he looked up, Stefan Dunham's body swung from the Hanging Bridge, still twitching after death.

"Gods, Justus," Sonja said, her voice hoarse. "Take me away from here, please."

The crowd was silent; the drums began their steady beat again. The Guard quickly and efficiently removed the body from the bridge to take it off down Coffin Canal for burial.

It was over . . . the example made, the lesson taught.
Lord! What of Stefan's family?
What of us?
Who's going to be next, and where will it stop?

Justice turned to go, his arm still protectively around Sonja's shoulder, and his eyes met Krishna's. For a brief moment, Krishna seemed about to speak, but he swallowed heavily, bowed his head, and lost himself in the dispersing crowd.

DON'T LOOK BACK

by Mercedes Lackey

The footstep outside the door to his room at Hilda's was a familiar one, so Raj didn't start—or reach for his knife—when a voice hailed him.

"Hey, Raj—"

Rigel—"Raj," to most who knew him—Takahashi stretched out his leg and pulled the closed door open with his foot.

"Justice, I thought you were in Life class." He raised an inquiring eyebrow at his tall, skinny roommate.

Suitemate, actually. Lord and Ancestors. Still hard to believe that I'm actually in the College, that I'm rooming with Justice . . . on the other hand, maybe I was safer in the swamp, all things considered.

Justice shrugged his shoulders, barely rippling the gray-black material of his shirt, and put his sketch-pad behind the bookcase beside him. "They canceled it. The model was another student, and they made him go to the—"

Raj swallowed hard. It didn't help his nausea any.

"Anyway, he got sick, so they told us to go home."

Raj tried to make a feeble joke. "Are you sure it wasn't 'cause he had to look at you for too long—"

Justice grimaced at him. "Oh, thanks. Thanks a lot. I like you, too. Here—" the art student tossed a smallish, brown-wrapped package at him. "This is for you. Kamat sent a messenger over with it. Hilda had it up front."

Raj caught it before it hit the bed; it was awfully heavy for such a small packet, and he *knew* as soon as he had it in his hands what it was.

And that he didn't want Justice to know.

Things were bad enough already. And more than dangerous enough already.

"Ready for the Testing?" he asked, to forestall any questions—and to distract Justice with another topic.

"I sure hope so." Justice threw his box of pencils into one of the two chairs in their "sitting room." There could only *be* one test that would be on both their minds—the Test of Faith. Pass it, and they were both certified as good little Revenantists.

Fail it, and—Raj didn't want to think about *that*. Getting tossed out of the College would be the least of his problems.

The artist stretched, and favored Raj with a wry look. "So. How about you?"

Raj swung both legs over the side of his iron-frame bed and shrugged. "I'm trying my best. Huh. Kind of funny, you know? Remember when I first thought of tryin' to get in the College? And I asked you how to pass for Revenantist?"

Justice raised his long eyebrows. "Yeah? What's funny about it?"

"Just this: if I pass this test of theirs, it'll mean

I'm *thinking* Revenantist. So what's the difference between thinking like one, and *being* one?"

Justice wrinkled up his nose. "Too deep for me, friend. Think you've been hanging around the Philosophy crowd too much. Tea and hair-splitting, yuck."

"Safer than running into Karle Hendricks," Raj replied bitterly. "Maybe they're dull and pretentious, but they aren't after me all the time."

Justice frowned sympathetically. "Yeah—you managing to avoid him? Is there anything I can do?"

Raj shook his head when Justice looked like he was going to say more. "Don't worry about it; there's nothing either of us can do about him. And you damn well *better* study that math. If you can't pass that, what the hell good will passing the Testing do you?"

Justice sighed, and shrugged again. "Too true, Raj. You know, my idea of hell is being forced to spend eternity doing story-problems." The young artist turned toward his own door, and Rigel toed his shut again with a heartless chuckle.

Two bedrooms and a sitting room. And even if it isn't Kamat, it's a world away from anything I've ever had before. Yeah, and I'm earning my way.

He pulled himself back into the middle of his bed, sitting on the handsome wool blanket cross-legged and pondered the silk-wrapped, sealed package that Richard Kamat had sent over by messenger. There was more than enough light from his tiny, airshaft window to read the inscription on the package. By what means it had come to Richard's hands, only the Angel knew.

Had Richard Kamat guessed the contents, he might not have been so quick to put it in Raj's hands.

Raj opened the outer paper, then the box it had wrapped, tipping out the package inside. Two handspans long, narrow, and heavy; and Raj had hefted too many blades in his time not to know the weight and balance of a knife, however well-wrapped in wooden box, umber silk, and crackling paper this one was.

Silk cords twisted about the final wrapping in complicated knots; red silk cords in patterns Raj knew, patterns difficult to duplicate. The final knot had been sealed with a wax stamp, imprinted with the Takahashi *mon*.

Hazard, those knots said, and *Be wary.* You only tied a package coming out of Takahashi with those knots when you thought there might be a possibility the package would be opened by unfriendly hands somewhere along the way.

All of which meant that *this* could only be the blade that had gone upriver to Nev Hettek and Granther Takahashi, the clan's iron-spined ruler.

The knife that had slain Cardinal Ito Boregy. The *Takahashi* blade, a signed blade with the *mon* etched proudly on the pommel nut for all to see, pointing straight to Takahashi—and another clan, a *Merovingen* clan.

House Kamat. A new Power, and rising, which made their situation more precarious than if they had been established movers-and-shakers.

Guilt by association implicated House Kamat; and most especially Richard Kamat, who had taken in two long-lost Takahashi boys and was even now about to tie silken cords of tighter binding to Raj, and so to the silk-and-steel House of Takahashi.

Someone had used a Takahashi blade to sever more than Ito's life. Someone had gone to expensive lengths to bring a signed Takahashi knife downriver to assassinate the Revenantist prelate. Which damning fact was known only to three: Rigel; Richard Kamat, to whom the blade had been entrusted—

And Cardinal Willa Exeter. Ito Boregy's successor.

The one who had *discovered* the body; who had given Richard Kamat the incriminating evidence with instructions to keep it safe. Who was, doubtless, playing some deep game of her own that involved Kamat debts and Takahashi debts and the ultimate calling in of those debts.

The cardinal wants her own tame Nev Hettekers? he hazarded. *Or is it more than that? Like something so complicated I can't see it?*

Raj rested his elbows on his knees and stared wearily at the thing, bright on the dark wool blanket of Kamat weaving.

I didn't expect an answer so quickly. Maybe I ought to put off opening it. My life's complicated enough as it is.

But the knots, and the message in them, did not permit any such evasions. Particularly not now, not when Richard Kamat needed *any* scrap of information, however hazardous, to counter that indebtedness to m'sera Cardinal.

Slowly, reluctantly, Raj reached for the packet; slowly broke the seal, and gave the cords the proper twist that freed them.

The silk fell open, falling on the oiled parchment

that had been holding the box. Raj pulled the silk away and the knife slipped free of it. The knife, and a tube of closely-written paper. But it was the knife that held the eye; shining, beautiful in its way, like a sleeping snake.

There was more in the way of an answer than Raj had expected. He'd thought to get a simple note. Instead—instead there were several pages here, all in Granther's hand.

Raj picked up the letters and began to read.

Richard Kamat's private study was bright as only the best room in a wealthy man's House could be; walled on two sides with clear, sparkling-clean windows and high enough to catch all the sunlight available. Polished wood, fine leather—an expensive retreat fitting the head of one of the rising stars of Merovingen.

But an incongruously young man for such an important post.

" '. . . purchased seven months ago by Desideria Chamoun,' " Richard read, his words dropping into the silence like pebbles into a quiet backwater. " 'Cousin to Michael Chamoun.' " He looked over the top of the letter at Raj, who was seated stiffly on the other side of his desk. "How certain can your grandfather be of this, Rigel? How can he tell one knife from another?"

Raj still had the blade in his hands, and chose to show him rather than tell him. He unscrewed the pommel nut and slid the hilt off the tang, laying bare the steel beneath. He tilted the thing in his hands so that it caught the light from Richard's windows, and touched a hesitant finger first to the tiny number etched into the metal just beneath the threads for the nut, then to the maker's mark that was cut into the steel below the quillons, where it would be visible. "This's a *signed* blade, m'ser Richard," he said softly. "Signed means special, and special means numbered. Takahashi has always kept track of what special blades went where. Of course," he added truthfully, "unless we get a blade back into our hands for sharpening or cleaning, we can't know who gets it after the original buyer."

"How many people know about this?" Richard Kamat's eyes were speculative; darkly brooding.

"That we keep track?" Raj considered his answer carefully. "Not many, outside of the clan. Not many inside the clan, for that matter, 'cept the ones making the signed blades. I don't think Mother ever knew, or if she did, she'd forgotten it. I doubt Denny was ever told about it; he wasn't really old enough when we left. Granther, me, Cousin Pauli, and whoever is working in the special forges. Maybe a dozen people altogether; *that* much I'm sure of. I'm pretty sure Granther was counting on me remembering."

The right corner of Richard's mouth lifted a little. "That remarkable memory of yours at work again, hmm?"

Raj nodded. "Granther showed me once how the signed blades were registered, when he took me through the forges. He'll remember that, I know he will. So he'll be pretty well certain I do, and probably figured that was why I sent the knife to him."

"So we at least have a tenuous link right back into the Boregy household; one that our enemies don't know exists. Interesting."

Raj held his peace for a moment, while Richard Kamat silently continued to read the letter that had been addressed to him. Until Kamat's brow creased for a moment, and the dark eyes flicked up at Raj—

"Granther told me what he was going to tell you, m'ser," Raj said with a lift of his chin. "About Denny, I mean."

The humor returned to Kamat's expression, and a bit of rueful, embarrassed approval. "What did he tell *you?*"

It had hurt, those words. At first. The old Raj would have dismissed them out of hand, and run off to sulk.

The new Raj maybe had a little more sense. It wasn't betrayal—it was sound thinking. Sound thinking kept Clans alive. Granther had to think about the welfare of the whole Clan. And—maybe he was sparing Raj; still protecting him. Second rank could go *be* a doctor. Second rank wouldn't be a target for assassins.

Provided those assassins didn't know for certain that he was Angela Takahashi's boy. The one with the "remarkable memory."

Second rank can get away with the minimum one year contract needed to keep Kamat's honor intact.

"That Denny's his first choice for Takahashi heir, if he can shape up. That I'm not—uh—sneaky enough to be a good House Head." The words Granther had *actually* used were "ruthless, tough and unprincipled," but Raj did not deem it politic to use *those* words to another House Head.

"You will serve better to advise your brother, and keep him from overstepping the bonds of Honor,"

the letter had continued. *"It was so that Aldebaran Takahashi served my father. It has often been so in our family, one to act as Head—but the other to act as Heart and Conscience."*

"He was a bit blunter with me," Richard Kamat said, putting the letter down and smoothing the page with one hand. " 'Denny has the brains and the mind-set, but not the sense,' " he read aloud. " 'Young m'ser Kamat, I do not entrust this task lightly to you, and I would not if I dared bring the boy home. But I do not; he would be a danger to all of us here, and not even realize it. You have said openly to me that you would gladly have even stronger ties between our Houses than those of obligation and the one-year contract marriage of your sister and young Rigel. So, I say to you now—if this is truly your wish, I tell you that you are training the heir to Takahashi—and that is Deneb. But every House Head has more than one plan, and I have more than one heir. Deneb is my first choice; but if he fails, it would be better for all of us to let the streets have him back again. I advise you to entrust his education in reason and caution to Thomas Mondragon. The man is a survivor, and surviving takes excellent sense, the same good sense Deneb lacks so woefully.' "

Silence again, as Raj pondered the implications of everything that had been said to him so far.

Richard's treating me like an equal. Like I deserve to have all *the information.*

He licked his lips and looked Richard Kamat right in the eyes. "Granther's right," he said reluctantly. "About everything. Including about Denny."

That had hurt as much as all the rest. But the

past few months had taught him a bit about his reckless little brother—

—and convinced him that without *some* kind of intercession, be it the hand of Thomas Mondragon or the hand of fate, Denny was going to get himself into some kind of trouble that *no one* would be able to get him out of.

"Lord knows I love Denny," Raj continued ruefully, "but he could make some serious problems for everybody. And Tom's about the right person to beat some brains into his head—Tom's got his respect, and he'll likely listen to him. And Tom'll knock him up against the wall if he *doesn't* listen—"

Like he's knocked me up against the wall for not listening.

"What about the rest?" Kamat asked quietly. "Don't you—resent being dealt out of your position?"

Raj shook his head emphatically. There *had* been a moment of resentment, yes, but it had been so quickly followed by relief that now he had no regrets at all. "I—I don't do that kind of thing well," he replied. "I mean—trying to figure policies, juggle people—what I *feel* about them keeps getting in the way."

"Given that you're contracting to Marina, I can't say I'm unhappy to hear you say something like that. Right now I think she needs a friend more than anything else in the world." Richard massaged his temple as if his head hurt.

It probably did, given that Marina had entertained everyone at dinner last night with an hysterical outburst over the dessert.

At least she waited until dessert. Last week she had a fit before the second course.

"She's all right this morning, m'ser," Raj said as confidently as he could. "She sent me a note, apologizing for the way she acted last night."

After I sent her a flower this morning. At least once in a while I'll get a notion about what will make her feel a little happier, cheer her up. Poor Marina.

"It'll be better once the ceremony's over," he told Richard earnestly. And then felt a lurch in his stomach, himself.

Lord and Ancestors. Me and Marina, married, even if it's only in name. When what I want—now—

What he wanted would not satisfy anything or anyone but himself.

What he wanted was time—time for himself, and Kat Bolado. The "Girl in the Boat."

He knew who she was now. Denny had arranged a meeting.

Lord. Kat. If I had any choice—

But he didn't have a choice. By the time he'd finally *met* his ephemeral girl, he'd already given his word to Richard Kamat and Marina. And it was too late. He couldn't back out of the contract, not then, not when so many people were relying on him to keep his word. Kat, thank God, had understood. Really, honestly understood, not just pretending to understand. And they'd made a kind of pact; while he was honor-bound to Marina they'd be friends and *stay* friends by never, ever going anywhere alone together. He met her two, three times a week, down in John's Tavern, and they'd talk—

Seemed like Kat understood him better than anyone. He kept no secrets from her. Maybe that wasn't wise, but with Kat, he didn't much care about being smart. And maybe, in a year or so—

Maybe they'd do more than just talk.

But that was for later. Right now he had Marina, and all the commitments he'd made to her.

Ironic that he was taking credit for her baby, who hadn't so much as seen her unclothed.

Well, at least we're *friends. And this* really *cancels out Takahashi debt*. He was under no illusions about why Richard had made the marriage offer—or why Marina had accepted it. *No way is she gonna get Tom to lay claim to the kid. So this's about the only way that baby is going to get a daddy that wouldn't bring* all *kinds of karma down on Kamat—and if Marina didn't* name a daddy, anybody who wants to put the screws on Richard could come along and claim it.

But that didn't make what was going to happen any easier. His eyes went without any conscious thought on his part to the shadowed nook of Richard's office that held the ceremonial sword marking the alliance of the two houses. Cords of Kamat blue and Takahashi scarlet hung at a precise angle from the hilt. Getting *married* wasn't exactly what Raj had had in mind when he'd been *in love* with Marina—and now that they were just friends—

And hell, I'm only seventeen—

But this was duty, and much more important than his own feelings. This was Clan business, and for the sake of the Clan and Takahashi Honor Rigel could no more back out than fly to the moon.

"I can't say I blame you for staying roommates with that friend of yours over on Kass," Richard continued, looking up with a wry twist to his mouth.

"There are times lately when *I* wish I could move off the island. By the way, those herbal teas you brought do seem to be helping Mother."

It was an oblique sort of "thank you," but neither of them particularly wanted to openly allude to Andromeda's addiction to deathangel—nor the flashback she'd had that had revealed the addiction to Raj, the outsider.

"I'm glad Doctor Jonathon was willing to trust me," Raj replied.

Richard smiled faintly. "He *was* rather dubious at first, but you've convinced him that you know what you're talking about. In fact, he's invented an 'old herb-doctor' to account for the things you brought him, and he's been leaking the information over to the College since the remedies seem so effective."

"I'm . . . glad to hear it. That—stuff—it's still a problem," Raj said soberly. "Nothing seems to keep people away from it, not with the Boregy girl eating it like candy. You'd think people'd have learned by now—" He shrugged. Richard shook his head.

"People never seem to learn."

By his face, unguarded for the moment, Raj could read the unspoken words.

Not even Mother.

Richard looked up, and caught Raj's eyes on him. After an awkward pause, he cleared his throat. "By the way, how are your studies with Father Rhajmurti coming?"

Raj swallowed. "All right, I guess. This stuff— it's not anything I can *memorize*. It's—I'm not sure, m'ser, I'm afraid even if I *do* pass, I'm never going to be a *good* Revenantist. When—when people I know are in trouble, I—I've got to help them, and hang karma.''

Richard smiled, his earlier cool poise restored, and stood up. "For Marina's sake, I wouldn't want to see you act any differently, Rigel.''

Raj knew a dismissal when he heard one; he stood likewise, edged past Richard to the door, made the right polite noises, and took his leave.

But he didn't go very far.

Just down two floors and over a few corridors, to another office—one not nearly so opulent as Richard's, but possibly more important to Kamat prosperity.

". . . Michael Chamoun's cousin," Raj concluded; he sat back on the hard wooden chair, then continued with his own speculation. "Not enough to convict anybody, but maybe enough evidence to be embarrassing?''

"Could be.'' Thomas Mondragon leaned back in his own plain wooden chair and interlaced his fingers behind his blond head, looking deceptively lazy and indolent. Raj knew that pose. He also knew what it meant. Mondragon was thinking. Hard. "So why bring this news to me, Raj?''

"Because I still owe you," Raj said bluntly. "Because you may be playing m'ser Richard's game, but that doesn't mean his coat'll cover you if things get *real* sticky. Because I don't know if m'ser Richard will bother to tell you or not. He didn't tell me *not* to tell you, and my debt to you comes first.''

Mondragon smiled, very slightly, and pointed a long index finger at him. "You're learning.''

"I'm trying, Tom," Raj replied earnestly. " 'Tisn't

like the swamp, and it is. There're still snakes, only they don't look like snakes. There're still gangs, only they don't act like gangs. There're tests—and they're just as serious. Like this catechism stuff—"

"How are you coming?" There seemed to be real warmth in Mondragon's murky green eyes; real concern.

Of course, that *could* just be concern over the Revenantist Inquisition taking up one of Thomas Mondragon's best informers, and one of the few folk who knew *who* and *what* he really was—but Raj didn't think so. As much as Mondragon could—and more than was safe or politic—he cared for Raj's welfare.

"All right, I think," Raj gave him the same answer he'd given Richard Kamat. "It's kind of hard to tell, but I think Father Rhajmurti figures we'll make out all right. Well, I *know* Justice will, but he's had a lot more practice in thinking Revenantist. The only thing that seems to help *me* is to try to think like I was God's own accountant."

Mondragon laughed at that, a deep-throated chuckle. The past few months had been good to Mondragon; he'd recovered from his near-fatal illness and more. And he and Marina were, if not on friendly terms, less at odds. Thanks to Raj's work, she no longer blamed *him* for her mother's perilous addiction to deathangel. There was still tension in the air whenever they met, but Raj wasn't certain what the cause was.

Could be just 'cause it's really Tom she wishes she was marrying. And not for a paltry year, either.

That might be what kept setting her off into hysteria, seeing as she and Tom met at least three or four times a week, since Mondragon had moved into quarters on Kamat at Richard's urging.

Jones had not much cared for that. Raj wasn't sure how Mondragon felt about it. But, at least to Raj's eyes, the suite of rooms that the new head of the Kamat-sponsored Samurai occupied *looked* more secure than Tom's old apartment on Petrescu. Raj could only hope that they were.

What Mondragon made of the situation, he couldn't tell; he could read the man a little better these days, but—well, Mondragon was Mondragon, and when he chose not to be read, there was no catching him out.

But for this moment, it seemed, his concern was on Raj.

"Richard tells me you're doing well enough in your College studies—" He smiled as Raj's jaw sagged a little. "Yes, Raj, we talk about you. And that scapegrace brother of yours."

"You're gonna have to do more than talk about Denny," Raj said bluntly. *Might as well let him have the bad with the good.* "Granther's got the notion of making Denny heir to Takahashi—*if* he can get some sense pounded into him. And Granther reckons you to do the pounding. He told m'ser Richard as much."

Raj managed *not* to grin at the dismay that briefly flashed across Mondragon's face. The renegade Sword sighed and cast his eyes up toward the ceiling.

"Why me?" he muttered. "Why *me*?"

"Father Rhajmurti'd say it was your karma," Raj said impudently.

Mondragon's green eyes lowered and gave him a piercing glare—but there was a touch of good humor behind the glare. "Save that Revenantist cant for when you need it, boy," he warned. "Did anyone bother to think that your brother might not survive my gentle lessoning?"

Raj absently rubbed a bruise that ran across his bicep—legacy of one of *his* recent lessons with Mondragon. He was learning the art of keeping himself alive at the sometimes too-efficient hands of Mondragon. The down and dirty art of street-fence, which had very little to do with the proper fencing studies he was getting at the College.

"Granther told Richard that if Denny didn't shape up—it was better for him to dump Den back on the streets."

"Which means, eventually, the Harbor." Mondragon sobered immediately. "A very . . . efficient, man, your grandfather. A very realistic man."

"Tom—" this was very hard to say, but Raj had come to a few hard conclusions himself over the past few weeks, talking things over with Justice. And this was his first opportunity to talk to anyone except Justice about them. "Tom, you know I'd die for Denny. I really would. But—I can't keep him from going off and killing himself, can I? He's either gonna grow up, or—or he isn't. Either way, it's his doing, and not mine, and there isn't a damned thing I can do about it. Because right now he isn't gonna listen to me. I proved myself a fool too often for that. And even if he'd listen to me, that doesn't mean he'd believe me."

Mondragon blinked. "Well. You *are* learning."

Raj sighed, and rubbed his bruised arm. "Yey. And it isn't easy. The learning, or believing it."

*   *   *

Raj let the crowd of students take him along the corridor while he concentrated on the material for his next class. Philosophy—like the things Father Rhajmurti was trying to drill him in—was not something you could handle by memorization.

He was so intent that he didn't bother to pay much attention to who was around him.

"Well, if it isn't the *Doctor*." The voice behind Raj held a sneer. Raj stopped, and turned—carefully— to face his newest tormentor.

Seems like there's always one. Back in the swamp, it was MacDac and Big Ralf. Tree had it in for me and Denny until Wolfling dumped him in the canal. So now it's Karle Hendricks. A new kind of game, different rules, but the same end. And I can't, I daren't fight him. Not physically, anyway.

Karle Hendricks; tall, dark, incredibly handsome. Captain of the fencing team. Son of the up-and-coming Hendricks family.

Certainly one of the most popular, if not *the* most popular, young man in Raj's class-group, not the least for the reason that he spread his silverbits around freely. Until Raj had arrived on the scene.

Raj was different, exotic—and good-natured. Scion of a foreign Nev Hetteker family perhaps, *but* under the aura of the rising star of the Kamats. The Kamats were *there*; which presumably meant that held true for the Takahashis. The Hendricks were only aspiring. All these things conspired to steal some of Karle's followers and make them Raj's adherents, at least at first. Karle was *not* noted for his good nature; the friends he bought generally ended up being reminded at some point or other how much they owed to Karle. Karle was inclined to back his reminders up with unpleasant words, and sometimes more than just words.

Raj never asked anything of anyone, which state of affairs was novel, and somewhat attractive to some of Karle's more reluctant "admirers."

Karle was not amused.

If you were one of Raj's friends—you could find yourself facing Karle along a blade, at least in fencing practice. And Karle had his retaliations timed to a hair, for precisely when Father Abdi wasn't looking.

If you were one of Raj's friends, you could find yourself waylaid on the bridges some foggy night, and beaten up. While Karle and *his* friends were demonstrably elsewhere.

"Hello, Karle," Raj said, carefully, making sure he got his back to the corridor wall. "How did the competitions go?"

Karle smirked, his chiseled features painted with self-satisfaction. "I'm still team captain. Double everyone else's points. When am I gonna see *you* on the strip, minnow?"

So far Raj had managed to avoid being at any lessons shared by Karle.

He shrugged, and clutched his books a little tighter. "I just don't know, Karle. You know I've got a lot of studying to do for Father Rhajmurti's test."

He was trying to keep face and voice as neutral as possible. But he steamed inwardly, wanting to smash that insolently handsome face, longing to see that perfect body up to the ass in swamp mud. *Eight, nine, ten. I'd still like to rub your face in muck. You bullying bastard.* He ground his teeth as Karle made some remark about foreigners, insinuating that Raj and some of the perfumed delicates of the Chattelan might have a few things in common.

If I get into trouble with him, it'll come down on Richard's head. I could get thrown out of the College. It isn't gonna hurt me to let him bully me. So what if people think I'm a coward? What's it matter?

But it rankled, it rankled, particularly when he was remembering how he had faced down both MacDac and Big Ralf. Both of them killer-crazies, both encountered in the mud and filth of the swamp; madmen who'd been out for his blood. Not dancers along a fencing strip, in the clean, well-lit salle, with rules and judges overseeing everything; no, this had been in rotten weather, with knives and bare hands, and no rules except that the winner lived a little longer.

And Raj had killed them both with his own two hands.

"Of course, our doctor couldn't possibly be a coward, could he?" Karle asked the four or five students crowding around him.

They grinned. Raj fought down the impulse to *say* something.

Like, "Try me in the swamp some time, I've killed tougher crazies than you." Lord and Ancestors, that would get me in trouble. Right now I'm like Tom Mondragon. They know the name, here; they know I'm sort-of from Nev Hettek. But let it be known I'm that Rigel Takahashi, and the word'll be upstream faster than a steamboat. Then the Sword won't be able to ignore me.

He bit his tongue, and his stomach churned.

"Maybe he's a lover, not a fighter," suggested

one of the others snidely. "I hear tell Marina Kamat must think so."

Raj's face flamed as they all snickered.

"I dunno, he don't look like much of a lover, either," Karle replied, circling around him and looking him up and down, critically. "*I* think Marina got herself somebody else on the side."

Raj felt a cold lump in his guts, and clutched his book until his hands hurt. That was too near the truth.

Way too near—

"Hendricks, are you and your little social club gonna block the corridor all day?"

Karle jumped as a hand came down on his shoulder. The hand was attached to a plump brown arm that belonged to Gopal Raza.

A senior student and one of the Rimmon Isle Razas. Standing beside him was ethereal Lelani Yakunin, another senior, and from another of the Elite Isle Families.

Raj could read Karle's face like the page of a book. Frustration—anger—then a conciliatory smirk. Neither of these two were people lowly Karle Hendricks dared to provoke.

"Don't pay any mind to this blowhard, kid," Lelani said maliciously. "Everybody knows Hendricks lets his mouth run while his brain's on 'idle.' You're the Kamat protege, aren't you? Takahashi?"

Raj nodded dumbly. Gopal squinted as he took a closer look at the badge on Raj's College sash. "Medicine, huh?" He laughed. "By the Wheel, Hendricks, you're even stupider than I thought!"

Karle scowled. "What's that supposed to mean?" he snapped.

"Well, first of all, you've been blocking the corridor for about five minutes. As a senior student, if I was feeling mean, I *could* hand you down some demerits for that. Second, baitbrains, you've been picking on somebody who's gonna be a *doctor* some day. You ever bother to think about what *that* could mean in a couple of years?"

Karle's bafflement registered in the blank look he presented to Gopal and Lelani.

"Look, fishbreath—you wave that fancy rapier of yours around all the time. One of these days somebody is gonna take you up on a bridge-duel. Probably a *lot* of somebodies. And one of them is *real* likely to be better and sneakier than you." Gopal's round face and bland expression made his indifferent tone sting Karle all the more; Raj could tell by the tensing of the younger boy's shoulders. "And when that happens, you're gonna be looking up at a doc, and hoping he can keep you from bleeding to the death, or going infected, or maybe losing a leg or an arm. Ever stop to think that the doc you'll be looking at might *just* be Takahashi, here?"

From the glazed look in Karle's eyes, that was a scenario he'd never bothered to entertain. The two seniors laughed, and pushed their way past Raj on down the corridor.

"I can tell *you* something, Hendricks," Lelani called over her shoulder. "If *I* stood in that pair of shoes, I'd think real hard about what kind of karma I'd been earning. Remember what's happened already. Remember, 'what goes around, comes around.' "

Raj wriggled out of the press of bodies while

their paralysis held, his own jaw aching, his teeth clenched, his throat tight with anger.

What goes around, comes around. Yeah, sure. But not soon enough.

The room between his bedroom and Justice's was six strides wide and twelve long. Not much room for walking out the anger that threatened to turn Raj inside out.

Raj paced the narrow confines of the sitting room, as Justice watched him with a worried expression.

"God, I'd like to get him up a dark cut some night!" Raj fumed between clenched teeth. "Up a dark cut and get my hands on him—" He reached the wall and turned jerkily, as he drove his fist into his palm. "Coward, am I? Stinking Chat boy-lover? Just one chance, that's all I ask—just *one*—"

"Raj," Justice said unhappily, "You aren't *really* thinking of—"

"Getting him alone, then pounding his face into a walkway?" Raj stopped pacing abruptly, and pivoted to face his roommate, his shoulders sagging with sudden resignation. "No. Damn, though, I'd like to give him a real taste of instant karma. Man-to-man, at hand to hand I could beat him."

Justice's expression of skepticism stung.

"I *could!*" Raj snapped. "All *m'ser* Karle Gupta Ivanovitch Hendricks knows is *school* fighting. Most of it by the rules—and then he only knows how to *bend* the rules, he don't know how to break 'em. Where *I*—"

He stopped, before he could say "where I come from," and changed his choice of words. "—he *don't* know street-fighting. I could have him down on the floor inside five minutes, an' I could beat him black and blue without *him* laying a finger on me."

"And what would *that* prove?" Justice asked quietly.

"That I'm as good as he is! Better!"

"*He'd* sing a different tune. He'd tell everybody you ambushed him, say you cheated. And by his way of thinking—by the way *most* of the hightowners think—you would have cheated. And he might give you trouble with Administration. That's not too healthy, these days. Especially if anybody finds out you were the source of those Crud-medicines."

"Yeah—but dammit, Justice, he'd *never* forget what I did to him!"

"Exactly," Justice replied. "Exactly. He'd *never* forget. And he'd make sure nobody else did, either. There's a canaler saying for situations like that. 'Don't look back. There might be something gaining on you.' "

"You don't *understand,*" Raj cried, clenching his hands into fists at his sides.

Justice just sighed. "Raj, I've got a tutoring session; I've got to go. Why don't you take your foil over to the gym and work some of that frustration out?"

Raj watched in silence as he picked up his books and notepad, and reached for the door handle. And hesitated for a moment, then looked back over his shoulder.

"Whatever you think, I *do* understand, friend. I really do. And—never mind."

Raj sagged down into a chair as Justice left, closing the door softly behind him. For a while he just sat, stomach churning, head aching, trying to calm himself down. When all his best efforts failed, he decided to follow Justice's advice, and go work some of his frustration out physically. If he went to the salle at the gym, he'd probably be able to find someone for fencing practice. At the least, he could take out his anger on the target-dummy. He grabbed up his foil and mask from the corner, checked to make sure that his keys were still in his pocket, and stalked out, slamming the door to the suite behind him.

It was still hot, even with the sun long down; the air was deathly still. The flames of the torches lighting the bridges rose straight up, unwavering. Somewhere below, Raj could hear people talking, laughing; the sounds of boats being poled along the canals. No sound of motors—not under the new Edict. Merovingen was the quieter for that.

Raj got all the way to the College, and was actually on the wide, paved walkway that led to the gym, when his sense of *something wrong* made him tense and look around.

Just as Karle and three of his friends stepped from a doorway ahead, blocking his path.

He whirled—to find his escape route blocked by four more.

The sound of a slow footstep on the walk made him turn to face Karle again, jaw clenched tight.

"Nice night, hey, Doctor?" Karle had fencing mask and foil tucked under one arm, and his hair was damp with sweat, clinging limply to his forehead. "You know, we never got to finish our little discussion this afternoon."

"That's—true, Karle," Raj managed to get out. Suddenly it was very hard to breathe.

"And you never did tell me when I was gonna see you on the strip. Now I *don't* suppose you were on the way to take me up on that invitation, were you?"

"I—" Raj rasped. "I—"

"I think maybe he was, Karle," one of the others said gleefully.

"What a pity. The salle is absolutely full of seniors tonight. They even booted *us* out, didn't they?" Karle made a sad face as he looked from one to another of his friends. "I guess we'll just have to postpone our little meeting."

The rest made noises of disappointment. Raj waited, heart falling to his boots. There was no way Karle was going to let him off *that* easy, and he knew it.

"Wait! I know!" Karle snapped his fingers and beamed. "We can have our little match right here! There's plenty of light, plenty of room—how would that be?"

Grins met this announcement, grins and exclamations of glee.

"What a perfect solution! Come on, Takahashi, you wouldn't want to disappoint everybody now, would you?"

"No," Raj croaked unhappily. "Of course not."

At a signal from their leader, the rest spread out and back; Karle smirked, pulled his mask on over his head, and saluted Raj mockingly. Trying to keep his hands from shaking, Raj did the same.

The feet scuffled on the worn surface of the walkway as they danced around each other for a bit. Raj could feel sweat running down his back, but he wasn't hot—he was cold, cold.

This isn't the swamp. He isn't gonna kill me.

He's only gonna humiliate me. . . .

Like hell he is.

They feinted, made a pass; blades hissed against each other, but both parried successfully, and Raj danced back, curiously short of breath.

The first exchange was inconclusive; the second was not. Karle came in with a low-line attack that was illegal as all hell; if Raj had twisted desperately aside at the last minute it would have hit somewhere *very* personal and left him gasping on the walkway. As it was, he'd have a bruise in a very tender area.

Karle disengaged and came in again, like a hunting shark. This time he backed Raj right up into the line of his friends; one of them shoved him and sent him sprawling at Karle's feet; both knees hit the walkway with a *crack*.

And Karle "accidentally" kicked him in the stomach as he got out of the way.

"So sorry," Karle mocked, backing up enough to give him room to get to his feet again.

Raj coughed, and did his best to pretend that nothing had happened. But he could feel Karle's grin behind the mask, he could *feel* it. And he wanted to smash that grin—

Karle made another rush; this time Raj stood his ground. Blades twined around each other; bells met with a *clang*, and they wound up staring at each other through wire-mesh; *corps-a-corps*, blades locked at the hilts.

Which was precisely the beginning of one of the

bridge-fighting tricks Mondragon had just gotten
through drilling into his brain.

*Sucker-punch his gut, pommel to the chin, kick
his knee in, and finish him with pommel to the back
of the neck as he goes down.*

It all flashed through Raj's mind in a split second.

*I can do it. Now. I can beat him, I can hurt him
and there's no way any of his friends can get here
fast enough to stop me—*

Time froze—

And he heard other voices in his head.

*"And what would that prove? He'd never forget.
And he'd make sure nobody else did, either. There's
a canaler saying for situations like that. 'Don't look
back. There might be something gaining on you.'*

"What goes around, comes around."

Raj stared into the mesh, into the faint shadows
that were Karle's eyes behind the mesh—and delib-
erately did nothing.

That was the beginning of the end. Less than five
minutes later he was beaten; exhausted, bruised,
and disarmed at least twice. Karle was moving in
for a third time when an angry voice froze him
where he stood.

"What is going on here?"

Raj stumbled back and leaned up against the
support of the wall to his right as Father Abdi
pushed his way through the huddle of Karle's friends
to stand between Raj and the fencing captain, face
flushed with anger.

"Just *what* is all this? Brawling? On *College* property, no less? Karle Hendricks, this is going to cost
you—"

I can let this go on. I can even say Karle forced me

into it. Father Abdi will believe me, especially after the way Karle came after me in the hall this afternoon in front of seniors.

"And what would that *prove?"*

While Father Abdi continued his strident lecture, Raj's mind explored a hundred pathways—and came up with something that just—might—work.

From somewhere he found enough breath to speak. "Excuse me?" he interrupted humbly.

Both Father Abdi and the sullen Karle flashed startled looks at him.

"Excuse me, Father, but it wasn't—what you think. The salle was full, and Karle had promised to give me a lesson."

Absolute truth, every word of it. Right down to Karle's own words.

Karle had pulled off his mask, and Raj got a fleeting bit of satisfaction watching the conflicting emotions racing across his face.

Didn't expect to eat your own words quite like this, did you?

"There wasn't anybody out here, and there's lots of room. Karle didn't think anyone would be bothered."

Father Abdi impaled each of Karle's friends in turn with his rapier-gaze. "Is this true?" he demanded.

They nodded, confused.

"I swear Father, every word of it is absolutely true. Why would Karle bother with me otherwise? Everybody *knows* how good a fencer he is, and how bad I am." From somewhere Raj found enough strength to push away from the wall, and advance on Karle, hand outstretched. Karle took it, face absolutely blank with astonishment.

"Thanks, Karle," Raj said, with complete sincerity. "I learned a lot from this." Then added, forcefully. "There's some real karma owed here."

And he saw Karle's face go from blank to pale, and smiled a thin little smile comprised of equal pain and satisfaction.

Because I just saved your tail from a real twisting, didn't I, Karle? And you're a good little Revenantist. Best you would have gotten is thrown off the fencing team. If I'd really squealed, you could have gotten thrown out of the College. And you just realized that, didn't you?

Father Abdi blinked. "Well, Raj Takahashi, if this is *really* what was going on, I guess I owe young Hendricks an apology for the dressing-down I just gave him. I'm sorry, Hendricks. I think it's very commendable, using your spare time to give some of the less experienced fencers a hand. I'll see to it that it goes in your record."

Karle flushed.

"He really gave me a good workout, Father," Raj said with just a faint touch of maliciousness. "He beat me three times, fair and square." *Cheating and all.* He shook his head. "I'm no match for you, Karle, and I'm afraid I never will be. You're really the best."

"Good boy." Father Abdi clapped him on the back, making him stagger. "A real gentleman knows how to lose graciously; that's as important as winning. Keep that in mind, young m'sers."

The boys shuffled their feet and muttered uneasily. Karle flushed a deeper red.

Raj smiled. "Hey, Father, I know when I'm outmatched! Anyway, thanks, Karle. I need a bath. I'll see you in classes tomorrow. Goodnight, Father Abdi."

"Goodnight to you, Raj." The priest turned his attention toward Karle again. "Now about that low-line attack you were starting—"

Raj managed not to limp until he got out of sight—then he used the railings to help get himself home. Halfway there he ran into Justice and Sonja Keisel.

"Ancestors! Raj, what *happened* to you?" Justice stared at him; Sonja bit her lip.

"Nothin' much. Just a little—exercise. With Karle Hendricks."

"Hendricks! But—"

"Just bruises. Honest. And I think maybe this came out all right." Raj explained as well as he could while they accompanied him across the last bridge and into Hilda's.

By then he wasn't limping quite so badly. They all crowded into the sitting room, and he eased himself down into the chair nearest the door. He rolled up the legs of his breeches, and prodded the bruised knees. They looked like hell, but they *weren't* swelling.

"It'll be okay," he told them as they hovered over him anxiously. "Nothing broken. I'll be stiff in the morning, that's all—and I'll probably need a beer or two to get to sleep."

"So—you *let* Hendricks beat you up. And then you pulled his fish out of the fire." Justice brought him the pair of scarves he asked for, and Raj began improvising a couple of knee-wraps.

"I guess so." He looked up from his wrapping, feeling some of that smoldering resentment that had led him out into the city in the first place. "Well, how big a fool was I? I *still* want to beat his face in, Justice."

"Uh-huh. But you didn't. Now he owes *you*. And even if he didn't—you made a big show of how much better he is than you are. So now if he tries bullying you again, everybody's going to *know* he's being a bully."

"The story will be all over the College by noon," Sonja put in. "Enough people are going to read between the lines to know what you did to keep Karle out of trouble. And what did this cost you?"

"Stiff knees," Raj admitted. "Not much, really. That—and people are gonna figure me for a wimp. A smart wimp, but a wimp."

"So?" Justice raised an eyebrow. "No reason to pound on a wimp, is there?"

"Not unless they get high or drunk and go out looking for somebody to beat up. And the day I can't outrun a drunk—" Raj snorted as Justice laughed.

"Exactly." Sonja smiled. She had a lovely smile. Raj could very easily see why Justice was rather smitten with her—even if Justice wouldn't admit that he was.

Like Kat, really. Bet they've got a lot in common.

"I guess it doesn't matter what they think of me," Raj said reluctantly.

Justice grinned. "Welcome to the club, Raj."

"What club?" Raj asked, confused.

"Smart people, who've figured out what *does* matter. There aren't a lot of us around." Justice headed toward the door with Sonja. They both stopped for a moment, when Raj spoke again.

"I suppose. But Justice—"

"Uh-huh?"

"I *still* want to pound his face in."

Sonja laughed, and Justice grinned as he replied. "There's no rules in the club about *wanting*, Raj. Good night to you. I'll bring you that beer after I walk m'sera Keisel home."

Raj pushed himself up out of his chair and over to his own room, and began massaging the bruised knees so they wouldn't stiffen up *too* much. *So it didn't cost me too much. And now Hendricks'll leave me alone, like Krishna leaves Justice alone. It was worth it.*

I guess.

Ah, hell. Don't look back, Takahashi. There might be something gaining on you.

FLOOD TIDE
(REPRISED)

by C. J. Cherryh

Two sick fools was how it had turned out, both hung over, neither one of them wanting to move for several hours, and having not a shred of interest in the fancy breakfast Jep had set outside. Which meant neither one of them had exactly won: she never would say yes to Mondragon's stupid notion she was going to run, and Mondragon never would tell her what he was into, only swore that he was staying close about Kamat except as he had to be out about town, and insisted he wanted her there, too, with him.

She'd said no, she'd explained to him all over again for the dozenth time at least how Moghi didn't hand out any damn charity, she had to haul his barrels and fetch his supplies, and the same for her other regulars, or figure they'd go to some other skip-freighter as could deliver—and Mondragon had said pay Del to do it, and looked upset, and they'd yelled at each other until he yelled, "Did you like it that much at Megarys, Jones?" and then shut up, because that was nothing she ever wanted to think about again, and it nearly made her throw up.

That was how it ended—he held her, he said he was sorry he yelled, she kept her mouth shut, Mondragon went to Kamat and she went there till nightfall and said her work was waiting.

So they yelled at each other quieter this time because they were in Kamat House, and he finally saw it was no good, unless he was going to lock her up—like Megarys, she'd said. I don't like roofs, Mondragon! I hate 'em! I can't breathe in here—

And he'd let her go, the way he'd let her go the last time he'd taken this notion to take her off the water and wrap her in cottony-floss.

But it was because he got the willies himself when she talked about roofs and walls, and that was why he gave it: that went straight to a sore spot—

His own damn fault, she told herself glumly. He was the one that brought up Megarys.

But she felt sorry she'd won that way, all the same, even if it was one crazed thing they both understood.

So she made up her mind she was going to do something nice; and she got down in the first drop-box on the stern of her skip, and she got the key to the Petrescu place, which Mondragon still had time on, and she went before she made her rounds and slipped over to Hoh's and got Denny.

"I want you to burgle," she said. At which Denny's eyes grew quite amazed. But they were old partners in misdeed.

"Megarys?" Denny asked, standing in the well—he'd learned right smart about getting in her way when she was poling.

"Ney," she said. "Want you to slip some stuff down to the skip."

"Yey, well, if I do?"

"Just I got this notion Mondragon'd like his stuff took care of. I got the key."

"That ain't burglary."

She shot Denny a look. "It ain't my apartment, it ain't yours, ol' Petrescu's got th' door locked. Even if it's Mondragon's property. Wasn't any time to move anythin' but clothes. But I just got the notion it'd be nice if that nice bureau got t' Kamat."

"Lord! 'At thing weighs a damn—"

"Ye bring the drawers down the steps one at a time, an' I'll help ye with the main piece. Easy. She's dark, ain't nobody goin' t' see us."

Denny scratched his head, looking doubtful. "Want I get some help?"

"Might do. We get that bureau, then I leave ye the key, a'right, and you and the lads just go get the light stuff. —An' no pilferage! I give a dece f' the job. Ye do it right!"

"Ney," Denny said meekly. "What d' we do wi' 'at stuff?"

"Ye just filch it right in t' Kamat. Right in t' Mondragon's sittin' room. Can ye do 'er?"

"Yey," Denny said. " 'Oo pays th' lads?"

"I paid *you*, ye connivin' sherk, you pays th' lads!"

" 'Ey, 'ey, I got t' give 'em a share."

She paused in mid-course across the halfdeck, held up four fingers. "A whole damn lune good sil'er, and ye doesn't filch anythin' off o' Kamat when ye takes it up!"

"Deal," Denny said.

Thump! in the hall, and Mondragon sat right up in bed. "Ney," Jones said, and put her arms around his neck, and pulled him down again on that soft brass bed. " 'At's nothin', I just asked th' man t' bring me personals up from the skip. I had m' hands full."

"That damn bureau—"

"She's pretty, Mondragon, all them carvin's up and down, don't care if they are naked, she's a pretty piece."

"I don't want you around Petrescu! I don't want you near that place!"

"Well, she's 'ere, ain't she? All that shiny wood, ain't goin' t' let ol' sera Petrescu have 'er. . . . 'Ere, now—"

There were, thank the Lord, no more thumps. But Mondragon wasn't listening anyway.

A little upset in the morning, he was, with a whole pile of pretty stuff from Petrescu in the middle of the sitting room floor.

He looked at her, a quick mad look, hands on hips.

She shrugged. "Guess it *was* burglars."

"Hell, Jones!"

She lifted a hand. "Hey, I didn't do 'er! Guess Denny just thought it'd be nice."

"Nice, God help me. Denny?"

"Ye shouldn't waste things, Mondragon, ye buy all this nice stuff, just leave it lyin'—" She shook her head, bent and picked up a pretty enameled box. Lord, money was still in it. "Good on him. —Done a turn at honest hire last night, him an' his lads."

"Denny?"

"Fair rates, too."

THE TESTING (REPRISED)

by Nancy Asire

"It's out," Alexiev said, leaning closer to Rhajmurti in the all but deserted hallway of the priests' private floor. "The testing's to begin tomorrow morning."

Rhajmurti took Alexiev's elbow and steered him closer to the wall.

"And?"

Alexiev darted a look around. "I tried, Alfonso . . . I *truly* tried. . . ."

"What do you mean, you tried? Are you telling me that I'm *not* to be one of the testers?"

"No . . . no. There was never any doubt about that. It's the students you're worried about. . . ."

Rhajmurti's heart lurched.

"What about them? I'm not going to be one who questions them, is that it?"

The look on Alexiev's face was enough to tell the story.

"Why not?"

"I couldn't change Tremaine's mind. He's got you set up to test the day following." Alexiev met Rhajmurti's eyes. "Believe me, I pushed until I knew if I pushed any harder, Tremaine would notice."

"O gods." Rhajmurti leaned back against the wall. Now, not only was the testing to begin sooner than anyone would have guessed, but he had only given one catechism class, hardly enough to fully prepare his students for the questions they would face.

"I *did* get you named as a backup," Alexiev said. "That's the best I could do."

"A backup?"

"Each priest has another priest named to take his place if he should fall ill, or—"

Rhajmurti stared. "And who's testing my students?"

"Father Jonsson."

"Gods, Pytor . . . he's nearly as bad as—" He bit his lip. "He's as reactionary as some other people I don't need name."

Alexiev spread his hands. "I'm sorry. I tried. I did the best I could."

"Don't worry about it. I'm sure no one could have done a better job." Rhajmurti rubbed his chin, stared at his feet, then looked up again. "You're *sure* I'm the backup?"

"Oh, yes. Tremaine said some kind things about you, by the way. He likes you, Alfonso. You should take more advantage of that."

"Whatever. I don't do well in the circles of the mighty. I'm just a simple priest, Pytor, and very content to stay that way."

Alexiev snorted. "Simple priest, is it? Ha! You're more convoluted than a canaler's knot. What the rest of us achieve in broad daylight, you do behind the scenes with no eyes to see."

"I'm hurt," Rhajmurti said, affecting a wounded expression. He set a hand on Alexiev's shoulder. "Thanks for what you've done. I owe you a favor."

"You can pay it back by letting me know how

you're going to get yourself into that testing room tomorrow morning despite the odds."

Rhajmurti lifted an eyebrow. "Your faith in me is humbling, Pytor, though I fear it's a bit misguided."

"Perhaps." Alexiev smiled slightly. "But you've never let me down yet."

Justice and Sonja stood leaning against the railing of Kass walkway, letting people pass behind them unnoticed. He glanced sidelong: Sonja had been silent ever since the hanging. Now, moody-eyed, she stared down at the canal, seemingly no more inclined to talk than was he.

The hanging had been depressing enough, but bad news kept on coming. The testing was scheduled for tomorrow morning, and Justice Lee's name was right smack in the middle of a long list of other students who would be questioned.

Including Raj, and Sonja.

"Damn!"

Sonja looked up at Justice's curse.

"Sorry. I've had about all the rotten luck I can deal with right now." He took a deep breath. "Gods, Sonja. I'm damned scared. I converted long enough ago that I think I'll do well in the testing. It's Raj. . . ."

"He's smart, Justus," she said, pulling a strand of hair from her eyes. "He'll do all right."

"But these are tricky questions. Father Rhajmurti showed us just *how* tricky they can be this morning. This is one time he won't be able to use that perfect memory of his. He's going to have to *think* like a Revenantist to please the tester, and I'm not sure he's been converted long enough to do it easily."

"The list said we're going to be tested by Father Jonsson. Have you ever had him for a class?"

"Several of them, earlier in my schooling. He's stricter than any other teacher I know."

"Wonderful. I've managed to escape him. Probably because I'm an accounting major." The first smile he had seen on her face all afternoon came and went. "He's an old friend of my mother's. They're some kind of distant, and I mean *distant*, relatives."

"Lucky you."

She stuck out her tongue at him. "Don't mock. Sometimes it's advantageous to know who all your relatives are."

He shrugged and looked down into the canal again. *Damn! There's not one blasted thing I can do to help Raj! And I'm afraid Father Jonsson will chew him up and spit him out without even a second thought!*

"Justus!"

He glanced up at the sound of his name, and saw Father Rhajmurti threading his way through the afternoon crowd.

"I'm glad I caught you," Rhajmurti said. "Is there somewhere we can talk?"

Justice looked around. "Here's probably the best place I can think of. We should be ignored."

"Not good enough. I need somewhere I *know* we won't be overheard."

"There's always Hilda's," Sonja said. "It shouldn't be too crowded there this time of day."

Jason brought three beers to their table after they had taken their places. Only a few customers patronized the tavern: two shopkeepers sat at a table by the door, and a student and his girlfriend commanded a table in the darkest corner of the room, interested more in each other than their drinks.

"What's going on, Father?" Justice asked after a token sip of beer. He sensed he would need a clear mind to deal with the answer to that question.

"I'm going to trust the two of you . . . trust you beyond what I should. If you breathe a word of what I say, the three of us could be in *big* trouble. Do you understand me?"

Justice nodded slowly, as Sonja did the same.

"You've seen the schedule for the testing, haven't you? I thought so. Here's the problem. I tried to get myself set up as the tester for you, and for several other students. But mostly for Raj."

"It didn't work, did it?" Justice asked, already knowing the answer.

"No, it didn't. But I *am* the backup for Father Jonsson. That means if he should take sick, or— gods forbid—have an accident, I would be the one to test you."

Time for the beer. Justice took a long swallow. "Why are you telling us this? What do you want us to do?"

"There's nothing you *can* do. I honestly think the two of you won't have any problems tomorrow."

"But Raj. . . ."

Rhajmurti nodded. "That's one of the reasons I tried to manipulate the system. I'm worried about him."

"Me, too."

"I know he's newly converted," Sonja said, "but why should he be picked on more than anyone else?"

"He's Rigel Takahashi, former Adventist, from Nev Hettek. What better reason than that?"

Sonja stared down into her mug. "That's damned unfair. I *like* Raj."

"So does nearly everyone he meets. He's a very likable young man. But his likability can't erase what he is or where he came from."

Justice scooted forward to the edge of his chair. "Father, you're telling us things we shouldn't know . . . that no student should know. I've never seen you do anything without a reason. What exactly *is* it that you want us to do?"

"Priests aren't made of stone, Justus," Rhajmurti said. "We have to share our troubles, too."

"Have you talked to Raj?" Sonja asked. "I haven't seen him all day."

"I'll get a message to him." Rhajmurti sat up straighter in his chair, took a swallow of beer, then pushed the mug aside. "I want the two of you to be at the College tonight in the same classroom where we met this morning. One last catechism class can't hurt any of you."

"I suppose not."

"And keep this in mind . . . if, for some reason, I *do* end up testing you in the morning, I'll not go easy on you. I just won't be as devious as some other tester." Rhajmurti shoved his chair back and stood. "Remember," he said. "Not a word of this to anyone, hear?"

"We hear," Justice replied. "We'll see you tonight."

Sonja watched Rhajmurti leave the tavern, then looked back at Justice.

"I know what he wants," she said softly.

A sinking feeling in his chest, Justice nodded. "So, I'm afraid, do I. But does he? I honestly don't think he wants to involve us. And if we try something, he doesn't want to know what it is." He met Sonja's eyes. "I've never thought of doing anything like this before."

A thin smile touched her lips. "Nor have I. But being a member of a Family, I know how to do it, and I might as well start practicing now."

The wind had dropped at nightfall, but the evening had grown damp and chill. Justice and Sonja sat close together on the left side of the steps to the College, both wrapped tightly in their coats. A fine mist filled the air, making the night seem colder.

Rhajmurti had dismissed the catechism class not a quarter hour before. The students attending had seemed stunned that some of them would be tested in the morning; that very fact, however, made for an intense two hour session.

Justice and Sonja had left the College as if they had nothing more on their minds than a late dinner and more study. Once outside the doors, they had darted into the shadows to take up the positions they now held.

"How soon?" Justice asked, leaning close to Sonja so she could hear him.

"Any time now. My sources tell me he leaves the College every night at this time. I think he's got a lady love somewhere."

"Gods." Justice wrapped his arms around his knees. Celibacy was not demanded of priests, but he found it hard to imagine Father Jonsson having a love life. For a Revenantist, the karma gathered in such interpersonal relationships was considerable. "I feel rotten about what we're doing. Utterly rotten."

"Think about Raj, and the feeling will go away." She turned her head and he felt her staring at him, but it was too dark to see her face. "Do you think certain students have been singled out by the cardinals as potential troublemakers?"

"I wouldn't doubt it. After Cardinal Ito's death and Cardinal Exeter's ascension, I haven't been sure of anything. That's probably why Father Rhajmurti's trying to protect us." He scratched his nose, trying to prevent a sneeze. "How much did you have to pay your hirelings, Sonja?"

"Enough to make sure they do a good job. And don't worry . . . they never saw or spoke to me."

Justice shivered, and not from the chill. "I know things like this go on every day, but I never knew how easy it would be to do it ourselves."

She laughed quietly. "Money talks, sometimes very loudly. And don't worry, Justus . . . nothing terrible is going to happen to Father Jonsson. That was an inflexible rule I insisted upon."

"Still, it seems—"

"Hssst! Here he comes!"

Justice burrowed deeper into the shadows beside the stairs, Sonja leaning closer beside him. He recognized Father Jonsson's voice as the priest called out to the poleboats gathered at the edge of the College. One of the poleboatmen jumped up onto the quay.

"Good evening, Father," Justice heard the man say. "The usual destination?"

"Yes, and let's make it quick, man. This chill's getting worse."

Father Jonsson walked into view, following the poleboatman to the edge of the canal. Back turned to a sudden gust of wind, the priest waited as the man pulled the boat closer.

"Watch your footing, Father," the poleboatman said. "Slippery here."

"Damned weather." Jonsson edged his way forward, put one hand on a piling to steady himself, and stepped out into the boat.

Justice never could recount exactly what followed, or how it happened. Another gust of wind whipped down the canal; the poleboat swayed out from its ties. Suddenly, Father Jonsson lost his footing, flailed at the piling to catch himself, and fell headlong into the canal.

"Gods! Help me!" The poleboatman knelt, leaned over and reached a hand down to the struggling priest. "Gods fry you," he screamed to his fellow boatmen, "the priest's going to drown! Help me!"

Immediately, three of the other boatmen ran to the edge of the quay, and between them, they hauled a dripping Father Jonsson out of the dangerous waters.

One of the poleboatmen rushed up the steps to the College, bellowing for help at the top of his lungs. Justice held his breath, leaned tight against those stairs, and pulled Sonja closer.

Two of the remaining boatmen had Father Jonsson supported between them, while the third was wrapping the priest in a heavy blanket he had pulled from his poleboat. There was a clatter of shoes on the steps as four members of Security dashed down to the quay.

"Damn! It's Father Jonsson! Is he hurt badly?"

"No," one of the poleboatmen replied. "Wet, cold, that's 'bout it, m'ser. Hit hisself on his head, though. Have a nasty knot there next morning, that's for sure."

The security man fended off the boatman's eager companions, each of whom was trying to hold the priest upright. "Get him inside, quick. He's already taken cold."

The boatmen gave up their burden, and College Security carried Father Jonsson up the stairs into warmth and safety. For a moment, the four pole-boatmen stared after them, then held a quick, hushed conversation, and returned to their boats.

Justice shut his mouth. His tongue had gone dry and he tried to swallow.

"He's all right, isn't he?"

Sonja nodded.

"He could have been killed," Justice said. "Falling in the canal like that at this time of year. . . ."

"They fished him out quick enough," Sonja pointed out. "He'll be left with a bad cold and an aching head, that's all."

Justice settled back against the stairs. There was no point in getting impatient; he and Sonja would have to wait at least half an hour before they could take a boat back to their respective domiciles.

"You frighten me a little," he said to Sonja. "You spread some money around and boom! Father Jonsson takes a swim and conveniently hits his head on the way down."

She stirred at his side. "I'm probably going to

ruin your estimation of my prowess, but I didn't plan on it happening this way."

"What?"

"Exactly that. Father Jonsson wasn't supposed to fall until he'd reached his destination. I wanted his woman friend to see the accident."

"And to have it happen off campus, removing any suspicion from us students." Justice shook his head. "Maybe Takahashi luck *does* run true: after what happened here, Father Rhajmurti will be our tester for sure. The gods must be watching over Raj, that's all I can say."

Sonja laughed quietly. "The gods often watch over men," she said, leaning back into the curve of his shoulder. "It's just that sometimes they like a little help."

WALKING ON THE WAVES

by Leslie Fish

Jones was making a last check-up trip back to the old Petrescu apartment when she heard the familiar whistle. She froze for an instant in a shock of recognition, then hunched her shoulders higher and bent harder to the boat-pole. Maybe if she ignored it, the whistle wouldn't come again.

It did. The quick, casual sound cut through the gust of rain-laden wind like a bullet, and as tightly aimed. Jones would bet that nobody standing ten meters to either side of her would hear it.

How does she do that? —No, never mind. Rif was a professional musician, after all: probably knew a dozen tricks ten times fancier to do with music and voice and words. Beware of Rif's tricksy words. Don't get involved in her damn dangerous business any more. Don't look up, or you might meet her eyes on the nearest walkway.

Then something fell with a small, ringing thump on the nose of the skip. Habits as old as life on the water made Jones ground her pole, stop the boat and look to see where the coin had fallen. Oh, there it was: a silverbit, winking like the moon on the skip's nose. Nobody in Merovingen-below could just leave it lie, no; level the pole, walk or run up

the length of the skip and grab the damn coin.
Jones went for it, cursing, knowing all too well
from whom, if not where, the coin had come. She
picked it up, stood up, looked, half-determined to
fling the coin back—but even to do that much, she
had to look.

Sure enough, there was Rif on the nearest walkway where she'd probably been pacing the skip
since its last turn, wearing that same indigo cloak
with the dark blue sweater and shirt, darker blue
pants and black soft boots.

But her look was different this time. No half-
playful smile now; that face was grim, almost chal-
lenging. It was change enough to make Jones
reconsider throwing the coin back, hesitate just for
a moment.

A moment was time enough. "You wanted me to
do something 'bout them weeds, Jones?" Rif tossed
at her.

"Yey. Did." Jones lowered her hand, half cursing
herself for it. Damn, but now she'd get dragged into
Rif's business again, no way around it. "Whatcher
want this time, Rif?"

"Take me out to the lagoon, an' back." Rif slid
into the skip in a single fluid motion. "Just the one
short trip, and that's all."

The lagoon? Oh, damn, not the lagoon! Even
now, at the height of flood-tide, the once-clear water was fairly choked with those damn weeds Rif
and her Jane friends had brought in: the tangle-
lilies that yes, right enough, cleaned the poison out
of the canal water so that even down in the Tidewater you could fall in and climb out again without
much chance of dying. Those same lilies got their

name from tangling boat-poles and rudders and propellors of boat engines—except, of course, the
shrouded propellors of those new engines Rif's friends
were selling. Those same tangle-lilies died on the
water and piled up in odd canal-corners until folks
just had to go rake the mess out—and more than
one hightown family had made good money collect-
ing the raked weed, drying it, packing it into bricks
of cheap fuel that sold well in the lowtown. The
same weed, not dried, thrown into brewing tanks,
distilled into cheap fuel-alcohol—chugger they called
it, because you could run boat-engines off it, which
meant more speed, more competition, more engine
wear, folks sooner or later having to trade in their
old engines for the new ones Rif's friends made,
and all the engine use drawing attention from the
College, maybe adding to the trouble clamping down
on Merovingen-below from the priesthood, maybe
trouble from the hightown families who imported
gasoline-fuel from upriver, all that, and the deathangel multiplying in the lagoon because the baby
ones fed off the tangle-lily roots. All that, just from
a seed-sowing trip Rif had made last year in this
very skip, and now here she was back for more.

"*Damn* yer, Rif!" Jones briefly considered giving
Rif a hard jab with the boat-pole, remembered
Rif's gun, and thought better of it. "Thanks t' you,
the lagoon's too damn dangerous fer swimmin' nor
anythin' else. Whatcher gonna do t'er this time?"

Rif flicked a brief smile and settled comfortably
down below the gunwhale. "I'm goin' ter throw
somethin' else in the water," she said. "Somethin'
that eats the weeds—the dead ones, anyway. Meant
ter spread it in the city, after flood-tide—will

anyway—but this bit's gotter be done now. No swimmin', don't worry. Hazard pay: five lunes."

"Make 'er six," Jones grumbled, already shoving the pole in the water. "An' don' take too long. I got other work this is holdin' up."

"I know." Rif nodded toward the island-buildings downstream. "Movin' yer man outter Petrescu. Good idea."

Jones swore, pushing off with more vehemence than anywhere near necessary. "Ye watchin' my man, now?" she snapped. "Y'got plans fer him, too?"

"Ney," Rif yawned and stretched, all apparent harmlessness. "Denny works fer him, also fer me an' Rattail. No big secret, Jones. Hell, if anything, I'd like ter thank 'im fer rammin' hell outter that Sword o' God shop last season. Beautiful piece o' work, that."

Jones shrugged. Mondragon's "accidental" sabotage of the machine-shop had been done in front of, and with the unknowing help of, half the population of Canalside. No secret there, either.

That casual admission about Denny, though . . . that deserved a comeback. Jones fought the temptation for a moment, then gave in. "Yer know, he knows 'bout yer work, Rif. The weeds, I mean."

Rif only raised an eyebrow. "Figured ye'd tell 'im," was all she said.

Jones opened her mouth, then shut it again. No, no point pushing this game any further. No point threatening Rif on the best of days, and no point hinting that Mondragon might sell the news of Rif's work for the Janes to any bidder; they both knew damned well that one Altair Jones had been piloting that skip when the tangle-lily seeds were sown. Hang Rif, and hang Jones. Rif guessed, or knew from talking to Denny, that Mondragon wasn't about to do that.

Jones steered through the narrow canals toward the lagoon, still angry with Rif, looking for some chink in that damned woman's armor. "Yer know, flood-tide's washed them damn lilies out ter sea," she tried. "Can't find 'em in the canals no more." *And don't ye ask me to help seed the next crop!*

"Just the dead plant tops," Rif yawned again. "The roots're set well. Besides, they've seeded out all over town. Come warm weather, ye'll see 'em pokin' up again. It's the lagoon we gotter worry 'bout now; they don't wash outter there."

Jones thought of the lagoon covered, meters deep, in floating masses of dead and rotting weed, and shuddered. "So whatcher gonna do?"

Rif tapped her fingers on her shoulder-bag. "Sow somethin' else," she grinned. "Two somethin's, ter be precise. Eggs from a kind o' water-flea that eats the dead weed—that'll clear up any weed that folks don't harvest fer fuel. Then there's eggs from a kind o' crawdad that eats the water-fleas. Keeps things nice an' balanced. Crawdad eats deathangel eggs, too, so there won't be as many o' them in the lagoon next year."

"Nice," Jones begrudged. "An' what eats the crawdads?"

Rif laughed, genuine and merry. "Folks do! Poor folks eat crawdads. Ye scoop 'em up in fish-traps or bag-nets, grab 'em by the bucketful, steam 'em or boil 'em or eat 'em raw if ye're in a hurry. Cheap food, Jones. All over the lagoon, an' next year all over the canals, too, now the canals're clean enough ter grow food in."

"Lord an' Ancestors!" Jones stopped poling for a moment to stare at Rif. The whole plan was so simple, so elegant, she could almost forgive Rif the scare and worry of the past year. Almost.

"They look like little-bitty lobsters," Rif went on, "maybe seven, eight centimeters long. Cute little things. Crackin' the shells is a pain, but the meat's worth it." She looked back at Jones, smile turning intense. "Ye came an' told me, last season, we were gonna have poor folks goin' hungry what never was hungry before, 'member? An' didn' I tell ye then that Jane would provide?"

"Damn." Jones dropped the pole back in the water, suddenly tired. She didn't want to get into this game; keeping herself and Mondragon safe was work enough. But still . . . The visible hints were so tempting. "Rif, what's yer game? I mean, all the Janes. What th'hell d'ye *want*, really?"

As if she'd been waiting for the question, Rif raised three fingers. "Food fer the poor," she ticked off. "Medicine fer the poor. Tech fer the poor— simple an' widespread an' hidden, so the damn priests an' hightowners can't stop 'er an' the sharrh can't see 'er, not 'til she's way too late."

"Too late fer what?"

"Too late ter stop us goin' back ter space again, gettin' off Merovin, goin' back ter the other worlds an' all they've got. Most like, we won't see that— but our children er gran'children will. Meanwhile, we can do better nor bein' poor an' sick an' hope- less an' lorded over. Now, how's that sound ter you?"

"Dreamin'," Jones muttered. But she knew that the front edge of the dream was real, real as the tangle-lilies and chugger and the new engines and now, maybe, free food growing wild in the canals. "Here comes the lagoon."

The skip slid out through a screen of reeds and tangle-lily stalks, a stretch impassible in dry summer but deep enough now, into the deceptively calm water. Lily stalks rattled and fell before the skip's prow, a thick forest of them, tall enough to hide a low-riding boat. There hadn't been this many last time she'd come here; now, there seemed to be no open water at all.

A flock of gray-teal rose flapping and honking in sudden thunder, surprising Jones so badly she nearly dropped the pole. The birds circled out over the lagoon, arched back to rest somewhere less than fifty meters off in the dense screen of lilies, and settled grumbling.

"Sweet Jane!" Rif breathed, "There must'er been forty-fifty birds there. We hadn' expected that—not so soon, anyway. Goddess! This time next year, should be 'nough birds here ter feed most o' Merovingen-below. Oh, hell, don't tell anyone, Jones—least no one but a few close-mouthed friends— not 'til there's enough of 'em ter breed big. . . ."

Jones only nodded, staring. She'd never seen so many gray-teal in her life. And this was only one flock. Oh, yes, by the Ancestors, let them breed up their numbers! She'd wager there was a good kilo of meat on each bird, and the eggs. . . .

"Must nest in the lily-tangles," Rif was saying. "Where they grow thick, twine inter mats, be good fer water-bird nests. Goddess, what next? Neoswans?

We knew she'd encourage water-wildlife, but this. . . . Ah, steer fer the middle, Jones. Let's see what else's come back here."

Jones did so, steering by memory through the unfamiliar forest of lilies and reeds. Something about the lilies must have encouraged the reeds, too—unless more of Rif's friends had done that.

Ahead, the smell of rotting lily-stalks grew stronger. She steered that way, wondering if the center of the lagoon was completely covered by the pesky stuff. The thicket of standing reeds and lilies thinned, showing open water for the first time.

Sure enough, right ahead of them floated drifting mats of the dead weed. Jones swore, knowing all too well what it was like to pole through the nasty stuff.

"Looks like I came just in time," Rif muttered, reaching into her shoulder-bag. "Try ter pole right around 'er, an' I'll throw the eggs as far inter center as I can."

"Yey, do 'er." Relieved, Jones cut hard to port and began shoving the skip through the interface of dead and living weeds. It wasn't easy: gluey dead tendrils clogged the pole, snagged on the underlying engine propellor-cowl, bunched at the skip's nose. Still, it was a damn-sight better than trying to push into the main mass of that central sargasso.

In the bow, Rif pulled two boxes out of her shoulder-bag, set them on the thwarts and opened them. The contents appeared to be some sort of coarse grayish powder. She took handfuls from both boxes and tossed them high overside, in the general direction of the central mass of dead weed, while muttering about wind directions and probable spread.

Circling the border of the weed mass took long, and disturbed another colony of water-birds—long-legged brown heronets, these—which made Rif practically gloat at Mother Jane's bounty. The shocking abundance of wild food made Jones oddly uncomfortable. She hadn't wanted anything more to do with the Janes and their bizarre business, but damn, seeing the effects out here made Rif's hints and promises dangerously seductive. Cheap fuel and cheap food for the taking, apparently no karmic debt involved . . . Lord and Ancestors, yes, that would be hard for anyone in Merovingen-below to resist.

"She's gettin' late," was the best defense Jones could come up with. "I got people waitin' fer me. How much longer's this gonna take?"

"How fast can ye finish the circle?" Rif replied, dusting off her hands above the water. "I'm close ter done now."

Jones leaned on the pole and shoved hard through the weeds. There—ah, there, right ahead—lay the fresh channel the skip had flattened on its way in. Rif saw it, too, sighed in relief, and simply dunked the boxes and their lids into the water.

"That's done 'er. Let's get outta here."

Jones leaned to the pole and shoved gratefully into the channel. Bit by bit, the clotted weed reluctantly slid off the bow and the pole. The skip was almost clean of weed by the time it reached the first line of the old sea-wall that marked the city proper. Nobody appeared to notice as they slid out into the backwater canals; traffic was light back here, and Jones made good time.

"I notice," Rif murmured, in that for-your-ears-only pitch, "that yer engine-prop didn' hang up much in the weeds. She's shrouded, ney?"

Jones hitched her shoulders, almost missed a stroke, jabbed the pole down with a muffled curse. Yes, trust Rif to notice a little thing like that. "All right, damn ye," she snapped. "Yey, I had ter trade in my old engine fer one o' them new ones yer friend makes. Ye happy now?" That had hurt, giving up that engine that'd been Mama's, and her mama's before her, but trade was competitive, and engine use meant engine wear, and after too many breakdowns there just hadn't been any choice.

"Runs better an' lasts longer, don't she?" Rif shrugged. "Look, Jones; we made them things fer folks like you. They run simple, clean an' cheap, an' take ferever ter wear out. They'll stand ye in good stead. What more d'ye want?"

What answer to that? "Well . . . They carry lots less metal nor the old ones. Ye know what good metal's worth."

"Sure." Rif grinned. "If we'd traded old-fer-new with the same 'mount o' metal, folks would've thought 'twere a gift. Ooh, karmic debt! Seems there ain't nothin' a Merovingian fears more nor a free gift. We had ter look like we was makin' some kind o' profit, ney?"

No, there was nothing to say to that. Jones gritted her teeth and poled onward through the seagate that would take her back toward Petrescu. No doubt Rif would say where she wanted to be let off.

An odd, hollow thumping echoed through the canyon of close-set buildings: somewhat like troubled-engine noise and something like the sound of bad plumbing. There'd been a lot of that noise around in the past few weeks, since the beginning of flood-tide. Jones frowned and eyed the buildings warily, wondering if one of them were about to dump a mess of sewage right in front of her skip.

"Hey, pull up at the next corner, Jones," Rif said. "I gotta do somethin' there."

Mystified, Jones shoved the skip close to the building at the corner. She could see nothing there worth noticing: not even a tie-up ring, nothing but a bit of ceramic pipe sticking up out of the water.

"Little further, little further," Rif urged. "There! Stop."

Jones did, seeing that Rif leaned over the gunwhale within reach of that standing pipe. And then Rif pulled a long knife out of her sleeve and banged on the pipe, medium-hard irregular beats. Tap, tap-tap, tap . . .

The sound echoed through the water. Same sound as before. What the hell?

"Rif, what'n hell're ye doin?"

"Uhm, nothin' much." Rif sat back in the boat, put her knife away and looked out over the water. ". . . Just knockin' loose some blocked-up sewer-gas, like a good citizen should. That stuff backs up, she can make 'er real bad inside a buildin'. . . ." She wasn't looking at Jones. "Hmm, can ye make a small detour an' let me out at East Dike?"

"Ney, I can't. I got business at Petrescu, an' she's already overdue."

Rif shrugged. "Petrescu'd be fine."

All the way down the canal, Jones wondered what that had really been about.

"You're late," said Dr. Yarrow, as Rif came trotting through the door of the school-barge's office. "We've had the pipes ringing for two hours, now."

"Sorry," Rif panted, dropping into the nearest chair. "I was out in the lagoon, sowing the eggs. Y'know, the wildlife's downright exploded out there. I saw flocks of gray-teal and heronet, near a hundred of 'em. It's comin' faster'n we expected. An' even Jones's got one o' the new engines now, an' I'll swear I smelled pressed-weed fuel-blocks hidden somewhere on 'er skip. I know I smelled a workin' slurry-tank. . . ."

"Later," said Yarrow. "We have a small crisis here. Cardinal Exeter's been sniffing around the school."

"Hell," Rif snapped, sitting bolt upright. "She got somethin' against Farren Delaney, or what?"

"No, this seems to be part of the general slap-around-in-the-dark." Yarrow picked up a slateboard covered with notes. "One of the kids—McGee's, no less—was grabbed by priests on the way home and questioned about what's being taught here. Fortunately, McGee's one of our late-starters—just learning letters and numbers, couldn't tell them anything but the basics. Also, he's in the habit of throwing crying fits whenever he's in over his head, and that worked, too. The priests let him go quickly. Problem is, he ran straight home and told his mother, who told other students' mothers, before the word got back to us. A couple of parents have already hauled their kids out of school for fear of worse."

"Damn." Rif leaned back in her chair and thought hard. "I don't know how t'lure the parents back, but I've got some idea what t'do about the sniffin' priests."

"Very good." Yarrow smiled wearily and dropped into her own chair. "If you can keep the priests off, I can get the parents back. What's your idea?"

Rif grinned, nastily. "Farren Delaney's kids still comin' here?" she purred.

Yarrow raised an eyebrow. "They are. Go on."

"Simple, then. Tell me where the priests're likely t'lurk fer kids, an' let me talk with the oldest Delaney kid. With luck, we can pull this off right this afternoon."

Yarrow shook her head. "First tell me, Rif. I'm not risking a child with anything heavy."

" 'T'won't be heavy." Rif grinned wider. "We simply tell the kid we're layin' a trap fer some nosy priests who want ter discredit his daddy's project. That'll put the kid's back up, right proper. Then we just tell him what to say, and where to go—and just when ter drop the word that his daddy's the Prefect of Waterways. Now, will that back them bastards off?"

Yarrow's shoulders shook for a moment before she finally gave up and laughed. "Lovely, lovely. We'll also have to warn the boy what not to say, too . . . and make certain he's not under any pressure to reveal it."

"Hey, we've been spreading the pipe-code as a kids' secret game, haven't we? One kid ter another? Y'don't haveta say a thing; kids'll keep kids' secrets from the grownups come hell or high water."

"True . . ." Yarrow considered. "Hmm, we already have the high water. And here's another bit of hell. Rif, one of our College sources says that Exeter's sent down word to have you and Rattail questioned. They could hit anytime in the next few days—sooner, if you stick to your uptown-parlor circuit. Do you want to have Ariadne change it?"

Rif thought about that for a long moment. "No," she finally decided. "I'll see Rattail in an hour anyway, tell 'er what's goin' down. We got plans fer somethin' like this, no fear."

"You realize you may be picked up at work tonight?"

"Hmm. Well, the sooner the better. Longer we wait, the more questions the high-bitch'll think t'ask —an' maybe the hungrier she'll be fer someone else ter hang."

Yarrow shivered. "You," she said, "have a weird sense of humor. Very well, let's go talk to the Delaney boy."

Alexis Delaney, nine years old and raised in a family that rewarded wit, came home from school a good hour later than his younger sibs, sporting a righteous and determined air. Only his mother, Ariadne, might have detected a touch of theatrical swagger in his walk, and she was not the first or second person in the household to meet him. To the porter's greetings—half scolding, half dithered relief at the boy's return—Alexis only said: "I was forcibly detained, and I want to talk to Papa at once."

The porter complied with alacrity, marching the boy straight to Farren Delaney's study. Farren, who hadn't realized that Alexis was late in coming home, only looked up from his papers and smiled.

"Yes, son?" he asked, setting a tablet aside. "What can I do for you?"

"Papa," said Alexis, unconsciously assuming a

stolid parade rest position, "on the way home from school I was stopped and nearly molested by a gang of priests."

"*What?!*" shouted Farren, almost bolting out of his chair.

"I was coming up the main walkway from East Dike," Alexis proceeded with the story as he'd been practicing it for the last several bridges, "and some priests stepped out and barred my way. There were three of them, and the first two took hold of my arms and wouldn't let me go."

"And the third?" Farren seethed. "What did the third one do?"

Alexis frowned in concentration, being careful to remember details clearly as Ariadne had always taught him to do. "The third one leaned down close and smiled, and told me not to be frightened, he just wanted to ask me some questions. I said that what *I* wanted was to go home, but he wouldn't let me. He asked me my name, and I said it was Alexis and I wanted to go home."

"And then?"

"He said . . ." the boy unconsciously mimicked the questioner's voice and stance. " 'In a moment, Alexis. There's a good boy. Just tell me about school. What did you learn in school today?' "

"The school. . . ?" Farren frowned thoughtfully, mirroring his son.

"I said: 'I learned how to do fractions, and the ge-ogerphy of the Det River valley, and how a hand-pump works, and we started on the history of the founding of Merovingen, and I made only two per-nunciation mistakes. Now can I go home?'

"And he said: 'Oh, that's very good. You're quite

a clever little boy. But didn't they teach you anything about Mo-rality, or Family Values or the Duties of the Soul?' And I said—"

"Oho," Farren muttered.

"And *I* said," Alexis forged on, " 'no, that's church
stuff. I learn that at the church-school on Sunday
when we go to church. *And*,' I said—" The boy
couldn't help grinning a bit. " 'The church-school
doesn't teach us anything about fractions or ge-
ogerphy, either.' "

"Good point," Farren acknowledged. "What did
he say then?"

"Then one of the other priests pinched my arm,"
Alexis glowered. "I yelled, 'Ouch! He hurt me! Help!
That man's hurting me!' good and loud, and people
on the walkway started slowing down and looking.
The third priest looked real worried, and he stood
up fast and shook his holy-stick and shouted 'Church
business!' at all the people. I think he 'spected
that'd make them go away, but they didn't. They
kept on standing there and looking. The priest wag-
gled his fingers at the other two, and they started to
pull me away toward a doorway, but I yelled, 'Where
are you taking me? Let go! I want to go home!' and
the people started muttering real loud and angry,
and they started moving toward the priests, so they—
the priests, I mean—stopped right there."

"Heh! Smart of them," Farren chuckled. "Did
they have the sense to let you go?"

"No. The third one still wanted to ask me some
questions. He asked me if I knew my catechism,
and I did, so I recited it. Then he asked me if the
teachers at the school ever made fun of the catechism or the List of the Duties, or anything like

that. I said: 'No, they're too busy teaching fractions and reading.' Some of the people laughed, and the priests didn't like that."

"Indeed they wouldn't," Farren muttered. "Sanctimony can't bear ridicule."

"So then I said: 'My school's a *good* school. It has to be, or my father wouldn't have got it that barge for a school building.' Then everybody looked at me, and one of the priests asked: 'Who's your father?' I said: 'My father is Farren Delaney, the Prefect of Waterways, and he won't like the way you grab his children and bother his school.' "

Alexis paused and looked up shyly to see what his father made of that boast.

Farren raised both eyebrows, smothered a brief explosion of laughter, smiled warmly at his son and asked, "What effect did *that* have?"

"Well," Alexis preened a bit, "all the people laughed, and some of them even cheered. The priests didn't say anything, they just looked at each other, and the one with the holy-stick looked as if he'd bitten into a bad piece of fish. Then he gave a sort of phony smile and said: 'Now, now, boy, we haven't done you any harm. You're quite free to go.' And he waved real quick at the other two priests, and they let go of my arms. Soon as they let go, I jumped away and took off running. All the people made way for me, but I looked back and saw that they closed up the crowd afterward so the priests couldn't follow me. I ran as far as the first bridge, and then looked back, and I saw the priests walking away fast and all the people following them and watching to see where they went."

"In . . . deed . . ." Farren murmured, eyes narrowed. Then another idea lifted one of his eye-brows. "But tell me, son, if you just now came in, you left school more than an hour and a half ago. This business with the priests, as you've told it, couldn't have taken more than, hmm, ten or fifteen minutes. Why, then, were you all of an hour late coming home?"

"Uh, well . . ." Alexis shrugged, blushing a little. "Once I stopped running, some of the people came up and asked me if I was all right, and did the priests do me any harm, and was I really Farren Delaney's son, and weren't you the one looking for people to work on his fire-stopping boat, and all that sort of thing. I had to stop and answer them, Papa; it was only polite."

Farren's shoulders shook with hard-held laughter. "Lord and Ancestors," he murmured. "You're practicing for a political career already."

The boy looked up at his father's face, wondering how that was meant. "Did I do the right thing, Papa?"

"Oh, yes. Yes indeed!" Farren got up, stepped forward and swept Alexis into his arms. "Yes, yes, absolutely right, my clever lad." He bounced the boy in a bear hug for a few moments, much to Alexis' delight, before regretfully setting him down. "Now go off, my lad, and tell that story to your mother. I think she'll enjoy hearing it as much as I have."

Alexis gave a whoop of joy and scampered off, eager to recite his tale to another appreciative audience.

Farren watched the boy go, then waved to the porter who'd been waiting at a discreet distance down the hall. "Send up two runners," he said. "I'll have some letters to dispatch shortly."

The porter nodded and hurried off. Farren returned to his desk, took out pen and paper and began writing furiously. The first missive was addressed to Governor Kalugin. The second was dispatched to Cardinal Willa Exeter. After that Farren had to stop and think a bit, but then he wrote up a list of names and set off to talk to his wife.

The soirée at de Niro's didn't break up until midnight, by which time the watchers at the house dock were cold, wet, and thoroughly miserable. When the doors opened and the guests began to depart, the little coterie of watchers scrambled into place clumsily, drawing the unwanted attention of the household guard.

"You, there!" snapped the lead guard, "Step forward—yey, all four of you. Who are you, and what's yer business here?"

The embarrassed clerics stepped forward into the light. The squad leader fumbled out his staff of office and waved it like a desperate banner. "We, ser—" he tried to sound imposing, "are a delegation from the College of Cardinals, here on Church business."

The rest of his cohort peered past him at the emerging party guests, trying to spot their quarry in the growing crowd.

"Well, ye're too late for the party," growled the guard, shifting his long billy club to passive-shield position. "Everyone's leaving. If you've a message for Master de Niro, hand it over and I'll send it up."

"The Church's business," the cleric simmered, "is with the entertainers whom your master hired. Are they leaving also?"

The guard gave him a narrow-eyed look, then shrugged. "Sure. That's them over there." He pointed with his club at a knot of people just coming out of the building. "Y'can't miss 'em. They're right in the middle of that bunch of fans."

He stepped back with an ill-concealed grin, revealing the sight of two elaborately cosmeticked and costumed women in the center of a slow-moving cluster of admirers. The women, carrying bookbags and instrument cases, were chatting merrily with a good score of fancily-dressed men and women, most of them young, loud, and carrying functional-looking swords. The crowd showed no sign of dissipating as it crept down the walkways.

The priests looked at each other, dismayed. This would be no quiet, discreet snatching. The squad leader frowned, considered following the singers until their protective crowd thinned out, wondered where and when that would be, considered the lateness of the hour and the distance to the College, and made his decision. With a resigned hand signal to his cohort, he stepped forward.

"Church business. Let us through, please. Church business . . ."

Surprised, the crowd stopped. There were multiple dark looks and mutters, several hands reaching surreptitiously for sword handles, as the mob slowly and grudgingly gave way.

The priests hitched their shoulders higher and kept close together as they worked their way toward their targets in the center of the crowd.

The two singers seemed to share none of their supporters' dismay. If anything, their poses looked somewhat theatrical and amused. The squad leader blinked rapidly as he stopped in front of them. He really hadn't expected, when he'd set out on this assignment, that he'd find himself trying to make a formal announcement to two vacuously smiling women with iridescent-blue eyelids and sequinned, keyhole-cut shirts.

"You are the singers known as Rattaille and Rafaella?" He had to stop and cough to get the annoying squeak out of his voice.

"*She* is Rattaille," said the taller one, slowly blinking eyelids laden with centimeter-long eyelashes. "*I* am Rafaella."

"Oo-*oo*-ooh," drawled the other, turning her head so that her enormous chandelier-earrings clashed and chimed. "Are we so faaamous that the Caaahllege wants to hear us?"

"You are summoned to the College! Immediately!" the cleric announced, certain that he could hear snickering somewhere in the crowd.

"It's after midnight," blustered a burly youth with a jeweled sword-sheath jingling at his belt. "Let them come tomorrow."

"Immediately!" the squad leader repeated, shaking his staff of office again. Behind him he could almost feel the other clerics fumbling for the butts of the pistols hidden under their robes.

"Oo-*ooo*-ooh," Rattaille crooned louder. "Maybe some cardinal wants to hiiiire us."

"*They'd* pay really good *money*," Rafaella agreed. "Not to *men*tion the *fame*."

The priests relaxed a trifle. Maybe the targets wouldn't give them too much trouble getting away.

"Careful," snapped a glossily-dressed young woman in the crowd. "It may be a trap."

The other fans grumbled agreement. The clerics fumbled for their guns again.

"But whaaaat in the world fooor?" Rattaille drawled. "I don't think they'll haaang us for singing loooove songs."

The priests shuffled uncomfortably at that, while the crowd grumbled some more. The recent hanging of that loud-mouthed tavern lout had not quite had the intended effect on the populace, and the College was full of recriminations over it.

"I really *doubt* that they'll *hang* us at all," Rafaella agreed. "After *all*, we're due to sing at Tre*maine*'s, on The *Rock*, tomorrow."

The squad of clerics hastily looked at each other. Tremaine's was the smallest household on The Rock, but that was still at the very top of hightown. The singers had friends in, literally, very high places. And now the rest of this mob knew about it. There could be none of the usual techniques to encourage proper submission, not with these two.

"So, we'll go see what the Caaaallege wants," Rattaille decided. "If we don't show up tomorrow, daaahlings, then it'll be time to complaaaain."

The crowd turned to mutter confusedly to itself. The squad leader grabbed the advantage while he could. "Come this way . . . please," he waved the two singers toward the dock and his waiting boat.

To his immense relief, the singers followed him—but they followed slowly, pausing to shake hands, chat, give autographs, take compliments and suggestions from their coterie of admirers, all the way into the boat.

The priests shoved off from the dock as quickly as they dared, taking exquisite care not to shove or splash any of the crowd of well-wishers—also trying to keep their faces hidden from calculating eyes that just might memorize their features. The squad leader, noting the number of watchers who seemed likely to follow the boat along the walkways, decided to dispense with the usual discreet silence and use the engine. The small courier-boat took off with a lively roar, spreading a huge wake behind it, doubtless drawing the attention of all the neighbors—as, no doubt, so did the loud farewells of the crowd on the dock. The chief cleric hunched down in his seat at the prow and tried to rub his chilled hands warm; nothing about this snatch had gone well. And now, if you please, the two targets were yattering about possible jobs at the College and what music high-church employers would want to hear—no more intimidated than the weeds in the water. He sincerely hoped that the cardinal's interest in these two was marginal, that he wouldn't be called in to explain just why this simple operation had gone so badly.

And it wouldn't do to keep Cardinal Exeter waiting much longer, either.

Shivering, the squad leader signaled to the boatman to turn the engine up full throttle. The sooner the problem was out of his hands, the better.

Cardinal Exeter rubbed her eyes and wondered if the lateness of the hour and its attendant fatigue were responsible, or perhaps the quality of the chamber's ancient lighting, or if these two singers really did look that way. The taller one wore her moused, teased, flaming red hair swept up into an unbelievable fountain of countless braids, interwoven with glittering blue and silver cords and silver beads, obviously intended to match the skin-tight blue lamé trousers side-laced with flame red cords strung with silver beads—and never *mind* that impossibly-cut flame red shirt with the silver embroidery on the collar, or the iridescent makeup that almost obscured the shape of the woman's features. As for her partner, how could the woman possibly walk in those unbelievably high-heeled boots? How could she breathe, let alone sing, in that skin-tight gold lamé jumpsuit with the alarming holes cut in it at unexpected places? How could she move her arms with all those goldstone-studded bracelets climbing from wrist to elbow and beyond?

How could she sing or even turn her head with her white-blonde hair pulled up into that ridiculous rooster crest through that array of goldstone beads? How could she play an instrument with all those laughably fake bezel rings on her fingers?

The two singers glittered and flashed in the lamp-light so that it was almost painful to look at them. And they *gushed* so.

"My *dearest* Cardinal Exeter," the taller one was burbling. "It's such an *honor* to meet someone of your esteemed *em*inence, let *alone* to be invited to your very *off*ice. Why, I can't *tell* you how very *priv*ileged we are to make your ac*quain*tance."

"Oo-*oo*-ooh, yes," the other cut in, obviously not wanting to fall behind in the flattery. "We've sung before high and loooow, but never at the Caaallege of Caaaardinals before."

"Why, we can't *imag*ine a finer vocation to sing for the *Col*lege, as *of*ten as possible," the red-blue-and-silver dressed woman (which one was she? Rafaella?) nudged. Lamplight flickered off her glossy-painted artfully-batted peacock-blue eyelids.

Cardinal Exeter decided that, yes, the singers really did look like that. No illusion of hers could ever be so appallingly tasteless. "Enough!" she snapped. "I did not summon you here to offer you employment."

Both painted faces fell. Then a flicker of hope dawned on one of them (pale hair and goldstone: Rattaille?) and the woman asked: "But you miiight consider the possibility, naooow that you've met us?"

"If you'd *like* to hear us *sing* . . ." Rafaella offered, flicking a glance at her instrument case.

"Not now!" Lord, no, don't let them start cater-wauling at this hour of the night! "You were brought here to be examined on the subject of heresy."

That was a blunt and clumsy opening, but all she could think of to shut up their mercenary chattering. Now, see how they dealt with that.

Both women looked blank. They blinked—easily seen, with those idiotic false eyelashes—and turned to look at each other.

"*Here*sy. . . ?" said one.

"I don't know anything abaooout it," said the other.

"Don't we have *any* songs about *heresy*?"

"Well, maaaaybe we can faaake it."

"I'll *try*," muttered Rafaella. She turned back to

smile hopefully at Exeter. "I *think* I know *one* song about it." She took a deep breath, squared her shoulders and pealed out: "Heresy, Oh Heresy; Beware the sting of Heresy . . ."

Cardinal Exeter recognized the tune. It was centuries old; the earliest known title was "O Tannenbaum."

" 'Oh, strive for virrrtue all thy days,' " Rafaella wailed on. " 'And shun the paaaath of evil ways. Oh Heresy, Oh Heresy—' "

"Enough!" snapped the cardinal, rubbing her forehead. "No more of that."

"I'm suuuure we could write a better one, given tiiime," Rattaille promised. "We'd gladly accept pay by the sooong, not by the daaaaay."

"We can *write*, or *find*, songs on *any* subject," Rafaella agreed.

Oh, no doubt they could, and would, for the promise of a penny. "I am not concerned with songs *about* heresy," Exeter pronounced crisply. "I am concerned with songs which *contain* elements of heresy. Songs such as yours, m'seras."

Again, the two produced, and traded, that blank look.

"Just what *is* heresy, ex*act*ly?" Rafaella whispered. "I never was *up* on *that* one."

"Me neeeither," her partner muttered back, "But oooobviously it has sooomething to do with baaadmouthing caaardinals in public."

Exeter rubbed her forehead again. Oh, Lord, now Rattaille was squaring her shoulders and taking that telltale deep breath!

" 'Oh, speak no ill of holy folk,' " she bayed—to

the tune of 'O Tannenbaum' again. " 'They will not take it for a joke . . .' "

"Enough!" Exeter roared. "If you sing that tune again in my presence, I'll have you both whipped!" Oh, stupid, stupid! Imagine how she'd look trying to carry out that threat. Imagine the gossip: "publicly whipped for singing 'O Tannenbaum' three times in front of a cardinal . . ."

The singers traded knowing looks this time. "Try 'Greensleeves,' " Rattaille whispered.

"The *lines* are too *long* for quickie rhymes," Rafaella complained.

Cardinal Exeter took a deep breath herself, and let it out slowly. "To repeat," she said, "I am concerned with heretical elements *in* your songs, and wish to examine them. Closely. Do you take my meaning?"

Obviously, the two did not. They exchanged idiot grins of delight, and simultaneously reached for their bookbags. Rafaella got hers open first, and drew out a thin folder full of sheets covered with writing and music script. "*These* are all the songs we brought *with* us," she burbled happily, handing them over. "If you find *any*thing heresy—uh, heretical in *there*, just *tell* us and we'll be happy to re*write* them."

"They'll wooork like neeew on the same aauudiences," Rattaille added gleefully. "Oh, you wooon't get the full efffect without the muuusic. We could sing them all if you'd liiiike." She turned another hopeful glance to her instrument case.

"No," said the cardinal quickly. "Leave your instruments in your cases, please." She peered at the first song in the thin folder, sourly wishing that the collection squad had caught the women at a time when they had their complete book with them. The song was a ballad, titled "The Wreck of the Edwin Fitzwilliam," and was at least twenty verses long. Exeter shuddered at the thought of having to listen through it. The next was an almost-equally long ballad called "The Jam on Jerry's Rocks," followed by "The Ballad of Sir Patrick Spens." Clearly it had been a night for long, sad shipwreck tales. Of course de Niro had made their fortune on the sea-trade, and perhaps the younger de Niro might take some illicit adolescent thrill in hearing about shipwrecks, but all this was politically useless.

Then again, the singers might have sung other, memorized songs.

"Are these all the songs you sang tonight?" Exeter asked, in her best ominous tone. Just let them say yes, and she'd hint they were lying, threaten to haul in the guests from that party.

"All but the *dance* tunes," Rafaella shrugged. "*They're* very *easy* to memorize, being so *short*."

Damn, that threw the line of intimidation off. "Recite the words, please," was all the cardinal could think of for a quick retort.

A moment later she regretted it.

The two singers patted their hands on their thighs in timing rhythm, then began to chant—Rafaella taking the chorus and Rattaille on the . . . well, it might possibly be called the verse.

"Baby, baby . . . whoa-oh. Baby, baby . . . yeah, yeah. Oh, yeah.' "

"Ooh, c'mon baaaby, whoa-oh. Sweetest looovin' you'll everrr seeee."

"Baby, baby . . . whoa-oh . . ."

"Enough!" yelled the cardinal, shoving the folder

of songs back. God, that one was worse than "O Tannenbaum." No, this was getting nowhere. High time for a different tack. "M'seras, what are your opinions regarding the subject of religion."

Again, that blank look.

". . . the *sub*ject of religion?" Rafaella puzzled. "*Sub*ject? *Ob*ject?"

"Well, there are lots of sooongs abaoout it," Rattaille offered. "The problem is getting sooomeone to paaay you to siiing them."

"Oh, *yes*," Rafaella brightened, assuming she understood. "If the church would like to *hire* us, I'm *sure* we can come up with *scores* of religious songs."

The cardinal took another deep breath. Lord, not this again! Did these fools think of nothing but singing and money? . . . "I mean, m'seras, what are your religious beliefs?"

Another swapping of blank looks, mutual shrugs.

"*I* was raised *Re*venantist."

"Sooo was I."

"And do you attend services regularly?" This was like pulling teeth; hard and slow and painful, with damned little gold to be found therein."

"Oh, not *re*gularly. Too *of*ten, we have to *work* on Sunday."

"And uuusually the hoooly days, tooo. Thaaat's when you find sooome of the best paaaid jobs."

Not much silver in that tooth. The poorer half of Merovingen could say the same. "Do you remember your catechism?"

"Oh, suuure!" Rattaille brightened.

"We even have a *tune* for it." Rafaella took that giveaway deep breath again.

"Not now!" Exeter ran a hand through her gray

hair. "Have you ever sung religious songs other than Revenantist?"

"Oh, suuure. We've been aaasked for Adventist hymns just scooores of times."

"Just *all* over lowtown. You just *have* to learn *some,* you know, singing for pennies and *sil*verbits canalside."

Exeter looked ceilingward, searching for inspiration, for some question that would uncover a shred of real political meat. Some of those songs she'd heard at Ariadne Delaney's were so close to heretical, she'd been sure there was more beneath the surface, something more than artistic whoring, singing anything for anybody who paid . . . "Have you ever come across songs defying or ridiculing religious beliefs?"

To her amazement, the two women laughed knowingly.

"*Lord,* yes!"

" 'Revenantist Maaan'! Oo-ooh, you want to hear it?"

Before the cardinal could think to stop them, Rattaille hummed a starting note, they both drew deep breaths, and then they took off.

> "He was a Revenantist man, lived a Revenantist
>   life,
> He surely was a Revenantist with a Revenantist
>   wife.
> He had Revenantist karma and it piled up by
>   the day,
> He drowned and came around again, and it
>   was all to pay.
> He was a . . ."

Exeter listened, with steadily glazing eyes, while they sang through verses that proclaimed their collective victim to be Adventist, Old-Church-of-Goddist, Retributionist-With-Janist-Tendencies, and Sharrist-With-New-Worlder-Leanings, but when the increasingly sprung lines got to Sword-of-Goddist-Infected-With-Immaterialist-Revisionism she slammed her hand down on the desk and bellowed: "Enough!"

The two singers stopped and gave her puzzled looks.

"But isn't *that* what you *want*ed?" Rafaella asked.

"It's the fuuunniest religious sooong we knooow," Rattaille promised.

"Enough of this!" the cardinal roared, feeling the headache spring to full bloom behind her eyes. "Get out of here! At once! And no, before you ask again, you will *never* be hired to sing at the College, or any where else in the city, if you cross my path again. Out!"

It must have been the last sentences that got through to them. The singers drooped like wilted hothouse flowers, sighed monumentally, shoved their music-folders back in their shoulder bags and picked up their instrument cases.

"We've *blown* it," Rafaella murmured to her companion as she pulled on her cloak. "If *on*ly we could've hit on the right *song*."

"Ohhh, maaaybe we should've triiied 'When Retribution Comes.' Thaaaat's got a looovely melodic liiine."

"*Out!!*" Exeter insisted, jabbing a finger toward the door, which the cleric waiting outside quickly opened.

The two singers shambled away, the picture of

dejection, still humming the tune Rattaille had started.

"Your Grace," the cleric offered timorously, "Shall I order the boat?"

"No, let them walk home," Exeter snapped. "And shut that door."

Sad voices harmonized faintly down the corridor: " 'Oh, when Retribution comes. Oh-oh-ohhh, oh, when Retribution comes . . .' "

The door mercifully closed. Exeter rubbed her throbbing temples and snapped off a few epithets that would have startled her household staff. "Artists!" she muttered.

There was, she remembered, some good brandy in the side cabinet. She got up and went to fetch it, not bothering with a glass.

Rif and Rattail plodded on down the walkways, looking tired, miserable and harmless as any entertainers might who had just lost a chance at a really big contract. Passing clerics and blacklegs gave them scarcely a look. Down the lower walks through the Signeury they went, around the boat-slip and across the bridge to Borg, then on to Porfirio and Wex, among thinning crowds, without once breaking from the role.

Only when they reached the shadows of the Wex-Spellman bridge did they stop, look to see that no one was watching, then wrap their arms around each other and stand for a long moment, shivering in the thin early morning rain.

"Oh Mother, oh Mother," Rif panted, as they eased apart. "That was *so* close. I damn-near lost the accent once'r twice."

" 'I'll have you whipped,' " Rattaile quoted, gig-gling hysterically. "I thought I was gonna lose ev-erything, right there. Oh, Goddess . . . Heh! 'O Tannenbaum'!"

"Na, it was 'Revenantist Man' that did it. Mother, did you see her eyes bugging out?"

"I wish I had a picture . . . Ah, damn, can we flag a boat this time of night? My feet are killing me. These damned boots—"

"Be careful with 'em. They gotta go back t-yer friend without bein' too badly messed up."

"They will, they will. Just let me take them off." Rattail sat down where she was and tugged at the high-heeled boots. "I can't wait to get out of this whole crazy get-up . . ."

"The de Niro kids loved it. Hmm, I hope they have the sense t'tell the others that story 'bout goin' ter Tremaine's was a fake."

"Oh, they will. *I* just hope they remember, if anyone asks, to sing 'Baby, Baby' for example of all the, heh, *dance* tunes."

"They should. That one's dead-easy t'remember. All the dangerous ones're really complex . . . Hey!"

The two women crouched fast, reaching for hid-den knives, as a silent walking shadow detached itself from the darkness of the walkway and moved toward them. A very tall, slender shadow.

"Rif," said an unmistakable quiet voice. "Are you all right?"

"Oh. Yes." Rif sagged in relief.

Rattail didn't. She stared at the oncoming silhou-ette as if unable to believe her eyes. ". . . never wanted to see him this close," she whispered.

Rif frowned at her partner, then walked toward

the speaker. "Ye shouldn've come this close, Cal," she said quietly. "Anyone could've seen ye."

"Didn't your partner know about me?" Black Cal stepped out of the darkness and took Rif's arms.

"She guessed, but I didn't confirm." Rif cast a warning glance back at Rattail. "Now she's seen."

Rat shook her head fast, fingers semaphoring promises: I see nothing, I know nothing, I don't want to get involved.

Rif grinned, turned back to Black Cal, then frowned again. "How'd ye know where t'find us?" she asked.

"A little black cat told me about the scene on de Niro's dock. I went to the Signeury bridge and waited 'til I saw you come out, and then followed you here."

Rif leaned into his arms, grateful at the thought of the unseen escort, shivering at what he'd just revealed. "A little black cat, huh?"

Black Cal smiled faintly. "One of Master Milton's minions. He owed me for that East Dike permit I got him, and I took it in, hmm, news service."

"I wish ye'd told me ye were gettin' inter this so deep!"

"I wish you'd told me you expected to be grabbed by the priests tonight."

"We were prepared. I didn' wanter worry you . . ." Rif leaned back in his arms and looked up at him. "Cal, what would ye've done if we hadn't come outta there t'night?"

A hardness swept over his long elegant face and shadowed green eyes. "I would have come in and gotten you," he said.

Rif stared at him. "What, blowin' away the guards an' the cardinal an' all?"

"Yes." He said it so calmly, as if he were talking about the weather, as if he knew as sure as sundown that he really could do that.

Rif shuddered. "What a load o' damn foolishness," she grumbled. "Rat n' me talked our way outta there, an' the cardinal doesn' wanter ever see or hear from us again, an' maybe she'll even lay off botherin' other singers, an' that's what we pulled off with words an' music an' these stupid getups—an' without riskin' yer life, Black Cal!"

She hugged him, very hard. He hugged back. Rattail looked away, anywhere else, at the rain, at the canal below, as if anything were more interesting.

Rif wiped her eyes and coughed. "Y'know, we gotta go home an' get outta this crap . . ."

"I have a boat waiting." He slid his hands slowly down her arms, reluctant to let her go.

"Aw, Cal, if I come back t'yer place afterward, we won't get any sleep before dawn. . ."

"Tomorrow's my day off." He kept his grip on the ends of her fingers. "Besides, I want to hear the whole juicy story—and also how the search for the cat-whales is going."

"All right," Rif gave in. "Hey, Rat, we've got a free ride home."

"Free ride . . . with a dynamite keg," Rattail muttered. But she got up, and came along.

All the long ride down to Fife she sat in the prow and muttered to herself about the crazy stunts Rif got her into and how she really ought to take a safer career, such as fishing for deathangel or preaching pacifism to the Swampies.

Rif and Black Cal, in the stern, paid her no attention at all.

Old Uki—it was short for Eucalyptus, but only a select few in Merovingen knew that—sat huddled at her usual spot in the niche between the old and new support pillars on the lowest level of Calder Isle. There was room here for a handmade awning to keep out the rain, room under it for a stool to sit on and an earthenware firepot to tend, room on the firepot for a small brewing kettle, and space enough besides to store the clay jugs of chugger that the old woman sold to any passersby who were interested. The tiny brewing booth provided excuse for old Uki to be sitting here all night, warming her hands at the fire, muttering about the rain and cold, and incidentally watching the walkways and bridges from an excellent vantage point. There was also room to reach to the waterline—and the upright clay pipe sticking out of the water—with a long enough pole, which Uki also had. Not a boat or pedestrian passed this corner of Calder Isle but that Eucalyptus McLandon noted, recorded, and often transmitted the fact. She was one of the best reporters, and night watchmen, in the Janes' network.

Just now, there wasn't much to see or report: no boats had gone by in an hour, no pedestrians in longer still. A quiet night in lowtown, but still old Uki listened and watched. There could always be something, at any time.

Ho, *there* was something. A figure: female, barefoot as a canaler, pants-cuffs ragged, walking slowly, stooped—as if with pain or illness rather than age—wandering indecisively down the walkway, and unconsciously wringing her hands. Aha, a poor lowtowner in trouble.

Uki slipped quietly out from behind her simmering brewing kettle and slid closer to the walkway, watching.

The woman fumbled her way close to the water's edge and stood there, rocking forward and back, as if trying to make a decision, or as if trying to summon the will to act. Oh, yes, all the symptoms were clear.

Uki glided forward and tapped the woman on the shoulder.

The woman flinched violently, almost slid over the edge into the canal, recovered her footing and whirled around. Her face was pale, hunger-pinched, hollow-eyed and, at that moment, startled half out of her wits.

" 'Ey, m'sera," Uki offered, showing her kindliest benign-granny face, "Ye wouldn' be thinkin' o' throwin' yerself inter the water, now would ye?"

"I—I— None o' yer karma!" the woman gasped. "What ye mean, botherin' me? Lemme 'lone, an' go 'way."

"Ah, hush, now," Uki spoke to the woman's distress, ignoring her shield of words. "Yon's no way ter clear yer karma. Whatever yer trouble, there's better ways ter deal with'er nor a quick jump inter the canal."

"Oh, t'hell!" The woman turned to look back at the dark water, hands clenching into fists at her sides. "Where's the cure fer bein' poor? Ain't no end ter that, this side o' the water."

Uki clicked her tongue. "Tush, there's plenty o' ways outta poverty, do ye bother ter work at 'em.

And there's plenty o' folks live poor without divin'
inter the water. An' don' tell me yer trouble's so
bad that nobody can help."

"Help. . . ?" the woman considered, then shook
her head. "There's no help down here."

"Ney? Now, how would ye know?" Uki chuckled. "There's more ter luck an' karma an' all nor
any scholar nor cardinal could tell. Help can come
from the damnedest places. . . ."

"Luck!" The woman spat. "My luck's been nothin'
but bad, this whole year'n more. Karma done shot
me down. I wish t'hell I could remember my past
lives, like them fancy uptowners with their deathangel
drug, so I'd know what I did last time 'round t' earn
bad luck like this."

"So bad nor that, ey?" Uki ventured to pat the
woman's rigid arm. "Why not c'mon over ter the
fire, warm yerself a bit, an' tell me what the trouble
is. I'm an ol' woman, an' I've seen much. P'raps I
can think o' somethin' or someone as could help
ye."

"Ney, I've karma-debts enough." The woman
pulled away, face cold and desolate with hopeless
pride.

Uki clucked her tongue again. Ah, dear: too miserable to live, too proud to take help . . . but believing a lot in luck. Possibility there. "Well, then,
tell me now, m'sera; y'have any sportin' blood?"

The woman glanced back, surprised but not of-
fended. "Ey, sure," she admitted. "Jus' no luck."

"Why then, I'll offer ye a wild gamble ter get yer
luck back. 'Twon't cost ye anthin' but a bit o' time
an' silliness. Ye game ter listen, at least?"

"What gamble?" the woman asked, intrigued in spite of herself.

Careful now: reel her in slowly. "Did y'ever hear the old legend o' the black cats?"

"Black cats? They're s'posed ter be bad luck ter cross."

"Bad luck ter cross, good luck ter speak ter." Uki grinned. "Ye've heard th'old tales o' the witch, Althea Jane, ain't ye?"

"Oh, aye. Hanged in the north, weren't she? And didn' she curse 'er judges, sayin' they'd all die within the year? An' they did?"

Good, good: that tale had made the rounds. "Aye, that an' more. It seems she had the gift o' speakin' ter animals, an' even plants. She got along best with cats—black cats—so before she died, she blessed 'em with somethin' special."

"What's that?" The woman took an unconscious step nearer.

"A strange power o' luck," Uki said. "Do ye cross a black cat, an' yer luck goes bad. But do ye make friends with a black cat, an' yer luck goes good. What's more—an' this part may int'rest ye—if yer luck's already bad, then do ye tell yer trouble ter a black cat. Just tell 'er all, out loud, like ye was speakin' t'a person—an' yer luck will change fer the better. Whatever yer trouble is, she'll get better—or even go 'way alt'gether. Yon's the power o' the black cat."

The woman stared for a long moment, then burst into laughter. "Lord, Lord," she sputtered, "ye really had me on there, fer a bit. I oughtta thank ye fer the laugh. Talk ter black cats . . . Oh, my flamin' bunions, that's good!"

"She gets better." Uki didn't cease to smile. "D'ye see yon doorway there?" She pointed at the building across the canal. "Down by the water, third from the right. Ye see 'er? Well listen now: back o' that door lives an herb-doctor, a right good doctor, too, an' if anyone's got luck, she does—fer all her patients come out better nor they went in. An' she's got a big black cat."

"So?" The woman shrugged. "That proves nothin'."

"There's more. I meself had real trouble not long back; a dirty blackleg 'e were, tryin' ter drive me outta my little shop-hole here, er else squeeze every penny outta me."

The woman grunted sympathy. She'd seen that, often enough.

"I was run near distracted, didn' know what ter do, desp'rate enough ter try drinkin' chugger—"

The woman winced, likewise in sympathy.

"An' then I got this crazy idea. I'd heard the tale o' the cats, an' I knew 'bout the herb-doctor's cat, an' I had nothin' ter lose, so I says ter meself, why not? I went an' found the cat, lured 'er close with a bit o' fish an' coaxed 'er inter my lap with a bit o' pettin', an' then I told 'er all my trouble—aye, talked t'er like she was a person, an' damned if the cat didn' listen."

"Just sat an' listened?" The woman marveled, edging a little closer.

"Aye, she did. When I was done, the cat got up an' trotted off, jus' like she was off on business. I figured, hell, that's th'end o' that, an' went lookin' fer somethin' ter drink. Fergot 'bout it . . .'til next mornin' . . ."

Uki stopped to roll her eyes in a dramatic pause.

"Well, what happened next mornin'?" the woman insisted.

"I went ter work as usual." Uki waved a modest hand toward her firepot and still. "An' I waited fer customers or that blackleg ter show up. Customers did, he didn't. By noon I had almost enough ter pay 'im off, but he still didn' show. Come afternoon I got worried an' started askin' around. Guess what I heard." Pause again, and smile significantly.

". . . That 'e was dead?" the woman asked, eyes wide.

"Better nor that." Uki grinned triumphantly. "It seems that with the Crud goin' 'round, the blacklegs was runnin' short o' muscle, so's he got extra work guardin' some warehouse that night. Now that would'a been good luck fer him, with the extra pay an' all, an' bad luck fer me, since he'd've got off work come dawn an' come lookin' fer me real early. But somehow, right 'bout an hour after I'd talked ter the cat, his luck went an' changed."

"An hour after. . . ?"

"Aye, maybe as long's it would'a taken fer a cat ter run from where I'd been ter where he was." Uki hitched nearer and dropped her voice to a conspiratorial whisper. "About then, it seems, somebody came by an' knocked 'im inter the water."

"In th'water?" the woman gasped. "Somebody? Who?"

"Turns out she was a hightown lady, an' 'twas 'er word 'gainst 'is that 'e didn' fall in by himself. An' she gets better." Uki nudged the woman with her elbow, and grinned wider. "So 'e hauls himself outta the water an' tries t'arrest the lady, an' who should come by but . . . Black Cal himself."

The woman shivered in appreciation.

"Black Cal takes one look at this big, blusterin' blackleg threatenin' this little hightown lady, listens ter both their stories, an' makes a righteous guess that the blackleg's lyin'. He tells the blackleg ter shut up an' go back ter mindin' 'is proper business, or go on report. Black Cal sees the lady home, an' the blackleg's too scared ter do anythin' but keep on guardin' the warehouse. So comes mornin', and he's got one awful case o' the Crud. All he can do is crawl home an' report in sick. He never comes back ter bother me, an' they say . . ." Uki dropped her voice a fraction lower. "They say he's been sick, on an' off, ever since. Never got 'is full strength back, never enough ter go out hustlin' poor folk in lowtown, not ever again."

Now sit back, wait, watch for reactions.

The woman slowly nodded her head. "What the hell," she sighed. "She can't hurt. Where d'I find this cat, again?"

Uki pointed out the door and watched while the woman plodded away toward it. Once she was alone on the walkway again, she reached for the pole and tapped out a code on the standing pipe down in the water.

Willow, Dr. Yarrow's night guard and secretary, heard the tapping clearly. By the time the tentative knock fell on the front door, she had everything ready. When she opened the door, wearing her too-large bibbed apron over rumpled clothes, she looked like a perfectly harmless servant.

"Yes?" she said politely to the hollow-eyed woman on the doorstep. "Do ye need to see the doctor?"

"Er, not the doc exac'ly . . ." The woman seemed on the verge of turning back, but then shrugged almost fiercely. "I'd . . . like ter see . . . yer cat."

"The cat?" Willow blinked innocently for a moment, then smiled. "Oh, that one. Lost of folk come t'pet the cat for luck when they're sick. I think 'tis the medicines really do 'er, but aye, come on in." She waved the guest into the dimly lit waiting room.

The woman hesitated a moment, then followed.

"Ye can sit here," Willow pointed to an ancient but comfy armchair in a corner, near a raveling but still handsome wall hanging. "Ye can have some tea if ye like, while I go fetch Mouser."

"Aye, thanks," said the woman, sinking gratefully into the chair. "I'd like that."

Willow poured a good cupful of the strong herb tea kept constantly ready in the waiting room, and went to pass the word to the proper ears.

The woman warmed her hands on the mug, then sighed and drained it.

A few minutes later Willow came back, toting a large and faintly-annoyed-looking black tomcat in her arms. "Here, now," she said, plucking the animal down in the visitor's lap. "Ye just pet 'im all ye like, an' get warm if ye need ter. I've got ter go ter the john, so watch the door for me, will you?"

"Oh, aye." The woman's look of delighted bewilderment, as she watched Willow leave the room, was priceless.

Willow grinned to herself as she clomped out the doorway, then quickly kicked off her shoes and tiptoed down the hallway that ran behind the wall of the waiting room. A chair sat near the wall, waxboard and stylus waiting on it. Willow took up the board and stylus, sat down in the chair, and put her ear to the conveniently-placed hole in the wall.

From behind it, at first, came nothing but the creaking of the armchair and the growing, thunderous purr of the tomcat. Then words:

"I s'pose this is crazy, but I've done crazier things . . . Ey, hello, cat. My name's Hope Blenski, an' I live on Ventani Isle, second door west, bottom level, fourth room down the left corridor . . ."

Willow scribbled quickly, in Janist shorthand. Very good; she wouldn't have to send someone out to track the woman home, or get her name from unreliable neighbors.

". . . I got this trouble, cat," Hope Blenski went on. "There's this damn under-priest . . . Y'know, one o' the kind they send out ter check on ever'thin' ye make or sell, name o' Prossa, carries a holystick. Well . . ."

Pause, no sound but the cat's purring and the faint whisking of what was probably a gentle hand on sleek fur.

"Well," the voice resumed, "He's blackmailin' me. Business-license crap, y'know. I make rope, buy the fibers cheap, soak an' wind an' dry 'em meself, go out an' sell 'em ter the Trade. Simple, ney? No harm, ney? Not what Prossa says."

A long heartfelt sigh. The cat meowed sympathetically, as if on cue.

"Damn, if I don't think ye *do* understand," Blenski marveled. "Well, like I'm sayin', all I do is buy fibers, wind 'em, go out an' sell 'em. What records'm I gonna keep, hey? I sell down by waterside, dunno who-all I'm sellin' ter nor what they're gonna do with 'er, and how'm I s'posed ter know anyway? That's what I says ter Prossa when he grabs me off'n a walkway an' wants ter see records an' College stamps an' all."

"Mrrrrp," commented the cat.

"Aye, 'tis no more nor common sense. But Prossa leans on me. 'Show records'n stamps,' he says, 'or get locked up.' Now what'm I gonna do? I begs an' pleads an' crawls like dirt, an' don' think 'e don't like seein' that, the scumball."

"Wrrraaa," growled the cat.

"Damn right. But 'e finally says t'me, 'Two dece an' I'll overlook yer past follies'—follies, my bleedin' ass! —'just have yer paperwork filled out next time we come 'round.' I ask when 'e wants the two dece, an' 'e says, 'Tomorra.' "

"Urrrrh," said the cat.

"Right, tomorra. I don't get 'im two dece by then, I go ter the bad room in the College basement. That's why I was 'bout ter throw meself in the canal. My luck's been bad fer the past year, an' this is the cap on 'er. So tell me, cat—witch-Jane's cat—can ye help me? Or should I just walk back ter the water?"

There was a long moment's silence, broken only by the purring of the cat. Then a rustling, and a louder purr. Then a whistle of surprise.

Willow stifled a giggle. Mouser, feeling comfortable with the kind-handed visitor, must have pulled his party trick of rolling over, staring up soulfully into the human's face, and bobbing his chin vigorously. It looked remarkably like a human nodding yes, and never failed to win Mouser more attention and petting.

"Damn," whispered Blenski, awed. "I never seen a cat do that b'fore! . . . Is that a sign? . . . Hell, gotta be a sign . . . All right, cat. I'll trust t'yer witch Jane, go home an' ferget the canal. Maybe tomorra, things'll be different. Hey?"

Willow entered the final note, set down the board and stylus and got up quietly from the chair. She tiptoed down the hall, slipped her shoes back on, made a few increasing foot-clomping noises, then walked around the corner and into the waiting room.

There sat Hope Blenski, petting the ecstatically-purring cat, with her expression at last fitting her name. She looked up almost guiltily as Willow came in, but didn't leave off petting the cat.

"Thanks fer mindin' the door," said Willow. "An' was Mouser a good boy? Did 'e let ye pet 'im for lotsa luck? Aw, was ums a good kitty-kitty?" She said the last while tickling the cat's chin, which made Mouser wriggle with joy.

"Oh, aye, he was real good, m'sera." Hope reluctantly handed over the happily-limp cat to Willow's waiting arms. "I think I got lotsa luck from pettin' 'im."

"Ye sure ye don' need ter see the doctor?" Willow offered, settling Mouser on her shoulder. "I can wake 'er up, if 'tis an emergency . . ."

"Ney, I'm fine now." Hope Blenski got up and edged politely toward the door. "All I needed was a bit o' luck, an' I think I got that now."

"Take care o' yerself, then." Willow opened the door and let the visitor out into the night, and watched her walk rapidly away. Then she put the cat down on the still-warm chair and headed for a certain back room.

"Raven," she said to the gray-haired man bent over a desk full of papers, "I think we've got a live one off the cat-tale circuit."

Raven stretched until his joints cracked, grateful for the chance to do some active planning. "What distress-story have we got this time?" he asked.

"A blackmailing priest named Prossa. And—"

"Prossa? I know that name." Raven fumbled through various papers and cards. "Nasty piece, that one. Shakedowns, worse'n most blacklegs."

"This time he's blackmailing a poor rope-maker who sells to the Trade. A good lowtown connection there. Trouble is, the victim needs relief by morning; either Prossa gone or two dece to pay. What can we do?"

Raven leaned back in his chair and thought hard, saying nothing.

"I've got the victim's name and address, if we want to do the moneybag-through-the-window trick again . . . if we've got the money to spare." Willow paused, looking doubtful. "We don't have a black kitten handy either, do we?"

"It's not that," said Raven, rousing himself to decision. "We only give a black kitten to somebody who's already gossiping regularly with one of our reporters. Otherwise, when they tell their troubles to the kitten and nothing happens, the legend loses power. Besides, I've a better idea."

He pulled out a particular list of names and studied it, frowning grimly.

"The College's bullying has roused enough resentment for this to work now,"he said, quietly. "Also, our . . . termination team needs practice."

Willow pressed a finger to her mouth, and said nothing.

"Go out and beat the pipe, Willow. Send the code, and Prossa's name—also his description and probable whereabouts, here, from his card. Be sure to stress the time factor."

Willow took a deep breath and stood up straighter. "Prossa, dead by morning," she said. "So it'll go."

"Hmm, and when you've finished with that, do a report for Yarrow. She'll need it first thing in the morning to set up the recruiter in time."

"Recruiter? In time for what?"

"In time to catch and work on our night visitor, when she comes back tomorrow to thank the cat."

WHERE'S THE FIRE?

by Roberta Rogow

Merovingen was suffering from a lack of gossip.

The list of safe topics of conversation was rapidly approaching the point of terminal silence. There was the weather, but after a while even the most literate student ran out of synonyms for "wet." There was the building program at Megary's, which was rumored would replace the burned-out structure with one to rival the Justiciary for impregnability, and the Signeury for grandeur—but no one really wanted to discuss Megarys in these days of too many mysterious disapperances: no one wanted a firsthand look at the interior.

There was the burgeoning pregnancy of Marina Kamat, and the inevitable speculation as to the father of the prospective Kamat heir, but one of the three most likely candidates had just thrown a magnificent ball in honor of his Third Contracting, and the other two candidates were *very* close to Kamat. After a few hostile glares and puzzled stares the witticisms stopped.

No one wanted to be clever at the expense of either the College or the Militia. Lord, no!

This left only one safe topic for conversation in Merovingen-above: Farren's Folly, the Firewatch.

Plenty to chortle over, snicker about, speculate on, and generally chew up and down at dinners and parties and small gatherings above and below Merovingen's thousand bridges.

In the first place, the very idea of hearty, genial Farren paired with feckless Mikhail Kalugin in any endeavor was beyond belief: and the two of them coming up with this elaborate bureaucratic arrangement of a permanent paid firefighting squad added to the exquisite humor of the situation. And, Lord and Ancestors, the squad consisted of Red Moze and his bridge-boys! The laughter resounded as far as midtown and below.

Merovingen had watched as Farren and Mikhail struggled with their supplies. Farren poled himself all over the city, cornering the market in sail-canvas and tar. Mikhail himself, dogged by scores of anxious blackleg security, haunted a canalside carpenter's shop, bringing in elaborate diagrams of ladders and clamps—every one of which had had to have the seal of the College (another nervous attendance of harried security, on both sides)—and more diagrams and more visits to a sailmaker's shop on harborside (security was apoplectic).

Meanwhile, the Trade had had its own thoughts about a gang of erstwhile bullyboys and ruffians who put themselves into the hands of a hightown penpusher and the governor's feckless firstborn, and who, discarding their flash and raffish style, let themselves wear bright red sweaters. The Trade had watched and snorted derisively as Moze and his sister Liz the Snitch and the rest of them ran up and down those rickety ladders, hauling heavy sacks, while the rain poured off their backs. Rumor was all over town that Moze was gallows-bait, that a certain injudicious prank about the aforesaid carpenter's shop had gone too far, the dumping of a barrel of sawdust on Mikhail's over-nervous guard— Moze himself had been caught up along with his ruffians, and a most humorless Signeury had damned the wretches to swing—except—except Mikhail's deciding aha! here was an organized, hale, and agile lot that might be spared to better purpose—

So from Hanging Bridge to Mikhail's employ had come Moze and crew—from clowning ruffians to raffish clowns: and all that long, wet grim summer Merovingen had watched and laughed at Farren's Folly and its salvaged crew. A firewatch? In this sopping, drenching summer and soggy fall? And with bridge-boy riffraff for a crew? Never! said hightown. Wear those bright red sweaters, and those silly looking caps, tied under the chin? Take orders from Mischa the Clockmaker, idiot savant, whose practical sense was nil, and Farren Delaney, whose brains were all in his wife's head? Never! said the Trade: Moze and his crew were born to hang: they were only biding their time till they filched fool Farren's wallet or Kalugin gold. Hightown and canalside were agreed on one thing: The Firewatch would never work.

While Merovingen snickered, Farren and Mikhail had slogged on. When the hose split (titters from the sailmakers' apprentices) under the pressure of the water, Mikhail had tested thickness of canvas and tar until he got a hose that would withstand the force of the pump. When the merchants cavilled at paying for the bridge-bully Firewatch, fearing pilferage and arson, Farren had knocked on doors in the Second Tier, pointing out to shopowners that they were the most vulnerable to fire, should it break out—and whether some signed for fear of Moze and some for Mikhail's promised patronage, the list had grown.

Farren and Mikhail had drilled their crew in person, wonderful sight! They had demonstrated hoseholding, ladder-climbing, and basic life-saving until spectators rolled laughing on the boardwalk. But the squad had persevered, Farren and Mikhail against the snickers, and Moze and Liz and crew against the nighttime hoots and taunts from their old rivals around the town.

And at last the Day, the great demonstration: Farren and Mikhail had decided to let the governor and his advisors see how things were going. And suitably surrounded by his blackleg guards and with attendant hangers-on and entourage genteelly snickering behind their hands, Iosef Kalugin dutifully watched from Golden Bridge as Moze fired up the pump and Liz took the hose. Josh and Axel hauled the ladder up, clamped it to the bridge-struts, nipped up and slid back. The ladder folded back down, the hose came reeled in sans disasters, and the Firewatch stood to motley attention as the governor and Cardinal Exeter conferred.

"Well?" Mikhail asked, unable to keep still any longer.

Governor Kalugin nodded. "Not bad," he said slowly—personal triumph, this: Mikhail his heir, Mikhail the notoriously feckless, had evaded public debacle. The disappointment in the crowd was palpable: and dare one hope—there might be some public reassessment due?

Cardinal Exeter nodded. "Acceptable," she declared. "The technical questions—"

"Only what we already have," Mikhail said, eager to show off his ingenuity. "And there's a bell to clear the way, once the boat is on the water."

"We can go operational when you give the word," Farren said.

"Then consider the word given," Iosef muttered. "I'll have notices posted today. The Firewatch is official. Mind—if there's one bad report on this crew of yours—"

"Not that there's any likelihood of a fire," Cardinal Exeter said, considering the dripping, still soggy bridge-timbers. "For all the College officially determines, all the tech is legitimate. —And, ser Delaney, do tell your wife I'll attend the reading of the next cantos of Lukhacz's Epic. I'm very interested in the depiction of Delaney's's Last Stand. . ." Exeter *promoted* Mikhail's causes: delicately *supported* his patrons and his attachments—carefully kept lists and investigated each and all contacts . . . for purity of thought and associations.

Farren smiled as the governor and the cardinal marched off. Once they were out of sight he whooped out, "We're chugging!"

Moze smirked at his bridge-bullies. "What next, m'ser?"

"We float the fireboat out to the dock, right next to the Firewatch barracks," Farren began.

"Eh?" Liz said suspiciously. "What's this barracks?"

"It's that big barn I had them build next to the dock," Farren explained hurriedly. "It's part of your pay. A lune a week, and found. That's a dry bed, a roof over your head, and staples on the stove. You want anything fancy, you'll have to come up with it yourself."

Liz shifted uneasily on her feet. "You didn't say nothing about found. Just the money, you said. Put out the fires, run the boat. That's all. We don't like takin' without givin' back."

There were snickers among eavesdroppers. A more critical sort might have doubted this nobility in Liz the Snitch—and Liz cast a foul look in those directions. " 'At's so," she said, fingering her knife—and it was, one knew: it was one thing to take and snatch, but *nobody* liked to get charity.

Farren understood that. "This isn't charity," Farren was quick to tell her. "I want you to be on that boat when the call comes in—" ("Not out lifting wallets on the bridges," someone whispered in the crowd.) "I want you fast to answer. Once the weather dries up you'll earn that lune."

("Lord," some said, "honest work. What's Moze an' his sister comin' to?" And others: "Arson, most like. What's wrong with the volunteer brigade, ain't never asked f' money . . .")

Moze took off the hated red cap and scratched his head. "Make it two?" he asked.

"Two," Farren conceded. "All I want is to make this Firewatch work. Just be on the boat. Tomorrow."

"Tomorrow," Moze said, as Farren and Mikhail loped up the stairs to the Signeury. Above them, the sun struggled to send a few watery rays through the thinning mist.

The firebells rang at sundown.

For the first time in months there was no rain, not even a wisp of mist hanging over the canals.

Axel was dishing out supper in the new barracks when they heard the sound.

"A'ready?" Moze asked aloud. "Damn!"

"What do we do?" Axel asked. "Soup's hot."

"We gotta," Moze said. "I ain't goin' t' Hangin' Bridge, damn, I ain't! Josh, get up and spot 'er. Where's the fire?"

The rail-thin pickpocket trotted up to the sighting-station "Moze, it's Megary's."

"*What?* You sure?"

In answer, Josh pointed to the plume of black smoke that hung over Rimmon.

"Now what do we do?" Axel asked. "We can't save Megary's. The Trade'll lynch us theyselves, wi'out no judge!"

It was a moment of truth, for sure and all. Even Axel sensed it. And Moze smacked his cap on his knee. "Damn, damn—we got no choice, lads!"

"So," asked Liz. "What do we do?"

"We go out and fight that fire," Moze declared. "But not too hard, boys. Not too hard."

With deliberate speed, the bridge-bullies fired up the engine of the pumpboat. Bell clanging, motor chugging, pump wheezing, they steered into the thick of the traffic on the canals, well sure that the Trade would do everything in its power to stop anyone giving aid and comfort to Megary's.

Every canaler seemed to be on the water that evening, and none of them would give way to the sweating, cursing Firewatch. They passed the Delaney dock, where Farren was already in his red sweater and cap, and it took them five precious minutes to get through the crush to reach him. More time wasted while a barge-load of kegs turned completely around in the narrow channel under Fishmarket Bridge. By this time the plume of smoke had begun to spread into a haze. The afternoon strollers on Ventani High Bridge saw the fireboat and its red-backed crew, and pointed down and laughed.

"It's Farren and his Hanging Bridge Ferry!" someone called out. The word was picked up and followed them down the canal. Farren grabbed the tiller from Moze.

"What the hell do you think you're doing?" he hissed. "Get over to that fire!"

"I'm doin' my best, m'ser, but it's too crowded."

"Just get through!" Farren muttered, through clenched teeth. One skip left a gap of a few inches. Farren nosed the fireboat into the gap, while Liz rang the bell on the bows.

By the time they reached Megary's, there was only a charred ruin left of what had been a brand-new building. Old Megary glared at Farren in disgust.

Mikhail was there on his sleek polished-wood powerboat. With his blackleg escort. "Where have you been?" he asked, while Megary raved and cursed and called his ancestors to witness he had paid the fire-fee, and where was his protection?

"We ran into a little traffic on the canal," Farren said uncomfortably, trying to evade eavesdroppers. "We'll have to do something about that. I hope no one was hurt . . ."

"He hopes nobody's hurt!" someone took it up, and relayed it to the crowd. There were hoots, wishes for all Megary to perish, with anyone who would deal with them.

Megary howled: "I want my money back, Delaney!

I didn't pay your Firewatch to get jammed up on the water!"

Farren smiled blandly. "We'll discuss that in the morning, when we've had time to reflect a bit. In the meanwhile, is there anything the Firewatch can do to help?"

"You and your red-backed Firewatch can go . . ."

"We'll try, m'ser Megary. Moze, back to barracks!" Farren pushed the boat back into the canal. Moze fired the engine. Liz did not clang the bell. They cruised back through Archangel, under the bridge, to the hoots of Trade and hightowners alike.

Once they were there, Farren waited until they were all back in the barracks, staring at their cold bowls of soup before letting loose on them.

"What the hell was that about?" he began, his voice dangerously gently. "I thought we had a deal. I paid you, I trained you, you get the boat out and fight the fire. That *was* the arrangement, wasn't it?"

Moze stared at the floor. "Ay, that was it. —But you didn't say it would be Megary's."

"What difference does it make if it's Megary's or some swampy's hidey? I don't care if the fire's in the Grand Castle of the sharrh! It is our job to go and put it out!"

"The Trade'll carve us in fishbait," Liz said flatly.

"Liz," Farren said, "if I had my way, I'd see Megary and his ilk at the bottom of the Det before I lifted a finger to save their worthless hides. But they paid their insurance fees, and I'm bound to honor it. Personal feelings have nothing to do with it."

"What's the odds, then?" Moze asked. "The Trade don't want Megary's, you don't want Megary's—"

"Don't you people understand? We do not have the right to pick which fires we put out and which we let burn. We fight all of them! Megary will want his fee back, and soon all of them will, and the whole Signeury will call it Farren's Folly. D'ye know what your choices are? Do you remember your appointment on Hanging Bridge? Or do you think they won't blame *me* for your mistakes?"

Farren stopped for breath.

"We got the rope on this side," Moze said, "we got the Trade an' their hooks on t' other. We got to walk th' canalside, m'ser, an' it don't matter what Megary's money says, ever'body knows what them Megary boats do, I mean, we snitch a few wallets an' all, an' we got Hangin' Bridge—and them Megarys snitch kids and sell 'em, an' they bought th' judge—"

"And Karl Fon doesn't have to march against us," Farren said bitterly. All he has to do is wait until hightown and low tear each other to pieces, and then he can take over what's left."

"Eh?" Liz said, wrinkling her brow. This was too remote a connection. "What's this about Karl Fon?"

"What have we got?" Farren began to pace around the central table, scattering the bridge-bullies as he moved. "Bought judges, people arrested for a joke in a bar . . . that Boregy woman preaching class against class—don't you understand? This isn't about Megary's . . . it's about the way things are in Merovingen. How do I make you understand? We can do more than just sit here and wait for the next turn of the Wheel! There's *got* to be a way to get out of this *swamp* we've gotten into!"

Moze and Liz edged closer together. "Cardinals

say we wait for karma," Moze said with cautious and currently advisable piety.

Farren ran a hand through his hair. "Karma? Hell, we can rearrange our karma!"

Liz spoke in the dead silence after Farren's ringing words. "That there sounds a scary lot like heresy, m'ser."

"Then turn me in to the College," Farren said, slumping against the table. "You do things the same damn old way. No change. You sit here and let Megary's burn and they just build back. Don't you see there's a way to put a stop to 'em?"

"How?" Moze asked. All this religion and politics was a scary idea. He liked smaller problems. "How'd you deal with Megary's, m'ser?"

"I wouldn't burn 'em out," Farren said. "I'd tax them! I'd find a dry rot in their roof and mildew in their cellars. I'd fine 'em for dumping garbage into the canals, and I'd run inspections on their damned boats. By the time I was finished with 'em they'd have a hell of a lot of judges to buy. My office *can* do it. Can do a lot of things, 'long as I stay in it. *That's* the way to deal with Megary's!"

"Maybe, m'ser. But you got not to talk that way." Moze found himself unaccustomedly worried about his patron—found himself with an honest hightowner on his hands, and the sure knowledge if this man went down, so did Moze and Liz and the boys. "You got to be careful—"

Farren smiled ruefully. "I know."

"Way-hen?" came a voice from the door—canaler cant in a hesitant, hightown accent—Mikhail Kalugin himself, with his blackleg guard. Mikhail was smudged with smoke, his hair wildly waving in the wind, his face flushed with fire-burn or good-natured excitement. "Well, well, first day problems, but all in all a success, eh?"

"M'ser Kalugin," Moze greeted him respectfully.

"Why did you leave me there?" Mikhail asked peevishly. "I had to explain to that disgusting Megary why we couldn't get to his fire on time. Just as well, just as well—the reputation of the Firewatch and all. My security tells me the whisper is, the Firewatch has to be honest, eh? I mean, the whole canalside's buzzing with it."

"Has to be honest?" Farren asked.

"Why, sure it wasn't any accident, but wasn't the Firewatch that did it; and them coming late—that's marvelously politic, as my brother would say. Anastasi himself couldn't time it better. Sister Tatty's just going to be livid. She so wanted me to be a fool!"

"That's . . . quite fortuitous," Farren said.

"Ah, yes." Mikhail had an unaccustomedly smug look on his smudged face. "And since of course we did show, eh? I maintained there's no question of a refund. And since it's clearly arson, we won't pay a silverbit until we prove where culpability lies. Eh? Most of all, the equipment works! It works and the whole town's seen it does!"

"It did that," Farren said, more cheerfully.

"It must! It's going to stop the burning, you see." A feverish look came into Mikhail's eyes. He assumed a conspiratorial tone, including Moze and Liz as well. "It has to work, to stop the burning."

"The burning," Farren said. Moze and Liz seemed to draw closer to him, as if to seek protection from a possible madman.

The words tumbled out of Mikhail: "Cassie's seen it all. There's going to be burning, and the canalers will try to come up and kill us all, but if there's a Firewatch, then we'll stop the burning, and if the Firewatch is mine, then they won't kill me or Cassie, because I won't let them, you see, and she'll love me for it!"

With which Mikhail sailed out of the barracks, gathering his guards as he went.

"Is he daft?" Moze asked Farren as the footsteps left the boards outside.

"Only about Cassie Boregy," Farren told him. "But you see what's happening up there?" He jerked his thumb upward again, implying hightown, and hightowners, and the Signeury. "Give it a chance. Trust me!" Farren's blue eyes held Moze for a minute. "You've got a chance, Moze, you and yours. Do you want it? Or do you want to throw everything away?"

"We'll do it your way fer a bit," Liz the Snitch said finally. There were nods all round, a sober, worried lot of rogues.

It was, Farren thought, at least a hope of a beginning, a single sandbag laid, against the deluge.

WHEELS WITHIN WHEELS

by Bradley H. Sinor

"Kali!"

Kali Duquesne stirred in her bed and rolled to one side, not all that certain she was even awake. Outside her window a thunderstorm was venting its wrath on Merovingen. That was like any morning this week. If it were morning—which it wasn't.

"Kali!"

This time the sound of her name brought Kali fully awake. She pried her eyes open to stare at a dim candle, in the hands of someone standing a few feet from the side of her bed.

"If it's anything short of Jane herself returning or a personal message from the sharrh, why don't we just leave it all until morning?" she muttered, and pulled the sheet halfway up over her face.

"I really wish I could do that, little one."

Kali smiled. There was only one man, Miles Quincannon, security chief for Greely House and Greely and Company, who called her little one.

For a long moment the big man stood there, staring at Kali. "Come down to your father's study as soon as you're dressed," he said finally, then turned and headed out the door.

Kali lay there staring at where Quincannon had

stood for several minutes. At that moment all she wanted to do was listen to the sound of the rain.

"Damn it." She shook her head angrily. Surely it couldn't all be starting again. In the six months since her return to Greely House, nothing—nothing of the intrigues she had married to escape. Kali realized she should be used to this. It had been going on all her life. Only with Darius it all had taken on the aspect of a bad dream.

"Darius, Darius," she muttered as she groped around on the floor for the sweater and trousers she had dropped hours earlier. "Damn—if we'd ever had a chance . . ."

"Do you m'sers know what time it is?" Kali demanded as she came down the circular staircase into the main room of Greely House.

Quincannon looked up at her briefly. In this light the big security chief looked older than she had ever seen him. The left sleeve of his shirt was ripped and bloodstained.

He stood to one side of the study door with two of the security staff whose names Kali hadn't bothered to learn. A few feet away was her older brother Simon Greely, looking bleary-eyed from too little sleep—or too much drink.

The big study door was a bastion of childhood memories and challenges. No one was ever permitted inside without a direct invitation from Marcus Greely himself. Kali could well remember several very painful reminders of that rule.

On the fingers of one hand Kali could count the number of times she had been admitted to her father's sanctum. Once had been the night, three years ago, that she had informed him she was defying his wishes and contract-marrying Darius Odell. The last occasion, a scant six months before, the day of her return to Greely House after Darius' funeral, when Marcus Greely informed her that the Family would do nothing to find out who had killed her husband.

The door itself was a huge piece of carved hardwood, hung on the strongest hinges available . . . a sealed, windowless sanctum beyond that door—which was exactly the way that Marcus Greely liked it.

"It's just into second watch, Kali," said Simon. "It's Father. No one's seen him for hours."

"So?"

"He'd returned from a meeting with Kamat, about that merchant's association thing, just before sunset. He was madder than I've ever seen him. I don't think it was anything to do with Kamat, it was something else. He wouldn't say what was the matter and when I asked him he seemed almost on the point of slugging me."

It couldn't have happened to a nicer person, Kali told herself.

"About a half hour ago this arrived," Quincannon said, holding up a leather portfolio case. "Your father's been expecting this case for days. He'd left orders to have it brought to him no matter what the hour, so I went to his rooms. The bed hadn't been slept in. I knocked here. I even checked the kitchen. The study door is locked, apparently from the inside. Ten minutes of yelling and we still haven't gotten an answer."

"And you haven't gone in there yet?" demanded Kali.

"I wanted the two of you here before I broke in on him." Quincannon held up a slim silver key. "I do have this."

That surprised Kali. "So," Simon said, "let's do it, dammit."

Kali Duquesne stared at her father's body. He lay half across the huge desk that stood at the center of the room. From this angle it might have appeared that he was only taking a moment to rest.

Kali leaned against the edge of the table, not all that certain what she was feeling just then. She and her father had never been all that close. Marcus Greely hadn't been all that close to anyone. The last time they'd faced each other in his study they'd ended up screaming. Now the only thing left was a queasy feeling in the pit of her stomach.

Quincannon lingered near the door. He walked forward finally and bent over the desk. Kali heard him speaking but couldn't tell what the words were. Then he reached out and closed the dead man's eyes.

The killing had been done with a single blow to the side of Marcus Greely's head, a blow that had caved in the side of his head.

"Whoever did it," Simon said from beside the door, "he had to have let him in himself."

"Someone he felt comfortable with, even trusted," said Kali. "—As much as he'd ever trust anyone."

"Including us," said Simon, turning toward Quincannon. "What kind of a security chief are you, old man? It's your job to keep things like this from happening."

Kali heard the distinctive sound of a wrist sheath

spring: she knew that it had deposited a stiletto into her brother's hand.

Quincannon didn't wait for Simon. He closed the gap in two strides, his fist slamming into the younger man's chin. The stiletto clattered onto the floor and he kicked it away.

Before anything else could happen a small figure appeared in the doorway, staring at all three of them. Except for a bushy mustache the newcomer was clean shaven, and dressed in a heavy sweater, pants and knee-high boots, all black.

"God," he said, "I thought I was walking into a tavern brawl."

"A blackleg, that's all we need now," said Simon. "Just who are you anyway, and who let you in, dammit?"

The officer stared at Simon for a long moment, then turned toward Kali. "M'sera, I'm officer Ian McVoy. Here at the request of Marcus Greely. The storm, unhappily, delayed me."

"Father called for you?" said Simon.

"Under his own seal."

Kali saw Quincannon grimace. "It seems m'ser had more planned for tonight than we knew—I'm afraid, officer McVoy, that there has been a slight change in plans."

"So I see, so I see," nodded McVoy. "M'sera Duquesne, if you would be good enough to escort one of these two m'sers somewhere to cool off. I'll have questions for you all, but they can wait awhile— one killing at a time is more than enough for me."

"I must be doing something right," said Quincannon. "Counting Simon, it's the fourth time someone's tried to kill me in the last few weeks."

Kali rummaged through the medicine and bandages in the small wooden box she had taken from the cabinet. She had the ruined shirt sleeve off. The cut on Quincannon's arm wasn't deep, and not even an inch long, a lot of blood, hardly deep enough for a scar.

"You keep pulling stunts like this thing with Simon and we'll be having to plan your funeral, not to mention hiring a new chief of security."

"Make it something elaborate," he said. "You know . . . a small something along the lines of Cardinal Boregy's this summer . . ."

"Should we be ordering up an orange robe for you?"

"Never!" said Quincannon.

If the security chief had any religious beliefs, Kali had never heard him voice them. The Greelys were nominally Adventist, although her own mother, Isadora Duquesne, had dabbled in secret Janism.

"Would you like me to lie and say this won't hurt?" The disinfectant was a paste made from plants and fish oil. Effective, but it did have that one drawback.

"Smells awful."

"So what happened?" she said as she began to spread it on his skin. "You been drinking in the wrong bars again?"

"Hardly!" said Quincannon indignantly. "For the last few months I've been trying to sniff out who's behind those hijackings . . . you know, the lading and damage bills that don't match. Greely and Company isn't the only House who has been feeling the sting. —So I was down near East Dike, second level, talking to some other warehouses . . . and some damn bridge-bullies jumped me. Out after some money and a bit of fun."

"They made the mistake of picking you."

"Exactly."

"So where are they now?" she asked, knowing full well the answer.

"I gave 'em to the Det!" he grinned. "—And, do you know, not a one of them could swim."

"This looks as if it happened several hours ago. Why didn't you have it attended earlier?"

"It wasn't that bad and I had to report to your father. More than likely I was the last one to see him before he was killed. —Damn, I should have been there!"

"So why didn't you tell that to the blackleg—about talking to Father?" She measured a long bandage into her hand and began carefully winding it around his shoulder. "It might help him."

"I don't really know," said Quincannon. "Let's just say I didn't have much use for McVoy. Never did have much use for blacklegs in general."

"Hmmn. But you were a blackleg once."

"Maybe I didn't like the kind of company that I was keeping."

"This house is better?"

The key was still where Kali remembered— wrapped in a stiff piece of leather, hidden under the loose board beneath the leg of her bed. She couldn't keep from a little shiver as she took it up, remembering the illicit thrill of the first time she'd gotten nerve enough to use it . . . oh, there'd been no doubt in Kali's mind that if her father had caught her he would have exploded—but that had been the fun!

Child games. These were not. Knowing what she knew of Greely house secrets, she entertained her own suspicions; so immediately after depositing Miles Quincannon where he and the blackleg investigator could talk in mysterious private, she'd headed elsewhere: McVoy had said he wouldn't need to talk with her for at least an hour—more than enough time for her to do her own investigations. *Her* key, thank the Lord, was still in its hiding place.

A trek to the downstairs hallway, then: the keyhole was hidden inside the mouth of a wooden gargoyle, part of a carving in the paneling. Twist it first to the right, then to left, with no little strength—and a lever elsewhere moved, counterweights dropped, and a section of wall a few feet from her pulled back on itself.

Kali stepped through into the pitch dark between the walls of Greely House, a space only wide enough for one person. The air inside was warm and dry, washing over her face like a shower.

She hadn't bothered with any kind of lamp. A shove at the lever from the inside to send the panel back again put the passage in total dark, but a hand on the wall was all the guide she needed . . . a careful walk then, though she remembered the way, and the passage dead-ended a few feet beyond that destination.

The passage brought her to a dark chamber that lay behind her father's study, complete with a pinholed glass mirror, minute source of light. All anyone in the study might see was an oversized mirror in a frame that Marcus Greely had always claimed to be pre-Scouring. But an eye close to any of several pin-hole flaws in the aged silver backing could see the study quite nicely.

An assailant coming from her vantage, from behind one of the bookcases, certainly solved the problem of the locked door. It also severely limited the number of possible suspects—uncomfortably limited them.

Looking into the study Kali now saw several black-legs conferring with a handful of staff in Greely livery. A small squat man bent over her father's body, carefully examining it with a magnifying glass . . .

Then her heart all but stopped at the sound of a footstep behind her in the passage. She held her breath, her fingers clenched on the cold metal handle that would move the bookcase and allow her escape—by the entry to the study she was sure the killer must have taken.

A moment later came a flood of lanternlight, a figure shadowed behind the lamp.

"Well."

She knew the voice. The lamp moved, showing her the face of the blackleg investigator, McVoy: in his other hand he held up a key. A rather formidable looking pistol protruded from his belt.

"You're good," she said, still shaking. "I didn't even hear the hall panel open."

"Thank you, sera Duquesne. Truth be told I've been in and out of here near on a half-hour. This place is fascinating. I got very curious when I heard you arrive. —Now, may I ask what *you* are doing here?"

A muffled thump!: the passageway carried it like an echo chamber.

"Where?" she gasped. "What was that?"

"Above, to the right! Follow me."

She expected a return to the hall panel. Instead McVoy went past her toward the dead-end wall. Playing his light across it several times: "Here?" he mumbled, then finally: "No, here!" His hand vanished into the darkness near the floorboard. Kali could only stand and stare as the supposedly solid wall she had been sure of since childhood swung open on hidden hinges to reveal an ascending staircase.

Passages within hidden passages.

"You coming?" McVoy said over his shoulder.

"How did you know this was here?"

"Quincannon told me."

The stairs led up to another narrow passageway behind the walls. Kali had climbed but a few steps before she smelled a strong odor of sulphur and cordite—and realized the nature of the *thump!* that had echoed through the passages.

"Whoever's doing the shooting," McVoy said, "is on the other side of that wall."

It took McVoy a little longer this time to find the lever. When the panel opened, Kali recognized the sitting room in Simon's quarters. Draped across the couch was Simon—and there was no doubt he was dead: his head lay at such an impossible angle that his neck had to be broken.

McVoy walked in, set down his lamp, and probed for a pulse at Simon's neck, but Kali knew he wouldn't find one. She let her gaze trail around the room. On the floor near the wall she saw Simon's

gun, and she went to pick it up, finding the barrel
still warm to the touch—a small-caliber pistol, it
was, small enough to hide in his hand, or in the
small of his back as Simon had preferred.

"I'd leave that where it is, sera Duquesne," said
McVoy.

Kali looked up. The blackleg had his own pistol
aimed point-blank at her.

"So, you've decided that I'm the one you're looking for?" Heart thumping, Kali gauged the distance
between them, wondering if she could possibly de-
flect the gun from its aim, get off a shot of her own
with Simon's gun . . .

Or, granted that blacklegs were notoriously cor-
ruptible . . .

McVoy didn't answer. He stood there, a shadowed statue, the barrel of his gun unmoving.

"You going to shoot?" she asked. "Or is it something else you want?"

"It's not you he wants, little one," said Quincannon's voice from her left, and Miles Quincannon
stepped from the curtained alcove into the light.
Blood dripped from the bandage Kali had wound
around Quincannon's arm.

"You?" McVoy gestured with the gun toward the
body.

"Aye."

"Then—" The gun found a new target. "Be so
good as to not make any sudden moves."

"I think not." Quincannon shrugged—then pivoted on one foot and hurled himself toward McVoy.
The blackleg investigator fired twice. The first shot
went wild, smashing into the couch above Simon's
body. The second caught Quincannon square in the
stomach.

"Now *why* did he have to do that?" McVoy asked plaintively, the barrel still aimed at Quincannon, where he lay in a pool of blood.

"Why don't you lie? Say that it's not bad and I'll get better?" asked Quincannon. A coughing fit followed. Then blood.

"You wouldn't listen. You never do." Kali helped the old man stretch out on the floor, and rolled up a blanket as a pillow.

"Damn fool," McVoy said.

"I was talking to her," Quincannon said. Another cough. More blood. "—You can put it down to sheer flamin' stubbornness, little one. Now I suppose you'll be wanting to know about your brother."

"Only if you feel like talking," she said, knowing Quincannon had at most a few minutes left. She took his left hand in both of hers and squeezed it, wanting—

—wanting no secrets, no confidences. But Quincannon said:

"I suppose I should say it was karma . . . 'cept I don't know that much about balances and karma and all that. —Truth is, I didn't want to run and I've never liked a hanging . . ."

"You, Quincannon?"

"Couple of months back your brother got me involved in some money-making schemes of his . . . supplies from the family warehouses. Spiting your father was Simon's reason. Me, I enjoyed the money . . . only your father tumbled to it . . . something he heard tonight at that meeting with Kamat must've been the stick that sank the boat. He called me into the study . . . fired me outright, he did. Only reward for so many years of service was . . . he wasn't going to call the blacklegs on *me*. They were for none other than his darling firstborn, Simon.

"We ended up shouting at each other. Then I hit him a good one and walked out. I guess Simon must have heard the whole thing up the passages. Probably having the time of his life."

The rest of the story was fairly easy for Kali to fit together: Simon coming downstairs, watching the whole thing from behind the mirror . . . and when he saw Quincannon walk out, seeing his sudden chance to be head of Greely House.

"He—" Quincannon began again, and coughed up blood.

"Don't talk," she said, pressing Quincannon's hand. "Don't try to talk . . . I can guess the rest."

But Quincannon was able to say: "Simon had the nerve to pin it square on me—damn if that wasn't what he was doing. *He* stole the seal, called the blacklegs . . . had the whole frame pat . . . had the face to tell me plain what he'd done . . ." Quincannon started spitting up blood. Kali felt the old man's hand stiffen and then go limp.

The rain had stopped, leaving a cold breeze behind it. Kali leaned over the railing of her bedroom's balcony.

She hadn't slept . . . had had neither the time nor the inclination. Along the canal skiffs were working their way through their daily rounds. In the east the clouds were beginning to clear.

It had been McVoy who had pointed out the obvious to the staff. With both Marcus and Simon Greely dead, Kali Duquesne was now Househead of Greely House. To her cousins' certain dismay.

Which meant . . . security problems. Old debts to pay. And collect. Which meant there was a need for Simon's pistol, tucked in the pocket of her robe.

The passages . . . Quincannon dead, Simon dead—and dear, miserly, murdering Father, of course.

So Simon had double-dealt Quincannon. And her. But now she had no shortage of funds without the income from Simon's petty chicanery—and silences were already assured, Simon's most importantly, the damned, double-dealing, greedy fool.

So the pilferages could stop now.

Quincannon she did regret—a Househead in Greely needed a man of his talents.

She watched the blacklegs below, on waterside, the inspector instructing the swarm of Signeury clerks in duties doubtless under-rewarded as his own. McVoy was a fine, good-looking man, a man of certain qualities—and sudden, bloody instincts. |

A man already in possession of too many Greely secrets . . . and well knowing his delicate position . . .

McVoy . . .

Indeed, McVoy.

MARRIAGE

by Lynn Abbey

House Kamat of Merovingen was making a marriage. Pity the residents of Kamat: the family, clients, and tenants alike.

Preparations had been underway for a month. Two gangs of carpenters hammered on the exterior, closely followed by painters trimming up in the traditionally lucky reds and golds. A veritable army of occupation descended upon the kitchen suite to prepare a feast for five hundred of Merovingen's finest—and this not counting those assembling to construct the penny-cake for the marriage largesse, nor the men installing hydraulics to get the two-meter-high confection from the kitchen to the mid-door where it would be divided among the ordinary folk.

M'sera Andromeda Kamat, mother of the bride, designed the marriage costumes herself. Rumor proclaimed that twenty meters of the finest First-Bath lace went into the bridal costume alone; a rumor m'ser Richard Kamat could confirm, if he had time to study the receipts landing daily on his desk. The invitations had been calligraphed in midnight-blue ink, of course, on parchment culled and cured from the family's sheep flocks. Incoming gifts had al-

ready forced the family to abandon the afternoon
parlor on the mid-level; by the Big Day, the upstairs sitting room would be useless as well.

Family and factotums steadily filled the guest
rooms, while everyone awaited, with some trepidation, the arrival of Great Uncle Bosnou who, as the
oldest surviving Kamat, would perform the traditional contract ceremony. The last time Bosnou came
to Merovingen—for Richard's birth some twenty-
seven years ago—he brought the entire *stancia* with
him . . . and three dozen sheep for roasting.

The memory of that event had made invitations
to the contract ceremony prized possessions throughout the city.

At Fowler's, a respectable dive in the Kamat
Gut, touts were making book on the activities Upstairs. The odds on the ceremony itself were even
and hadn't moved in two weeks. Kamat would get
this contract signed on schedule if the Det were in
high flood and the shaarh themselves were scouring
the sky. The action was on the bride and the likelihood that she would stand before the podium with
her firstborn in her arms or in her belly. Odds were
posted three times a day—after Marina's meal tray
returned to the kitchen.

Marina would have thrown a snit had she known
of Fowler's much-erased slate, but of that, at least,
she remained ignorant. For ten days she had been
confined to bed with her feet up, surrounded by
solicitous servants, most of whom had at least a
month's wages in escrow at Fowler's. It was not,
however, below-stairs money that kept Marina cush-
ioned from gravity's tug; those orders came from
Richard Kamat himself.

"It's not too late, Tom."

"It was too late when it happened, Richard," Thomas Mondragon replied from the sofa where he reclined with a glass of Kamat's finest brandy dandling in his elegant fingers. "I told you that first off."

"A lot can happen in a year; a lot *has* happened in a year."

"But nothing has happened since you asked me last week. I'm content to see the late Raj Tai, now Rigel Takahashi, take my place at your lovely sister's side."

Richard ignored the sarcasm. It had been a good three months since he'd had a kind word for his younger sister. If anything, Richard was harsher in his judgment than Mondragon. Richard knew how much of her behavior was theatrics. He knew what the theatrics were supposed to accomplish; and he knew, even as he put the proposal before Tom for the final time, that his own priorities forced him to dance to Marina's tune.

"Knowing the price?"

"Yes, Richard, even knowing the price—which you and I both damn well know isn't two tin pennies. Raj hasn't got your head for politics—" That was a barb that stung, although Richard was just good enough at politics to keep it from showing. "You've taken one heavy load off Elder Takahashi's back. Raj'll do your House proud as a physician . . . he might even be happy doing it."

Storm winds lashed the spire where Richard conducted Kamat's business. Logs shifting in the fireplace sent sparks up the chimney. The walls creaked. Richard was used to the precarious swaying of high-

est Merovingen; Tom was not. For once, the ice-
blooded assassin was visibly uncomfortable. He
clenched his glass and brandy sloshed onto his dark
twill breeches. Richard almost smiled.

"I suppose you're right. Happiness isn't part of
an heir's education, is it?"

Tom's expression was as sour as quinine. "You
speak for yourself."

"Has it occurred to you, Tom Mondragon, that
you just might survive? You might outlive your
enemies' interest in you. Not even the Sword of
God's going to chase you forever."

"You don't know the Sword."

"If they're like you, I do. It's not a revolution,
it's excitement, conspiracy, danger . . . and the lucky
ones die before the game ends. You haven't been
lucky, Tom; you're going to survive and if you're
not careful, you're going to be lonely and bored."

"I'm not going to sign that contract."

"You're going to have to sign something someday."

"Thanks for the advice. Can I leave now?" Tom
set the glass on the table and dried his hand on his
breeches. He was halfway to the door.

"You'll stand Angel for the kid." It wasn't a
question.

Tom's face was hard and angry when he turned.
"You don't know when to give up, Richard. I've
got no sentiment; it rotted away years ago."

"You've got no friends, either. There may still be
a handful of innocents who believe you're some
distant Boregy kin, but there's no one who doesn't
know you're out of Boregy and into Kamat."

"I feel safest when there's nothing binding me."

"When the Det rises, there's nothing too precious
to put on the dike."

"Another Merovingen homily?"

Mindful of the continuing rains and the monthly tide cycle, Richard shook his head. "*You* don't know the Det."

"I'll take my chances."

"But you will stand Angel?"

Mondragon might not be a karma-obsessed Revenantist, but there were few things he liked less than owing, and he owed Kamat more than money these days. Standing out on the balcony with a child in his arms—even his own child—while the names were proclaimed would retire a substantial portion of that debt. And, as Richard pointed out, Tom didn't believe in the future.

"Who'll be standing with me?"

"If it's a girl, Eudoxia Wex and Lidmilla Kuzmin-Exeter; if it's a boy, Eudoxia and Anastasi Kalugin."

Rain-heavy wind struck the spire again. Tom stiffened, but probably not because the floor listed beneath his feet.

"The midwives say it will be a girl. They say they can tell by the way it's dropped."

"I'll stand." Tom opened the door.

"One last thing . . . If we're going to put Rigel Takahashi's name on the contract, we'll need someone else from his house to witness it. Do you think you could deliver the Takahashi Heir for grooming tomorrow?"

"You don't want much, do you?"

Richard shrugged. "No. If I really wanted a favor, I'd ask you to keep my uncle Bosnou out of mischief."

"I've been hearing about him. Something to do with sheep, wasn't it?"

The tension broke. Richard laughed and Tom left the room smiling; Bosnou had that effect on everyone. Kamat's Househead was satisfied that he'd gotten the best out of the entire situation that he could, but he was in no hurry to tell Marina that the marriage plans weren't going to change.

Despite the fact that Marina was adamant that Mondragon was responsible for Andromeda's bout of deathangel addiction earlier in the year, and despite the fact that she hadn't said a civil word to anyone since Tom had moved into a flat above the dye-room, Richard was certain Marina loved Mondragon and expected him, not Raj, to sign the marriage contract on Satterday.

All traces of good humor faded from Richard's face as he stared at the fireplace. It would have been much easier if Marina had aborted the child, but she hadn't and reality ran a collision course with tragic romance.

Lineage and alliance determined the shape of Merovan civilization, and children were its chief currency. Maybe in Merovingen-below men and women loved and bore their children without regard to marriage contracts, but in Merovingen-above these things could not be left to chance. The men and women of the Great Houses had their highly visible affairs, but when it came to producing the next generation precautions were taken. Inbreeding was the official, and very real concern. The Scouring nearly evaporated Merovin's gene pool and the first few generations after the Scouring had consolidated the damage. Every family produced its share of simpletons and misfits—witness Kalugin's Clockmaker.

But the greatest concern in Merovingen-above was the sly opportunist whose genetic claims could not be disproved. Every formal government or religion on Merovin denounced the barbaric social customs of humanity's origins, but almost every formal government or religion drew its hierarchy from the wealthiest families.

Marriage contract bridged the gap between the ideal and the real: witnessed declarations of parental intent. In many houses each birth was the culmination of a different alliance. It could be said, albeit crudely, that a successful family traded the fertility of its women like any other commodity. It could be said that Kamat's rise had been slowed by its members' reluctance to make multiple contracts. Marina would not be the first woman in Merovingen-above to contract marriage after she was pregnant to a man who was not the father of the child, but she would be the first in Kamat.

Under no circumstances, however, would Marina be the first Kamat to give birth to an uncontracted infant if they had to hang her by her heels until the ink was dry. Marina had insisted the birth could not possibly occur before Falling, but anyone could see that was just another of Marina's numerous miscalculations.

Richard's pen snapped in two. He stared at the pieces, scarcely knowing where they had come from. "Dickon! Dickon . . . m'ser Kamat!"

Eleanora Slade rapped on the door as she opened it. Her face was flushed and she was gasping for breath. There were a hundred steps from the main floor to the landing outside Richard's office; she'd run up them two at a time.

"Dickon, he's here!"

Richard brushed the pieces into the waste basket.

Since coming to the household, Eleanora had taken a firm grip on the domestic reins. The young widow was the one who translated Andromeda's grandiose schemes into reality. She cossetted Marina when no one else would go into her rooms. Richard trusted Eleanora as he trusted no one else. The doors to his office and his bedroom were always open to her.

He'd never known her to be intimidated by anything Kamat before, yet it was clear by her hesitation that Great Uncle Bosnou had made her nervous. Understandable. Bosnou Kamat made everyone nervous. Richard got his jacket. He paused in front of the mirror, adjusting the lapels and the rolled neck of the sweater beneath them. Eleanora tucked a wisp of his hair back into line and gave him a kiss on the cheek.

"For luck," she explained.

Richard nodded grimly, heading down the spiraling stairs.

Sometime in the Scouring, or perhaps before—who knew what went on before the Scouring—custom decreed that, written contracts notwithstanding, a marriage wasn't a marriage without a performance. The woman had her part, and so did the man, but the most important part went to the eldest member of the family in which the contract originated. The eldest Kamat was Bosnou, youngest brother of Hosni who had founded the family's Merovingen branch.

Bosnou had loyally followed Hosni to the big city, and left it a month later. Life on the Det estuary wasn't for him. Had Bosnou been the eldest brother, they'd all still be herding sheep. Instead, Bosnou ran the *stancia* and came to Merovingen only when tradition demanded. He hadn't come to Nikolai's funeral, but Marina was his Angel's-daughter and that was an obligation Bosnou took seriously.

"Where is she?" he boomed once Richard reached the mid-level landing. "Where's my 'Ree?"

Bosnou hadn't changed. Though nearly eighty, he could pass for an active man in his early sixties. In his own terms, he'd dress out at just under two meters and just over 120 kilos. His hair remained more black than silver, and his eyes missed very little. He gave Richard an embrace that lifted the younger man off the carpet, and a kiss that reeked of mutton and garlic.

Richard was grateful when his feet touched the carpet again. He wrapped both his hands over one of Bosnou's. "Good to see you, Great Uncle. How was the journey?"

"Nothing for complaining. She's over and we're here until we leave, eh? Everybody got sick, yes, but no one died except one of the sheep. So we roasted her over a fire and everyone felt better."

"You brought sheep?" Richard asked with none of the authority appropriate to his position as Househead.

Bosnou opened his arms wide. "Great Uncle Bosnou comes to a feast with nothing but himself? Last time the Old Stick—" the distressingly accurate nickname Bosnou had given Richard's late father "—said we hadn't brought enough for everyone. This time, Dickon, we are prepared."

The mid-door opened. Richard honestly expected

a flock of sheep to trot into the vestibule. Instead
he got a flock of his cousins, none of whom he
recognized. The sheep, Bosnou said, the *fifty* living,
bleating, eating, and defecating sheep were being
ferried to the Kamat warehouse as they spoke.

Richard's stomach rebounded off his bowels. He
stood mute as a round-faced, round-bodied woman
barely out of her teens separated from the rest. For
a moment Richard thought his great aunt hadn't
changed a bit, then his intelligence reasserted itself.
This woman couldn't have been more than twelve
the last time he'd seen Bosnou. He had a new great
aunt—the sixth, or so he believed.

"Malaki," Bosnou said, confirming Richard's suspicion. The last one had been Belina.

With his thoughts still dominated by the sheep,
Richard embraced his great aunt, then shunted her
over to his pale mother. "We've set aside the third
level for you, Uncle Bosnou."

Bosnou turned to his brood. "You heard him.
Run along, then. Follow your cousins, they'll show
you where to go. I'll be along later."

Richard tried not to feel jealous of his great uncle.
Fowler's would never give odds that the Merovingen
branch of the family would ever scurry off to do his
bidding as Bosnou's folk did his. A spar of an arm
descended around his shoulders and Richard found
himself drawn into Bosnou's confidence.

"You tell me, now, how is my Angel's-daughter
doing? You know she got your mother's hips."
Bosnou cast a disparaging glance Andromeda's way.
"What good is a woman with skinny hips, I ask
you? Malaki—she's all hips. Good hips, good laugh,
good cook—everybody's happy. You remember that.

Now, your sister, why isn't she down here to greet her great uncle, her Angel's-father. Why not?"

"She's . . . resting."

Bosnou chewed that over. "She got her feet up, eh? Else something fall out?"

Reluctantly, very reluctantly, Richard nodded.

"Where's the father? Let me welcome him into the family, man to man. Is that tavern still down in the Gut?"

"Uncle Bosnou, there are some things you should know. Things you should hear from me . . . man to man."

Richard led Bosnou into the doorman's closet. The old man listened while Richard sketched in the situation: Tom and Marina; Tom and Boregy; Tom and Kalugin; Tom and Raj; Marina and Raj. The eldest Kamat leaned against the doorframe. He scratched his beard and adjusted his homespun breeches, then he began to pace the length of the closet—two steps each way.

"This is not good." He tugged on his beard again. "This you should not permit. Who is this Mon-Dragon that he holds himself so far above Kamat? He does not want a child; he does not have a child. He has a child; he stands by his child—"

Richard cleared his throat. " 'Ree admits she misled him, so Tom . . ." he cleared his throat again. "So he would use none of the ordinary precautions."

"He believes her? A woman with skinny hips and he believes her? Where's he from—a cloister? You let me talk some sense into him." He reached into his boot and pulled out a knife that was easily the length of Richard's forearm.

From his perch on the mail desk, Kamat's Househead silently swore that Bosnou would never be left alone with Tom Mondragon. "It's settled, Bosnou," he said in his firmest voice, ignoring the honorific. "Marina is going to sign a contract with Rigel Takahashi. It is a good alliance for her, for the whole family. We've made *arrangements* with Takahashi. There were no arrangements to be made with Mondragon."

Bosnou snorted. "Arrangements! Your arrangements! What of the child's arrangements? How does my Angel's child know who he is when your arrangements are more important than blood? You make a lie to serve maybe Takahashi and Kamat, but it is a lie just the same; it is karma . . ."

Richard shook his head. This was a three generations argument that had begun with his grandfather. "This is Merovingen, not the *stancia*. In Merovingen we do what other Merovingians do. That is our karma."

"Is that what do they teach in your *College?* Karma is paid in the blood. The survivors knew that, and they knew never to forget it. Like the sheep. We start with ten sheep. Ten sheep would not make three generations. But the shepherd knows about blood and karma. The shepherd knows the lineage of every sheep. We have made twenty generations of those ten sheep. Still we watch the blood."

"Merovingen is not a flock of ten sheep, Great Uncle. Times change—" a Revenantist got chills saying that to another Revenantist. "Merovingen doesn't worry about bad blood . . . we've got more important things to worry about," Richard added the last in a whisper he immediately regretted.

"Your soul will be mired on Merovin for all eternity if you forget blood and karma."

Richard made another mental note: keep Bosnou well away from Cardinal Willa Exeter. One preferred not to imagine her reaction to hinterlands theology while the College was renovating orthodoxy and every House in Merovingen was on its best behavior. With a cautious eye on Bosnou's still-naked knife, Richard relinquished his perch on the mail desk.

"It's too late now, Uncle Bosnou. What's done is done—that's karma, too. We've made arrangements with Takahashi—at least we've improved the mire a bit."

Bosnou hesitated, staring hard at his grand-nephew, wondering if the young man would flinch. Karma, blood, and family honor notwithstanding, he'd known the advantages inherent in the Takahashi arrangements.

"I figure you'll be needing a thousand more white fleeces a year, just to have something worthwhile in the dye-vats once we get all that fancy white mordant. Bred us twice as many Merin ewes this fall, and sent Malaki's folk to clear a new valley. We'll need maybe twenty families for settlement contracts by spring."

Richard shook his uncle's empty hand firmly. "Twenty? I think we can manage that."

"Thirty, if it's that easy to get twenty."

Richard nodded. Unlike most Merovingen island families, Kamat retained strong ties to its outlying territories. The city branch kept up appearances, but the cream of its profits went back to the *stancia* along with a steady trickle of emigrants hoping for a better life than the Det offered.

Bring on The Rock and the College—what could they do to Kamat when Kamat's wealth and fortune remained on a sprawling *stancia* five hundred klicks to the east? Could they bankrupt Kamat? Could they persecute Kamat? Could Merovingen send blackleg soldiers so far from home?

"Let me get you something to drink, Great Uncle."

"None of that dark water you cityfolk drink from spit-glasses?"

"No, no brandy. We'll go down to Fowler's. He's laid in a barrel of sour mash just for you."

Bosnou's face warmed with anticipation.

Marina Kamat flattened herself—as much as it was possible to flatten herself given her advanced pregnancy—against the passage wall. She held her breath as her brother and great uncle went down the other passageway. Her heart was pounding. She forced herself to breathe deeply.

Some primal instinct warned Marina that her next histrionics would send her irretrievably into labor, and she wasn't *that* foolish. In her own mind she wasn't foolish at all. She'd made more mistakes than she'd expected, a few miscalculations of character and timing, perhaps, but nothing foolish. Foolish was running away when the going got difficult—as it undoubtedly would before this evening was over.

She caught her reflection in a wall sconce. All the mirrors in her rooms—the rooms where her nurse and keeper was sound asleep—were covered over. Angel-on-high, none of her friends had blown up like cooked sausage when they got pregnant. Marina knew she'd gained fifteen kilos, at least, in the last three months—the tailors never stopped complaining about the fit, or lack thereof, in her marriage costume—but she tried not to think about them or see them.

She'd packed herself into the only clothes that still fit: imitation canaler scruffies from her College days. She tried a variety of expressions and poses. Nothing worked. A doubt glimmered in her mind: maybe she would play her last hand and lose. Her eyes glistened, her jaw trembled—and she finally had the expression to thaw Tom's heart.

She also had a key to the back door of his apartment. A key which like several others she'd kept hidden for many years; a romantic heroine never threw keys away.

"I waited for you," she began as the first tears slid down her cheeks.

Mondragon was studying account sheets. His pen left a trail of blotches across the next columns. "Marina—" he stammered. There were a handful of comments fighting for his tongue, and to his credit he swallowed them all.

"I thought you would come to tell me yourself."

"Tell you what?"

Neither the tears nor the trembling were pretense. Marina could see from the look on his face and the way that he gripped the back of the chair when he stood that he didn't know why she'd come. "My life is over and you're sitting here balancing accounts!" Her voice was shrill and rising. "What about my accounts, Tom? How can you do this to me? Don't you care about me?"

Tom inhaled. He didn't, but Richard would turn him out of the apartment if Marina had that damned baby in his livingroom before the contracts were signed. The apartment was Tom's last bolthole and, at the moment, he cared about it.

"I care, 'Ree, but it's better this way. Better for you and Raj." Tom Mondragon never sounded more sincere than when he was lying through his teeth.

"It can't be better for me. I belong to you! I love you!"

Her tone got behind his defenses and made him feel, for once, unjustly accused. "I find that hard to believe. For six months you've hissed and clawed at me. I believe you used the word hate yourself more than once."

"Because you hurt me. Angel's mercy, there's karma between us. Karma, Tom—we're bound for all eternity."

Mondragon's education did not include an understanding of a karmic spiral leading to a purified Merovin and the nirvana of the stars. In general, Adventists had a more precipitate view of eternity, and nothing in Tom's life led him to change his thinking. The intricacies of Revenantist theology, as interpreted by sheep-breeders and incurable romantics, eluded him. "You're a willful woman who can't stand not getting her own way. I told you how it was with me at the very beginning. You brought this on yourself, Marina Kamat. There's no *karma* here but your own."

"Is it my karma to bear the child of a man who hurts and abandons me?"

"Your choice, Marina, your words."

Her face was a dangerous shade of red. Her shoulders heaved with every breath, but she could not find a voice for her outrage.

"You'd best leave now, before you make a bad situation worse."

The room was silent for a fraction of a second, then a key clicked in the lock of the front door.

"Hey, Tom! Ye about, Tom?" A voice Tom recognized all too well boomed down the hall. "That outland Kamat brought *fifty* sheep with him. What a mess! You shoulda been—"

Altair Jones, scruffy, armed, and perfumed by the sheep she'd been moving since sundown, got one unsuspecting stride into the room before Marina launched herself at the father of her child.

"I *love* you!" she trilled.

Reflexes, not thought, guided Tom's arms. He caught Marina, stared at Jones, and felt like a man damned by circumstances far beyond his control.

"Marina Kamat," he said for Jones' benefit. "It's time for you to leave!" Tom jostled her in his arms, but Marina could not, or would not, stand up. "I'm going to call Richard," he threatened, but not even that could stop Marina's incoherent wailing.

Jones was fully occupied absorbing every detail of the scene into her deepest memory; she didn't twitch. Tom sought a better grip on his burden. He gave Marina another shake, released her. She wobbled, then caught her balance.

"Now you listen to me, Marina Kamat." Tom cupped his fingers under her chin, forcing her to look at him. "You're going to walk out of here and never come back. You're going back to your room and tomorrow you're going to sign the contract with Raj. And you're going to forget you ever thought you loved me. You understand that?" He loosened his grip so she could no or say yes. She did neither as her lips twisted into a grimace of pain and tears streamed down her cheeks.

"Your brother's put your whole damn House on the line for you—you *owe* him that much."

"I'll die without you."

"You're not the type."

Without taking his eyes off her, Tom stepped back. He folded his arms over his chest. Marina ran out the door. Tom emptied his lungs. He turned to deal with his other problem, but Jones was gone. The outer door clicked shut.

"She'll be back, or she won't. Karma." Tom heard himself and shook his head. "It's a damn disease!"

The outer door slammed and bounced behind him as he left. He didn't bother to go back to latch or lock it; everyone, it seemed, had a key to his bolthole.

Richard Kamat awoke well before dawn. The rain had stopped, the skies were clear. Eleanora had opened the balcony. The aroma of mutton roasting in spices seeped in. Richard leaned over the rail to fill his lungs with it. A wall of clouds hovered beyond the harbor. Kamat could contain the festivities with its balconies closed and its windows shuttered, but the next eighteen hours would be immeasurably easier if those clouds stayed where they were.

Considering what he had eaten and drunk at Fowler's, Richard himself felt remarkably fit, almost eager for the day's events.

"Dickon?"

"Out here, Eleanora. I wouldn't have believed it possible, but I think we're going to have clear skies and smooth going. I must be doing something right."

He heard her come onto the balcony and turned to take her in his arms. Her brows were drawn with anxiety. His arms fell to his sides. "What's wrong?"

"That boy—Raj's brother? Ashe found him in the mail closet—locked into the mail closet. He bolted the moment Ashe opened the door—"

Richard started looking for his clothes. "Did Ashe lose him?"

"No, but the boy bit him good. Doctor Jonathan had to put two stitches in—"

"Where's Tom Mondragon?"

Eleanora hesitated. "No one knows. The apartment's empty. Both doors're unlocked."

Richard stomped his foot into his boot. "Damn it all," he swore as much at Tom as at the nail coming through the heel.

"I think he's just scared out of his wits," Eleanora meant the boy, not Tom. She had children of her own and knew how to see past belligerence. "But none of us downstairs can convince him that there's nothing to be afraid of."

"Right." Richard paused by the mirror. His eyes were bloodshot; he hadn't washed or shaved—hardly the adult image to reassure the Takahashi heir. "How's Marina?" he asked as he opened the door.

"Sound asleep so far as anyone knows. There hasn't been a peep out of her or her nurse all night."

"—Grateful for small blessings." The rest of his comment was lost to the clatter of his boots on the stairs.

Ashe and two other men had Denny cornered in a lower house washroom. They'd separated him from his clothes and run him through the tub. There were puddles all over the floor, and water dripping from the ceiling.

"I ain't no Deneb Takahashi!" Denny shouted when he saw Richard standing in the doorway. "I ain't. You got the wrong kid. I never heard of Takahashi. I don't have any brother either!"

Richard's eyes rolled involuntarily. He'd never laid eyes on the young, already-legendary Takahashi Heir. He'd managed to convince himself nothing could be as dire as the portrait Tom and Raj pointed between them. Of course, if Tom, damn him to a Sharrist hell, hadn't bothered to explain anything to Denny before locking him in the mail closet, the boy's terror was completely understandable. And if Tom had said anything about the letter Elder Takahashi had sent down from Nev Hettek, the terror might well be incurable.

"Leave him with me," Richard told his servants.

"He's a mean one, m'ser," Ashe averred.

"I can handle him."

But he couldn't. The instant Denny saw a sliver of freedom, he dove around Ashe and made for the door. He led with a hard fist that caught Richard roughly where a man least likes to be hit. Richard lurched to one side and, naked as the day he was born, Deneb Takahashi squirted by.

The only path Denny knew led back to the crowded servant's hall, so he took the stairs up into uncharted territory. He went up a second flight before dashing down a hallway. If he could get outside the house, if he could find an air shaft or ungrated window, he'd be out of danger—even naked as he was.

Denny knew the exteriors of half the isles of Merovingen, including Kamat; his experience with the interiors was more limited. He'd always imagined that Merovingen-above was an orderly place with square-corner rooms and level corridors. Instead, the private quarters of Kamat were as convoluted as any canalside rat's nest and lined with heavy, locked doors. Finally, he saw a pool of sunlight.

The window grate should have opened from the inside—fire was as much a threat as theft in Merovingen —but Kamat's servants shirked their duties and the salt air had turned the hinge into a single rusty knob. Desperation overcame intelligence; he tried to squeeze through the largest opening. The scratches would have been worth it, if he'd gotten through, but he got stuck with his neck and wasted precious moments getting free. Even worse, he was in a cul-de-sac and the foot-echoes were getting louder.

"*Psst*, you there . . . boy, this way."

An old man beckoned from a doorway. He wore a baggy, striped shirt and a tasseled cap no Merovingian, no matter how cold or how poor, would have worn on a bet. Denny shifted his balance from one foot to the other.

"Boy, you got no chance standing there."

Denny made up his mind. He darted under the old man's arm, even knowing it was likely a jump from the frying pan into the fire. The window was wide open and so obvious that Denny distrusted it. He rolled under the bed with the dust devils and the cobwebs. The door closed; the lock tumblers clicked. Fleece slippers moved across the room to the window.

He bought it! Denny exulted, then froze as his pursuers came down the hall.

The slippers pointed toward the door. The old

man didn't speak when his door knob rattled. He didn't move until the hall was quiet again, then he sat in a chair. Denny's confidence crept back. He didn't know many old folks, but the ones he knew slept like cats the moment they stopped moving. All he'd have to do was wait, and wait some more.

Denny vowed to count to a thousand, but when he reached three hundred and the old man hadn't twitched, he eased out of his hiding place. His luck had definitely improved: not only were the old man's eyes closed, there was a fine wool flannel shirt draped over the doorknob. It was way too big for him, but down on the canals it would be worth as much as everything he'd left behind. With it tied tightly around his shoulder, Denny headed for the window and freedom.

"I wouldn't, if I were you—"

I wouldn't either, if I was you, Denny agreed, but he figured he had to be faster than ten old men until he got on the window sill.

"—Unless I had about fifteen meters of good rope."

If the drop went straight to the canal, Denny might have chanced it, but he was looking down on the steep, unforgiving slate of another roof.

"Nope, I wouldn't try that without a hanging rope, and, boy, hanging rope is one thing I didn't bring with me, so why don't you come back over here and tell me just what you've done to get yourself in need of hanging rope."

Denny was whipped. He undid the knot at his neck and slid his arms down the too long sleeves before facing the old man.

"I didn't do nothing. Kamat's got me mixed up with someone else."

"Do they?"

"I don't look like no House-Heir, do I?"

The old man chuckled, a surprisingly friendly, agreeable sound. "No, I don't guess that you do. How'd they come to make a mistake like that?"

Denny stayed by the window. There were circumstances under which the drop could look pretty good, though none of his survival instincts were tingling. Not that he hadn't misjudged the codger. Now that he studied the situation properly he could see that the pieces didn't add up to a doddering old man. In fact, they didn't add up well at all, but Denny was a canal-rat; *stancia*-folk were as alien as the sharrh to him. In the end he had to trust his instincts.

"They must've been looking for my brother."

The old man's brows tightened into a doubt ridge. "Your brother?"

Wildfire tingling shot down Denny's back. "Yeah . . . I got a brother."

The old man appeared to relax; Denny wasn't reassured. His instincts weren't exactly saying *danger*, at least not in a way that made the window attractive, but he decided not to say anything more. The room got very quiet—the way it had been when he was under the bed—and after about the same amount of time Denny got restless.

"Who're you? What you doin' here? Why'd you let me in?"

"You didn't look like a dangerous criminal."

"You didn't answer my other questions."

"You could say I'm an old friend of the family, everybody's Great Uncle Bosnou. What's your name?"

"My friends call me Denny, Denny Tai." He meant to sound confident, but it was difficult to swagger with shirt-tails tickling his calves.

"Denny Tai, is it?" Bosnou sat back in his chair. "You want some tea, Denny Tai?"

Bosnou began preparing breakfast without waiting for a reply. He counted on the smell of fresh food and Denny's age. Malaki had baked the biscuits before they left the *stancia*. A dollop of fermented honey and a tightly sealed tin kept them safe from the rigors of a sea journey. Bosnou suffered a twinge of regret as he set the last of them within Denny's reach.

Malaki's biscuits were like no biscuits Denny had ever seen before, and if they hadn't looked sticky and sweet he wouldn't have tried them at all. His life had enough adventure without eating unfamiliar foods. But they called his name and he knew he could eat all five from the first bite. Midway through the third, it occurred to him that they might be drugged or poisoned. If they were, he reasoned, it was already too late; the tin was empty by the time the water boiled.

Tea came in thick, opaline glasses set in silver-wire baskets. Ever the connosseur of easily removable property, Denny appraised their value canalside. His eyes narrowed.

"Who are you—really?"

Bosnou dumped dark crystalline sugar and dried peel into each glass. "How did you come to lose all your clothes?" he asked as he took away the empty tin and set a steaming glass of tea in its place. "A cap I could understand, even a sweater or shoes, but everything? You must have been in a pretty tight corner, buko."

Denny had no intention of telling anyone the humiliations he'd endured since midnight. He was sure he could resist any interrogation, but the old man only asked his question once. As before, Denny grew restless waiting for his tea to cool sufficiently.

"It's all on account of my brother. He thinks everything happens to him—but it rolls onto everyone else. . ."

The old man sipped his way through two glasses of the potent tea and Denny, who was unaccustomed to an attentive, adult audience, kept on talking. Most of the people and places meant nothing to a man who avoided Merovingen like the plague, but there was enough, along with what Richard had said in Fowler's the previous night, for a fair understanding of the boy's problems.

"But is it worth running from, Denny? Is it worth attracting *their* notice? These city people with their heads so far from their hearts—isn't it better to be part of the flock when the shepherd's awake?" Bosnou asked when Denny finally ran out of things to say.

The mid-morning peal began. Denny had a minute to gather his thoughts before answering.

"Would you want to be Deneb Takahashi?" he countered when the bells were silent.

Bosnou stroked his beard. "If I had a choice, no," he admitted. "But you don't have a choice. You *are* Deneb Takahashi."

"They're gonna cut my hair an' make me wear a starch-tie and shiny leather shoes with buckles!"

They'd finally gotten to the core of the matter. Bosnou shook his head sadly and went rummaging.

"Me, too," he confided, tossing piece after piece

of lace-trimmed linen onto the bed. When he turned around he held an old-style velvet jacket dyed the distinctive First-Bath blue of Kamat and crusted with gold braids. "Fifty years I've had this cursed thing, thank God it still fits or I'd have to get another." He put it carefully beside the linen. "But I wear my own boots. Family's family, but a man's got to draw the line somewhere."

Denny looked slowly from the jacket to the high leather boots standing in the corner. They were well-made and well-worn, and their stiff, thick soles would be downright dangerous on the rain-slicked wooden walks of Merovingen.

"You must be one of those *other* Kamats," he whispered. The dense wool flannel, sweet biscuits, and silvered tea glasses finally made sense.

"Did you think I was some old fool taking up space? Well, I'm that, too, when I come visiting."

Denny was on his feet and looking anxiously from the window to the door.

"Settle yourself, Deneb Takahashi," Bosnou commanded, and Denny sat down with a thud. "Dressing fancy won't kill you. You run now, you're no different from this brother of yours; leaving a mess for someone else to clean up." He glowered until Denny shrank within his borrowed shirt, then he softened. "Now, you take that linen and my boots. We'll find out what manner of torture my niece, Andromeda, has in mind for you to wear, and then we'll get through this day together.

Still looking like he was condemned to a fate worse than death, Denny did as he was told.

They found Richard Kamat on the catwalks above the huge dye-vats. Those few Kamat employees not needed for the festivities were getting ready for the First-Bath run that would take place, as it always did, on the new moon tide. Some things were more important than marriage contracts.

"We're ready," Bosnou shouted up from the work floor.

Richard was too far away for his expression to be easily read. Denny was immensely relieved to see that Richard wasn't limping.

"I see you found our young fugitive," Richard looked at Denny not his uncle. "Where's Tom?"

" 'Bout as far away as he can get."

Richard nodded curtly. If Tom wasn't signing the marriage contracts, he wasn't necessary. His absence would cause no more comments than his presence and, given his dubious relations with some of the people who had to attend, it wasn't surprising that he'd decided to light out. And he had, after a fashion, delivered the Takahashi Heir; Kamat itself had almost lost him.

"Mother will be inspecting the men in the library at fifteen-thirty. I think a buffet's been laid out there as well."

"And my young friend's clothes? He seems to have lost track of them."

"They're drying in the kitchen. I'll have someone send them up."

"That my clothes, or just the frilly stuff you want me to wear?"

The look Denny got from the Kamat Househead made him very grateful for Great Uncle Bosnou's presence. "I suppose we can find *your* clothes *after* the ceremony."

Denny's instincts told him not to press his luck.

They also told him to keep the old man between himself and Richard, which he did as they left.

The letter upstairs in Richard's safe consigned Denny's training and education—or retraining and reeducation—to Tom. Watching his uncle put a big hand on the boy's shoulder, Richard wondered if Denny's chances for survival would improve if he were sent to the *stancia* for a few years instead. Richard was already planning to send Marina there once the child was born. Marina *and* Denny might be more than even Great Uncle Bosnou could handle, though.

So Denny would be Tom's problem, for the foreseeable future. Richard's would be Marina with whom he should be having lunch rather than dawdling beside the vats.

But we can't both be acting like children, he chided himself.

Marina was surrounded by pillows on a daybed. The hairdresser had been and gone. A profusion of false curls, ribbons, and flowers framed her forehead and cascaded over one shoulder. The marriage costume—a confection of pale blue satin and midnight lace—stood beside her on a headless mannequin. The arrangement was coincidence, though for a moment Richard had the disconcerting sensation that his sister's head would simply be taken from one body and placed on the other.

"You'll be very beautiful," he said, feeling more sympathy for her than he'd felt in the last month.

"Mother's worked miracles to hide the fact that I look like a bloated fish."

" 'Ree—"

"Don't lie to me, Dickon. I'm over nine months

pregnant and I look like a slobbering cow. Angel's blood, I wish it were over. *All* over."

She sighed and pulled her bare feet under her dressing gown. Richard sat down on the cushion she cleared. Lunch was a wilted salad and sandwiches obviously prepared yesterday and left sitting in the cold pantry. Richard took a bite. The bread was stale, the cheese waxy, and the meat as dry as leather.

"You'll be back to your old self again in no time, 'Ree. In no time at all this will just be a bad dream—"

"With a contract and a child," Marina snapped.

Richard shook his head. "A contract marriage, 'Ree, nothing more. Raj understands, and so will the child. *We* are the exceptions, Ree, with a mother who lives only for her family: her husband and children. Has it made things any easier for either of us?"

Marina stared out the window. Everyone else in Kamat might suspect Richard and Eleanora, but she knew the truth. It was just about the only confidence she'd managed to keep throughout these long months of hysteria. "I love Tom. I'm in love with loving him—the hopelessness and the pain of it."

"You'll get over it," Richard said without very much conviction.

"I won't," she countered with plenty of conviction. "He's got another woman, you know. I saw her. Low class, but easy with Tom, even I could see that. She's living with him, right here, on *our* island. In an apartment *you've* provided."

Richard took Marina's hands in his. "The woman's

name is Altair Jones. She has a poleboat, and we give her work sometimes. She saved Tom's life before you knew he existed, and 'Ree—unless I miss my guess completely—Thomas Mondragon's hurt her more than he's hurt you."

"Impossible." She pulled free. "What could a poleboat woman know about love?"

"I'm ashamed of you, Marina." Richard got up. "What's happened to the rebel who thought life was so much more real Below? You've known the likes of Tom Mondragon all your life; this one's just managed to get in more trouble than the rest of us, and not managed to get out of it. Altair Jones probably thinks she dragged the Angel Himself out of the Det. You think she's got family some place to bail her out?"

"Is that why you're giving her work?" Marina asked in a small voice.

Richard gave it a moment's thought. "We hire among the boats in our Gut, and lately her boat's been in the Gut a lot." He did not say what he'd do if Tom disappeared and Jones didn't.

"It's not fair, Dickon. It's not fair that it turns out this way." She'd said this often enough before, but always with tears streaming down her cheeks and her voice rattling every piece of glass in the room. This time there was a hint of maturity in her whisper.

"Didn't you listen to the cardinals when you were a child? This is Merovin, nothing's fair." That, too, was an axiom that had been shouted before, though now it was said with deprecating humor.

"I think that in a previous life I must have been a mass murderer."

"And the rest of us were saints," Richard added as he leaned over to give her a kiss on the forehead. "Keep telling yourself it will be all be over by sundown."

She squirmed and pressed a hand against her belly where the child had kicked her. "Don't I wish it would *all* be over by sundown . . ."

Richard left Marina feeling better than he had imagined possible. He made an obligatory call to the library where Bosnou and three valets had turned Denny into a presentable, if sullen and uncomfortable, contract witness. They were about to perform the same magic on an anxious Raj.

"I won't embarrass you or your sister, m'ser Kamat," Raj insisted.

The valet sprayed him with cologne. "Close your eyes and don't breathe," he barked as the cloud rose inevitably upward.

The warning came too late. Raj sneezed violently and a pomaded forelock flopped between his eyes. The problem, Richard recalled from his own youth, was not embarrassing yourself, and the solution didn't come until you were old enough, or powerful enough that your mother didn't dare tell you what to wear.

Rank did have its privileges and Richard was ready to make use of them.

"I'll wear the jacket," he informed his valet when he was back in his own rooms. "Put the rest back in the box and hide it."

"Yes, m'ser Kamat. Anything else, m'ser ?"

Richard gave the formal jacket a look Denny would have envied. "Get rid of all that lace, and the bombast. I'm not going downstairs looking like a Nev Hettek fancy-boy—"

"But m'ser, the m'sera, your mother . . . ?"

"Just rip it off, Ralf. By the time she sees me, it will be too late."

"Yes, m'ser Kamat," Ralf agreed without twitching a muscle toward the offending jacket.

"Off, Ralf, every last centimeter by the time I'm done shaving—unless you think my mother's allowance will pay your wages."

Ralf didn't and when the menfolk of Kamat gathered in the library for inspection shortly before fifteen-thirty, Richard was the only one without lace tickling his ears. Andromeda scowled when she beheld her son.

"Dickon . . . you don't *match*."

"I look fine, as do you, Mother." Richard embraced her properly, careful not to crush the flowers on her collar.

She shook free. "Everything was planned, Dickon, and now you don't match. What will our guests think?"

"No one notices men at a marriage," Richard replied without revealing his honest opinions. "Everything is perfect. How is Marina?"

Andromeda rolled her eyes. "The waist's bagging and the hips are too tight. We had to rip out the seams and sew them back around her. You'd think she was carrying twins . . ." It was the first time the thought had occurred to her. She covered her mouth. "Oh, Dickon, not twins . . . the contract isn't written for twins."

Suppressing a weary shrug, Richard put an arm around his mother's waist and guided her toward the door. "No, Mother, not twins. Doctor Jonathan would have known and told us long before this.

Ree's going to have a single, healthy child born within the bounds of a duly empowered marriage contract. Stop worrying."

One might as well tell the Det to flow upstream. Richard spotted Alpha Morgan, Andromeda's personal maid, hovering at the end of the hall. Richard's affection for the stern old Adventist was tied to her ability to keep his mother on an even keel; today he loved her. "Find my mother something harmless to fuss over," he whispered.

"We've done the flowers five times over," Alpha Morgan replied. "An' the kitchen. It was you or your sister . . ."

"What about the parlor? Can't she rearrange the gifts?"

The maid-servant brightened. "Endlessly," she agreed. She turned to Andromeda. "I saw more boxes arrive in the vestibule, m'sera. Do you think we can trust that clod Ashe to put them in their proper places?"

Andromeda's expression was eloquent. The two women headed for the parlor where an unconscionable number of expensive trinkets was arrayed under the watchful eye of Ashe and two other burly men. Richard rejoined the other men. They had Raj in Takahashi crimson with deep blue lace hanging past his knuckles. The young groom was muttering and his eyes were tightly closed. He'd committed the entire contract to memory, not trusting himself to find, much less read, his portion when the time came. Richard could think of nothing to say that would reassure Raj, so he opened the nearest book.

He read and reread the same poem until it had, despite everything, wedged itself in his memory.

Denny was eating his way from one end of the buffet table to the other; Raj ran to the close-closet and came out paler than a corpse. Reaching into his pocket, Richard flicked the catch on his repeater watch. A little hammer struck the case four times; he frowned. The repeater, which used the ancient meridian system for convenience, told him only that it was after the sixteenth hour and before the seventeenth. Usually that was all the time a man of Merovin needed to measure, but not today.

He paced to the balcony. The clouds that had hovered beyond the harbor since dawn were gaining height and growing darker. There'd be rain before midnight; there might be rain in the next hour. A small crowd milled outside the mid-level door waiting for a share of the largesse. Kamat's reputation would suffer if delays within the house overlapped with rain outside it. Of course, there were other delays that could damage their reputation even more. . . .

"Sit down, buko," Great Uncle Bosnou commanded. "Your pacing makes the rest of us worse."

In the moment while Richard framed a terse reply, the bell above his office finally began to ring. Marina had left her room. It was time for Kamat to assemble for the ceremony.

Andromeda Kamat's great design began with the sounds of a hidden string octet. Those fortunate enough to have an invitation crowded into the vestibule and halls. The luckiest of the uninvited jammed the doorway. All eyes focused on the broad landing where the parchment contract overflowed a small podium. Two liveried servants brought in the banners of Merovingen and the blue ram of Kamat.

After hanging them where they would block no one's view, they took their positions at the base of the staircase.

Traditional protocol brought the host family in from the left and the guest family from the right, but as Takahashi was represented by Denny and the groom against some two dozen Kamat scions, Andromeda made a less traditional division by gender. The deviation not only allowed her to balance the numbers on either side of the podium, but made it possible to slip Cardinal Willa Exeter and Mikhail Kalugin onto the landing without drawing unwanted attention to their presence.

Marriage was a family affair, but a marriage contract wasn't ironclad until the proper civil and spiritual authorities witnessed it. Ordinarily it did not matter if hours, days, or even weeks elapsed between the signing above the seals and those below. This contract was not ordinary; everyone who was privy to Kamat's secrets, or Tom Mondragon's secrets, recognized the possibility of a messy challenge down the line. Exeter came of her own free will; Mischa came because the cardinal had her favorites among the Kalugins. Anastasi stood with the other guests in the foyer; Iosef claimed a last minute attack of gout; Tatiana was nowhere to be seen.

Raj's trembling made the brocade of his jacket shimmer in the sunlight while Denny, who'd made them all so nervous, soaked up everything like a well-behaved sponge. The music stopped when Bosnou braced his hands on the podium. The house was silent except for the distant tolling of its bell.

Whatever Bosnou thought of Merovingen or fancy

clothes, it was clear he loved marriage contracts. He recited the Kamat ancestry so the least canal-rat waiting for the largesse outside the door could hear each name clearly. He called for the grantor of the contract, and beamed with pride when Marina made her way to the landing.

"My Angel's-daughter!" He helped her down the last few steps.

Andromeda had worked wizardry with satin and lace. At a first or second glance no one noticed the precipitous bulge below Marina's waist. They noticed her uncertainty, the trembling of her hand as it rested on her uncle's arm. But that was nothing unusual. The most promiscuous sower of wild oats confronted that first marriage contract with trepidation: the assumption of adult responsibilities was implicit in the signature.

Bosnou returned to the script. He called upon Richard to give Kamat's assent; he called on Deneb Takahashi to attest Raj's legitimacy with the Nev Hettek house. Richard could not help but notice wide-eyed stares on the faces of those who thought they knew the name of every skeleton in Merovingen. Denny had no trouble until he came to his mother's name which brought a quaver to his voice. If it meant the boy gained some understanding of who, and what, he was, even that boded well.

So far as anyone could tell, Raj said everything he was supposed to say, exactly as he was supposed to say it. Bosnou nodded, at least, when the youth was finished, and he was the only one who could possibly have heard him. The quill pen dropped a huge blot on the parchment the moment he lifted it.

"Don't worry," Great Uncle Bosnou said, letting

his sleeve absorb the excess. "Take a deep breath. Take your time." It was wasted advice. Raj's signature was illegible—another reason to have Exeter and Kalugin close by. "Now turn around and face everyone."

Raj could not have looked less happy if he'd faced the noose on Hanging Bridge. He was numb from the navel down. His eyes were watery. Then something by the door caught his attention. It took a moment to recognize a neated-up Jones waving a foil-wrapped marriage gift. Jones! And behind her, looking neither sullen nor happy, Tom himself!

The tension drained from Raj's neck and shoulders. He could feel his knees again, they hadn't turned to jelly. But—damn—his eyes got all cloudy again when he heard Marina read her lines.

". . . It is my free given will that Rigel Takahashi be my marriage partner until one child is born between us and for so long thereafter as we do both consent." She took up the quill and signed her name with an audible flourish. "Marina Melora Cassirer Kamat."

She joined Raj at the edge of the landing. She did not resist when Raj took her ice-cold hand in his. She did not seem to notice him at all—or anyone else despite the slow rotation of her head from the left to the right.

Bosnou read the text of the contract: the rights and the obligations of the signatories to each and their respective families to each other and to their offspring for the duration of the contract and through karma to eternity. It omitted significant details—like the alum mordants Takahashi promised Kamat—and dwelt for several interminable clauses on the unlikelihood of Marina's barrenness.

Raj's thoughts wandered to the future; Marina's gaze wandered toward the front door. She let out a shriek that actually shook the chandelier. It was a primal sound full of fear, rage, and blackest hate. Jones knew it for what it was, and that it was directed at her. She was gone before the sound had died away. Tom understood when he felt her leave. Raj understood when he saw Tom's expression and the emptiness where Jones had been. No one else had a clue.

Marina screamed a second time, an equally primal sound of pain that stopped as suddenly as it began. She grabbed her bulging abdomen, lost her balance, and collapsed headlong down the stairs.

The Angel of Merovingen looked after drunks, fools, and Marina Kamat. Her thrashing and sobbing confirmed that she hurt, but they also confirmed that she was alive. Anastasi Kalugin, at whose feet she'd wound up, was among the first to recover. He barked at the honor guard who pushed the guests back while he helped Marina into a more comfortable position. Richard shouted for a doctor.

In other circumstances—out in the swamp or down along the canal—Raj might have come forward. It was not, however, professional discretion that kept him rooted on the landing carpet, but stunned disbelief. His eyes watched his wife move; his brain said she hadn't hurt herself badly; but his emotions simply screamed that he'd failed to protect her. Since Raj was ashamed of himself, he interpreted the wet smear on the back panel of Marina's costume shamefully, as well. Several moments passed before he understood that it signified something entirely different.

"Her water's broken," Doctor Jonathan confirmed the moment he reached her. "Get the midwives. Get her out of that *thing* and start boiling water."

The midwives were quite willing to deliver the baby right there at the foot of the stairs in front of the highest and lowest members of Merovingen society. Marina had other ideas. She used the doctor's cravat to haul herself upright. A contraction brought her to her knees, but not before she'd grabbed the banister. She dragged herself and one of the midwives up two steps before Richard gave the order to have her carried to the library.

"She's gone into labor . . ." Raj murmured to no one in particular. "We didn't even finish the wedding. . . ."

All who heard him lapsed into silence.

". . . Before the contract was proclaimed . . ." Raj was miserable, wallowing in his own sense of failure, with no inkling of what he was actually saying. ". . . I might as well not have signed at . . ."

Raj's soliloquy ended abruptly as Richard hauled him back up the stairs. "Finish the ceremony," he commanded his great uncle.

Bosnou shrugged and gestured toward the men carrying his Angel's-daughter from the foyer. This sort of complication simply did not happen on a well-run *stancia*, but for that very reason he did not argue. Clearing his throat he returned to the unfinished paragraph. " 'Whereas the purpose of marriage is the procreation of healthy children of known ancestry—' "

"—This is outrageous. A travesty. An affront to all decent people and decent marriages." In a virtually unprecedented display of self-assertion, Mikhail

Kalugin tore the parchment from Bosnou's hands.
"It's not legitimate. I won't have any part of it."

Some people watched the faint smile on the face
of Mischa's younger and very ambitious brother,
Anastasi. Some people watched the tight brows of
Mischa's patron, Cardinal Willa Exeter. One or two
caught the disbelief on Richard Kamat's face. But
no one in his right mind spared a glance for Mischa.

"*I* witnessed Marina Kamat give a willful consent," Anastasi said in a silken voice. "That's what
matters, isn't it? The Signeury shouldn't have a
problem accepting the contract." He was looking at
the cardinal; he didn't need to look at Richard
Kamat.

Exeter wasn't in as tight a corner as Kamat, unless she gave weight to all the mercantile househeads
waiting for her next words. Kamat and its ilk could
accommodate any orthodoxy, so long as it did not
impinge on the truly sacred—and for a merchant
only trade and contracts were truly sacred. Quash
the Kamat-Takahashi contract, a contract she'd
known from the beginning was strictly trade, and
she'd have the Clockmaker's support. Quash Mischa
and she might as well climb in bed with Anastasi.

"Marina had given her consent," she reminded
Mischa, playing on his sentimentality. "Even now,
she thinks the marriage is valid. She thinks the
child will be within the lines. Would you deny her
that?"

Mischa crushed the parchment. "Within the lines!
The ink's not dry *on* the lines."

"A second contract child takes nine months,"
Richard took up Exeter's cause. He'd pay Anastasi's
price, but not if he could get Mischa for nothing.

"The first born is when God wills it. That's the *law*, m'ser Kalugin."

They didn't call him m'ser Kalugin very much: Mikhail, Mischa, Clockmaker, and worse—those were the names he heard most often. He rather liked the difference . . . the deference.

"The law's not right," m'ser Kalugin replied almost reluctantly.

"You can change the law when you're governor," Willa whispered. "But first you must *become* governor."

The standoff ended wordlessly as Mischa spread the wrinkled parchment across the podium. He signed and passed the pen to Exeter. "The laws must tell the truth," he said as she dipped the quill in the ink.

Cardinal Exeter didn't comment on the likelihood of *that* happening any time soon—not with Anastasi an arm's length away and grinning like a cat.

"A marriage!" Bosnou Kamat shouted, lifting the battered parchment for all to see.

"A girl!" echoed back from the stairwell.

There were cheers, there was laughter. There was largesse in the form of penny-cake and largesse in the form of mutton. There was the restrained music of Andromeda's string octet, and the far more infectious music of the *stancia*. There was a thunderstorm of appropriate proportions which instead of dampening the celebration simply concentrated it— along with the mutton and the cake—within the house.

For the first time since Hosni Kamat bought the

island from the Adami, the new moon tide came and went without a First-Bath run. Richard didn't remember he'd forgotten it until almost dawn when he had, frankly, more important things to consider— like could he walk . . . could he stand . . . could he *crawl* to the nearest window?

Fresh air revived him, as did the gentle rain. He faced the room, and regretted it immediately.

There were bodies everywhere. Any surface not covered by a sleeping body was piled high with debris. Richard walked through the middle level of his house like a man in a nightmare. He vaguely remembered laughing when the huge penny-cake tipped off its cart and spilled across the hall carpet; it seemed less funny now. Nor was he amused to see the remains of the mutton sprawled across the vestibule.

"Luck to you all," a man Richard didn't recognize at all said as he left. "Karma!"

"Karma," Richard muttered back.

"This is the worst. We made barricades at the top of the stairs after midnight. We let no one up, not even the family."

Eleanora handed him a large glass of juice. Richard gulped it down.

"Wise . . . very wise," he said between swallows. The refreshing liquid unlocked a few more memories. "Angel have mercy . . ." He handed the glass back to her. "Sour mash . . . I was drinking sour mash, wasn't I?"

"Until midnight when Fowler ran out."

"And after midnight?"

"I don't really know. It was something your uncle brought with him."

Richard leaned against the banister. "I want to die."

"You can't, not yet. There's the naming. You can bathe and dress, if you wish, but you have to hold the naming before the noon peal."

"I'll be dead by then. Oh, God, I hope I'll be dead. If I'm not dead, I'll have a head the size of the Chattalen."

He started up the stairs. Eleanor slipped her arm under his and guided him to the rightside branch. "Your uncle's in the library. He said you'd feel that way. He's got something for you to drink." Richard swerved to the left. "No, no . . . it seems to work. Raj was much worse than you and he's eating breakfast."

The image of breakfast superimposed on the jangled memories of the previous night moved Richard's face several shades toward green. It also took away his strength. Eleanora was able to get him into the library with no further protests. The glass they handed him smelled of turpentine and looked suspiciously like raw sewage. It packed a wallop that, mercifully, numbed the palate.

"*Yetch!* What was that?" His voice was already clearer.

"Don't ask," Mondragon advised from the bay window overlooking the mid-door behind an upraised hand. For one frightening moment he thought he was going to be ill, when that passed, so had the hangover. Richard looked around in slack-jawed amazement.

Marina looked calm and comfortable on a bed improvised from two chairs and an ottoman. Raj and Denny were in mid-attack over a platter of sausage and eggs. Bosnou was smug with a jug of his miraculous concoction in the crook of his arm, but nothing compared with the radiant smile on Andromeda's face as she wiggled her fingers above her first grandchild's eyes.

Richard Kamat was not one to gush over infants, especially newborns. They were, as a rule, bruised and misshapen, courtesy of their mother's labor contractions. By the time they were appealing, they'd also begun to smell. But his niece had slipped into the world without battering. She was the color of rose porcelain with storm gray eyes and a crown of pale gold curls. She looked up at Richard when he got closer and he was sure she smiled when Andromeda put her in his arms.

"What's her name?"

"Natalya Fumiko," Marina advised from her bed. "If you approve."

Richard nodded and returned the infant to his mother. Beautiful or not, Natalya couldn't compete with the aroma of breakfast. By the time he'd eaten, washed, and changed his clothes, everyone necessary for the naming had gathered in the library. The Kamat bell began ringing; the glass doors of the bay window were opened.

Marina was blonde and the fairest of all the Kamats, but when they handed Natalya to Tom for the proclamation, it was apparent that she would take after her father.

"Use both hands. Always keep a hand beneath her head and neck!" Andromeda chided. "Haven't you ever held an infant before?"

Mondragon rearranged his arms without answering the question. His feelings, if he had any, toward the smiling, helpless creature who was also his daughter went undetected by those who looked hardest for them: Marina, Raj, Richard, and Jones—who was foremost in the small crowd on the walkway beneath the balcony. With one hand carefully framing her head, Tom raised Natalya above his head for everyone to see. The two women standing as her Angel-mothers caught the cascade of the naming gown as it caught the breeze. Mondragon's face was hidden, but not his voice.

"A child is born today." Tom turned her from side to side. The sun struck her eyes and she began to cry. "Natalya Fumiko . . ." Was that a hesitation because she squirmed, or a heartbeat of regret? ". . . Takahashi. The lineage of Hosni Kamat declares her. Her karma is their karma. Angel protect her now and forever."

fish's Tavern was unusually quiet, unusually empty.

WITH FRIENDS LIKE THESE

by Mercedes Lackey

Hoh's Tavern was unusually quiet, unusually empty.
Of course it was early—and the two bar-singers,
Rat and Rif, were not due to start their "show" for
another hour. But still; there were only eight other
people here besides Denny and the younger singer—
and one of those was Wolfling, the strange Janist
who had attached himself to Denny and his brother
as a kind of bodyguard, for reasons best known
only to him.

Denny rather wished *he* hadn't come at Rat's
urging. He'd had no idea she had wanted something
this risky out of him.

"Come *on*, Denny," Rat hissed urgently over her
beer, thin face looking even thinner with the light
from the candle hollowing her cheeks. "You've *got*
to get me in there!"

Denny squirmed uncomfortably in his chair. "I
can't, Rat. I *tol*' ye once—"

"You got those bridge-brat friends of yours jobs
as runners for Kamat." She scowled—then glanced
out of the corner of her eye at Wolfling, sitting with
his back to the wall not two tables over and staring
at her.

"What's with your friend?"

Denny resisted an urge to chuckle. "He don't like th' way yer talking t' me. I reckon he's thinkin' about fergettin' ye're both Jane—"

"Shh!" She glanced around quickly. "This may be Hoh's, and it may be where we hang out, but that *doesn't* mean it's safe to throw *that* word around." She scowled again, then recalled Wolfling and changed her expression to one of pleasant sweetness. "Besides, Rif may be—that—but I'm *not*. I'm just her partner, not one of her congregation."

"Ye better ferget that when *he's* around," Denny pointed out impudently. "Th' only reason he's lettin' ye talk t' me like this is 'cause he thinks ye *are*."

Rat smiled dulcetly at Wolfling, who continued to stare stolidly at their table. "You're trying to change the subject, brat."

"Look, gettin' those jobs fer th' other kids was *different*," he said desperately. "They wasn't askin' me t' do anythin' but get 'em real work! What ye been askin'—I *can't* get ye inta th' Kamat warehouse! Ain't no way!"

"You work there," Rat pointed out. "You could get your hands on the keys easy enough, long enough to get me a wax print."

Right. With a supervisor starin' down at me all th' time. Sure, friend.

"Besides—dammit Rat, I give *up* thievin'! Ye tol' me yerself t' give up thievin'!"

She sighed, and downed the rest of her beer, signaling the waiter for another. She waited until he'd placed it in front of her before continuing.

"Look, Denny, would it help if I told you that we won't be taking anything Kamat *knows* is there?"

He stared at her, dumbfounded. "Anythin' Kamat

knows—ah, hell! This *is* Jane stuff, ain't it?"

She winced, but didn't deny it.

"Why in *hell*," he snarled, "didja haveta go usin' *Kamat* t' do yer smugglin'? Kamat's the one that *started* them Samurai! He's gonna be *double* careful on his own ground!"

"It isn't smuggling," she said, combing her fingers through her short, white-blonde hair. "It's—something we were keeping in the warehouse until things cooled off a little. Then Kamat started this Samurai thing, and now we can't get at it."

" 'It'?" Denny said suspiciously. "Just what's this 'it'?"

"You don't want to know."

"Ah, hell." He wanted to tear his own hair out in fat handfuls. *If Rat says I don' wanna know—then it's Trouble. Big Trouble. Just what I needed.*

"Can they trace it back t' ye if anybody finds th' thing?" he asked, dreading the answer.

"Nobody's *going* to find it," she replied resentfully. Then added, "Well, yes. Maybe."

"Ah, *hell*." He clutched his beer to keep from clutching his hair. "Look, I can't *promise*. Okay? But maybe. I'll see."

Rat's sour expression melted into pure happiness. Denny's heart sank a little farther. *Great. Even Bigger Trouble than I thought.* "Look, I didn' promise *nothin'* except that I'd try!"

"That's okay, bridge-brat," she said, standing up and finishing off her beer, then reaching out with one long-fingered hand to ruffle his hair. He glared. "Anything you *try* to do you usually manage. I have faith in you."

She sauntered off to the back room where Rif

was presumably waiting, tuning her gitar. Denny
stared down into the mug of beer that no longer
held any appeal at all.

*She has faith in me. Wonderful. Just what I wanted
t' hear.*

It was a little like old times. Denny perched on
the edge of a roof overlooking the Kamat warehouse, legs dangling over the precarious drop below,
Raj sitting beside him with his knees tucked up and
his chin resting on them. They'd both escaped up
here after dinner, and it didn't appear that anyone
was going to miss them any time soon. The breeze
was fresh up here, it wasn't nearly as hot, and the
evening sun was just starting to descend. All in all,
very peaceful. Unlike the rest of their lives, lately.

"So what's it like, bein' a married hightowner?"
Denny teased his older brother.

Raj sighed. "About like it was being an unmar-
ried student," he replied. "Nothing much's changed,
except that I have to help answer all the congratula-
tion cards."

He looked at Denny out of the corner of his eye,
and Denny grimaced.

"Don' go volunteerin' *me* fer that, big brother.
My scribblin' ain't *that* good."

"At least you can write." Raj smiled faintly. "Not
so long ago you'd have had a hard time doing more
than signing your name."

"Yey," Denny replied sourly. "Sometimes I wisht
I was still back then. Things was simpler.

Raj didn't reply, but his expression grew more
thoughtful.

Like maybe he wishes the same.

"Lissen," he said awkwardly. "What'd ye think if I mebbe took a trip upriver fer a bit? Not home—" he added hastily at the startled stare Raj gave him. "That crazy old uncle of m'ser Kamat's asked me t' come along when he leaves. I been thinkin' 'bout it. I like 'im."

"Besides," he continued hastily. "Old bird needs somebody t' look after him. He's crazier than a Sharrist."

An' I don't much like what's been goin' on around here lately. Could use a break.

"I'd—miss you, little brother," Raj said slowly. "I really would. But I don't get to see you much anymore, what with one thing and another. I think you'd do pretty well out there. And I like the old man, too—he's kind of like Granther, in a way."

Denny snorted. Granther was no more like *that* old crazy than Denny was like m'sera Cardinal!

"I think Granther got a chuckle out of my story— you know, my imaginary blond father? I guess he must have heard about what I've been telling people, 'cause his note said 'it appears you have succeeded enough in your studies to have a thorough grasp of genetics. Your application of same is quite inventive.' "

"Huh?" Denny replied. He was concentrating on the sudden appearance of someone from the Kamat warehouse. The figure was in Samurai uniform, but Mondragon had told him to make sure everybody he saw *in* that uniform was someone who was supposed to be wearing it.

"Too often people look at the uniform, assume everything is all right, and never notice the face."

Got that right, Tom. Happen you've used that dodge a time or two, hmm?

"About the only way the baby could *be* a blonde— and mine—would be if my daddy was blond and Marina had some blond ancestors somewhere—" Raj broke off as Denny frowned with recognition and distaste. "What's the matter?"

"Nothin'." He looked at Raj's lifted eyebrow, then relented. "Well, nothin' important. Just that Sammy down there. Brian Delaney. Likes t' throw 'is weight around. Been hasslin' me when I'm on duty at th' warehouse."

To his surprise, Raj frowned. "Delaney?" His brother leaned over and peered down at the man. "Delaney? Damn. That *sounds* familiar. And he *looks* familiar—"

Raj's face got that funny-absent look it always did when he was trying to remember something. "Delaney," he muttered. "Now where—"

He suddenly went white.

"Sword," he whispered. "He's a Sword, he has to be! His older brother Darryl was one of Mama's contacts—"

"He can't be!" Denny protested. "Mondragon passed him through!"

"Mondragon wouldn't know him," Raj whispered. "He's *not* Nev Hetteker, he's from here. Local recruit. Denny, we've gotta tell Tom!"

He started to scramble to his feet; Denny stopped him with a pull on his sleeve.

"Take it easy," he said, his mind going six ways from Satterday, and coming up with a notion that had a grin tugging at the corners of his mouth. "He ain't done nothin' yet. Reckon he's waitin' on somethin'. Bet we've got some time yet; I'll tell Tom. That way ye don' haveta get inta it, an' maybe have m'ser Richard wonderin' how come ye're so familiar wi' th' face an' name an' all. Hmm?"

Raj sank back down to the roof. "You sure?" he said doubtfully. "You will tell Tom? You promise?"

"Oh, yey," Denny chuckled. "I'll tell 'im, all right."

But first I wanta tell somebody else.

This was his second trip to Hoh's in a week; in some respects, it was identical to the first. The tavern was mostly deserted (again) and Wolfling nursed a beer after having popped up behind Denny out of nowhere and following him to the place. Rat sat across from him, candlelight making sculptures of her cheekbones. Both of them had mugs of beer in front of them.

But this time it was Rat's that was virtually untouched. She was staring off into the space beyond Denny's ear, arms resting on the table, hands clasped on the mug—and she was humming.

Rat hummed when she was thinking; the harder she thought, the more inane the tune.

Right now she was humming a kid's counting-song.

It hadn't taken her long to see that Denny's information was as good as having a key to the warehouse, if not better. She'd more or less promised Denny that she and Rif wouldn't be taking anything out of the Kamat's keeping that they didn't have title (however precarious) to. But if somebody else could get the blame for a theft—

And if that somebody could *also* be proved Sword of God—

Denny could hardly contain his glee.

* * *

A note to the warehouse brought Denny to the roof of Kamat two days later. It was quite dark—and *quite* past the time he was supposed to have been virtuously in bed.

But virtue and Denny had seldom had more than a nodding acquaintance.

Rat was waiting, in the shadow of the big kitchen chimney; garbed head to toe in close-fitting black, only someone who was *used* to looking for her would have spotted her, even with the moon to help.

"Hey, kid."

"Hey, yerself." Denny arranged himself on the rooftiles in the same long shadow. "So, what's the deal?"

"This Delaney has a break-in set up for ten tomorrow night, right before the watch changes at midnight. We—ah—arranged for his message to get altered. Rif and me'll show up at ten, use the *conveniently* unlocked door, and get our tails out. His folks'll come in at eleven." She chuckled, and shifted a little, noiselessly.

She looked like a giant black cat lounging in the shadow.

Wonder if she's the one as wrote "Cats of Jane"? Think she's more 'n half cat, personally.

"So I tell Tom tomorrow. Figger he'll set up a watch on this guy. How ye gonna get by that?"

"You don't tell him until ten tomorrow. Even if he can get a watch set on Delaney that night, we'll be long gone."

Denny pondered that one. "If he don't—how ye gonna get Delaney?"

A long, thin shadow-hand reached over and ruffled his hair. "Pillow-talk, my naive young m'ser. Black Cal's getting the same information as Delaney's cohorts. Does that suit you?"

Denny patted his hair indignantly back into place. "I guess it's gotta, don't it? You follered Delaney. An' figgered out what he was up to." Denny made statements rather than real questions, and Rat nodded. "What I can't reckon, is how you made his buddies think the time was gonna be later—"

"Hmm." The voice in the darkness sounded very thoughtful. "Well, you're not too young to understand . . . Men, my young protégé, can be damned fools where an attractive woman is concerned. Of course, women can be damned fools over attractive men—and my beloved partner and her current liaison illustrate both those points."

Denny's snort of agreement brought an appreciative chuckle from the shadow.

"Let's just say that when a man is being a damned fool, someone who *isn't* a damned fool can play interesting tricks with his memory. Delaney *thinks* he said 'ten' and that's when he'll leave the side door unlocked. He didn't. And you are now off the proverbial hook."

"I wisht ye wouldn't use all them big words, Rat," Denny protested. "When ye get fulla yerself ye use them big words, an' I don' unnerstan' half of what yer sayin'."

"Better get used to the 'big words,' kid," she replied, uncoiling herself from the shadow. "That's the kind of circles you're moving in now."

And with that, she was gone.

I didn't even see 'er go, an' I was watching. Huh. Denny scrambled carefully down the slanted roof to the gutter that led to his bedroom window. *"That's the kind of circles yer movin' in,"* hmm? *Yey, I guess so. Maybe I better start tryin' t' talk hightowner better. Maybe then th'Delaney's wouldn't think so quick about hasslin' me.*

As he made his window and slid inside with scarcely a sound, another thought occurred to him.

So what kind of circles did she useta move in, I wonder?

And another, as he stripped off his clothing and got into bed.

I wonder if this gets me off th' hook with her now? Or is she gonna keep comin' back for more favors?

Bet she keeps comin' back.

Hell. With friends like Rat. . .

Yey. This's a damn good reason t' go visitin' upriver. Mebbe I get gone long enough, she'll forget about me. An' even if she don't—I won't be around t' go askin' favors of.

Denny turned over and stared at the wall. *Think mebbe I take old Uncle up on that invite.*

Yey. Think mebbe I better. . . .

FLOOD TIDE REPRISED

by C. J. Cherryh

Weather was about to turn, one hoped, Lord! Rain and more rain, till Old Det was swole up and running fierce through the town, till Mantovan corner marker was under and a canaler-boat and a Gallandry motor-barge came to odds, on account of the canaler finding more current than wanted to be, there on the Port Canal turn.

"Should've heard 'em yell," Jones said, while Mondragon helped her with the barrels, down by Salem, on the Gut, where the current was especially fierce. "Barge hit Pardee corner a hell of a swipe, ol' m'sera Pardee herself was yellin' out the window, an' all. Took the pilin's right out, whole skip-length of Pardee waterfront, them big logs floating free, canaler yellin' th' barge pushed 'im short. Hell, if the barge caught the pilin's he was short, if he were short that close t' shore it weren't his fault if some damn fool come to grief on his waterward side. Never should've given that canaler room."

"Instinct," Mondragon said. That was one of his big words Jones knew. "Didn't want to ride the poor fool down."

"Instinct, hell, there's legal traffic an' there's damn-fools committin' suicide. Big ol' barge, a fool can hear 'im, ain't no cause that canaler comin' ahead on that corner—Lord, he was comin' *off* o' Grand, had hisself all the room he wanted. Ney, he was a fool, he crowded that barge, damn sure, but ain't no way Pardee'll sue *him,* he ain't got the money Gallandry's got! An' let all them landers get to arguin' in the court with Pardee's lawyers, bunch of canalers all callin' each other liars—I dunno, I'll be surprised if the Gallandry don't give up an' pay Pardee t' save 'em worse.''

"Money counts," Mondragon said.

"Ain't no justice," Jones said. "I tell you, what: the Trade is goin' t' file a paper."

"File a paper?"

"With them judges." She caught the last barrel, swung it into place and walked over to the waiting store-front, where the night-boy waited to make his mark on her tally sheet. "Thank ye, Jonny. G'night, Lor' bless." And to Mondragon as she jumped aboard and caught her balance on the slats of the empty well: "Folks is just gettin' so damn legal nowadays—the Trade took a vote, an' if nobody calls any meetin' to oppose, there's goin' t' be this paper writ up, sayin' how it is, the current there an' all, from them as know that canaler's a fool. Ain't fair on Gallandry. An' those lander judges ain't goin' t' know it."

"Expert witness," Mondragon said. A fancy word she didn't know.

"What's that?"

"It means you know what you're talking about. It means somebody like old Jobe could go to the court and tell them the situation there. Jobe should talk to Gallandry."

"Dunno. Expert witness, huh? That the law?"

"That's the law."

She cast off the bow-tie, he cast off the stern; they sorted out the two poles and shoved away.

"Jobe said ask ye."

Mondragon made a noncommittal sound, and shoved with the pole. "Hin. Mark."

Gotten right handy with the skip, he has, Mama.

He likes it right well that Jobe asked—ain't no hightowner that Jobe'd ask, now is it?

Mama was back to silences again, having said her piece. Mama was probably mad about the engine.

She said, "Hey-hin, bow a-starb'd, there," as they hit the Gut current, and the way Old Det was running, the skip's bow hove over a good bit. " 'Ware pole! Hey!"

She poled off the wall at the swing of the current, Mondragon ducked the pole-end and crossed right smart over to portside to shove as she trod on the stern-case. Neat as could be, the skip got her lightened bow up, swung over in a poleboater's maneuver and Mondragon's pole went right in where it had to.

"Good," she said, "that's good, that."

Storm-tide, a good wind blowing: the Gut's current shot them into the Grand, and after that it was just hard, fast work, to bring a light skip upcurrent— no using the engine after hours in this stretch, and after Mantovan corner it was just a bit on past Ventani to Foundry, and after that just a little ways to Kamat. They were at a good clean clip.

"Seen old Muggin lately?" Mondragon asked. She reckoned it was Mantovan corner put him in mind of crazy Muggin, who had had this bad habit of night-tying there, where the barges came.

She said, "Seen him over t' Arden Cut, last week. Smelly as ever."

"Wondered if he was still alive."

"Don't know what keeps 'im goin'." A stop for breath. The current came hard, and the pole warmed in her hands. "Him an' Min. Lord."

"I know what keeps Min going. Bottle of whiskey a week."

"That ain't fair. You know she's in love with you. Knit you that sweater an' all."

"For two bottles."

"Ye're a hard man."

Mondragon laughed. It wasn't often he laughed. She liked to hear it. It meant things were going better, that maybe whatever was going on with him was going better lately. She didn't ask.

But on a certain thought she said, "Cute kid, that."

"Who?"

"The *baby,* Lord, who else?"

"Marina's?"

Marina's. Like there was else. But it seemed for a moment he hadn't thought of that. She *was* a pretty bit. And Jones thought: Could've been mine an' his. Would I want that?

Ain't ready for any kid.

Mama wasn't either. Damn, she wasn't. Didn't pick my papa, either.

"Jones, *what about the baby?*"

Damn, the man was honestly worried. She saw his face in the light off Hanging Bridge, and laughed, to ease his mind. "Hey, not me, Mondragon."

He let out a breath and missed his rhythm with the pole.

"Scare ye, did I?"

"Out of a year of my life." A few strokes more of the pole. "You're not having thoughts like that, are you?"

"Me? Hell. Just wondered if that was the change in ye."

"What change?"

"Ye ain't jumpin' at shadows."

"Say things have calmed down a bit." A breath. "Maybe we'll take that trip to the rim."

"Ye want to? I'll do 'er."

"Next week, I think. Way things are going—maybe next week some things'll be settled."

"Deal." They were coming up on Fishmarket Bridge now. They needed their wind. She savored that last thought awhile, all the way up to Foundry, both of them breathing hard and the pole grown more than warm in the hands.

"Ye'll have blisters."

"Had them before."

Gasp.

Up Foundry North Canal, then, and an easy port swing up into Kamat West, and the blank forbidding face of Kamat warehouses and dye-works. And a wooden gate standing wide into the black recess of Kamat's water-port. "Here we go, now, trick bit comin', bow sharp a-port, hope t' hell ol' Richard ain't tied his fancyboat in here t'night—the damn lantern's out."

"Better swing out a bit."

"Ney, ney, trust me, just like th' Gut, Det'll push 'er hard. Ya-*hin,* yoss, yoss, yoss, there!"

He shoved hard. She fended off the wall. The skip sailed true right into Kamat's water-gate, neat and even clearance on either side. The fancyboat *was* there. They missed her clean, glided right past for the landing. "See?" she said.

And *did* see, shadowy movement in the depth of the cut, against the faint reflected glow of the garde-port. She had the pole out of the water, she called out, " 'Ware the shore!"

"In the cardinal's name!" came back, hollow off the walls.

And Mondragon: "Jones! Easy!" before she had time to swing.

She stood, shaking in the knees and cold, while the skip tossed and ground against the pilings of Kamat House. They were all in shadow. She counted five, maybe more of them, and Mondragon was saying, "What's the trouble here?"

"Thomas Mondragon?" one said. "You'll come with us."

"What charge?" Jones asked out, with a mind to finding targets for the pole. Six of them. She could do for two or three, before they knew what hit them. But Mondragon said, "Jones, easy, Jones." And to the cardinal's slinks: "*Is* there a charge?"

"None yet. You'll come along, ser."

"Mondragon," Jones protested, knowing dammit, *knowing* he was thinking of her in the middle of it. He put his hand on her shoulder.

"Just take it easy." He squeezed, hard enough to bruise. "Listen. Just drop a word to Richard, all right? Probably just some questions, same as his. Nothing to hide and no reason not to answer."

A second squeeze, that hurt. He meant, Shut up, Jones. Don't be a fool, Jones. He was saying—Tell Richard. You didn't fight the cardinal's slinks, you ended up dead for that. And he'd be in it.

She said, "All right." He let her go and racked his pole and went ashore while she stood there. They told him go on out along waterside, she heard that much. She watched them go, watched them round the corner against the glisten of the canal's dark water, and she had this sick shivery feeling, hearing them walk away.

She threw down the pole, jumped down to the well and grabbed up the boat-hook, then ashore, with only the hook to keep the skip at hand. She rang the garde-port bell, rang it and rang it.

A shadowy face showed there, furtive and frightened. She said, "It's Jones. Tell m'ser Richard they arrested Mondragon, the cardinal did—they took 'im, just now, ye hear?"

Give 'em credit, the man started to unlock the door for her; but she pulled the skip up hard and was back in the well, headed up to the half-deck and trading the hook for the pole.

"Where are you going?" the Kamat servant asked.

"T' find help. Tell m'ser Richard—tell 'em Mondragon's in the Trade, remind 'em that, hear! He ain't alone!"

Hell with the pole, she thought. Hell with the quiet-laws. She flung the pole down in the dim light the door cast, threw up the engine cover, put up the tiller bar and started the new-fangled engine up.

She took, damn, she took, the water boiled and bubbled up white behind and she reversed the screw, cast a look back at the Kamat man.

"Move!" she shouted. "Fool!" And backed her out, fast and hard.

*   *   *

They said walk, Mondragon walked. They said face the wall, and he faced the wall while they searched him and took the knife he had: his sword was still on Jones' skip. So long as they were on Kamat Isle he hoped that word might have sped upstairs to Richard Kamat and that Richard might move to find out what was going on—maybe even to stop it.

But when they headed him for the bridge to Sofia and he was walking with a hard grip on either arm, shock began to set in, a physical kind of shock that turned him cold and made everything unreal, their steps on the boards, the sound of the water. He was back in Nev Hettek again, on that walk between the prison and the commandant's office, he could see Merovingen around him, its wooden towers and its lacework of bridges, but the sound of their footsteps on the boards overcame all other reality. He thought, Richard will get Jones away. There's the money at Moghi's, there's that safe place upriver—she won't like it, but she'll be alive . . .

Then common sense tried to say, But maybe there's no need. There's still the chance this is nothing more than Exeter pulling Richard in for a warning, it could even be Richard this is aimed at, nothing about me at all. . . .

It brought him a little calm, thinking that, but they hurried him down the bridge steps on Sofia and along the flooded walkway toward a waiting poleboat. He had seen that damned thing up and down the canals too often. No charges yet, they had said; but there had been no charges against Delaree, either, when they were asking him questions. Less and less chance it was the College they were going to. This boat belonged to the Justiciary.

They shoved him face against Sofia's wooden wall. He heard the rattle of chain as they pulled his arms back.

Then he was not in Merovingen, it was Nev Hettek, it was small spaces and bars. He twisted half free and, remembering the canal-edge, drove straight for the water and escape, but something slammed into his head, buckling his knees. More than one body hit him, bore him sprawling back against Sofia's brick foundations. His head hit, stars exploded, time jumped from that impact to a second blow across his face, a sudden powerful whiff of something chemical.

He thought in panic, Professionals—as the icy cloth covered his nose and mouth and fumes flooded his lungs. The long, long slide started. He felt one of them kick him in the leg, but there was no feeling there, no feeling from anything they did.

Jones cut a wake all the way down the Grand, zigged the skip around a slow canaler-boat and shot the Eastdike Gate at a rate that doubtless raised curses behind her—hope to the Lord there was no fisherman out on this windy night: she headed out into an inky black harbor where there was only water-sheen to tell her what was ahead, no stars, no moon, nothing but the lights of Rimmon Isle and its docks.

But that black yacht was there, she knew it was, she had heard the gossip about the canals, how it had come down from Archangel—it never moved these days but what word went with it, where Anastasi was, Anastasi who had run down a canaler cold as could be. That great black ship had a limited dockage: it could only clear the bridges on the Grand, and only turn about up by the Signeury, whenever Anastasi thought the climate wanted changing.

Now it sat at its other dock near Nikolaev, the way it had come in the time she and Mondragon had first run afoul of Kalugin business. There were electric lights all up and down the dock, brighter than the lights of Rimmon, there were fancyboats and yachts of all sorts, but that one was the only one lit up like noonday.

And when she got closer she could see guards—a godawful number of them: Kalugin defending himself, damn him! while Mondragon got taken up by the cardinal, Lord only knew why, except Damn-'im Kalugin had put him somewhere to make him get aslant of the cardinal's business.

Maybe Kalugin *knew* it—maybe Kalugin damn well expected trouble, and let Mondragon walk into it.

The guards took sharp notice of a skip powering up to the docks. She saw the militia blacklegs with their guns running down the water-stairs to point them at her like she was the Angel come for 'Stasi's soul.

She cut the engine and yelled at them, "Tell 'Stasi Kalugin it's Altair Jones, and I'm a courier, hear?"

"On what business?"

"Kalugin business!" she yelled back. "An' a hurry on it!"

Mondragon always said, if you bluffed, you bluffed like there was no tomorrow, you did 'er high and wide and ye walked like you knew what you was doing. So she skipped down into the well, she grabbed up the tie rope and jumped ashore among the blacklegs to make a jury-tie to a piling.

"Where's the message?" one said, jabbing her with a gun.

She pointed at her head. "Here! An' damn little time for it. Ask 'Stasi."

"Report it," that one told another man, who headed up the steps in a hurry. But the guns stayed aimed at her, except the blackleg captain's, that waved her up the stairs.

Damn, she thought, never saw so many so'jers down t' Rimmon.

What the hell's goin' on? That's what I want to know.

She climbed the wooden steps, barefoot and quiet, while the blacklegs came thumping up after her and the ones still up on the high dock met her with a solid row of gunbarrels.

"I got to see 'im," she said, waving a hand toward the yacht and the gangway, and started walking that way, but the militia showed no sign of letting her. "Move!" she said, reaching a point it was come ahead and get shot or beat. "Out o' my way, damn ye!"

"You wait a damn minute, canaler! Nobody's walking in there without orders."

"*Urgent,* man are ye deaf?"

"Stand still!"

She stood. She waited while the man the captain had sent ran up onto the yacht and found whatever damn secretary they could wake up to talk to at this hour.

"You better wake 'im up!" she said. "It's Anastasi's neck we're talkin' about!"

"Shut up!" the captain yelled at her, and guns clicked.

So she shut up, quick and quiet, and waited with an eye to the gangway.

It seemed an age before the blackleg that had gone up came running down again, to report to the captain in words she couldn't hear.

But the captain got a funny look on his face then and glared at her and motioned her with a wave of his hand.

So she strode off to the gangway and up it, wobbly-kneed, onto the deck of a ship that gave her the willies sure and proper, *bad* memories, those—and there were more blacklegs on the deck, that made sure she went straight where the captain directed her to go, down the companionway into that inside corridor all lit with electronics.

But not down to the stowage this time: this time they showed her to that fancy door, and they opened it wide for her and stood up straight when she walked through.

Anastasi himself was there. She felt weak in the knees from relief she had never thought she would feel to see that black-hearted, handsome bastard.

"Mondragon's arrested," she said, right off. "Ye got to get him free, m'ser."

"Arrested by whom?" Anastasi asked.

"The cardinal. We was makin' night runs, just put in t' Kamat, an' there they was waitin' for us. They took him with 'em. He said t' me, Jones, get help, so I came here."

"You came here. What precisely should I do, sera Jones?"

"Get 'im out o' there! It ain't any good for you either, 'Stasi Kalugin!"

There was a door half open, behind Anastasi. It moved, and a tall, red-haired woman walked out— all in blackleg kit, she was, and wearing a gun.

"There's a problem," Anastasi said to her.

"I heard," the woman said, calmly and coldly; and of a sudden, matching that red hair with the distant sight of Tatiana Kalugin, Jones knew who she was dealing with.

Tatiana and Anastasi all in one room, and no throats cut.

And Mondragon in Exeter's hands.

"Ye got to do something," Jones said. "M'ser, he ain't never played you off. Ain't never. You c'n get 'im out."

But she was thinking: what in hell kind of double-cross is this, Tatiana here, Lord an' my Ancestors— what's up?

Is *that* what Exeter's sniffin' after? Oh, Lord, what've I gone an walked into, like a fool; an' what am I seein' here that I ain't supposed t' see?

Anastasi said, looking at his sister, "We'd better take care of it." And to the guards that were standing around, "See sera Jones has a cabin to herself—"

"I ain't stayin'!" Jones yelled.

"No breakables," Anastasi said without a flicker, "and no weapons."

Light flared and flickered about the walls of Mondragon's black sky, became stonework, a narrow place like a cut into some building, lamplight on the walls as the boat glided in. Mondragon blinked, tried dimly for control of his limbs, and was not sure whether they answered at all. "Get him up," someone said, over the splash of water and the sound of hurrying footsteps on wet stone.

He thought, Where in hell am I? and could not remember what had happened to him, or whether some vast amount of time had not elapsed since his arrest, in Merovingen's dark underside. It *was* Merovingen, the water-sound told him that. He had a canaler-girl and a few friends who had not betrayed him: they were all right. He was relatively sure of them and he was happy with that memory—but hereafter, for himself, the rules were different, there were stone walls, there was no way to get word to anyone, and God only knew how long he had been here or how many more days he had.

"Come on, come on," voices said. They gathered him up off the bottom of the boat and a vision out of hell swung about him, oil-light and black-cloaked figures. They stumbled over a body in the bottom of the boat, someone that wasn't moving— they said, handing him on to someone else, "He killed Depagian," and that echoed through his head along with a sound like some massive working engine, that might have been his heart pounding. His head swung helplessly, he could not get his feet under him and the grip hurt his arms: he thought he was going to fall as they passed him ashore and a gap of water opened under his feet—he could not have saved himself; but they hauled him up the steps and into a great open doorway, more oil-light, blond stone, a desk, a cleric sitting there with a book open in front of him.

The priest said, "Canon court," while they held him on his feet, and the words rang in his hearing, over that continual engine-sound. The priest said, "Thomas Mondragon. Place of birth?"

He kept his mouth shut. They jerked at him and brought his head up.

"Place of birth?"

He thought, They already know who I am, this is a damn game. . . .

The priest wrote something down. The priest said, in the disinterested voice of record-keepers everywhere, "Thomas Mondragon, a Falkenaer, resident of the city, charged with conspiracy, with espionage, with sedition, with theft, with murder of one Everett Depagian, with resisting arrest, with—"

The voice came and went in his hearing. He watched the pen move on the paper. The priest said, "Put him in number three," and made another note in his book—after which the cardinal's men dragged him off and tried to make him get his feet under him. As long as they shook at him and cuffed him, he tried, but it was not smart to acknowledge he was aware of anything: if they knew he was, they might decide to question him now and right now he couldn't remember the right, the safe answers. So he made the minimal effort, endured the acute pain in his arms and only half tried to stay on his feet as they dragged him down a narrow stairway into a vaulted hall.

Big room, lamp-light, ropes and hooks and a clutter that might have been some warehouse, except he knew the use of things like this, and he knew this was the place in the Justiciary you never, having seen it, got out of. The townfolk were wrong, it wasn't any little room the Justiciary had in its gut, it was this place with barred cells at one end, a place of echoes and strange noises that might be voices from elsewhere. He felt cold of a sudden, not sure what sounds he was hearing and what he was remembering: one thing blurred with the other, one

prison was very like the other, and all that kept it
focused was the surety that he had no great deal of
time left.

"Stand up," they said, and pushed him against
the iron grating of a cell—someone took his hand
and closed it about a cross-bar head high, and he
held on and grabbed another, because they were
letting him go and if he fell down they would kick
him, he had had experience enough of irritated
guards. He held on while they stripped his clothes
off, not sure what they would do then, and he
wanted to be no more conscious than he was.

But they shoved him into the cell, that was all.
He stumbled sideways and fell, skinning his arm on
the rough stone, hit his shoulder and his head, and
heard the door slam shut and chain run through.

Nothing in the cell, not even a ledge to sit on. His
jailers said something about a bench, wood scraped
over stone, and he heard them walk away—except a
single footstep, the rattle of the bench. He opened
his eyes a slit to see that one of them had sat down
outside his cell.

Here and there again. Consciousness came and
went in a steady flux, sound droning in and out of
his awareness. Eventually he realized the man sitting outside was a priest, and the rhythmic sound he
was hearing was the priest swinging this kind of
stick and ball arrangement and praying in a steady
monotone.

Go to hell, he thought, but he had still no wish to
move and let them know he was conscious.

We can get someone to him in his cell, Anastasi
had said, speaking of Delaree.

But the priest out there was a suicide watch, no

doubt of it. They had lost Delaree, and they had no intention of losing him before they could ask their questions.

Wrong choices, Mondragon told himself, a string of wrong choices, starting with the one to temporize with the situation. He should never have stopped Jones, he should have used a pole-end himself, killed a handful of the cardinal's men, and used the time to get himself and Jones—

—where? Where, that a faster boat could not overtake them, or frightened people turn them in, or assassins find them? He knew too much, had gotten far too high, the list of people who had to fear what he knew had grown impossibly long. It was his own survival he could not believe in any longer—Jones hadn't a chance in hell of living any-where, so long as he was with her, and he accepted that fact. Jones—

—hated roofs, she said: more than hated them, she panicked. He had tried once and again to keep her off the water and away from his enemies, had watched her die a little every day she tried to live the life he was asking of her, shut away from sun and weather. That was how it was. You didn't hold Jones, you kept her only if she was free; and if he had sworn one thing since that last futile attempt, it was that Jones was never going to die in a place like this. He had to: that had been laid down a long time ago. But, dammit, she didn't—and that, he decided, was the real reason why he had walked ashore like a fool—because Jones still had a chance, at Kamat's door, within reach of friends who had their instructions. Everything had added up against him, and damned if he was going to take her down with him.

Maybe she was on a ship by now, maybe it was morning. Richard Kamat might have to knock her cold to get her there, but get her there he would, between his resources and Moghi's—Richard had promised him that in exchange for his sworn silence on certain matters, and if he was any judge of men at all, Richard would keep that promise, that after all cost him so little. He had not dropped bodies at Kamat's door, he had kept his bargain with Kamat; and there would be no city-wide hunt for a canal-rat who had vanished, except among the Trade. No one would follow, no one would investigate, no one would care, in the halls of power in Merovingen; and when a week or so had passed and Jones, safe upriver, heard that he was dead, maybe it would occur to her that there was sun and wind on the river, and that the Det was wider and longer than Merovingen's dark canals. Maybe when she saw there were places like that—she would know there was more to do with her life than throw it after his.

He kept trying to believe that. But, God, it was hard . . .

RAPPROCHEMENT

by Janet Morris & Chris Morris

"What do I *want*, Chance?" Tatiana Kalugin repeated Magruder's question softly. "I want Mondragon dead. He's still in that same cell in the Justiciary basement. Anastasi's assassins can't get to him the way they got to Delaree . . . it's too dangerous. So is Mondragon. He knows too much about us—"

Perhaps it was something in the set of Magruder's jaw that silenced her. Chance Magruder was supposed to be her lover. She'd made the rules of their relationship clear. Everything in Tatiana's life had rules.

She would help Magruder in Merovingen, and he would help her. She was helping him—had been helping him since he'd come here to establish a Nev Hetteker embassy and trade delegation. She'd done for him what he never could have done on his own. She'd secured him the very embassy he was standing in, clothed in Chattalen velvet and sitting on a Kamat House chair. She'd risked her father's wrath when they were found together—risked everything, over and over, for this man.

Partly because she'd known, in her heart of hearts, some day there'd come a time when she'd need the help of someone like Magruder—an outsider, a Nev Hetteker, a provocateur and the only man in Merovingen who could command, however covertly, Karl Fon's revolutionary Sword of God assassins.

When he didn't answer, just stared off into the distance, as if the tapestry on the far wall was a window, she knew she'd misjudged him.

"Is it so much to ask, to take care of Mondragon for me?" she prodded. She wasn't accustomed to asking favors. Favors, unlike orders, could be refused.

Chance Magruder had a face of slightly crumbling planes and aging angles. In lovemaking, it was beautiful. Right now, it was a death's head. "Is it so much to ask me to kill a man for you? Yeah, it's . . . something. It's . . . more than a casual request. It's an overt act that could get me the cell next to Mondragon's, for one thing. For another, he's a Nev Hetteker, just like me. . . ."

Each word seemed to pull something from her body: her heart, her soul, her stomach, and finally, her bowels. At last, feeling totally emptied, she sat sideways on the ormolu desk between them. She'd given him that desk when he'd moved in here. She'd raised his fortunes beyond anything he could have dreamed without her.

"So you think Exeter will prevail, is that it? You think you don't need me any more? You think it's time to change partners— throw in with Mikhail, perhaps—shift your allegiance to what seems now to be the winning side?"

She could barely command her tongue to move. Betrayal was the final horror. Betrayal was what you feared the most. Betrayal was ignominious. Betrayal made you a fool. Betrayal made you a target. It was always betrayal that got you in the end. So you made alliances, outside the family, because the family was completely dedicated to betraying one another. God had betrayed her and made her a woman; if she hadn't been, perhaps her father wouldn't have betrayed her in favor if her idiot clockmaker brother, Mikhail. And Anastasi was the soul of betrayal.

But Magruder? She'd opened her heart to him, her legs to him—done whatever she could, at the greatest possible risk. And all because, when this moment came (as she'd known it must) she'd known she'd need one man like Magruder on her side. An unquestionable ally. Someone who owed her too much to betray her. Someone to count upon when no one could be counted upon. . . .

That Magruder betrayed her was too cruel a trick even for fate. It made her a slut, a fool . . . a tool. It meant that Magruder counted her as an expendable ally, that he had neither enough fear of her nor respect for her—forget affection; never count on affection, or morality, or strength of character or ethics—

Magruder said, "It can't be done, Tatiana."

—She would have to humble herself before Anastasi, after all. After she'd made such a show of being unafraid of everything that Anastasi feared. Exeter. Iosef, loving father of Mikhail and them both. Discovery, because of Mondragon. Indictment for treason. The Justiciary cells. Even a death at the hands of Exeter's priests on Hanging Bridge. . . .

"How dare you say 'can't' to me?" she managed to ask. Barely more than a whisper. Badly enunciated. Words that wouldn't rise to her nose, but seemed to tumble right out of her throat.

She couldn't look at him. She'd let him use her. He'd lied to her and she'd believed him. She had never been more surprised by a betrayal in her life. She'd been so clear with him about the price of her aid. . . . Perhaps she'd been insufficiently clear with herself about the price, to herself, of her own affection for him.

"I told you, Chance, some day it would come to this."

"There must be another way. Somebody else—"

"I'm not asking somebody else. I'm asking you."

Her eyes were closed, because she didn't want to see even her pale hand on her black-clad leg. She was wearing the battle dress of her militia, these days. She had a pistol on her hip. If only she could make her body obey her mind, she could shoot Chance Magruder. Shoot him in the face, if she opened her eyes and saw him smiling that cynical smile of his. She recalled their recent lovemaking, and squeezed her eyes shut harder. How could she have so misjudged him . . . herself . . . everything?

"Tatiana, I'm telling you: this isn't the way."

"You're telling me you won't help me," she corrected. "I made myself very clear, from the beginning, that it would come to this. Over and over, we discussed what we'd do when it did . . ." She clamped her mouth shut. She wouldn't plead. She didn't want to look at him. She had an impulse to tell him to leave, to throw him out. But this was *his* embassy. Nev Hetteker territory. Nev Hetteker soil in Merovingen. She'd seen to that, to bind her lover tighter in advance of this moment, so he'd never be able to say all the things he was saying now.

"I thought you were . . . hyperbolizing. All ruling classes are paranoid. You've got to calm down, Tatiana. Murder won't solve this."

"Hyperbolizing? You're a coward," she said dully.

"So I'm a coward. I'm a live coward who's lived through one revolution and can help you live through another one, if that's what it takes."

She would not look at him. The pale eyes. The deep shadows around them in which his lids hid. Somewhere she'd heard that people whose eyelids were hidden were duplicitous. Magruder's duplicity was never in doubt, never a problem—always an asset, until it was turned on her rather than turned to her service. "You're a betrayer. Everything I've done for you was predicated on an agreement . . . now that the time is here, you tell me to find someone else?"

"That's not what I'm saying. I'm saying, *don't* find anyone else. Don't *do* this. It will lead Exeter right to your door. If you kill Mondragon—or your brother does—or Kamat does, or Boregy does— whosoever does it, will swing from Hanging Bridge. Believe me. If there's one thing I know, it's revolutions. Exeter's trying to thin the pack. She doesn't care which of you takes the bait. But that's what Mondragon is—bait."

"You're lying. You're a liar."

She had to open her eyes to find the door. She slid stiffly off his desk and started out of the room, still not looking at him. If she caught him smiling at her, or even smirking, she would shoot him in his own embassy. She could say he'd tried to rape her, if she had to. Everyone but her father would believe that.

Of course, her father was in league with Exeter,

paving the way for Mikhail to become Iosef's official heir, and thus prolong Iosef's own life with an
insurance policy called Mischa the Idiot.

Old Iosef would be tended solicitously by one
and all, once it was mandated that Mikhail would
succeed him. And then she and Anastasi, as Anastasi
had succinctly put it so recently on the boat, could
suck Det water, for all the good it would do them.

Magruder's hand came down on her shoulder,
hard, and hers went to the service revolver on her
hip. As he spun her to face him, she jerked the
revolver from its holster. By the time he started to
pull her against him, she had it firmly in both hands.

The gun was cold.

Heavy.

Its muzzle thrust against his navel.

There was a revolver's length between their bodies.

Time stopped.

Her breathing nearly stopped as well.

It would only take a little squeeze, and there
would be one less wild card in Merovingen. . . .

His embrace lost its fervor when the gun poked
his hard belly. She could almost see, under the
velvet he wore, the graying hair on his stomach,
parted by the gunbarrel. All she had to do was
squeeze the trigger. . . .

He knew that, too.

He didn't pull her closer, or put any pressure on
her at all. But he didn't let her go, either.

The sensation of being frozen in time grew
stronger. She couldn't truly banish the temptation
to let the gun remove him from her list of problems.
She was humiliated by his very existence. If he
ceased to exist, at least the one man who'd truly

made her as much a fool as Mikhail would die before he could spread the word or act on the knowledge.

"Tatiana, look at me."

She couldn't.

But then, of course, she did. She had to. She was not some canalside trollop whose fare had seduced her and stolen her poleboat. She was, if nothing else, still a power in Merovingen. So far.

And powers didn't shoot their enemies personally. One didn't give an enemy that much importance. She had the whole blackleg militia to do that sort of thing for her. This creature whom once she'd trusted would see his final moments in deep water, cough out his last breath into the Det, and she'd be nowhere about.

Looking up to meet Magruder's eyes, she wondered how she ever could have considered him handsome. His conniving, narrow mouth; his cruel, downturned nose; his empty eyes full of artifice. . . .

She'd found it all exciting, fascinating—even titillating—while she had herself convinced that she was master of his unsavory skill, of all the violence embodied in Chance Magruder. She'd found him intriguing, dangerous and sexier for all of that.

Now she saw the self-serving expedientist, and realized that no man was attractive without moral courage, without honor, without loyalty in his soul. How could she have been so blind?

In her mind, she pulled the trigger, so much did she want to see the pure surprise on his face. In reality, she said, "Take your hands off me, thug."

He did. Very carefully. Then he stepped back one pace. Two. She felt the pressure against her wrist and arm lessen as his stomach and the gun barrel parted company.

His voice, so husky, seemed to shake when he said, "Please, Tatiana, you've got to listen to me."

"Don't whisper at me, you bastard. You think you can whine and mewl and I'll melt because you're so overswept with remorse and honesty? You don't know the meaning of emotion. Go try that trick on someone of your own class."

His eyes were pale and pale-eyed men, she'd always known, were lacking something. The pale folk from Nev Hettek were not like the rest of them, not like the Merovingians.

Tatiana Kalugin knew all about pale eyes; she saw them every time she looked in the mirror. She shook her red hair back and looked at her gunhand. Somehow, she'd cocked the hammer. With the gun still pointed at Magruder's midsection, she brought the hammer down, slowly and carefully, with the thumb of her other hand, on a live round in a full chamber.

He didn't even flinch. He only watched her. He said, "You've got to let me help you find a way through this. I—" His voice broke.

If she thought she could have kept control, she'd have pistol-whipped the smile from his face. But if she tried, someone would get hurt tonight. The violence inside her, aching to get out, was a surprise. She wanted to hurt this man for not being what she needed him to be—what she'd warned him he must be, and what, so many times, he'd agreed he would be.

"Fine," she said instead, denying herself even the little joy of slapping him with gun hand or free hand. "You show me that you know a better way." She holstered the pistol. "Teach me the Nev Hettek skills that have turned you into so much less than a man." She let her eyes run down from his face to his crotch, and then back up.

Then she shook her head. "All the times I let you clamber around on me . . . I should have known you hadn't the manliness to follow through—"

He looked at the floor. He held both hands up toward her, tentatively, palms out, forfending something.

Then he let them drop. And turned away. And said, "You've got to join forces with Anastasi on this."

She started visibly. Anastasi and she had talked about it, on the boat. But of course, Magruder with his spies would know. . . . But Magruder couldn't know how difficult an alliance with Anastasi was, especially with both their intelligence organizations paralyzed because of Mondragon, who knew too much about everyone.

Magruder hadn't noticed that he'd hit a nerve. He was still talking: "Find a way to get Mondragon out. Legally. *Then* kill him, if you want. But make Exeter release him first. Find a loophole, an inequity. Cry false arrest and scandal. Decry an open attempt to play politics with a man's life. . . ."

"Tell the truth?" She tried to say it with haughty disbelief that he, of all men, should suggest such a thing, but the words came out amid a throaty, half-hysterical giggle. "How novel. How utterly un-Merovingian. Who'd care? Who'd know the truth when they heard it? Why bother, when no one would credit the truth enough to be surprised by it? What's the use of—"

"Try to find a way to get Mondragon out of the Justiciary. With Anastasi's help. Or without him. I'll help you do that much. . . ."

"Oh? Now you'll help me. And how will you do that?"

"I'll petition the court—Exeter's office. Mondragon's a Nev Hetteker, after all. I'll say he's a protected person. I'll contrive some papers to prove that he is, and date them appropriately. Show him as part of my staff, an ambassador at large or a dignitary of some sort—I'll think of something—I can probably ram through a plea of diplomatic immunity. Exeter doesn't want to be seen as the force that destroys relations between New Hettek and Merovingen. If it comes to it, I'll have Karl Fon recall the whole staff—me, Chamoun, everybody—Mondragon included, back to Nev Hettek as a result of Mondragon's unilateral detention without trial. We'll demand the right to dispute and disprove all allegations. Break off diplomatic relations, or threaten to, unless they release him into our custody and drop all specious charges. How's that?"

"Words. Paper." She spat. "You think you can save yourself by pushing paper around from one desk to another?"

"Can you sell it to Anastasi?"

"I'm not selling anything for you. And I'm not asking my brother for anything." She would not be impressed. She refused to admit that the plan was good, perhaps even workable. Let him go to Anastasi. Let Magruder crawl on his knees to her brother.

And then let Anastasi come with Magruder in tow and both of them crawl on their knees to her—after they'd taken the risk, once the deed was done.

For then she'd know their secret. If they implemented Magruder's plan, they'd pay dearly themselves for the privilege, after the fact. And then, perhaps, if she liked the show, she would let the man called Chance Magruder live. But only if she had Thomas Mondragon as a gift from him. . . .

"Deliver Mondragon to me, Magruder, and you'll keep your embassy, your standing here, the rest. But I won't lift a finger to help you, actively. You and Anastasi do what you will. If Mondragon is not in my personal care by the end of the week, pack your things. As easily as I created all this for you," she waved a hand around, "I can destroy it."

"You won't have to, if this doesn't work," Magruder reminded her as he went slowly to the tapestry and pulled it back, to reveal a window onto Merovingen. "If we can't get Mondragon out using this strategy, I'll have no choice but to close the embassy, return to Nev Hettek, and take Michael Chamoun and the whole trade mission with me."

"Good," she said through gluey lips. *Threaten me, will you?* He was rattled, to take such a risk. This was better than shooting him. A bullet hurts only for a short time. "Too bad you can't take crazy Cassie Boregy, the prophetess you and Chamoun made, and her baby with you. Now get out of my sight—"

Too late, she remembered that she was in his office, not her own—on his turf.

But he bowed his head and said, "I'm sorry. I'm so sorry."

And she thought she heard him mutter, almost wonderingly, as he headed for the door, "But I really did love you," before he went through his own doorway and shut the door behind him, leaving her alone in his sanctum.

He'd never done that before. When she'd wanted him to show his trust by giving her the run of his embassy office, he'd never allowed her to contrive to be alone here.

Now, she didn't care. And here she was. She went over to his desk, which she'd given him, and sat behind it.

Wonder of wonders, it wasn't locked. He hadn't been expecting her. He'd been working. She looked at the papers stuffed hastily into his top drawer.

One of them was a letter from Danielle Lambert, the Nev Hettek physician he'd brought down to attend to Mike Chamoun's child.

These two—Magruder and Lambert—were old friends, from the tone of the woman's letter, which asked for a quick return to Nev Hettek.

She sat back, holding the letter in her hands. Nothing overtly incriminating, but something in the tone, nevertheless . . .

Cassie Boregy, who prophesied revolution whenever she'd chewed enough deathangel, was Michael Chamoun's wife and entre into the powerful house of Boregy. The baby was the cement of their union. And the way this glorified wet nurse talked about that baby to Magruder made Tatiana wonder about the child.

The child was addicted to deathangel, this was clear. Why the physician was distressed, was not clear. The mother was a deathangel addict. Everybody knew that. Even Cardinal Exeter, who was ignoring the fact. So why should the physician be disturbed about the child being an addict? This was natural. And yet the physician was disturbed. And what was stranger, was that the physician would entreat Magruder to allow the baby to go back to Nev Hettek—back. This was very strange. Unless the Nev Hettekers were ready to start the war that Anastasi longed for between Nev Hettek and Merovingen, there was no way the child of Boregy House could be taken from its mother.

Unless, of course, the child wasn't Cassie's at all. One heard rumors. One heard all sorts of rumors. But Michael Chamoun's baby out of Cassie Boregy was referred to, throughout the document that Tatiana was holding, as "our Hope."

Code words, of course. Nothing more, certainly. The baby's name was Belle. Belle Boregy. And yet, this letter was a letter from a distraught woman to a man who was privy to her most intimate concerns. And the most pressing of those concerns was the rapidity with which the baby, suckling at Cassie's teat, was *becoming* addicted to deathangel. Tatiana was no Nev Hetteker physician, but she naturally assumed—anyone would—that, if the mother was addicted, the child would have been born addicted. So, even if they had withdrawn the child from the deathangel after birth, what did a little more deathangel matter now, one way or the other?

The letter was so strange that Tatiana sat for a very long time with it in her fingers, until she realized that the perspiration from her thumb had smudged the signature.

Then she carefully put it away and left Magruder's embassy. She would have plenty of time to think about what use she could make of the letter from Dr. Lambert to her old friend, the ambassador.

Plenty of time. If Magruder's plan worked and Anastasi came into line and all three of them didn't find themselves swinging from Hanging Bridge some fine morning.

"Mike," said Magruder to his protégé, "I want to you to ask your father-in-law to support anything and everything that Anastasi comes up with to get Mondragon out of the Justiciary basement."

"Whaddever y'say, m'ser. Whaddever y' say." Mike Chamoun trolled his hand over the side of the fancyboat that Magruder had sent for him as the boat cut black water and white froth boiled back to the stern.

They were reasonably safe from eavesdropping on the boat, with just one trusted Nev Hetteker at the helm, in the dark, with low running lights and a reasonably fair wind as they headed toward Rimmon Isle where, once arrived, they'd turn around and motor back. All Magruder needed was privacy, for a talk with this boy who was coming apart under the strain at just the wrong moment.

Young Chamoun had been drinking heavily ever since Magruder had sent him out with Kenner to assassinate Ito Boregy. Although the action had been necessary and justifiable, if Ito hadn't died, Willa Exeter couldn't have begun her current reign of terror.

Starting a revolution in Merovingen was only a little more dangerous than starting one in Nev Hettek had been; and that, because Magruder was older, calmer, and farther from home. He didn't regret anything that was happening here and now—except, perhaps, Tatiana's reactions.

When it came down to it, Magruder didn't care who the hell ended up at the top of Merovingen's heap, because he meant to incite Merovingen-below to burn the whole heap to the ground. But young Chamoun did.

The boy looked up at him and took a defiant swig from a bottle of Boregy's private stock that he'd brought along.

Damnfool kid. Whatever pain it had caused Chamoun to lose his real child because his wife was a dope-fiend, and have another baby smuggled in to take its place, that pain was less than what the living child's mother was feeling, as the attending Nev Hettek physician to a purported Boregy heir.

"Chance," Mike Chamoun said, "we can't hold this together much longer. Y'know it. I know it. Even Vega knows it. Only Cassie," he sniffed and rubbed the back of his hand under his nose, which seemed red even in the boat's low running lights, "doesn't know it. But she knows that Mikhail's her bosom buddy. Bosom buddy . . . boson muddy . . . gotta get Cassie's buddy outta our hair, over there, or everythin's gonna go splat in our faces. . . ."

"Mike, what are you trying to say?"

"What if she divorces me and marries Mikhail, takin' that kid with 'er?"

"Then it's a good thing that kid's who she is, and not who she's supposed to be. Think of your own parents." He had to pull on Chamoun's leash, somehow. "Back in Nev Hettek, your folks are sweating this out. Everybody is, right now. I don't want you to screw up over there, Mike. I'm going to send Kenner over to you, full time. Call him your cousin. He's half a hero as it is, for opening that machine shop. I want him bunking in there. . . ."

"Him 'n' Dani Lambert, too? You need both o' them t' keep an' eye on me? Then you don't need me and I can go home. . . ."

Even Chamoun knew that was ridiculous. The only way that Michael Chamoun was going home, now that he was in this deep, was in a box. The kid took another swig of Vega Boregy's wine.

"How'm I supposed t' get Vega to—"

At least Michael wasn't completely brain-dead. "Remember that flashlight you gave Cassie as a betrothal gift? Get it. Give it to me. Then report it stolen—but just to Vega. Mess up the room where she keeps it so it'll look like an inside job, some servant in a rush rifling her things."

"I don't get it," Chamoun said.

"Willa Exeter is declaring everything more sophisticated than a hatpin as illegal technology and prosecuting on those grounds. I want Vega spooked. And I want Mikhail to find out—not be told—what happened, and get spooked, too. If we can get Mikhail thinking that Willa Exeter is his enemy, then her whole initiative is going to fall right apart."

"I still don't get it."

You poor dumb, drunken bastard. "Mikhail's in love with your wife," Magruder said, leaning close to the boy in the stern, even though he could see almost full around him and no boat was anywhere near by. "In case you hadn't noticed. If he thinks Exeter's going after Cassie—which she surely would have by now, except for Mikhail's fascination with her—then he's not going to want or accept Exeter's support, at best. At worst, he'll cause enough embarrassment and suspicion within the ranks of those Old Families that Exeter's trying to form into a coalition to support Mikhail that it'll come to a grinding halt on its own."

"Okay," Chamoun nodded with shitfaced solemnity. "I'll get you the flashlight."

As if Chamoun had a choice. That was what Magruder was sending Kenner into Boregy House for. With Kenner in there to ride herd on Michael Chamoun, Chamoun was going to find out what it meant to be Sword of God. Until now, he'd been only a pampered tool of the revolution. Now he was going to become a soldier in the army called Sword of God.

There was one hell of a difference.

In Cassie's powder-blue bedroom filled with golden ormolu cherubs, Michael Chamoun rifled bureau drawers like a thief in the night.

Where was that foolish flashlight, anyway? Kenner, newly introduced into the household by the simple mechanism of Michael's bringing him home, was outside the door. If anyone came by, Kenner would knock on the door, purportedly looking for Michael.

So that was all right. Michael had a right to be in here—it was his wife's bedroom; it was his bedroom, too, although he'd taken to sleeping on the other side of the baby's room. So it was all right, he told himself again. Then why did he feel like a thief—a real thief, a thief in the night? He'd given her the flashlight, hadn't he? Then it was all right.

Kenner wasn't all right, though. Kenner was dark as Merovingen-below on a moonless night, all tanned skin and black eyes and with a perpetual shadow he carried with him that no light seemed able to dispel.

Kenner was a born killer. Chamoun had seen that

for himself, when he and Kenner had gone after Ito. Magruder was a man capable of anything in the service of the revolution, but Chamoun was aware of the difference between a man and an animal, and between an omnivore and a carnivore. And between a battle-weary veteran like Magruder, and a hungry young wolf like Kenner.

Kenner was pure carnivore. They should have picked somebody like Kenner to do Michael's job—to come here and marry Cassie and have a baby and lose his heart and soul. Well, soul, because Kenner didn't have a heart.

And neither did Mike Chamoun, anymore.

As he swished his hands through a drawer of Cassie's silken underthings in the dark, feeling for the hard cylinder of the flashlight that had announced his intentions to marry the Boregy girl, Chamoun kept thinking, *My parents did this to me.*

Others people's parents were like Cassie's parents: staunch, loving, giving, competent, protective. Michael had gotten into this whole Merovingen adventure because his parents needed to be protected from their own screwed-up lives. He'd been doing things to help his parents all of his life. Now his parents had all but ruined his life. They might even have managed to get him in a position where he'd die out here.

He couldn't have said no to Chance tonight, any more than he'd been able to say no back in Nev Hettek—because his parents were virtual hostages to the revolution. The whole Chamoun shipping empire was a fabrication of Karl Fon and Chance Magruder and the rest of the revolutionary council.

Michael Chamoun's parents were still living—and

living marginally well—because Chamoun was willing to do whatever he was told. He was chosen for this specifically because he could be controlled through his family, and because he looked likely, and because, probably, he wasn't a Kenner. He wasn't somebody who knew how to fight back. The only thing he'd ever known how to do was take orders, work his heart out for his family—and now for the revolution.

Had he been picked to come here because he'd fixate on Chance and take Chance's orders the way he'd taken his father's all his life? He didn't know. He couldn't have said if his life depended upon it. Everybody always needed him to do something. Nobody around him could ever get along without him. He always had to pitch in and forget his own wants and needs and put off his life till later.

Well, maybe there wasn't going to be a later. Maybe, this time, his parents had finally destroyed his life while he was trying to save theirs one more time.

He couldn't even remember his mother's face. That was funny. Or his father's. He remembered their hands. The shaking, old, gnarly hands with the undernourished nails all ridged and yellowed. They'd been teachers, before the revolution. They'd taught him to respect knowledge and respect his elders and respect all sorts of things that soon became the stuff of treachery and work camps: truths that the Fon government didn't believe in; values that the revolution didn't share.

But then his parents had learned the new ways, and taught him to love the revolution. His father had said to him, "If you like Karl Fon, you're going to love Chance Magruder."

That was so long ago. Nearly a year before he'd come to Merovingen. And this was the first time he'd heard the words with the sarcasm that his father might—must—have intended.

But you did what you could to keep the family alive. You protected your blood. And you kept in mind that these people down here in this hellhole of superstition and ignorance were willfully ignorant, vicious fundamentalists at odds with each other and the tiniest bit of technology that could make life better for the average sod.

Half of Merovingen was so afraid that the alien sharrh would come back and raze their planet again that they didn't dare light a candle at night. The next largest majority was sure that you were stuck on a wheel of eternal rebirth like a butterfly glued to paper. And it went on. . . .

Superstition was the enemy, Karl Fon taught. Intolerance was the enemy. It was the revolution's job to give man back his heritage, or at least a chance at it.

It shouldn't be illegal to make a flashlight. It shouldn't be immoral to try and clean up the rivers. It shouldn't be a capital offense to say something critical of the government. But all those things were so here.

He slid his hand under one more pair of undies and there was the flashlight—hard, round, and intact.

He lit it to make sure. He put the contraband in his back pocket and headed for the door. This place was a pit of fools. And the worst thing about it was that each fool supported the worst things about the government:

They believed that they lived over and over, so

they were willing to suffer now, make some kind of deal with God so that they could live in hightown later. It not only made them tractable, it made them passive. They were sheep.

The Adventists believed that the statue on Hanging Bridge was going to come alive, draw a foolish wooden sword and—*blam*—the new age would begin.

Whether or not the sharrh were really coming, Michael wasn't sure. He'd been drugged during catechism and dreamed he was a fighter in the defense force when Merovingen had been attacked from the stars. But all the sharrh had done lately was get his wife started prophesying doom.

Living here was like living in a world where everything was upside down: Ignorance was exalted; the poor people, the uneducated, the martyrs, criminals, and the enduring clods were the venerated ones; the few educated hightowners were the evil that must be tolerated, because without the hightowners, even the pathetic subsistence in Merovingen-below would come to a grinding halt.

So all your sinners were up on the upper levels, and all your good people below. If you believed. If you could equate ignorance with goodness. If you thought that moral arrogance was the same thing as moral exercise.

Michael Chamoun shined the flashlight once around the room. He'd been smitten with puppy love for one of his wife's friends, and thought, being from a degenerate technological culture, that when he got here, he'd have a chance to cultivate a relationship with this girl, named Rita.

But there weren't relationships, here. There were matings. Ritual couplings. Women didn't hold their bodies in any great repute. They made love to everyone. They screwed around like sailors—which, in a way, they all were.

All Merovingen women were sluts, in Michael's estimation. Even beautiful Rita. And his wife was a drugged-out crazy. She'd killed their child with her drugs.

In Merovingen they'd say that the child died as retribution on Michael's head for letting himself and his loins be used to make a merger, for making Cassie fall in love with him, for swearing vows he didn't intend to keep and living as his wife's husband under false pretenses.

But what did they know, in Merovingen, about anything? Technophobes had come to disgust him. He was so tired of lace at his collar and ritual and exaggerated manners that he could scream.

His wife had killed their baby with her drug-taking and Nev Hettek had foreseen it, sending in a replacement baby just in time. Well, thanks, Dani. Thanks, Chance.

Dani Lambert had given her own baby to Michael, for the sake of the revolution.

If it was Revolution or Retribution, Michael would still take Revolution every time: change over superstition. Superstition was the overt sign of an unwillingness to accept change. And what didn't change, died.

As his baby had died. Dani Lambert's kid was either Karl Fon's daughter or Chance Magruder's daughter, so Kenner had told Michael with that wolfish grin.

"Ain't that a bitch and a laugh on 'em? They've got this real hotsy totsy daughter of the Boregy

House, hightown's top of the top, bound to inherit a whole chunk o' this place—wait till she grows up and one o' her daddies comes to see her."

Kenner was something Michael could never be. He didn't know how or when he'd done it, but he found himself lying on Cassie's bed, shining the flashlight at the muraled ceiling: off, on; off, on; off, on.

And Kenner finally knocked, and stuck his head in: "What's the matter with you? Blinking that light. Shows under the door."

Kenner hit the wall switch. Boregy House had lights, when it wanted to use them.

"Come on, Chamoun. Shape up. Let's get out of here and I'll buy you a drink."

Kenner thought that all Michael cared about was liquor. Well, it had been, almost, since Cassie's real baby died.

Kenner moved toward him with a litheness that Michael Chamoun would never possess, all readiness and speed. And aggression. Chamoun told himself, as he rolled off the bed before Kenner could lift him up by the collar, that it was just training. Magruder hadn't given Michael that kind of training because he wasn't supposed to move like a fighter, like a soldier: he was supposed to be a pampered son of Nev Hettek's first-generation merchant-class aristocracy, which existed only in the mind of Magruder and Fon, until they'd made Michael Chamoun into what they needed to get into the pants of Merovingen's hightowners.

Kenner wrenched the flashlight from Michael's unresisting hands.

"Right, a drink." He started to get up, but Kenner

pushed him back down. "On second thought, fancy pants, you've had enough to drink."

"You'll never get out—and back in—without me. Chance'll have a fit if you leave me."

Kenner was squinting in the bright light. He shook his head and said, "Yeah, okay. Come on. But try to look like you're not scared to death, hear? This is your damned house, isn't it?"

"Not exactly."

Maybe Chance had taught Kenner something, but not enough about Merovingen. Finally seeing that there was some need for him—that somebody, somewhere, needed him—Michael Chamoun levered himself off his wife's empty bed to escort Kenner out of Boregy House safely.

Cassie was off with Mikhail, as usual.

Maybe they could get to Magruder with the flashlight before she got home. Then there was only a little more to to do: making sure his wife missed the gift, and told her father.

And, of course, told Mikhail.

The thought of Cassie in the Justiciary's fabled basement ought to have rankled more than it did.

As he followed Kenner down the stairs to the water-gate, Chamoun admitted that, as far as he was concerned, his wife had murdered his baby.

So maybe, if things got out of hand the way they often did when Magruder played long shots, and Cassie ended up in the Justiciary, it would prove that the Merovingians were right and he was wrong: then he'd believe in karma, and in Retribution.

But until then, he was going to stop drinking and start paying attention. It wasn't just the footing on the stairs down to the water-gate that was treacherous tonight.

Merovingen wasn't a place you could roam around freely, any longer. Unless you had a Kenner by your side, or unless you were one of Willa Exeter's witch-hunters.

Since Chamoun was probably one of the people whom Willa Exeter would most like to get into the Justiciary, he needed to watch his step.

Not just figuratively, either.

With Cassie fast becoming the apple of Mikhail's eye, one easy way to dispose of an unwanted husband would be through Mikhail's supporter, Cardinal Exeter.

He hadn't thought it through until they'd reached the landing and the boatman at the garde-porte greeted him with a show of deference and a sniff at Kenner.

And then, finally, Chamoun understood—or thought he understood—why Magruder had assigned Kenner to stay with him.

And his eyes nearly filled with tears of gratitude and embarrassment. Chance cared about him. Chance was looking out for him. Chance was doing more for Michael than Michael was doing for himself.

He really was going to stop drinking. He really did have a stake in things here. Even though the baby was dead, the Revolution was alive and well.

As the water-gate rumbled and Kenner hopped into a waiting boat, Chamoun nearly shook the hand Kenner offered him. Then something happened—he wasn't sure what. Kenner slipped. He slipped. The boat rocked.

And the flashlight fell.

It hit the water with a splash and both of them plunged their hands in after it.

But it was too late, and the Boregy retainer was right there, looking at them.

Had he seen? If he had, did he know what he'd seen?

Kenner said, "Never mind, I'll buy the next bottle. Come on, let's go."

And there was nothing for it but to ready the boat and push off.

Chance wasn't going to like this. Not at all. That flashlight, if it turned out to have sunk in the mud of the water-gate, could turn out to be a real problem.

Or not. It depended on what the retainer had seen, Kenner said. "He's good as dead. Trust me. He won't live till morning. As a matter of fact, he might not live another couple hours. All depends on how long it takes us to get back there, say we forgot something, and finish him. After all, the place was supposed to have been burgled. . . ."

Chamoun closed his eyes.

He wasn't a killer. He'd found that out the last time he'd gone out at night with Kenner.

But he knew Kenner was right. The Boregy retainer, who'd seen the flashlight drop, had to die. Or else he might. And, worse, the Revolution might. And if the Revolution died, Merovingen would live on in superstition unending, while women like Cassie chewed deathangel and killed their babies, and men like Mondragon sold their partitioned souls to the highest bidders, and the rest waited to be born rich or fried by the sharrh, whichever came first.

"Mondragon will talk, freely and inventively, dear sister," said Anastasi to her as they walked together along the bridge to the College. "If he believes there's no hope. No help. He'd even deal with Exeter exactly the way he's dealt with everyone else . . . and no one wants that."

"So we'll try to make sure," she affirmed the arrangement, "that he talks to no one we'd rather not have him talking to. But it's agreed between us, then: keeping him alive and a threat to all others beats having him dead and losing the, shall we say, constipating effect he has on so many whose secrets he knows."

"Agreed," said Anastasi Kalugin, nodding his proud head once. Tatiana's brother was beautiful in the moonlight. Or beautiful because he was trying to cut a deal with her and Anastasi had powers of persuasion that were nearly more than mortal. Tatiana reminded herself that his so-called deal would extend only so far as its explicit limits, and no farther.

They'd use Magruder's plan to make Exeter release Mondragon into their custody, or into Magruder's.

She shivered. That was the difficult part: One wanted Mondragon under one's personal protection. But Magruder was the most likely person to whom Exeter would release him.

Were they slitting their own throats in order to keep Mondragon's whole?

She didn't know. She couldn't say. She was still smarting from her encounter with Magruder.

"Why so quiet, sister? This is what you wanted, isn't it? What your pet Nev Hetteker proposed?"

"He's not my pet."

"Then what is he?" Anastasi stopped, turned, and a wisp of disturbingly pale hair blew across his forehead as he peered at her. "What is he, Tatiana?"

A spy. A provocateur. An insurrectionist. But she couldn't very well say that.

"Chance? He's a useful tool. Like Mondragon. Exactly like Mondragon—a blade sharp on every side." *Be careful, brother, for all our sakes.*

"So you're not as sure about releasing Mondragon into Magruder's custody as you pretend." Anastasi licked his lips. "That's something, anyhow, dear sister—you're not love-besotted, at least."

"Ha!" The derisive snort came out of her with too much vehemence. Thus, she had to cover the lapse as Anastasi looked closer: "Let the Nev Hettekers flock together. Let Exeter worry over them, not over eliminating all of Mikhail's enemies by dint of this inquisition. After all, brother, you and I are Mikhail's worst enemies. As the list grows short, our names come closer to the top of it. This way, those old families supporting Exeter's 'clean-up' will think twice: Mikhail and Cassie as a couple in ultimate power is a frightening thought."

"More frightening than handing into Nev Hetteker hands the man who knows the most dirt on every power worth mentioning in Merovingen?"

"At least our intelligence will be current, once again." *If Mondragon had been free, this meeting, and meetings like this, would never have had to be handled in person. Mondragon could have been sent from one Kalugin to the other.* "If you're worried about Mondragon's discretion—don't."

"Because it's never been in doubt? Never is a long, long time."

"Because," she said, taking a deep breath, "we can afford, once this Exeter matter is concluded, to arrest Mondragon and his Nev Hetteker cohorts on charges of high treason, espionage, and sedition, if we choose. Once there's an overt link between Mondragon and the Nev Hetteker embassy, the advantage is clearly ours." Mondragon would be theirs. Even better. Chance Magruder would be as much their hunting dog as Mondragon. He'd wear the Kalugin collar, or his neck would stretch. She wondered why Chance hadn't thought of that, when he offered to openly claim Mondragon as one of his own. But no one thinks of everything. No one.

She'd learned that lesson the hard way. If all went well, the question then would be whose creatures the folk of the Nev Hetteker embassy became: hers, or her brother Anastasi's.

Anastasi had long been looking for a pretext to make open war upon Nev Hettek. Such a war would consolidate his power base at home, since the army was his. He could declare martial law in a situation where a whole nest of Nev Hetteker spies and Sword of God agents was revealed to be working out of the Nev Hetteker embassy.

And she couldn't have that. So she said, as their bootheels cracked on the College bridge once more, "Look, brother. Don't think I can't envision you using the Nev Hettekers to act prematurely. I can. You mustn't. We must keep this alliance of ours as long as Exeter's in power. She's too dangerous to underestimate."

There. She'd said it.

And Anastasi chuckled appreciatively. "You have a bargain, sister—as long as you don't use Nev Hettek openly against me."

They were, after all, brother and sister. She sighed theatrically, "Done. Now, since neither of us are afraid to turn our back on the other for at least the next few hours, let us concentrate on how we can best approach the cardinal."

She was in there, was Cardinal Exeter, studying late the art of deception.

Tatiana had always hated the College. Always known it would unleash their greatest test, their most horrid danger.

The intellectuals of the College were all up late, it turned out as they entered, scurrying hither and thither with stacks of what she imagined to be incriminating documents in their hands.

A man dressed like a foyer table led them through the labyrinth to Exeter's study hall.

The woman was a wizened, sexless thing with hair cut as short as a boy's and enough fat on her that she looked more like a eunuch than a woman.

Her eyes were sexless, too, cold and tired and traced with lines.

"I cannot express my honor at your visit," said she in a water-snake's voice.

"Nor I, our pleasure," said Anastasi, pouring oil on those waters, "that you have granted us this late interview."

She offered them seats in gilt-framed chairs with fish-carved arms.

Tatiana saw Exeter staring at her, then realized why: the openly-carried service revolver on Tatiana's hip. "Cardinal," she said as she eased into the chair and crossed her black-booted legs, "it's come to the point where all of us must stop this feuding and work together for the good of Merovingen, I'm sure you'll agree."

"Oh, I do," said the chief inquisitor of the city

with cold amusement. "It does my heart good to see you two together, no matter the reason. It would make your father proud, if he could see it."

Now to light the oil on the water and burn the snake where she lurked: "He'll see us an hour after we leave here," Tatiana promised in a clearly threatening voice. "We have reason to believe that you'll soon be apprised that Cassiopeia Boregy has been harboring illegal technology among her personal possessions."

"And since we're concerned for Mikhail's reputation, as we know you are, we think that the matter must be handled with the utmost discretion."

Exeter didn't blink. She sat back in her chair. And she said, "Where did you get this information?" Very slowly. Very guardly.

"Through privileged sources. I'm sure you understand that those sources must be protected," Tatiana's brother said.

"And what is it you want?"

"We want," Tatiana said, "not to feel compelled to report this ourselves, officially, to you through channels. But since, given the ways of Merovingen justice lately, one must report such things, here we are. Of course, all of us should attend the letter of the law in these matters. Inquiries must be made by your office. Otherwise, we should have to report that, although we personally made sure that you were informed, no such inquiries were made. And that would discredit not only you, personally, but the whole process you represent." Couldn't say "witch-hunt." Too bad.

But pleasure was inching up Tatiana's torso from her groin, a pleasure that was nearly sexual in nature as the unblinking woman squirmed without moving.

"Yes, I see. Well, we must do what we must. Of course, in a case where a girl proclaimed by the College to have visionary powers is concerned, one must tread carefully."

"Indeed. But tread one must," Anastasi turned the knife in the belly of Exeter's inquisition. "Else all other parties under interrogation should be freed in a general amnesty, because then the process will be seen to be flawed and riddled with favoritism."

Kiss our collective asses, you childless, heartless, loveless old bitch.

"And I suppose you'll oversee this . . . investigation personally?" Exeter, gathering her wits, riposted at last.

"By my ancestors, no," Tatiana said fervently, looking suitably shocked. She placed a hand on her breast. "Why would we become involved? The Justiciary basement has too foul a reputation, at this moment, as a dungeon of injustice and partisanship, for us to venture down there. Neither of us have any intention of entering the Justiciary basement— for any reason—until all this . . . investigating . . . is just a poorly-remembered dream. After all, we've never been interested in ruling by fear."

Which was as bold an insult as Tatiana was willing to risk. And as open a threat. She was breathing hard now, as if she'd run a long distance.

But Anastasi was still fresh: "We also think you should know that the Nev Hettek embassy passed an official complaint to my office on the unwarranted detention of one of their citizens, a Thomas Mondragon. We heartily recommend that you release this person forthwith, into the hands of a suitable custodian, unless you have some clear and certain reason to continue to hold him."

"I see," said Exeter. She seemed to have grown smaller, or sat back farther than the stuffed chair behind her desk would allow.

Snakes curl up, arch back before they strike, Tatiana reminded herself. For one instant of vertigo, all the possibilities of failure and loss hiding in this moment were clear to her, yawning like hungry beasts in a chasm that suddenly opens underfoot.

But it was too late to turn back now. It had been too late, once she and Anastasi had solidified their plan.

And Exeter said, "If the Nev Hettek embassy petitions me, I will take their plea under advisement. Until then, let's hope this Mondragon person stays alive."

"Let's hope he does," Tatiana said. "I'll gladly give you extra blacklegs to protect him. The last thing we need now is an international incident." She looked pointedly at Anastasi.

And her brother said, "Well, I'm feeling better." He stood up and held out his hand to Tatiana. "I hope you feel better too, Cardinal Exeter, in the wake of our little talk."

Tatiana took Anastasi's hand and stood up. "We must be going. We do have an appointment with our father, as we mentioned. Have a good night, m'sera Cardinal. And a happy tomorrow."

Tatiana certainly would. The look on Exeter's face was inconclusive, but the unblinking eyes seemed so sunken as the cardinal watched them leave her chambers that Tatiana was sure that Cardinal Exeter was going to have a very unhappy tomorrow.

And nothing, at that moment, could have made Tatiana, or her brother, happier than that.

Kenner reached up as if to take the line from the retainer in order to secure the boat, and pulled the man into the boat.

The retainer hit the decking with a muffled cry and a thud, and Michael Chamoun blinked at the liveried figure writhing on the deck near the bow with a knife in his belly and Kenner bending over him.

Then Kenner stood up and Michael saw that the Sword of God agent had slit the retainer's throat as well as his belly.

The man's mouth opened and closed like a fish's mouth, but nothing came out of it save a thin trickle of blood that, as Michael watched, turned into a torrent.

Blood was streaming from his neck, too, down over his livery—black blood in the light of the garde-porte.

"Go. Out. Now," said Kenner, still crouching over his prize.

Kenner cast off the line with bloody hands—into the water, where it dangled.

Michael nearly crashed the boat against the stone of the water-gate as he steered it out into what was left of the night.

Somewhere near the Ventani Bridge, he vomited over the side, watching Kenner throw the lifeless, nearly bloodless body of the retainer overboard.

"Blood!" Michael nearly screamed over the engine. "Kenner, what about all the blood?"

Kenner waved a hand at him: Don't worry.

They bailed and scrubbed until Chamoun's hands nearly bled before they got the boat clean enough to bring back to Boregy House.

By then, everyone was awake and too worried to notice them—worried about Cassie and Mikhail and the men who'd come looking for Cassie only to hear that she wasn't at home, but at Mikhail's.

Even without the evidence of the flashlight, Michael realized, Chance had gone ahead with his plan when they hadn't appeared on time.

But of course, Chance would. The missing retainer, when he was discovered dead, would only further support the story of a burglary.

But Michael was the one that had to go to Vega, despite Chance's premature move.

And then he found out that Exeter's henchmen hadn't come because of Chance at all.

Vega Boregy, Cassie's worried father, said, "Go to your friend Magruder, Michael. Tell him I hold you two responsible for introducing advanced technology into this household. Tell him that if Cassie is harmed or frightened in any way, I'll make it clear to the cardinal that the flashlight was Cassie's betrothal gift from you."

Vega's black hair was falling out of its club. He brushed it away irritably. "Well, boy, what are you standing there for? Go!"

So he went, with Kenner as a dishonor guard, to the embassy, as everyone called the trade mission, and there Chance was waiting.

In the kitchen, while Kenner wolfed a steak nearly raw, Chance said, "Don't worry, Michael. Just Tatiana jumping the gun."

As he talked, Chance was continuing to make bullets for his 10 mm side arm. He had the bullet molds and the powder and the lead and the brass spread over the kitchen table. He also had a little bottle.

Kenner picked up the bottle, shook it, looked at it critically, opened the top and smelled it. Then he grimaced and nodded. "Mercury. Nice touch."

Mercury tipped bullets were deadly. Bullets with hollows into which a drop of mercury was placed before the slug was settled in its casing were pure poison.

"Expecting trouble?" Chamoun said to Magruder.

"Never can tell," said Magruder. "Actually, I'm expecting Mondragon. It's sort of the same thing."

Mondragon, in his cell, was certain of nothing. He was somewhere he'd always been. The rest of his life—everything he remembered—was but a dream. There'd been no girl who'd fished him out of the river—no river.

He was waiting for Karl to come and finish him. At least Karl could have the courtesy, because of their years of friendship, to do it personally.

Then there'd be no more bug-infested, moldy straw, no more questions coming from lights that talked in the dark, no more answers that begot more questions.

One thing Mondragon had learned in five years spent in Karl Fon's jail—or was it five months, five minutes, five decades, five lifetimes?—was not to give a talking light an interesting answer.

You could never tell when the lights were hallucinations, or actual lamps behind which inquisitors lurked.

They'd fed him today. Someone had. When they fed him, he always had a session with the talking lights.

Sometimes he thought they drugged his food. Since he was hungry, he ate anyway.

You had to keep up your strength. He had to keep up his strength. He'd get out of this. He'd get out of Nev Hettek. He would. It was just a question of time.

The talking light appeared. First it was a flicker that could have been something on the inside of his retinas. Or could have been the light men say they see near death.

It came closer like that light.

Funny, Mondragon had never expected to die in prison. Karl wasn't the sort to let a man off easy. The revolution needed villains. It was short on heroes. To make heroes, you had to have villains.

The light came closer, but it bobbled as it did. Did the light at the end of life bobble? Everybody who'd seen it said it was beautiful and steady.

There was nothing beautiful about this light. After so much darkness, looking at it made his head ache. His left eye began to tear, then to run.

He rubbed it. It hurt. He saw two lights, now, but that was only a result of rubbing his eye.

The eye was swollen; it was tender to his touch. The upper lid wouldn't open all the way and the lower lid felt as if it were twice its normal size.

In the face of the light, the eye closed of its own accord and he could feel tears running out of it. Sticky tears, not the salty tears of fear or sadness or repentence.

Of course, whoever was behind the light couldn't know that.

He lay his head back on the straw and ignored the light.

It said, "Thomas Mondragon, what day is it?"

"How should I know?"

"How old are you?"

"Old enough to know better. But I don't."

"Know better than what?"

Got to be careful. Sometimes, defiance just got you into more trouble. "Better than to think you're anything more than a hallucination. I don't talk to hallucinations. Go away. I'm asleep."

"You can sleep after you've answered our questions."

"Our questions? More than one hallucination? Funny, I only see one." Hallucinations didn't editorialize. At least, he didn't think they did.

He crooked an arm over his eyes. Pressure from his arm would keep his left eye from throbbing so. It would also keep it from popping out of its socket, which was what it felt like it might do any second.

"Can I have my regular eye back? The one that fits my head?" he asked the hallucination.

"Ah, um . . . if you speak the truth," said the hallucination.

"Speaking the truth was what got me in here. I may be foolish, but I'm not crazy." Not? Talking to hallucinations wasn't a sign of sanity. But sanity wasn't a sign of survivability, not in a situation like this.

"Speaking what truth?" the hallucination wanted to know.

"That there's no justice," Mondragon said.

"Then you do know where you are. And why. Say why you're here, Mondragon. Then food will come."

"I just ate." How long had it been? Hours? Days? It couldn't be weeks, or he'd be in worse shape even than he was. It could have been minutes though—he really wasn't hungry.

"Who are your accomplices?"

"In what?"

"Who are your accomplices in treason?"

"Oh, that." Mondragon nearly chuckled. "Well, let's see . . . there was Karl Fon—you'd know him. He's a bigwig in the new government. As a matter of fact, he is the new government. Then there was . . ." Maybe he ought to shut up. He'd been about to give Chance Magruder's name, and Dani Lambert's name, and a host of other names. Better watch it. He was too tired to play a game of wits, even with a hallucination.

"Do you want to walk out of here under your own power?" The hallucination was losing its temper. "Do you want to walk, ever again, under your own power? We can use physical means, you know. And we're getting tired of waiting. Very tired."

"I'd actually like to stay here until I die. If you don't mind. It's quiet, peaceful. I like the bugs in here. Every one of those bugs has his own story to tell. It's really quite fascinating—"

Something came out of the darkness and slammed his lips against his teeth and his skull into the stone beneath the straw. He spat blood.

"Tsk. Tsk. Mustn't lose your temper," he said when the colored lights which obliterated the single light hovering over him had finally faded.

So it wasn't an hallucination: hallucinations couldn't hit that hard.

"Who are your accomplices?"

"My mother; my father; my dog, Spot; my—"
Whack.

"Where is your allegiance?"

"To Nev Hettek, where it's always been. What do you think, fool? You think anybody ends up like this who doesn't believe in something?"

"So you admit you're a Nev Hetteker."

This was really crazy. "Of course. Born and bred. My papers are available to anybody. Ask Karl. Ask Chance. Ask—"

"Chance who?"

"Come on. Chance Magruder."

"And you would be content to be released into this Chance Magruder's custody?"

"Sure thing. Any time. Right after I tell you what you want to know—except I can't tell you."

"Why not?"

The light was bobbling closer and closer to his face, as if inspecting him.

He probably could have kicked at whomever was holding the light, if there really was someone holding it over him in the dark. Maybe he could have kneed that someone in the groin. But he was too tired to fight, too tired to endure any more pain simply because pain cleared your head and made you know you were still alive. Sometimes he used the inquisitors to make himself angry enough to last another day.

But today he really didn't care. He didn't care at all.

"Again—why not?" the voice behind the light said.

Exasperated, Mondragon shifted his legs—and felt a contact. There definitely was somebody standing over him. He wished he could see better. His night vision was shot to shit.

"Again why not what?" he demanded, almost coming up on one elbow. But it hurt too much. He slid back. "For an interrogator, you're pretty poor, you know that?"

"Why can't you tell us what we want to know?"

"Because I don't know what you want to know. I'm beginning to think that you don't know, either."

The light receded. He thought he heard a shuffle as a foot misstepped in the dark.

From a greater distance, the voice behind the light said, "If you were free, what would you say about your stay here?"

He had to turn his head to the left to face the light. That was where the door was. "Nothing. What's to say? I don't even know how long I've been here, let alone what's real and what I've been dreaming."

He had no hope for it, but he tried anyway: tried to cooperate; tried to grasp the straw of a chance he thought he saw.

"You've been dreaming. Yes. Dreaming. We think you've been too ill to realize that you're in a clean hospital bed. Is that so?"

"You got that right."

"If we were to release you to your friend Magruder, you would realize that you've been in a clean hospital bed, tended by professionals, and that you just keep falling out of bed and throwing yourself into walls in your delirium, but that no one has harmed you."

"I know that. I always knew that." *Don't believe them. It's a trick.*

And it was a trick, because the light went away then. It extinguished itself with a click and he was alone.

His eyes were tearing again. Now it was both eyes. He tried to sink back into his uncaring somnolence, but it didn't work.

Every time he heard a noise, his heart would leap. His gut would tighten. His ears would strain with expectation.

They were going to come turn him loose. Chance was going to come and get him. Chance had always been the best of the lot. Chance had finally talked Karl into realizing that Mondragon had never betrayed him: Mondragon had just been following his conscience, and the letter of the revolutionary code.

Chance would come and take him away and they'd go up into the hills and fish the way they used to do.

He'd see all his—

The door opened, bringing with it a flood of light that made him groan and cover his eyes with both arms: this light came into the room completely, filling every corner of the windowless cell.

He thought there might have been a man in the light, but he wasn't sure.

This was death, then: not a little bit of light, but a whiteout. As if he'd fallen and then been covered with an avalanche that was weightless, warm snow covering him. . . .

"Up. Let's go."

He couldn't see anything but green light when he opened his eyes.

Someone had hands on him. Arms supported him.

He was too weak to fight them. Anyway, you fought with your mind, not with your hands, if you wanted to win.

But standing alone would be nice. Having legs that could hold you would be nice. Going out into the Nev Hettek sunshine once again would be nice.

But it was dark, wherever they took him after they dressed him and hooded his head.

It was dark and damp and he could smell the salt air and rotting vegetation.

Someone steadied him against a rough wall and said: "Stay here. Somebody'll come for you."

Somebody did.

Chance Magruder did.

It was Chance's voice in the dark that said, "Easy, son. I'm going to take that hood off your head. Then I'm going to untie your hands. Then we're going to put you in a boat and take you over to my place, where you'll be safe. Do you hear me?"

"I hear you," he said, very quietly, in case it was yet another dream.

"Here we go."

He felt the hood come off. He felt the strong hands, untying him.

Chance took hold of his arm and slipped under it. Chance's shoulder was supporting him. "I can't see . . ."

"You will. Don't worry. You're not permanently blind. It's night."

"Good. Night. Thanks." They started to move, using Chance's strength and Chance's eyes. Mondragon's ankles felt like they were made of jelly. His feet slid around as he tried to use them.

"Don't thank me. I need you. Step down. Three steps."

"Are we going to Karl's?" Down meant into a boat of some kind. Or else it was a wagon and

Mondragon's concussion was going to make him vomit.

"You're going to the Nev Hettek embassy—in Merovingen. Remember Merovingen?"

"A bad dream."

"You could say that, yeah. But you're stuck in it. So are we. You're in my custody. Sit."

Magruder's support came away. His back was against a curving wall—definitely a boat, then. He leaned his head sideways and his cheek rested against a bench. A bad dream in Merovingen.

A Merovingian boat. Magruder's custody. Damn. Jones. . . .

It all came back in a rush. He tried to get up. He couldn't. That was no dream. Exeter's henchmen. The Justiciary basement.

Constant interrogation. . . .

The boat started. He tried to watch where it was going. Magruder's custody. He was seeing double when he saw anything distinguishable at all in the night.

"What—" It was a croak lost in the roar of the engine.

A shape came toward him. A face peered down. "You say something?"

Magruder's face.

"What do you mean, I'm in your custody?"

"You're released, pretty much cleared of charges, but on probation. We used a diplomatic immunity ploy. You're officially an employee of the Nev Hettek government. Congratulations."

The cynical humor in Magruder's voice chilled Mondragon so that he began to shiver uncontrollably.

The blurry Magruder went away and came back

with a blanket and a tin mug of something hot. When he tasted it, it was tea.

He had to hold it in both hands. "Jones?"

"Not my problem."

"I need to know if she's—"

"You need some sleep. Food. Medical attention. Then we'll worry about your girl."

Richard would have taken care of her. Richard would have. "What's this going to cost me, Magruder?"

"Everything. Your soul. Your allegiance. Maybe your life. Got any complaints?"

"What else?"

"Things are too unsettled here for me to talk to you now, with you in this kind of shape. We've owned to you. You, they say, have owned to us. It won't be so bad. No worse than you've been enduring. A little information here, a little there—"

"What else is new?" Mondragon muttered.

Magruder didn't answer. But something was new. He was alive again, free again—but free under Magruder's supervision. And that was very new, and very unsettling.

But maybe it would be all right. When you came out of prison, everything looked black. He remembered that from the last time. And in the truly black Merovingen night, with the moon setting, black was at its blackest.

"I don't like those shakes of yours," Magruder said after a while. "I'm going to have Dani look at you."

Dani. Danielle Lambert.

"No. I'm fine. Just underfed and overexcited."

"And scared to death," Magruder said softly, and squeezed his arm in wordless comfort.

That was the thing that always threw you about Magruder: when he wasn't being a bastard, he could be a nice guy.

Or make you think so. And Mondragon wanted to think so. Even though his mind knew that Magruder was trying to gain his confidence, Mondragon wanted to confide in someone. He needed someone right now. He needed to sleep without worrying about where he'd awake. He needed to eat without worrying about what was in his food— truth drugs or poisons or worms.

And he needed to gain back his strength. If what Chance said was really true, and Mondragon was officially recognized as a Nev Hetteker under the protection of the embassy in Merovingen, then everything was changed.

There might be some hope for him after all. As long as he could keep Magruder happy, that is.

And how long would that be, when Magruder was here fomenting a revolution and needed information badly?

Well, spying was what had kept Mondragon afloat in Merovingen this long.

He'd have to find a way to keep doing it. There was always a way to survive, he told himself. He could play one faction against the other here for years, he told himself. If Magruder wanted him dead, he'd have been dead by now, he told himself.

But he couldn't encompass all the changes that had come to pass while he'd been imprisoned. He sat in the bottom of Magruder's boat and shook. He was sure he had a fever.

Magruder was, too. He didn't protest when the big man helped him out of the boat, or when he was hustled into the embassy by the back door.

And there, waiting for him with her physician's bag in hand, was Dani Lambert.

The shock of seeing her was almost enough to convince Mondragon that he was still hallucinating, that he was back in his cell in Nev Hettek, and all this—everything he'd thought had happened in Merovingen—was a figment of a prisoner's imagination.

But Dani was no figment. Her strong, cool, sure hands took hold of his face. Her lips tightened, and orders for his comfort came out of them.

And Tom Mondragon finally relaxed: Magruder might be an expedientist and a sometimes-enemy, but Dani was the best of them all, had always been the best of them.

"What—what are you doing here?" he managed.

"Ssh," she said. "You just rest. Everything's going to be all right."

And he believed her. You had to believe Dani, or else stop believing in the human race altogether.

When the revolution had been a real ethical movement, Dani had been all of their best parts. Somehow, seeing her here, feeling her hands on him, looking into her clear eyes full of empathy, he knew he could sleep without fear, even under Magruder's roof.

"But, for Retribution's sake, why didn't Exeter release him back to Kamat?" Vega Borey wanted to know.

Cassie didn't understand the question. She didn't know what to answer. She and Mischa had just been . . . talking.

Mikhail Kalugin was toying with one of the watches

he'd made. It was as large as a cookie, held on his wrist by a strap. And the man no one but Cassie thought was smart said, "Probably because someone pulled a string somewhere. That's the way it goes, isn't it?"

Cassie's father had his hair pulled back in a club. They were in his office. She didn't want to be here. She wanted to go to her room, see Baby Belle, and perhaps have just a little deathangel before she went to sleep. She had to hide the deathangel from Michael, of course, but she hid so much from her husband these days, what was one more fib?

Michael had been someone named Mickey in his regression, when he was warrior against the sharrh. Mikhail was Mischa to her, now that he was a warrior against the evil forces of revolution and his horrid brother and sister who were driving Merovingen toward the vision of fiery retribution that Cassie had seen.

She wanted to go hold Belle. She stood up: "Daddy; Mischa and I just came over to see the baby . . ."

"Sit down!" her father thundered.

She sat, beside Mischa in one of the two chairs facing Vega's desk. Her father wasn't sitting behind his desk, he was pacing behind it, hands clasped in front of him.

"Cassie, Mikhail: there's been a murder in this house tonight. And a robbery."

"Oh!" Her hand flew to her mouth. Her heart nearly stopped. "Belle? Is Belle—"

"Your daughter's fine. One of the retainers, that's all. But down at the water-gate. Whoever rifled your rooms was an insider. That person must have been surprised by the water-gate boatman, and that's why the boatman was murdered."

"You've notified the proper authorities, of course," said Mikhail.

"Your sister? Of course the blacklegs have been informed. But we're concerned, Cassie. We're concerned about what might have been taken from your rooms."

"What might have been taken?" She didn't understand.

"When you became engaged to Michael Chamoun—his gift to you. Do you still have it, to your knowledge?" Her father's face was even paler than usual as he came around to stand before her, arms crossed, leaning on his desk. "You didn't happen to throw it away, did you?"

"The flash—"

"Don't say it." Vega looked over both shoulders. "I'm no longer sure that the house is secure. The gift. Did you, to your knowledge, still possess it?"

"Yes, of course." She was embarrassed, and uncomfortable. She never liked to talk about Michael in Mischa's hearing. Mikhail was so . . . sensitive. Mikhail was her devoted lover. Mikhail never criticized her the way Michael did. Michael didn't even love their baby as much as Mischa did. . . .

"Good," said her father. Mikhail was looking between her and Vega. "Cassie, are you in trouble? Vega, is she in trouble? I can help—"

"That's why we're so glad you're here right now, Mikhail. I think we can use all the help we can get with this. If you'll both come up to Cassie's bedroom while she finds the betrothal gift, perhaps we'll be lucky." As he spoke, he was shepherding them out of his study. "Perhaps the gift will be where Cassie last put it. Perhaps this is all a false alarm, to shake the tree and see if any overripe fruit should fall."

"Fruit?" Mikhail followed Vega up the staircase, a puzzled look on his face. "Cassie, m'ser Chamoun gave you fruit for a betrothal gift?"

"No, Mischa. Not fruit. A—"

"A figure of speech," her father interrupted. Vega was always interrupting her these days, except when she was prophesying.

Just tonight, she'd given Mikhail a private audience and tried to prophesy the wonderful future he saw for them both, with him at Merovingen's helm and her by his side and Baby Belle between them, but she'd had to force it. The vision she saw wasn't the vision Mischa wanted to have described to him.

It always made her sad to force a vision into some predetermined mold. But she'd done it, for Mikhail.

Someday, if things went well, Mikhail might be Belle's new father. Surely, if her husband kept behaving in so dastardly a fashion, Mikhail could find a way to save her from the misery of her marriage.

On that they were both agreed.

"What's happening, Vega?" Mikhail asked as they topped the landing. "Tell me what's wrong."

"I don't know what's wrong," said her father, rounding on them both. "Tonight has held a murder, the release of Mondragon into Nev Hetteker care for reasons I don't believe and only half understand, and a purported burglary. Whether the burglary is serious will determine the rest."

"What rest?" said Mikhail, who put an arm around Cassie's waist protectively, where her father could see. The gesture thrilled her.

Vega scowled at it. "Cassie, let's find it."

Slipping free of Mikhail, she went dutifully into her room to get the flashlight. She'd never bothered to truly hide it. It wasn't in one of her good hiding places, the way her deathangel was. She didn't have to hide the flashlight from Michael Chamoun—he'd given it to her.

As she was reaching for it in a drawer with her underthings, she said, "I don't know why you're so worried, Daddy. It's right— Oh."

And she looked harder, but she couldn't find it.

And then Vega said, "So it's gone," and sat down on her bed as if he were a balloon and someone had let his air out.

"I still don't understand."

"I've had an enquiry about Cassie's being in possession of illegal technology—a Nev Hetteker battery-operated device." He shook his head. "Damn Exeter, anyway. We can always say that the flashlight wasn't illegal when Cassie accepted it. . . ."

"Illegal?" Cassie asked wonderingly, as she straightened up empty-handed. The flashlight was truly gone. She knew where she'd put it and it definitely wasn't there.

"Flashlight?" said Mikhail Kalugin, his glance flickering from her face to her father's. "Exeter? What has Cardinal Exeter to do with—"

"If she arrests Cassie, Mikhail, I expect you to use all your influence to make sure that my daughter never sets foot in the basement of the Justiciary."

"The Justiciary! That's unthinkable," Mikhail demurred. "Willa Exeter is a good woman. My friend. I'll go speak to her—"

"Your friend?" Vega looked up, his face a mass

of lines. "If she's your friend, then you're safe. But she's no one else's friend. She's tearing Merovingen apart. So don't be so sure she's your friend, Mikhail."

"She is." He crossed his arms.

Cardinal Exeter, Mischa had told Cassie, was paving his way to become Iosef's successor, uniting the old families. . . . "Mikhail, you promised that our family would be among the ones that the cardinal—"

"I know what I promised. I'm going to see her. This whole thing has gone too far." He came to Cassie and took her in his arms right in front of Vega. He kissed the top of her head. "Don't you worry, little truth-seer. No one's going to hurt you. Nor your family."

He looked over her head at Vega. "M'ser, take my word for it. Your daughter will be safe if I must stand bodily between her and any agents of the inquisition."

"Good," said Vega Boregy with a nod of his head. "That's just what I wanted to hear."

Tatiana and Anastasi greeted the sunrise together on her balcony. Neither had slept all night. Their agents had been in and out with reports.

The last report, one of Mikhail going into Exeter's office and shouting at her so loudly that half the words had been heard through the cardinal's stout door, was cause for celebration.

Anastasi kissed her on the cheek and bowed low, toward a table set with flaky pastries and fresh eggs and fish. "Breakfast, sister? I do think we've earned it."

"After you, brother. And I dare say, yes, we did.

The inquisition may not be over, but it's lost its head of steam. Mischa will never trust that woman again, and with the Boregy girl's future in the balance, Mikhail will not bend an inch. The fool."

"So," said Anastasi, pouring her tea. "A toast, then, to business as usual and Merovingen's future under our rulership."

"A toast," Tatiana agreed, sitting down and feeling the revolver she still wore jab her flank as she did. They were going to carve a new alliance together that would solidify their gains of the evening. Alliances came and went. Neither of them was such a fool as to think that anything lasted forever.

When Exeter was a memory, there'd be time to worry about whether Tatiana or her brother would prevail and rule in Iosef's stead. Now was not that time. Now was the time to make sure that Mikhail was never, ever considered a serious contender for Merovingen power again.

They had Willa Exeter on the run. She clinked her teacup against her brother's and sipped the winey brew. Even if it had taken so extreme a measure as giving Mondragon, and all his information, into Magruder's care, they had done it.

Now, all they had to do was get Mondragon back out of the Nev Hetteker's clutches, and things would be as they most preferred them in Merovingen.

It would serve Magruder right, to find out he'd been used while he was trying to manipulate her. And it would serve Anastasi right, to find himself indebted to Magruder.

And, when the next few rolls of the dice were tossed, Tatiana would find herself just where she'd wanted to be, all along: with an edge on her brother in the deadly game they played.

And if gaining that edge had cost her a faithless lover, then what of it? Power was always lonely.

But power was what she wanted. And she would have it, by and by.

Dani was finished tending to Mondragon and lying on the little daybed in the embassy's third guest room when a knock came on the door.

She started guiltily. She should have gone back to Boregy House by now, but she was just too tired. Worse, she didn't want to go. Little Hope, her baby, was in good hands at Boregy House.

But Dani wasn't. Every time she saw that stupid drugged-out cow, Cassie Boregy, pick up Hope and croon to her and call her Baby Belle, Dani wanted to vomit, or throw something at Cassie, or take her baby and run.

But where did you run to, from here? Merovingen was the end of the earth, the bunghole of civilization, the bastion of what Karl called the "Fundies": the fundamentalists.

She couldn't run back to Nev Hettek with her daughter, Hope, not when Karl had sent her down here to do a specific job. She couldn't run out on the revolution and its leader. Not with her baby. Not anywhere that Karl wouldn't find her.

Find her and kill them both, if she did that. Karl Fon was a long-term planner. In fifteen years or so, when Dani was old and wizened, somebody would knock on the door of Boregy House and Belle Boregy, heir to Vega's empire, would be told that her father wasn't Michael Chamoun at all, but Karl Fon, liberator of Nev Hettek.

By then, if the revolution wasn't already a complete success, they'd have an agent in place to make it so. If Dani took Belle/Hope out now, the very least that would happen was Dani's capture and the baby's return.

Magruder himself would see to that.

The knock came again. This time, louder, more urgent. Knock-knock. Knock-knock-knockknock-knock.

Damn, she'd forgotten all about the fact that somebody needed to get in here.

That person tried the door she'd locked so she could get some rest, summon up the courage to go back to Boregy House, and play the professional physician to her only begotten child.

It sucked. She'd never thought it would hurt so much. As she got up to unlock the door, colored lights played at the edges of her vision, spiraling inward: fatigue signs. She'd better get some serious sleep or she was going to pass out, one of these times she stood up too fast. She'd never really rested up from her own pregnancy.

And damn the pregnancy, too.

Damn Karl and Chance and damn them all. You couldn't liberate these Merovingians from their superstitions, which meant you couldn't liberate them at all. Karl hadn't realized that, even when he came down here to take a look. He was too focused on his goal.

Magruder probably knew but didn't care: Magruder forced issues, that was his way. If you were unreceptive, stubborn, or hostile, he pushed harder. He always found a way. Dani could attest to that.

She stumbled on a carpet badly laid, and then turned the key in the lock and pulled open the door.

"Chance! I'm sorry. I just meant to take a short nap . . ." The look on his face stopped her cold.

Her blood rushed to her head. She slumped against the door, too tired for the adrenaline flooding her system to do more than dizzy her and make her pant. "What is it now? What's wrong?" she nearly gasped.

She must catch her breath.

He looked her up and down and shook his head. "You're a mess, you know that?"

"Screw you, Chance."

"You liked it that well the last time?"

"What's wrong?" she said again.

"Tatiana wants to see us."

"Tatiana Kalugin? Wants to see *us*? I don't even know—"

"Wants to see you, which means us."

"But, why?" Oh, her heart knew why. Her soul knew why. She took hold of the door's edge with both hands and leaned against it, waiting for him to answer.

"Probably what you think. She's found out about the baby swap somehow. Try to clean yourself up. The last thing I want her to see is a bereaved mother who's manipulable."

"I'm not manipulable. I'm tired. First I was up with the baby last night. Then there was that sloppy murder—your doing, no doubt—at Boregy House. Then Mondragon. I haven't slept for—"

"I don't care how long it's been. Clean up, I said. Take a shower. Make it quick."

"I don't need one."

He pushed past her into the room and somehow got hold of her wrist on the way. "You go in there and do it yourself, or I'll hold you under cold water and you'll wish you'd done it the easy way."

"Chance—" She bit off the half-sob that snuck out with his name.

He pulled her in against him and held her while she shivered.

She knew it didn't mean anything. Magruder's actions never meant anything—not the gruff ones or the gentle ones. Chance was all professional. But her body leaned against his as if it were hungry. And when he stroked the back of her neck and ran his fingers through her greasy hair, she nearly wept.

How could she be so hungry for human comfort that the touch of a man like Chance Magruder—a man you knew would sell anyone and anything for advantage—would feel so welcome?

He kissed the top of her head, after awhile, and gently pushed her away, both hands on her shoulders. "Take the shower. I'll wait. If we stay here any longer, we'll never get out of here without—"

"I know," she said.

She couldn't even hate Magruder. That was one part of her troubles here in Merovingen. If he'd really cared, though, he'd never have let things come to this. . . .

The shower was a blessing. He'd been right. When she came out, Chance was gone but he'd found her some clothes, somewhere: clean pants and a brocade shirt.

When she put on the pants, she realized they were his: she'd always been able to wear his pants, if she rolled up the legs. Today, she tucked them into boots.

When she looked up, Magruder was standing in the doorway. "Much better. Ready?"

"I suppose."

They didn't have far to go.

Tatiana was in the downstairs reception room of the embassy, dressed like a stormtrooper with shoulder-length red hair.

The woman looked Dani up and down and said, "I'd like to ask you a few questions, m'sera Lambert. Alone."

Chance closed the double doors from the inside. "I'm not leaving."

Tatiana nodded. "If you insist, Ambassador. M'sera Lambert, do you have anything to say about Cassiopeia Boregy's child?"

"Professionally, I can't comment," Dani said. "Physician/patient relationships are privileged."

"And you consider yourself physician to both, is that it?"

"That's it," said Dani, wanting desperately to sit down but not quite daring to while the other woman was standing.

Chance moved between them. "I got Doctor Lambert from her much-needed nap for this, Tatiana. Can we speak plainly?"

"I read the note in your desk, Chance—the other night."

Magruder looked at his boottops, rubbed the back of his neck with a hand, and said, "So, what do you want?"

"I want Mondragon back."

"Physically? Impossible. He's here under Doctor Lambert's care. Brutalized. Starved. He's one of our citizens officially, after all. . . ."

"Access to him," Tatiana said in a voice that told Dani that the other woman knew she was winning a point and glorying in her triumph. Gloating is never a pretty thing to watch.

"When he's up to it, which only *Doctor* Lambert can determine, you'll be welcome to see him, of course."

Chance was too mild. Dani wondered which letter Tatiana had read. Then she thought of the last, depressed, despairing one she'd written Chance, and she did sit down, putting her head in her hands.

"M'sera Lambert?"

"Tatiana, she's just exhausted."

"I can see what she is, Chance. M'sera Lambert, when will I be able to speak with Mondragon for an hour or so?"

"Two, three days, at least."

"That's not the right answer," said the queen of the blacklegs.

Dani didn't answer.

Tatiana called Dani's name again, and Chance actually stepped in front of Dani. "Tatiana, you don't want to talk to anyone but me about this."

"I needed to see if she was the baby's mother. Now I'm sure. And you're mine, Magruder. You and all of yours. What a wonderful, stupid, dangerous risk to have failed at taking." She laughed throatily. "I truly love you, Chance. You've given me exactly the hole card I need."

"Only good until you play it," Chance reminded her. "And then, only once."

"Just let Mondragon know that he's reporting to me, and I'll be back. As long as you and your slut-cum-physician behave yourselves, the baby can stay where it is. As a matter of fact, I'm going to enjoy knowing it's there in Boregy House."

She moved toward the doors and Chance turned on his heels to watch her go. He didn't say a word, just stood there, a living shield between Dani and Tatiana Kalugin, in blackleg uniform with a gun on her hip.

When Tatiana reached the doors, she said, "Oh, by the way, just tell me who the father is—you or Karl Fon?"

"Get out, Tatiana."

"Oh, Chance. Don't growl like that. You really ought to tell me. I have a right to know, don't I?"

"I'll come see you later," Magruder said.

Dani stared at her boots and they blurred. The doors slammed.

Magruder wasn't going to tell Tatiana what he didn't know for sure. Dani knew. Magruder should have known.

But men like Magruder ignore what they don't want to see.

And since the baby, her baby, was a Boregy now, a time bomb ticking in the very heart of Merovingen-above, it didn't matter who the real father was.

Belle Boregy was the child of Michael Chamoun and Cassie Boregy. The last time she'd seen Michael, he was drinking himself into a torpor. The last time she'd seen Cassie, she was chewing death-angel and trying to breastfeed another woman's child.

What difference did it make, whose baby was at that breast, really?

She kept asking herself the question, and not liking the answer.

It was going to make a difference to them all. It was already making a difference.

In all her life, Dani Lambert had never expected

to see Chance Magruder knuckle under to blackmail.

She just watched her boots, and a few pathetic tears fell onto them from her tired eyes. She was all hunched over and she couldn't straighten up or her aching stomach would give up its contents then and there.

And then, from somewhere, Chance was there, crouched down before where she'd have to look at him.

"It doesn't mean anything. Tatiana's made her first mistake. She's just become part of the revolution, though she doesn't know it yet. Don't worry. Don't worry about Mondragon, or the baby, or me. Or yourself. It'll be all right. I promise. And I've never lied to you, have I?"

"No, Chance," she said wearily, somehow able to straighten up at last. "You've never lied to me."

And that, at least, was the truth here where nothing ever seemed to have the slightest bit of truth to it.

Suddenly she didn't blame Michael Chamoun for turning into a drunk. "Chance, I know it's before lunch, but I'm prescribing a drink for myself—a strong one, if you'll be so kind."

"Good girl," he told her, and went to get it. "Prescribe one for me while you're at it," he said from the bar. "It's been one hellish night."

Two truths from Magruder in one sitting. It must, Dani thought dreamily, be a lifetime record.

FLOOD TIDE
(REPRISED)

by C. J. Cherryh

They came, held guns aimed at her when they brought her food, and in the beginning they had said, the chief of these blackleg-bastards, that if she broke any of the furniture or scarred any of the walls of Anastasi Kalugin's yacht, Anastasi might take offense at it, and if he did, it might go very hard for certain people.

That was the way Anastasi was, Jones believed that, except Mondragon was business, and business was more important to Anastasi than anything she could do to his fancy woodwork; but the threat still bothered her; and she spent her days going slowly crazy. There were books. There was one called *The Odyssey* that she read, page at a sitting, because though it was spelled odd and was real old, she could make sense of it more than the others, that she couldn't read half the words of. It was about places she thought must be down by the Chattalen, because they talked about wine. Except there were sheep, and islands, and that was the Falkens. It was confused as hell. She skipped around in it a lot, and when she got to the part about the pigs she was sure 'Stasi was crazy; but she thought—I'll ask Mondragon when I see him. Mondragon would be proud she read a book.

Mondragon would give her hell for being here, in this mess. That was all right. She was still alive. Every morning she woke up in that soft silky bed and every night when she went to sleep she thought, I'm still alive, and he is—because ain't no way 'Stasi'd keep me around if there wasn't a use, ain't no way he'd want me alive t' tell what I know, ain't no way in hell he'd turn me loose. . . .

But she kept thinking, when she was sitting in the fancy, soapy bath—Where's *he* right now? And when she was eating their fancy food and drinking Chat wine—What're they feedin' him, Lord? and when she felt the motion of the water under the ship, that told her she was still where tide moved and a body could breathe—Stone don't move, stone just sits, stone ain't alive, it's dark and it stinks and he's got all of that damn building between him and the outside, Lord, how's a man to think and breathe in all that stone?

And at night, when the electrics went out, and she was lying there in that fancy bed—Lord, what's happenin' t' him? What's happenin' and what in hell's Tatty Kalugin got t' do with 'Stasi and what's 'Stasi up to, that ain't got Mondragon out of there yet?

Mama, why ain't I dead?

But Mama didn't talk in this place, wasn't any way Mama was coming in here, Mama was thoroughly disgusted with her daughter.

Mama'd say, Fool.

Mama'd be oiling up that gun of hers and puttin' the bullets in and she'd say, the way she'd said when Jones was a little girl scared of that gun: Altair, this ain't t' handle careless, and ye don't let anybody know ye got it, and ye don't ever make a threat of usin' it. Ye make up your mind before ye ever take it out. An' ye know how many shots you got and you never get into anything that's got more fools than you got shots—and you count 'em less one. Ye always keep one, Altair. Ye never plan t' let this gun empty."

Yey, Mama, she'd said.

Damn gun was in her skip right now. If there was anything left of her skip right now. And she'd broken one of Mama's Rules, walked right in with no shot saved back, no more plan than that. That was why Mama wasn't speaking to her.

That was all the help she'd been to Mondragon.

Maybe she should have gone to Kamat, maybe she should have gone inside and talked to Richard and begged him—

And maybe Richard *was* doing something, maybe Richard was working with Anastasi and they had ways they was getting Mondragon talked out of that damn place.

But sometimes in the dark she saw Hanging Bridge and the crowds and the drummers and all, and she'd get up and walk the floor and have a light on, because it was too real, she'd seen it too often lately, seen a body drop, and the crowds go away, and the body lowered down on a rope to that boat that took it away under Coffin Bridge.

She told herself, They ain't never hanged a canaler, and he's that—

If the cardinal knew that, which she wasn't sure.

She thought, in those hours, If he's dead, maybe

'Stasi'll still let me go, if I tell 'im I'll go find
Exeter. If he's dead, I'll find 'er, just real quiet,
find myself a spot an' wait for a sight o' that woman
an' blow 'er t' hell—

She was thinking that when she heard the engines
start, like this big heart beating; and the whole ship
change its moving. She thought—

Oh, Lord, something's happened. We're moving.

And because they were down at Rimmon, she
knew it was into Merovingen proper they were going.

She threw her clothes on, she was washing her
face when the door opened and 'Stasi Kalugin was
standing there.

"Sera Jones," he said, "your skip is still at the
dock."

"M'ser?" she asked, very politely, with this sinking, poisoned feeling in her stomach.

"He's in the Nev Hettek embassy," he said, after
which she heard things all muddled.

"Is he all right?"

"In the Nev Hettek embassy," he said again, and
this time she heard it with everything he meant.
"It's public now—who he is, what he is—it'll be all
over town by noon. No, he's not all right. I've a
message for him."

"Yes, m'ser?"

"You're the message," 'Stasi said, this dark-eyed,
dark-hearted bastard. He said, "Go on. Go to him.
Tell him—I've work for him. Tell him—see me.
Soon."

APPENDIX

MEROVINGEN FOLKLORE 102
OR
SIGNS AND PORTENTS

by Mercedes Lackey

Even the most devout Revenantist is not immune to the *need to know*, to the search for a Sign that will tell him what is in store in his future, or the future of the entire city. Perhaps this is merely a reflection of Man's never ending search for ways to control his future; for whatever the reason, there are Portents associated with things and places all over Merovingen that the most orthodox, and most devout, still believe in their deepest hearts are nothing less than true and infallible.

THE ANGEL OF HANGING BRIDGE

The statue of the Angel Michael, copy of that stolen and lost, stands on Hanging Bridge as if he was watching over the entire city. And indeed, many believe this to be the case. The principle Portents associated with the Angel are concerned with Fire, Flood, and Earthquake.

It is said that when a Fire grows large enough to threaten the city, the Angel's wings move. The meaning of this Portent is unclear; the devout claim it is because he is fanning the fires to hasten the destruction of Merovingen and bring on Retribution; the hopeful claim it is because he is trying to put them out, and the cynical claim it is because he is trying to fly away and escape.

Obviously there is a purely physical cause for this apparent phenomenon; the flickering light, reflecting from the uneven surfaces of the Angel's gilded wings, could easily make the wings appear to move. It is noteworthy that those who claim to have seen this Portent also say that the Angel's garments (also gilt) stirred in the breeze created by the movement of his wings.

When a great Flood is about to descend on the city, it is said that the Angel can be clearly heard to weep and lament. Once again there is a purely natural explanation. Most devastating floods come after unseasonable rains, when the normal prevailing winds have shifted from out of the west to out of the east, holding back storms that would otherwise spend themselves at sea. When the wind shifts to this unusual direction, the Angel, being high enough to be affected by it, might well "cry" in the manner of an Aeolian harp, causing consternation among those hearing it.

When a devastating Earthquake is to strike the city, the Angel is said to groan out loud, as if in pain. This is a sound unlike the soft "lament" on the occasion of a flood, but is very loud, and quite unmistakable. It is said that once the Angel groans, the earthquake is heartbeats away.

The natural explanation for this phenomena lies in the Bridge and the Angel itself; it is gilded metal hammered over a carved wooden form. Most major earthquakes are preceded by minor temblors. Such temblors would most affect insecure structures such as bridges, or islands set on mud and wood rather than rock. During such a temblor, the Bridge itself would move, groaning under the stress. The Angel might well also groan under the stress of being twisted, as the metal rubs over the wooden form, which is doubtless beginning to suffer rot.

THE HARBOR ANGEL

The Harbor, or Lesser Angel, also has Portents associated with it. It is said to weep in Fever Season, weep poisonous green tears, symbolizing the poison in the veins of Merovingen. Again, there is a natural explanation. The Lesser Angel is bronze, which is well known to corrode to green verdigris. Although the Harbor Angel is kept polished, verdigris will collect in folds, such as those around the eyes. Fever Season is always marked by increasing fog at night—said fog will naturally collect on the surfaces of a metal object (by its nature cooler than the surrounding air) and drip from it. Hence, green tears.

THE WHEELS OF KARMA

The walk to the College is lined with representations of the Karmic Wheel. These are said to spin in the night when great change is to take place. There are some who even attempt to keep records on the positions of the Wheels in order to say whether or not they *have* moved.

The wheels being mandelas in which every sector is like every other sector, it is very difficult, if not impossible, to tell one sector from another. It would not therefore be possible to say whether the Wheel had *not* moved, and it would be *impossible* to convince the credulous that they had not.

THE GHOSTS OF DEAD HARBOR

During the worst storms, the specters of all the ships lost during the Great Earthquake and all their crews are said to rise and sail again. This is the "Ghost Fleet," and it is something no sailor or canaler wishes to see—for it is said that anyone who lives by the water that sees the Fleet in sail will die before the month is out. No amount of cajoling or explanation that what the superstitious person saw was likely swamp-fire, St. Elmo's Fire, or lightning on mist will convince him. Any number of Falken sailors—and more especially canalers—have pined themselves into death because they thought they had glimpsed one of the Ghosts.

M'SERA

She is known only as M'sera; no canaler will call her otherwise. She is only seen during Fever Season. She wears only scarlet; cloak, fine silk shirt, pants, boots, gloves. She appears only at night, but can be seen in any part of town. Her face is in shadow beneath the hood of her cloak—but the long hair which escapes is also red.

To see her means that the Fever has come; where she walks is where it will strike. Occasionally she can be seen to turn aside and touch someone or something; boat or dwelling. The Fever will strike there, and carry off at least half the inhabitants.

There is one strange sidelight to M'sera—*very* occasionally she will be seen to follow young men and women at a discreet distance. When the person in question has parted from companions, she will accost that person—and contrive to touch or kiss him. Such a one is doomed, but strangely doomed. His (or her) candle will burn briefly, but very bright— she (or he) is destined to become a brilliant artist, poet, musician, composer—and die at the height of fame.

MEROVINGIAN SONGS

Revenantist Man
by Anonymous
(A drinking song)

He was a Revenantist man, lived a Revenantist
   life,
He surely was a Revenantist with a Revenantist
   wife.
He had Revenantist karma and it piled up by the
   day,
He drowned and came around again, and it was
   all to pay.
He was a . . .

Verses *ad infinitum* (Adventist; New Worlder;
Adventist Revisionist; Sword of Godder; Janist;
Sharrist; descending in social acceptability until fi-
nal verse:

He was a little bitty worm, he lived a wormy life
He surely was a bitty worm with a wormy wife,
He had wormy karma and it piled up by the day,
He died and came around again and it was all to
   pay,

He was a . . .
[Fill in religions in reverse: at which point begin
all over again *ad nauseam*.]

Baby, Baby

by Unknown*

Baby, baby whoa-oh, baby baby yeah, yeah, oh
yeah,
Come on, baby, whoa-oh, sweetest lovin' you'll
ever see.

Baby, baby whoa-oh, baby baby yeah, yeah, oh
yeah,
Baby, baby whoa-oh, baby baby yeah, yeah, oh
yeah,

Sweet lovin', whoa-oh—

Baby, baby whoa-oh, baby baby yeah, yeah, oh
yeah,
Baby, baby whoa-oh, baby baby yeah, yeah, oh
yeah,

Yeah, baby, whoa-oh, baby, yeah.

*Lyrics believed to date from the 20th century.

INDEX OF ISLES AND
BUILDINGS BY REGIONS

THE ROCK:
(ELITE RESIDENTIAL)
LAGOONSIDE

1. The Rock
2. Exeter
3. Rodrigues
4. Navale
5. Columbo
6. McAllister
7. Basargin
8. Kalugin (governor's relatives)
9. Tremaine
10. Dundee
11. Kuzmin
12. Rajwade
13. Kuminski
14. Ito
15. Krobo
16. Lindsey
17. Cromwell
18. Vance
19. Smith
20. Cham
21. Spraker
22. Yucel
23. Deems
24. Ortega
25. Bois
26. Mansur

GOVERNMENT CENTER
THE TEN ISLES
(ELITE RESIDENCE)

27. Spur (militia)
28. Justiciary
29. College (Revenant)
30. Signeury
31. Carswell
32. Kistna

33. Elgin
34. Narain
35. Zorya
36. Eshkol

37. Romney
38. Rosenblum
39. Boregy
40. Dorjan

THE SOUTH BANK

Second rank of elite
41. White
42. Eber
43. Chavez
44. Bucher
45. St. John
46. Malvino (Adventist)
47. Mendelev
48. Sofia
49. Kamat
50. Tyler

THE RESIDENCIES

Mostly wealthy or
government
51. North
52. Spellbridge
53. Kass
54. Borg
55. Bent
56. French
57. Cantry
58. Porfirio
59. Wex

WEST END

Upper middle class
60. Novgorod
61. Ciro
62. Bolado
63. diNero
64. Mars
65. Ventura
66. Gallandry (Advent.)
67. Martel

PORTSIDE

Middle Class
74. Ventani
75. Turk
76. Princeton
77. Dunham
78. Golden
79. Pauley
80. Eick
81. Torrence

Upper middle class
68. Salazar
69. Williams
70. Pardee
71. Calliste
72. Spiller
73. Yan
88. Hendricks
89. Racawski
90. Hofmeyr
91. Petri
92. Rohan

Middle Class
82. Yesudian
83. Capone
84. Deva
85. Bruder
86. Mohan
87. Deniz
93. Herschell
94. Bierbauer
95. Godwin
96. Arden
97. Aswad

TIDEWATER (SLUM) FOUNDRY DISTRICT

---

98. Hafiz (brewery)
99. Rostov
100. Ravi
101. Greely
102. Megary (slaver)
103. Ulger
104. Mendex
105. Amparo
106. Calder
107. Fife
108. Salvatore

109. Spellman
110. Foundry
111. Vaitan
112. Sarojin
113. Nayab
114. Petrescu
115. Hagen

EASTSIDE (LOWER MID.)

RIMMONISLE (ELITE/MERCANTILE)

116. Fishmarket
117. Masud
118. Knowles
119. Gossan (Adventist)
120. Bogar
121. Mantovan (Advent.) (wealthy)
122. Salem
123. Delaree

124. Khan
125. Raza
126. Takezawa
127. Yakunin
128. Balaci
129. Martushev
130. Nikolaev

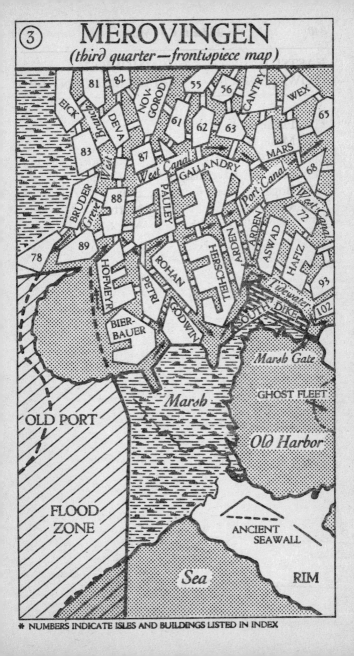

③ MEROVINGEN
(third quarter — frontispiece map)

EICK
81 82
DEVA
83
BRUDER
78 89
HOFMEYR
BIER-BAUER
PETRI
GODWIN
ROHAN
88
Crevé
West
Brauer
NOV-GOROD
87
West Canal
PAULEY
55
61 62 63
56
CANTRY
WEX
65
GALLANDRY
MARS
68
Port Canal
ARDEN
ARDEN
HERSCHELL
ASWAD
HAFIZ
72
West Canal
93
Tidewater
SOUTH DIKE
102
Marsh Gate
GHOST FLEET
OLD PORT
Marsh
Old Harbor
FLOOD ZONE
ANCIENT SEAWALL
Sea
RIM

✴ NUMBERS INDICATE ISLES AND BUILDINGS LISTED IN INDEX

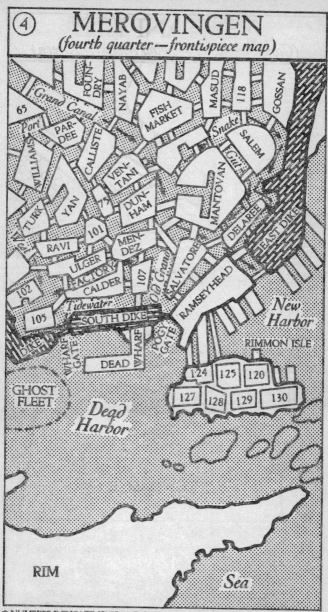

④ MEROVINGEN
(fourth quarter — frontispiece map)

Grand Canal

FOUN-DRY

NAYAB

FISH MARKET

MASUD

118

GOSSAN

65

Port WILLIAMS

PAR-DEE

CALLISTE

VEN-TANI

Snake Cut

SALEM

MANTOVAN

TURK

YAN

79

DUN-HAM

DELAREE

EAST DIKE

RAVI

101

MEN-DEZ

ULGER

FACTORY

CALDER

107

SALVATORE

Old Grand

102

Tidewater

105

SOUTH DIKE

WHARF GATE

RAMSEYHEAD

New Harbor

DIKE

POLE GATE

DEAD

WHARF GATE

RIMMON ISLE

GHOST FLEET

Dead Harbor

124 125 120

127 128 129 130

RIM

Sea

✳ NUMBERS INDICATE ISLES AND BUILDINGS LISTED IN INDEX

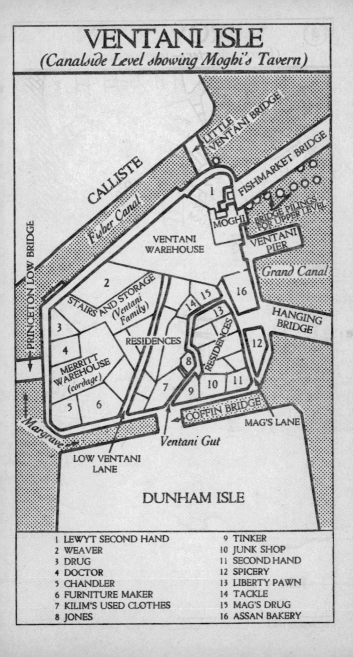

VENTANI ISLE
(Canalside Level showing Moghi's Tavern)

1 LEWYT SECOND HAND
2 WEAVER
3 DRUG
4 DOCTOR
5 CHANDLER
6 FURNITURE MAKER
7 KILIM'S USED CLOTHES
8 JONES
9 TINKER
10 JUNK SHOP
11 SECOND HAND
12 SPICERY
13 LIBERTY PAWN
14 TACKLE
15 MAG'S DRUG
16 ASSAN BAKERY

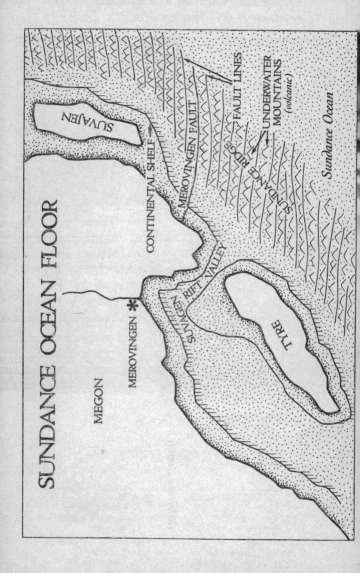

SUNDANCE OCEAN FLOOR

MEGON

SUVAJEN

CONTINENTAL SHELF

MEROVINGEN *

MEROVINGEN FAULT

SUVAGEN RIFT VALLEY

SUNDANCE RIDGE

FAULT LINES

UNDERWATER MOUNTAINS
(volcanic)

TYRE

Sundance Ocean

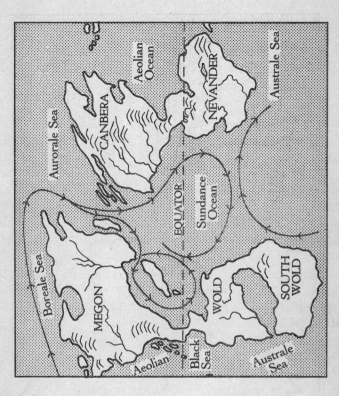

MAJOR EASTERN OCEANIC CURRENTS
(affecting climate)

N

Aurorale Sea

Aeolian Ocean

CANBERA

NEVANDER

Australe Sea

Sundance Ocean

EQUATOR

Boreale Sea

MEGON

Aeolian

WOLD

SOUTH WOLD

Black Sea

Australe Sea

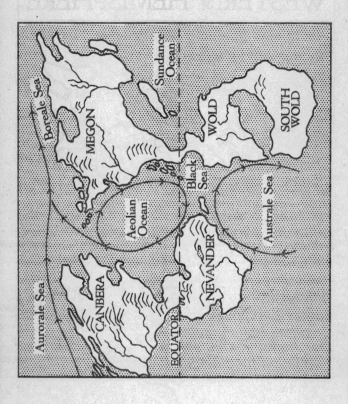

WESTERN

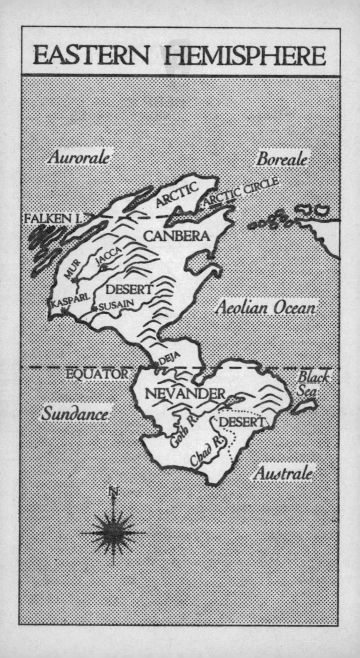

DAW

C.J. CHERRYH
THE ALLIANCE-UNION UNIVERSE

The Company Wars
☐ DOWNBELOW STATION   (UE2431—$4.50)

The Era of Rapprochement
☐ SERPENT'S REACH   (UE2088—$3.50)
☐ FORTY THOUSAND IN GEHENNA   (UE2429—$4.50)
☐ MERCHANTER'S LUCK   (UE2139—$3.50)

The Chanur Novels
☐ THE PRIDE OF CHANUR   (UE2292—$3.95)
☐ CHANUR'S VENTURE   (UE2293—$3.95)
☐ THE KIF STRIKE BACK   (UE2184—$3.95)
☐ CHANUR'S HOMECOMING   (UE2177—$3.95)

The Mri Wars
☐ THE FADED SUN: KESRITH   (UE2449—$4.50)
☐ THE FADED SUN: SHON'JIR   (UE2448—$4.50)
☐ THE FADED SUN: KUTATH   (UE2133—$4.50)

Merovingen Nights (Mri Wars Period)
☐ ANGEL WITH THE SWORD   (UE2143—$3.50)

Merovingen Nights—Anthologies
☐ FESTIVAL MOON (#1)   (UE2192—$3.50)
☐ FEVER SEASON (#2)   (UE2224—$3.50)
☐ TROUBLED WATERS (#3)   (UE2271—$3.50)
☐ SMUGGLER'S GOLD (#4)   (UE2299—$3.50)
☐ DIVINE RIGHT (#5)   (UE2380—$3.95)
☐ FLOOD TIDE (#6)   (UE2452—$4.50)

The Age of Exploration
☐ CUCKOO'S EGG   (UE2371—$4.50)
☐ VOYAGER IN NIGHT   (UE2107—$2.95)
☐ PORT ETERNITY   (UE2206—$2.95)

The Hanan Rebellion
☐ BROTHERS OF EARTH   (UE2290—$3.95)
☐ HUNTER OF WORLDS   (UE2217—$2.95)

NEW AMERICAN LIBRARY
P.O. Box 999, Bergenfield, New Jersey 07621

Please send me the DAW BOOKS I have checked above. I am enclosing $_____
(check or money order—no currency or C.O.D.'s). Please include the list price plus
$1.00 per order to cover handling costs. Prices and numbers are subject to change
without notice. (Prices slightly higher in Canada.)

Name _____

Address _____

City _____ State _____ Zip _____

Please allow 4-6 weeks for delivery.

DAW

More Top-Flight Science Fiction and Fantasy from
C.J. CHERRYH

DAW

Exciting Visions of the Future!

W. Michael Gear

☐ **STARSTRIKE** (UE2427—$4.95)
The alien Ahimsa has taken control of all Earth's defenses, and forces humanity to do its bidding. Soon Earth's most skilled strike force, composed of Soviet, American and Israeli experts in the art of war and espionage find themselves aboard an alien vessel, training together for an offensive attack against a distant space station. And as they struggle to overcome their own prejudices and hatreds, none of them realize that the greatest danger to humanity's future is right in their midst. . . .

☐ **THE ARTIFACT** (UE2406—$4.95)
In a galaxy on the brink of civil war, where the Brotherhood seeks to keep the peace, news comes of the discovery of a piece of alien technology—the Artifact. It could be the greatest boon to science, or the instrument that would destroy the entire human race.

THE SPIDER TRILOGY

For centuries, the Directorate had ruled over countless star systems—but now the first stirrings of rebellion were being felt. At this crucial time, the Directorate discovered a planet known only as World, where descendants of humans stranded long ago had survived by becoming a race of warriors, a race led by its Prophets, men with the ability to see the many possible pathways of the future. And as rebellion, fueled by advanced technology and a madman's dream, spread across the galaxy, the warriors of Spider could prove the vital key to survival of human civilization. . . .

☐ **THE WARRIORS OF SPIDER** (UE2287—$3.95)
☐ **THE WAY OF SPIDER** (UE2318—$3.95)
☐ **THE WEB OF SPIDER** (UE2396—$4.95)

Kathleen M. O'Neal

Powers of Light

☐ **AN ABYSS OF LIGHT: Book 1**   (UE2418—$4.95)

Only the Gamant people dared to resist subjugation by the Galactic Magistrates. For the Gamants knew they were the Chosen Ones, blessed with the gift of an interdimensional gateway to God. But were the Beings of Light with whom the Gamants communed actually God and the angels? Or were they an advanced race to whom the Gamants were mere pawns in some universe-spanning game? Either way, the Gamant faith would soon receive its ultimate test as the Galactic Magistrates mobilized to put an end to their rebellion, even as many among them turned to a messiah who might betray them all. . . .

☐ **TREASURE OF LIGHT: Book 2**   (UE2455—4.95)

With the Gamant worlds under siege by the military starships of the alien Galactic Magistrates, Jeremiel Baruch, commander of the rebel human forces, has seized the magisterial battle cruiser *Hoyer*, though not in time to prevent a deadly scorch attack on the planet of Horeb. Rescuing all who have escaped the attack, Baruch heads for the world of Tikkun to recruit others to his cause. But what neither Jeremiel nor the magisterial enemy pursuing him know is that far more powerful forces are about to take control of the future, beings capable of and prepared to destroy humans, aliens and the entire universe. . . .